This book is for my mother,
of course,

and
for my Grandmother Jane,
still a hot ticket at ninety,

and
for all new mothers everywhere.
May you have the time to read a book.

THIS LITTLE MOMMY STAYED HOME

A NOVEL

Samantha Wilde

BANTAM BOOKS

A Bantam Books Trade Paperback Original

Published in the United States by Bantam Books, an imprint of The Random House Publishing Group, a division of Random House, Inc., New York.

BANTAM BOOKS and the rooster colophon are registered trademarks of Random House, Inc.

Library of Congress Cataloging-in-Publication Data
Wilde, Samantha.
This little mommy stayed home / Samantha Wilde.
p. cm.
ISBN 978-0-385-34266-7 (trade pbk.) — ISBN 978-0-553-90667-7 (ebook)
1. Stay-at-home mothers—Fiction. 2. Motherhood—Fiction. I. Title.

PS3623.I537T47 2009
813'.6—dc22
2008050233

Printed in the United States of America

www.bantamdell.com

2 4 6 8 9 7 5 3 1

Book design by Helene Berinsky

Praise for **THIS LITTLE MOMMY STAYED HOME**

"Think of the funniest person you know, give her a baby and a month without sleep, multiply by ten, and you've got the incomparable Samantha Wilde rocking the hilariously appalling realities of motherhood and the modern marriage. This book belongs on the bedside table of everyone who's ever been a mother, or had one."
—KAREN KARBO, author of *The Stuff of Life*

"Here's a talent test: when a narrator's doldrums make a reader laugh out loud. Samantha Wilde's inkwell must be filled with truth serum, because this brave and funny book gets the postpartum peaks and valleys so very, winningly, right."
—ELINOR LIPMAN, author of *The Pursuit of Alice Thrift*

"[This] is the funniest novel I've read in a long, long time. What a treat! Mothers everywhere deserve this book."
—ELLEN MEISTER, author of *The Smart One*

"Samantha Wilde is the irreverent, knowing, laugh-out-loud, brutally-honest-but-most-treasured best friend that every new mommy craves and every reader relishes. They should issue this smart, hilarious novel along with newborn onesies and nursing pads."
—PAMELA REDMOND SATRAN, author of *Babes in Captivity*

"Riotously hilarious, unabashedly honest, and positively impossible to put down. Samantha Wilde's debut is a must-read for all moms and non-moms alike."
—JESSICA BRODY, author of *The Fidelity Files*

To my family and friends: This is a work of fiction.
I made everything up. It's not about you.
I promise. I just have an excellent imagination.
Really.

THIS LITTLE

MOMMY

STAYED HOME

I KEEP SLIPPING UP AND SAYING POSTMORTEM WHEN I mean postpartum. I'm two weeks postmortem now, so I guess I shouldn't expect more of myself. It's like my hormones are playing Pac-Man with my brain cells—eating them, one by one. But is that really the worst thing in the world? Not by a long shot. The worst thing in the world is the feeling I have every time I sit on the toilet. If I reach down I can feel my perineum dangling just above the water line. (If you don't know what your perineum is, lucky you. There are some body parts better left to obscurity.) The doctor who stitched me up didn't mince words: "There," she said, completing her work. "Now it looks like a vagina again."

What a relief, then, that it looks like a vagina and not, say, like an Australian sheepdog or a jar of moldy marmalade. I should be so grateful! I hadn't realized I could have walked out of the hospital with an etching of one of the presidents between my legs, like at Mount Rushmore. Or maybe it was more like Alice Cooper or another scary rock star way past his prime. What's black and blue with hair all over? Or maybe it wasn't black and blue from my son's overeager exit. Maybe it could have still made it into a book of feminist art, still looking like a pink orchid, just perhaps a new long-petaled variety? I'll never know what that doctor knew. Shucks.

At any rate, I'd imagine a vagina is a good thing for a vagina to look like. I haven't personally looked at it lately. I'm trying to medicate its existence away with the hard-core drugs the hospital gave me (Ibuprofen). I have a friend who did the *Our Bodies Ourselves* know-yourself-better-labia-look-squat over a mirror at one week postmortem, and I don't think she ever recovered. She said it looked crooked, misplaced, like her vaginal lips had migrated to her inner thigh. It was funnier than the *Vagina Monologues,* she told me, except she didn't have the heart to appreciate it, since, after all, it was *her* vagina giving the monologue like a fat old man with a lisp—not really the character you'd want your vagina to play in the show, if given the chance.

My husband hasn't bothered to check out the netherlands either. I would venture to guess he hasn't bothered to check out anything during his free time besides his Xbox and whatever large-breasted woman he can find on local cable. I don't mean anything against him. He can't help it, he'd rather be at work. I just mean to say: I CAN'T STAND HIM.

Am I screaming? I shouldn't do that. I'll wake the baby. Oh, God, I love that baby. I guess I only have so much love in my heart. There's no more room for anyone else anymore. Which is a surprise, since my breasts and my chest have all expanded so radically I could develop a new career in a carnival sideshow. My husband, the master of making lemonade out of—well, melons—took advantage of the moment of what is called engorgement and took pictures of my breasts. That's the time when your milk first comes in and each breast weighs more than the baby doubled. Hey! I guess my husband *has* noticed me since "the great event." Or parts of me, anyhow.

I love having a new baby. No, really, as much as it sounds like I don't, I do. It beats every other job I've had: shelving books in the library (college), catering (postcollege) and, my most recent, real adult-job, freelance editing (something to do with my English degree). Motherhood's the only job I've ever had where staying in your pajamas all day and spending as much time in bed as you possibly can is encouraged. That's got to be an overlooked benefit to having a newborn. It's just not pure pleasure all the time. It's not pure pleasure most of the time. But they tell me it will pass.

I lie down on the bedroom floor some days and weep while my husband locks himself in the bathroom with his Nintendo DS and takes an hourlong dump. I cry because I want that. I want to be able to do that. I want to be able to poop, and I want an hour to myself. But in addition to constipation, tearing and POP (pain on pooping), I am on call. I am the new 7-Eleven. I am open for business all hours of the day and night. When no one else is around, which is most of the time, I circle the house topless because there seems no reason to wear a bra or a shirt. My breasts have become a public commodity, at least locally. The baby nurses about every tenth breath he takes. I am the milk factory that never closes its doors. I am every man's wet dream. A busty babe on constant display.

Actually, I think that's too generous. I am most definitely nobody's wet dream. I've taken to calling my belly Lumpkin, to be affectionate. My abdominal exercises consist of lying on the floor and breathing. My aerobic activity is a walk to the mailbox. When I walk down the driveway to pick up the mail

I feel like a prisoner newly released. The sun offends me. Lying in bed, trying to nap, I hear the neighbors' daughters playing in the yard. I don't sleep; I lie still and think of how much I hate them. I think of how they have everything, even flat bellies. Even vaginas that look so much like vaginas no one would need to point it out. My only weapon is time and the pathetic hope that they will kneel on a gurney one day dripping feces, blood and meconium, begging for drugs, their slender white bottoms quivering ever so slightly as they bump into the elevator and head to maternity.

I've made a habit of calling and crying to my mother. I attempted to explain my sock metaphor to her.

"My sanity is a pair of socks," I said. "I put it away in a drawer about the time of the birth. What I want to know now is why do I only have one sock left?" After a long pause I decided to offer some clarification. Not everyone gets a sock metaphor. "What I mean is, when will I recover from my trip to postmortem hysteria?"

"Postmortem?" she said

"I mean postpartum. Whatever. It's essentially the same at this point."

She promises it will get better. I agree. By the time he is twenty, I will sleep through the night, I will have recovered vaginal elasticity, I will have time to brush my hair, I will not go to CVS alone and feel like a wild bandit on the loose, calling home after five minutes just to ask Is he still breathing? That reincarnation of Abe Lincoln (no, it's true, he really does look like him) I gave birth to—is he okay?

I can only talk to women who are mothers now. Nobody else makes sense. People without children, what do they do with all that time? I can't remember anymore. I called my friend Melody today for the first time. Until this moment I literally had not been able to figure out how to speak on the phone and hold a baby at the same time. Melody had a baby girl three months before me.

"I'm going to die."

"You're not going to die."

"I really, really need sleep."

"Can you nap when he naps?"

"He doesn't really nap," I tell her. "He has what I call the nipple nap. He'll sleep as long as my nipple is stuck in his mouth."

"Maybe you could learn to sleep through that. I know. I know it's hard. I kept telling Eric how horny I was those first few weeks, and he couldn't believe it. Women in our condition aren't supposed to feel *that* particular emotion. You know what I told him? I told him, honey, I've got someone sucking on my breast about twenty hours a day, get real. What am I supposed to feel?"

"I hadn't thought of that." I *really* hadn't thought of that. I wanted to have sex about as much as I wanted to compete in a triathlon. Not At All. "I don't feel sexy," I told her. "I can't feel sexy until I sleep. I can't feel sexy until my hair is clean. I can't feel sexy until my legs are shaved. Do you know how long my leg hair is? Besides, I hate Drew. Just the sight of him makes me furious." Drew is my husband of six years.

"Drew? What's he done?"

"Everything. I don't even want to get into the birth. I have the distinct feeling he wishes we could press rewind and put the baby back in my uterus for another few years."

"I'm surprised. You two have been talking about having a baby for years."

"Right. And that's the difference between reality and hypotheticals. Drew was an awesome dad until Zach came along. When we would *talk* about our imaginary children he looked like an excellent father. Now that we have a real one, he's developed an allergy to babies." I heard a snort from the other end of the line. "I'm not making it up. I'll give you an example. Whenever the baby cries, I run to his side. I honestly can't stand the sound of his cry. I'll do anything, anything at all to comfort him. In fact, I nursed him the other day in the grocery store while I was walking down produce. I didn't skip a beat. I just put him on the breast. The point is, sometimes, when I'm gone for say . . . sixty seconds to pee or get a glass of water, the baby will cry and Drew will—well, he'll walk slowly to Zach. Sometimes he walks so slowly I can't imagine what he's doing or thinking."

"Well, he's a man."

"That's dismissive."

"No," Melody said confidently. "I mean that. Men and women are different, especially when it comes to babies."

"But look at Eric—"

"He's an exception."

"Look at your friends Howie and Lily—"

"Exception."

"What are you saying? Are you saying I've got the norm?"

"Yes."

"How come I can't have the exception?"

"Sweetie, life's unfair. Did you miss that lesson? If you don't get postpartum depression, you can consider yourself lucky. Some new mothers can't even make it to the grocery store, let alone nurse while shopping. Do you ever want to throw the baby down the stairs?"

"God, no."

"Well, there you go. You're blessed. I know a lot of women who do."

"Does wanting to kill your husband count? Is that part of postpartum depression?"

"It can be. But what you've got sounds like normal life to me. Men have it hard too, you know. Drew's life has changed as much as yours."

"That's a crock of pop-psych sensitive-man bullshit. He didn't carry the baby or birth the baby, and he doesn't nurse the baby. I'm so angry about the birth, I could spit. I can't even talk about it yet."

"Well, tell me when you can. It's better to talk about this stuff. Holding it in—"

"Can make me constipated? That's already happened."

"Not exactly what I meant. Take a breath, Joy. It will get better. The first couple of months are always a little crazy, for everyone." Then I heard a muffled cry. "Sarah's awake. I've got to go. Try to get some sleep."

I went to high school with Melody so I give her special license to say terrible things to me like "life is unfair" because I figure she has my best interests at heart. Besides, she makes a living listening to people cry and complain. She's got to be wiser than me. Not only did she become a mother first, but she's a therapist. The kind who has a waiting list. She's that good. I wonder if she gets away with telling her clients that life is unfair. Is that what we're all dying to hear? Is that worth one hundred thirty bucks an hour? If it is, I'm lucky she's my friend and I get it for free.

Really, though, he's a good baby. He has that delicious new-baby smell, like a pastry roll just out of the oven. And he has that new baby skin, silky soft like good lingerie. He's so good that he slept four hours in a row last night. When I woke up, I searched the dark room desperately for the cradle, and searched the cradle with a searing gaze for the baby, for his rising, falling breath. A second after, my heart swelled. It's like falling in love. It's the worst crush I've ever had. Then he burst into hysterical tears.

"He's hungry," Drew muttered from his side of the bed.

"No shit, Sherlock," I told him, dragging my Lumpkin belly out of bed to retrieve Zach. I am working on mastering the art of nursing and sleeping at the same time. I am convinced it will save me from utter despair, divorce, and institutionalization.

The baby is tiny. Once I nestle him beside me, I offer him my nipple, which he takes like a starving animal. I fold one arm beneath my head. The next time I wake up, the sun is out. And the baby is still alive, beside me, asleep. My nipple stands out like a landing light, looking obscene and misplaced, as if it had forgotten where it belonged. I decide to look on the bright side. If I ever get lost in the desert and happen to have some finger paints with me, I can paint my nipples and lie on the ground, waiting for an airplane to land and save me.

My mother called this evening to celebrate Zach's two-week birthday. She asked what I needed. She'd served her duty as my footman for a few days after I gave birth, but in typical Madeline Steeley fashion she'd made a quick getaway after four days and hadn't made an appearance since.

"I need you to come visit."

"Oh, I don't think that will work. Not this week, and let's

see … not next week … oh, dear, we've got to go into next month."

"Mom."

"I do want to help you, Joy."

"You've got to come. I can't do it. I can't do anything. How can I do laundry? What do I do with the baby? If I sleep when he sleeps, how can I ever get anything done? When do I write my thank-you cards for all the toys and blankets and bibs? I still haven't shaved my legs. That's two weeks, Mom! Two weeks of hair growth. If that happened to you, you'd have a stroke. You'd have a stroke and die. Have some pity on me."

"I know how it is. I lived through it many times. I want to help you, really I do."

"Then find some time to come here!"

"Listen, Joy, I'm doing lots of traveling this month—"

"I NEED YOU!"

"Okay, let's not shout. We can plan this calmly."

"No, we can't do this calmly. I'm all alone in the world. I'm all alone out here in suburban isolation. I never see another living soul. All the women in this neighborhood work. I'm all alone with this tiny, ravenous, overgrown baby chick, and I don't have any clean underwear. You have got to help me," I insisted through my sobs.

"Joy, honey, maybe you should call Drew."

"He's useless."

"He's not useless. He's your husband. Tell him you need help."

"Mom, just listen to me. Drew's always at work."

"He has an important job. Being headmaster at Clarkville is no small potatoes." Clarkville Academy was once the most prestigious private boarding school for boys on the East Coast.

Rich boys, that is. In fact, it's so famous the town is named after it.

"Well, being a new father isn't small potatoes either. I feel like I have an exit sign strapped to my forehead. Every time I see him he's walking away." She laughed. "Please, Mom. I really do need you."

"Okay, okay, okay." A long pause. A deep sigh. "How about next Tuesday?"

My mother loves me, perhaps in excess. I am her only child. Actually, that's not exactly true. I think of myself as her only child because I was, for about ten years. Then she remarried and had three more children, but I don't think of them as counting. They aren't real children. She never liked her second husband as much as she liked my father. My father died, which makes him the favorite husband because as everyone knows, once someone dies you forget all their faults. I am the original child. The love child.

My mother also went on, after her second husband, to marry a third husband and, much to everyone's surprise, had another baby. She calls Danny her bonus baby. He's barely a teenager now.

My mother has also managed to find time, between marrying three men and divorcing two and having five children, to create a business, more aptly called a dynasty. She had some boyfriend before my father, a chemist, and together they created a serum. You don't have to know what a serum is. All you need to know is that they sell the stuff, in the smallest jars you have ever seen, for eighty dollars and change, to wealthy older women who want to look young forever. She grew her own line of cosmetics off that one product. You can even see her, sometimes, on QVC, which I do, occasionally, when I am lonely for her.

"Can I bring someone?" she chirped happily before she hung up. She sounded suspiciously happy, in fact, but I only thought so later, when I had time to ponder it. And ponder it I did. After all her husbands and all her boyfriends, I should have known what was coming.

"Someone? What does someone mean? Oh, God, Mom, I *know* what someone means. Don't tell me. I can't take it. I'm a woman on the verge."

"Joy, honey, be sweet. Be reasonable. Be sane for me. You'll love him. Absolutely love him."

Right. I'd love him. I'd love him like I loved husband number two and husband number three and every other temporary lover who usurped my mother's time.

"What's his name?"

"Donny," she said.

"What's he like?"

"He's a Texan."

"Ah," I said. And that was about as gracious as I could be.

I finally admitted to myself that the only thing I ever want to eat are M&M's. I'm not proud of this fact, but it's true. Considering the abandonment I was enduring on all sides— first by my husband and now by my mother—my chocolate craving felt entirely reasonable. I called Drew on his way home from work.

"Awful news from my mother," I said. "I'll fill you in later. Can you bring home some M&M's?"

"Huh? Sorry. I had the radio on. What is it?"

"I said I need chocolate."

"I think there's some baking chocolate in the cupboard."

"I don't want baking chocolate, Drew, because I don't want

to bake. And I don't want to bake, because I still find it uncomfortable to stand, besides the fact that I happen to have a baby. I have a baby who does not sit, or stand, or crawl. He requires that I be holding him, oh, I'd say, ALL THE TIME! So if you don't mind, could you please bring me some M&M's."

"Is something wrong?"

Silence.

"You seem a little testy."

"Really, do you think so?"

"Oh, listen, I'm getting another call. I have to take this one. I'll be home soon. I'll get some chocolate, okay?"

He brought home a Snickers bar. That's his favorite. He said I didn't specify what kind I wanted. When I sat down on the kitchen floor and started crying, he got the message.

"I'll just run back out," he said quietly. He did not hold me, hug me, kiss me, or console me. I think he feared me. Or maybe he just smelled me. It'd been a while since I had a bath. But he did go again to the store. When he came back he had three pounds of M&M's in his hands. I elatedly ate almost one whole bag. Then Drew and I curled up on the sofa to watch the comedy channel together. Zach snoozed in his bouncy seat. For about twenty minutes it seemed like old times. I almost thought about forgiving Drew. Must have been the chocolate.

The next day the phone rang, and I picked it up instantly, breathless for some conversation. I'd even come to long for telemarketers, just so I could hear the sound of another adult voice. "Can you say that again?" I'd tell them, after they went through a five-minute speech. There are a lot of disappointed telemarketers out there. I don't think any of them ever called someone with so much interest. I must have heard those sales pitches three or four times each. Then I'd say, "That's nice. Thanks so much for calling," and hang up.

I'm not proud. I did what I needed to get through. Besides, I don't think I'm in my right mind most of the time. Sleeplessness will do that to you.

At any rate, I answered the funny—I mean the phone. (Words get lost in here too. It's the Mommy Brain Sieve. Don't act like you don't know about it. We all know about Mommy Brain Sieve.) I was sitting on the couch, my feet up on the ottoman. Zach was on the right breast, which made it easy to hold the phone between my left shoulder and ear.

"Hello?"

"Joy, it's Beth. How are you holding up?"

"As well as any new mother, I think."

"I so wish I could be there to help you," she said.

"Come over any time," I told her resentfully. Beth laughed, I'd say a bit cowardly. Whose fault was it, after all, that she lived an ocean away? Had I made her move to London? I don't think so. I mean, after all our years of college friendship—we'd been like the Doublemint twins, with matching ponytails even—how could she do that to me? We even dated some of the same men. That's how close we were. We shared everything. After all that, she left the country. I've never forgiven her. I don't think friends should move away. It's bad etiquette. Someone should write a friendship manners book so I can send it to her.

"I did just book a plane ticket," she finally said.

"What?"

"You *know* I've been planning to come for our ten-year reunion. And then I'll get to see your little sprout."

"The reunion?" All of a sudden reality came down and sat

on the couch beside me, as real as anything, as real as the baby's spit-up. It was like, hey, look, there's a whole world still going on outside of your breasts! Everything didn't stop when you popped out the next generation. Yes, that's right, the little voice of reality said, YOU will have to attend your reunion and you will look like—well, like someone suffering a severe case of PM (postmortem, that is).

"Shit," I said.

"Oh, you can't have forgotten, Joy? We just talked about it last month."

"I don't remember last month. Last month I didn't have a baby. Last month I didn't know how to fold a stroller one-handed, or how a baby sling looks so easy and still comes with a five-page direction booklet, or how sleep is the only thing worth living for in life or how there are only two kinds of people in the world, those with children and those without." I realized as soon as I said those last words that I didn't mean them. I loved Beth and Beth was the other kind of person. We both knew she always would be. All of a sudden, I felt like we were on different continents. And not just because we really were on different continents.

"Look," she said after a pause, sounding solicitous and friendly again. "I've made my arrival date a few days early because I want to come see you and help you out. We can get ready for this thing together. I'll do anything you want, anything you need. Hey, I'll even do diapers, or laundry. We'll go shopping for something to wear." I thought for a moment about Lumpkin, my belly, and the elaborate measures we would need to go to to disguise its consistency.

"When is this again?"

"May tenth," Beth said calmly. In fact, I could hear her typing in the background, sending off an email, no doubt. Beth and her computer were rarely parted.

"That's in two months. Zach won't even be three months old!"

"Right. That's why I'm calling now. To give you time to prepare. Will it be okay with Drew if I come?" She sounded distant then, officious.

"Of course. That's not what I meant."

"I'm so excited," she bleated girlishly. "It will be like old times." But *I* knew that couldn't be true. I could never have old times again. I would never be me again. I loved Zach with that kind of burning mother love you read about in Greek plays—the kind that makes you swoon and murder. I knew I couldn't old-time it. I was a lunatic. I still wore maternity pants. I talked every day about bowel movements that weren't mine. I had a vagina someone patted like a puppy after giving it stitches. I was, in fact, a *mother*. "Oh," Beth added like a sidebar. "Jake is coming too. I already spoke with him. Apparently his sister lives in Mystic; he'll stay with her. He says he can't wait to see you again."

"Jake..." I looked down at my colossal bosom, searching for the baby's head somewhere between it and Lumpkin. When I found him, I realized he'd fallen off to sleep. He looked like a wizened cherub. A wizened gypsy cherub since he'd come out looking entirely like me—unruly black hair, skin like a green olive, opaque brown eyes.

"Oh, no! Not Jake. Tell me someone else is coming. Tell me Mary Bloom with her awful prissy nose and short temper is coming. Tell me Ralph is coming—"

"Who's Ralph?"

"That weirdo I accidentally slept with freshman year—"

"Oh, right." Beth laughed. "Talk about a mistake."

"I'd rather see him than Jake! I can't see Jake looking like this. I'm a mess."

"Joy, calm down. It's only Jake, remember? Your *friend* Jake. It's been ages since you dated. And you weren't even together that long."

"More than three years. Three years is a very long time. Especially when you're twenty."

"But you're married now. You're happy. You have a baby. You have a gorgeous house in the froufrou section of Connecticut. You couldn't possibly still be interested in Jake. I mean, how long since you've even seen each other?"

"Let's see," I thought about it for all of ten seconds. I remembered perfectly the last time I saw Jake, right before he moved to London. "It's been six years. He left just before I got married."

"You're overreacting. It's probably the hormones. Aren't they supposed to make you crazy?" She didn't stop for my answer. "So what? Your gorgeous college boyfriend is going to see you a little flubbed out. He'll love you anyway. He has to; he's your friend."

"We lost touch. We haven't talked in a year or more."

"He's still your friend. He asks me about you whenever I see him."

"Of course. You're right. I'm being silly." I sucked my belly in. It wasn't all that big, was it? "I'll be glad to reconnect with him. It's no big deal."

"It'll be fun," Beth said. I sighed. "Honey, don't stress it. I'm completely sure Jake is one hundred percent totally over you."

"I know that," I said impatiently. Of course I knew it. I didn't want to hear it. I'd heard it before, all those years ago, when he broke up with me.

* * *

I met Jake in college, the same place where I met Beth. We didn't go to Harvard, but then it wasn't one of these Davy Crockett Jones colleges either that no one has heard of except the people who work there. We did all right for ourselves. We planned on getting good jobs, maybe even great jobs. Ditto the expectation for husbands. In the meantime, college meant a fair amount of studying and a serious dose of attending parties where enough alcohol would be consumed to make everyone look attractive enough to sleep with.

Love at first sight would be a gross exaggeration. Okay, so *I* loved *him* at first sight and he found me very cute—like Cabbage Patch Kids cute. I don't think anyone has ever had a sexual feeling for a Cabbage Patch Kid (at least I seriously hope not), and that's because they simply are not sexy. I wasn't so bad in college, actually, and Beth gave me good advice on what to wear and how to use a lip liner so even after the lipstick faded you could find my lips in a dark room. It's just that Jake was a bit of a golden boy in college. Athletic. Intelligent. Drop-dead gorgeous. And I was goofy and silly and what some would politely call "eccentric." We had about as much in common as a squirrel and an elephant.

Somehow, Beth, Jake and I ended up becoming great friends. Maybe it was Beth's ability to get Jake dates with all of her bikini-waxed friends. I, for one, did not wear a bikini. I also figured if nature intended us to have hair in our nether regions, then it couldn't be such a bad idea to keep it there. Through no fault of his own, Jake slowly began to fall for me. Beth got involved with a guy we called "Rocket." With her over at his place most nights, our happy threesome turned into a much more intimate duo. Jake and I studied together many nights, and when we didn't study, we played endless games of War.

And then it happened. We made out. We had sex. The next day I woke up alone in my dorm room, horrified, with mascara train tracks on my cheeks. When Jake showed up a few hours later to bring me to lunch, he laughed at my melodramatics.

"You're real," he'd said. "That's why I want you." This would eventually be my downfall. "We're better as friends," he'd tell me, more than three years later. "We just don't have that, you know, spark."

We dated for three and a half years. But I always knew one thing: Jake was too cool for me. It was like sleeping with a Greek god. You realize at some point they're going to turn into a fox or a bolt of lightning, so you don't hold your breath waiting for a marriage proposal. Life with a bolt of lightning for a spouse seems a touch awkward. Never mind that a part of me wanted it, that a part of me imagined myself a little bit like a Greek goddess. That a part of me knew if I got to marry Jake, I would be the luckiest woman alive. But enough nostalgia for the good old days. Jake was one hundred percent over me. Obviously I didn't care. I had a baby to love.

If only I was one hundred percent over him.

Two

FOR ZACH'S TWO-MONTH BIRTHDAY, I THREW MYSELF a party. I pumped and pumped milk to save, mixed a margarita and drank it down before Drew even got home. Then I had sex with him for the first time in postmortem history. I ravaged him at the front door like a drunk woman, which is exactly what I was. I didn't feel much like ravaging anybody, but I convinced myself that we'd get along better if I could find the energy to attend to his manly needs, which, naturally, consisted of sex and—for a moment I couldn't remember the other one. Oh, yes, food.

Drew proceeded with admirable patience while I inserted the entire contents of a tube of K-Y Jelly into my motherly orifice. Then he paused and said:

"Ummm, I may not be able to feel much with all that goo in there."

Naturally, I wanted to slap him. Or maybe it was just that I'd wanted to slap him all the time ever since Zach's birth. I wanted to slap him for getting to be a father without having his body permanently altered. I wanted to slap him for lacking all maternal instincts, for callously leaving the baby to cry for minutes—minutes!—at a time. Instead, and I thought this mildly heroic of me, I said:

"Let's just give it a go anyway." After all, I didn't add, I'm only doing it for your sake.

Okay, how can I describe this experience? The term "rebirth" doesn't quite capture the sensation. All I know is that there is no tube of K-Y Jelly large enough.

"Was that okay?" Drew asked.

"About as okay as childbirth." I mean, I lived through *that*, didn't I?

I started at about the same time to earnestly think about exercising. I hadn't started the actual exercising part of the plan, but I'd accomplished a lot of thinking. The reunion loomed just ahead like a monstrous reminder of all I would never be again (single, skinny, able to speak in complete sentences). At another time in my life I would have kicked it into high gear. I would have started running every day and spent morning and evening by my bedside counting push-ups and sit-ups. I couldn't, this time, motivate past the extreme exhaustion. Not even by thinking of Jake. I simply could not make myself perform a sit-up. For that matter, I couldn't stop eating chocolate. I think it had something to do with being overwhelmed, between thinking about what to wear for the reunion (i.e., when Jake set eyes on me again), and the awful prospect of sharing my mother with her new beau Donny, all I wanted to do was eat myself into a muumuu.

My meeting with the latest object of my mother's attention turned out bad, like scary bad. Like B-movie scary bad.

He acted like a fool trying to make solemn small talk with the baby. "Does she crawl?" he asked. "He's two and a half weeks old," I pointed out. He merely nodded his head. My mother kept wrapping herself around him as if she'd had a mysterious transformation into a wisteria tree. I couldn't imagine what the attraction could possibly be. Donny was old, a touch overweight, and insincerely sincere. How can you believe someone who acts so serious all the time? I've made it a habit only to trust funny people. He depressed me enough that after his visit I sat down to a bowl of cookie dough (and no, I didn't make it, store bought is good enough for me), which I proceeded to eat with a spoon.

I figured on two alternate plans, then, for my diet. One, about a week before the reunion, I'd stop eating for a few days and take off five pounds easy. Two, strategic fashion. I'd buy something with Beth, something nonmommy. And I'd buy one of those modern-day girdles that gives you long-term intestinal damage, but at least holds in the Jell-O pelvis for a good five hours. Not a bad trade-off, I'd say.

"Am I still attractive?" I asked Drew one night. The baby had taken to sleeping, occasionally, for four or five hours. It felt incredibly decadent, almost sinful, to sleep so many hours in a row by myself. So I'd taken to reading in the night just to make sure I didn't get used to living that kind of luxurious life. No, no more of that for me. I was a mother! I kept martyrdom always in my sights. I'd learned to sacrifice. I'd learned that I didn't need to eat when I was hungry or sleep when I was tired or pee when my bladder was full. I'd learned I didn't need intimacy or adult conversation or clean clothes or even clean hair. My former life seemed impossibly depraved. Eight hours' sleep! Good grief, I'm sure Mother

Teresa never slept that long. She had lepers to attend to. And I had...I had little Zach, fruit of my womb, light of my life. "Oh God, it's been five hours. Is he still breathing?"

Drew looked over at the bassinet. The early dawn brought the first hint of light into the room. "He's breathing," Drew said. "And you're attractive. Don't fret so much, Joy. You're doing a wonderful job." He patted me. He'd taken up the habit of patting me. It made me want to slap him. I'd begun to feel less and less like a woman with him and more and more like an aging Labrador retriever.

"Don't pat me."

"Sorry."

Then a long pause. The things we weren't saying could have filled a moving van.

"You didn't forget my mother is coming tomorrow, did you?" Drew said, carefully sidestepping the opportunity to bring up any of the big stuff.

"Of course not," I snarled. Of course I had forgotten. I always forget when his mother is coming. It's an act of kindness. If I thought about it, I'd kill myself.

"She wants to help with the baby."

"Of course she does." Her idea of helping consists of criticism and offering baby care advice regularly doled out to mothers in the year 1256.

"Have you thought of something nice for dinner?"

"Of course." Yeah, honey, I'm really into the gourmet meal planning. Like every other stay-at-home mother, there isn't much for me to do but pore endlessly through Martha Stewart magazines.

"That's great." And then another pat. "Let's get some sleep while the little guy is still out."

I reached over and patted him back, just to see what it felt like. Then I rolled over and stared at the bassinet. I could barely make out the rapid rising and falling of Zach's chest. The sight of it made my heart flutter, like a teenager in love for the first time.

When I met Drew a year after I graduated from college, I didn't know what he saw in me. He was pretty much the definition of Caucasian, whiter than Fluff, and an only child. Meanwhile, I've always looked vaguely like a gypsy; I have uncontrollable tufts of curly hair, which is why I always wear my hair short. I have more siblings than most people have relatives, and I practically raised them myself while my mother worked. Drew was clean cut, wholesome, conscientious, determinedly liberal (despite his ferociously Catholic mother and her medieval politics), and poor—but the good kind of poor, the we've-worked-for-everything-we-have-and-we're-very-proud-and-climbing-the-ladder-of-success-one-rung-at-a-time-toward-the-American-dream kind of poor. I was messy, accident prone, and in deep political denial. (In other words, I never read the newspaper, watched the TV news or listened to public radio. I guess if I had, I might have realized I had a perineum before I ripped it open during childbirth. Perineum seems like the kind of thing you might hear about on NPR, maybe even with a French accent.) My family was also entirely nonreligious and well off. Of course, the money got spent almost as quickly as it came in. There were a lot of mouths to feed.

Still, Drew had a thing for me. On our third date he told me he wanted to marry me. I am not making this up to sound prettier than I am even though I am okay in the looks department. (When I get all done up, I can look quite good.)

Honestly, though, he just had a thing for me. We'd met at a party where we convened around a bowl of Fritos, which apparently nobody else wanted to eat; that's the kind of bonding to build a life on, isn't it?

Okay, so it might be worth mentioning that I had just been dumped by Jake and that I did, oh, maybe a teensy-weensy bit (like Barbie's bikini teensy), hope that dating and being engaged to Drew would bring Jake back to me. If I hoped a little more than that, it's hardly seemed to matter all these years. Drew and I have been happy.

We got engaged quickly. And I did think of Jake when I took the ring and said yes. I couldn't help it. It hadn't even been six months since he'd moved out of our apartment. We'd broken up before then, but we'd lived together for a while after we broke up for the obvious reason that since we hadn't had sex in a year anyway, and since I in no way tempted Jake with my alluring femininity, living together would work just fine. "Why not?" Jake had said. Imagine how awful it was for me. I spent the whole year trying to lure him back into my bed—until Drew came along, of course.

Before Drew and I had known each other a year, we were officially on our way to matrimony. I couldn't find a reason not to. (It turned out we had much more in common than Fritos on account of both having lost our fathers as children.) A year and a half later we went to the justice of the peace. All our friends joked about us heading off to the courthouse. Everyone we knew had a proper wedding. This translates as spending years of their lives looking through sample invitations (snore) and spending their future children's college savings on pâté, organic flowers and favors that your guests can plant in their backyards so they'll remember your wedding long after you've stopped being friends. Our friends said they were going to count nine months and wait for a baby. They couldn't think of any other reason that we'd go for a civil ceremony. But that wasn't it. We wanted to be married; we just didn't want the conventional stuff. Drew didn't want the fanfare; he thought weddings were frivolous and a waste of money. I'd been to enough of my mother's not to need one for myself. Then we took our honeymoon in Nova Scotia. We saw lots and lots of trees. Drew loves trees. I don't.

Secretly, I've always felt a little guilty. I've never admitted to Drew that I don't see any difference in color between a green oak leaf, a green maple leaf, and a green pine needle, though he swears every kind of tree comes in a different shade of green. I don't want to be the kind of person who doesn't like trees; it doesn't seem very . . . friendly. I've kept it a secret all these years. And you know what? He still likes to tour me around a forest—and I still go.

Let me be exact. My mother-in-law, Priscilla McGuire, would terrify the Dalai Lama. I don't even think the Pope would be able to maintain his—what is it he has? popishness?—with her around. She's like a Catholic dominatrix gone mad. And did I mention Drew is her only child? That means Zach is THE grandchild.

When I first met Priscilla, Drew offered a number of insights that he thought would help me to view her compassionately. She had, after all, lost her husband, Walter. He died of a heart attack when Drew was twelve. When they first married she hoped for a large family, like the one she came from. But no amount of prayer brought any fruit to her womb. After Drew she turned barren as the desert. Once Walter died the chance of another child evaporated completely. I doubt

Priscilla has even shaken the hand of a man in her widow-hood, let alone slept with one. Apparently, at one time, she had enough facial muscle tone to smile—at least she was smiling in her wedding photos. By the time I met her, well, let me just say, she isn't a pretty woman, in any sense of the word.

It's amazing what you can forgive a person when you are first in love. I forgave Drew his awful mother; he couldn't help having an awful mother. I told him he could borrow mine anytime. Besides, when we were dating, his mother seemed entirely irrelevant. I didn't see her much. We didn't talk about her much. When I did see her I could hold my breath and practice nonviolence. It was great. It made me feel very spiritual. I'd leave her company without once having sworn, shouted, or committed a homicide. You can imagine, I became very proud.

But marriage, then Zach's birth, changed everything. As conspicuously absent as my own mother has been, Priscilla has been present. Priscilla had, by the time Zach turned two months old, invaded every corner of my psyche. It was like Chinese water torture, only much much worse. It was Catholic widow torture.

The funny thing is, as long as I loved Drew with all my heart, I could manage her. It seemed a small price to pay for my larger happiness. And I did feel bad for her. She looked like a shriveled pea pod someone had left out for a few nights—wrinkled, narrow and curling at the edges. But as my affection for Drew began to wane, taking care of Priscilla seemed too high a price, with no foreseen reward.

So I made a thick soup for her, and bought a fresh loaf of bread, tossed together some spring greens, walnuts and cranberries. I'm sure Drew thought it should have been more, but it was just enough that no one could properly complain.

"Look at the trouble you went to," Priscilla muttered disparagingly as she took the lid off the soup pot. She'd dressed in her characteristic gray, which only served to enhance the dull gray of her short hair. For some reason, she'd worn black ballet slippers, a throwback, I think, to the days when Walter still lived. He'd been a short man, and Priscilla is almost Amazonian in height. Their marriage apparently contributed to the not-too-flattering Igor hump on her back. "Now, my Walter knew how to make a pot of soup," she said, still scowling into the pot. This *Walter,* who generally made an appearance in everything Priscilla ever said, had never, as far as I gathered from Drew, cooked anything in his entire life.

"Oh," I said. "Well." Then, because it's my job to pretend that I don't really want to take Priscilla by the neck and give her a good wringing, I said, "I hope you like it. I made it just for you. I know how much you like a good vegetable broth. Why don't you sit down? It's almost ready."

"You should have kept the baby up," she reprimanded.

"It's not really possible to 'keep him up,' Priscilla. He's still just a newborn. He sleeps when he sleeps."

"I had Andrew on a schedule. He was always up for dinner. That was important for my Walter. He always wanted to see his boy."

"Uh-huh."

"Of course he was sleeping through the night by three weeks."

"Uh-huh."

"He always had a full tummy. We never bothered with that foolish nursing. Everyone knows it starves the baby."

"Uh-huh," I said, giving Drew a meaningful glance. Meaning: Can't you do something about this?

"Oh, dear." She looked over the food I'd set on the table. "I can't have lettuce."

"You can't have lettuce?"

"No, it gives me gas. And you know I don't eat bread."

"I didn't know you don't eat bread."

"I've never eaten bread."

"I've seen you eat bread."

"I've never eaten bread."

"Doesn't your mother eat bread, Drew?"

Drew looked red with discomfort. He shrugged.

And that is why I hate him. I sat fuming and hating him all night. He'd somehow become as passive as a sorority girl on a first date. I didn't remember him being that way before the baby. It's as though Zach rendered him a pale, mute version of himself. And I distinctly remembered Priscilla loving bread. She ate some of the soup. Then she put her spoon down.

"Too spicy." She made a face, puckering her lips as she licked them.

After college, I took a job working for a catering company. I think it gave Drew the wrong impression—that I cared for cooking, or at the very least can do it. But I worked for a caterer because it was a job, and like all college graduates with English degrees, I needed a job in a field totally unrelated to what I'd studied because nothing I studied could ever earn me a single dollar. (Yes, Shakespeare makes for great outdoor theater, but reading all his plays doesn't necessarily give one a marketable skill.) Of course, at one point I'd had some big idea. I wanted to write either the screenplay or the novel of the century or, at the very least, if I didn't have enough time for either of those, the poem of the century. All of this seemed

like the appropriate aspiration for an English major. It hadn't
yet dawned on me that I would need more than your garden-
variety talent to pull off such a stunt. Not unlike childbirth, it
appeared that many, many people had written books, poems
and plays. How hard could it be? Look at the human race.
That's a lot of women giving birth. It makes it seem, well, at-
tainable. When actually it's all very selective. You just can't
take this stuff for granted.

I find it some consolation that while I can't really cook, or
really write, I managed to produce a child. Frankly, it's the
best, most interesting thing I've ever done, albeit a pretty
common accomplishment. Still, when he came out with all
his limbs, with ears and eyes and mouth, it was like winning
the lottery. "Look! Feet! Hands! Testicles! Eyes! Two of each of
them!" I felt very proud indeed that my body had managed to
put together an entire baby with all the right pieces in all the
right places. For a period of time there—say maybe the first
hour—I thought, I've got this mother thing covered. It's all
biology anyway. And then the little creature started screaming
and didn't stop. I looked around the room for help. I looked
at the little red berry in my arms that not a moment before I'd
been admiring with total awe. Then I did what most new parents do; I pressed the nurses' call button.

Don't misunderstand me. That one hour of complete confidence in my baby-making abilities is now the stuff of myth
and legend. I am officially incompetent. I'm not that bad at
diaper changing. I'm pretty good with the breastfeeding
thing. I like the little guy a whole lot more than I ever thought
I would. I don't mean love, because of course I love him. I
mean *like*. As in I *enjoy* his company. Sometimes. It's sleep I
can't get a good handle on. Oh, yes, and sanity. Which I'm going to need a good dose of if I have to meet Jake, deal with this

new southern beau of my mother's and somehow live peacefully with the man formerly known as my husband (before he
transformed himself into Allergic-to-Baby-Man) and the
woman who loves him most in the world—no, not me—his
mother.

Realizing that my life required more than the usual amount
of energy, I headed to the store to replenish my decreasing
chocolate supply. When we arrived, I strapped Zach into his
baby carrier, where he promptly fell asleep. I felt free to mean-
der through the aisles. When I caught sight of another
mother wearing a baby in a carrier, I practically raced to her
side. I knew she was a new mother; she looked unkempt, fragile, lost. Her stringy hair appeared to have been neglected for
a full ten-month term. When I came upon her, she was staring
at the peanut butter. For a long time. Without moving. It
looked like peanut butter meditation. It was so Zen, I didn't
want to interrupt. But I couldn't help myself. She had "kin-
dred spirit" written all over her.

"How old is yours?" I finally asked quietly. I startled her so
much she jumped.

"Excuse me?"

"Oh, sorry. I just asked how old . . . your baby," I gestured
to the infant attached to her front. Then, just in case she'd
missed it, I gestured to the infant attached to my belly. "How
old is yours?"

"Oh." She brightened. "Nine weeks."

"He's just eight," I replied. "What's his birthday?"

"February ninth."

"He's the sixteenth!" I practically shouted with glee.

"Wow. They're, like, the same age."

"Almost. Although I guess when we stop counting their age in weeks and months, it's not going to matter. They'll be the same age then. Just think when they're ten or twenty or thirty they'll be exactly the same age. These days, I guess, developmentally a week is a lot of time, but down the road it's not going to matter at all. I mean, anyone born in the same year as me I consider to be the same age. Actually, anyone born within a few years of me, I consider to be the same age. Don't you? Really anyone in the same generation. I guess I'm old enough to think of it that way now. But maybe I'm older than you. Am I older than you? I'm thirty-two. You look younger than that, though. If I had to guess I'd say twenty-nine." I stopped to take a breath, and a silence as big as King Kong filled the grocery store. Then the woman broke into squeals of laughter.

"You must be staying home too," she finally said through her laughter. And then, more calmly, "I know just how you feel. I'm at home too."

"Really? No one I know is. That's the best news I've heard in weeks."

We swapped a few baby puke stories and tips on how to sleep during the day (close your curtains, wear one ear plug—so you can still hear the baby—and always take your phone off the hook). My new friend read me like a three-page baby's first book. No explaining to do. No need to impress. I instantly liked her more than I'd liked Drew lately. It was as if she *knew* me, knew what I was going through. When she looked into my cart and saw the heaping pile of chocolate bars, we shared a belly laugh. In my case, a jiggly belly laugh.

We exchanged numbers, and I called her that night to set up a time to get together. I read her name from the back of my grocery receipt. Diana Walker. It might as well have said

Leonardo DiCaprio. It was like salvation. And she lived five minutes away. *Local* salvation. Practically like drive-through salvation. What could be better than that?

When Melody, my above-average-in-every-way friend, came over the next day with baby Sarah in tow, she acted offended by my new-mommy-friend story.

"What am I? Chopped liver? You should have called me if you were having such a hard time."

"I do call you," I said defensively, switching Zach from the left to the right breast. "Besides, it's not unreasonable to want more than one friend in my life, is it?"

"I guess." She sighed a bit. "I guess I just feel bad for not realizing you were still struggling."

"Look at me, Mel. My whole life is falling apart. I love this baby, but I don't know what I'm doing. I feel like I've totally lost myself. I can't remember what I used to do with all my time. The worst part is I feel like I've lost Drew in all this. We can't manage to carry on a conversation. My marriage is crap; my mind's a big mush pile. My mother's deserted me—"

"But all that is normal. Just par for the course."

"See, this is why I don't talk to you. You're a therapist. I can't talk to therapists. They don't listen."

"What are you talking about! I *am* listening." She picked up Sarah and plunked her down on the play mat. At five months she was an entirely different creature from Zach. She touched things, for one. She'd also developed a habit of smiling and cooing. She acted like a baby, in fact, whereas Zach hadn't left the amoeba phase.

"No offense, Melody. You know I love you. It's just that you have your life so together. No one wants to talk about their problems with someone who doesn't have any."

"You're crazy, Joy."

"Exactly, that's what I'm trying to tell you."

"No, not because of motherhood. Because you think I don't have any problems."

"But you don't! You're like the mommy professional. You've adjusted to motherhood effortlessly. You've never even skipped a beat. You and Eric still maul each other like newly-weds, as far as I can tell, and your maternal hormones are like Canada, they're so mild. Besides, you're back at work. You can't know what it's like to be home all day alone with a baby with no one to help you or talk to you. Drew's so caught up in Clarkville that I only see him first thing in the morning and last thing at night."

"I have all kinds of problems; they're just not interesting enough to talk about. And I only work part time," she said.

"Right. And when you're working, Eric has the baby. Drew would never do that."

"He would if he had to. You know Eric. He'd rather stay home. He's never wanted to work full time. And you know that I wouldn't be working if I didn't have to. We couldn't make it without my salary, not if we want to stay in Clarkville."

"Well, what about the baby then? How come you're so easy with Sarah?"

"She's older than Zach—"

"Barely."

"Hey, remember when I called you crying when Sarah was first born? Of course you don't. You were too busy being pregnant. I had a few rough days. It just gets better. I promise you. And you have to remember that I raised all my siblings, practically. And with Eric home so much I get lots of help around the house. Besides, my mother is close. I think she's over at least three times a week."

"Should I remind you that I also raised a bunch of brothers? Anyway, this whole conversation is making me sick to my stomach. I mean, how can I be friends with someone I am so jealous of?!" I made a gagging face and Sarah laughed at it. Melody just pouted.

"Okay," I finally say. "You know I'm happy for you. I just feel like I'm drowning here. I mean, I love Zach. I don't want to be doing anything else—except maybe sleeping. I certainly don't miss working. I liked editing, but it's not as though it satisfied my soul." I squeezed Zach gently. "I just feel like I'm losing it. I don't have it together like you. I can't seem to get my footing. I know if I could sleep for twenty-four hours straight, everything would be better." Melody had begun to look a little tired with my conversation. "Do you want to hear a funny story?" I asked her.

"Sure."

"The other day, while I was eating a pound bag of M&M's, I dropped one of the candies. I couldn't find it anywhere on the floor. You know what I did?" Melody smirked. "I got down on my hands and knees and searched for that sucker. I looked around for a good five minutes, but I still couldn't find it."

"The Tale of the Missing M&M. I can see the headline now." I could see Melody was enjoying my tale of woe.

"While I was making my search-and-rescue effort, I had to contort myself into all sorts of positions. During those contortions every part of my body came into contact with my stomach; it was unavoidable. It was so awful, it almost made me stop eating."

She raised her eyebrows suspiciously. "So what did you do with the rest of the bag?"

"I ate it. And then, at bedtime, I found the missing one."

"No!"

"Yes. In. My. Bra."

Melody broke into laughter. "You know," she said, "you do have some things I don't have."

"Like what? Stretch marks?"

"Like a really good sense of self-irony and a great sense of humor."

"Ha. I'd sell them for a nap. I'd sell my soul for a nap."

"Then go take one," she said. "I'll watch Zach."

"Really?" I began to salivate at the thought.

"Really. But I'll expect your soul in return."

The beauty of old friends is they forgive you for being yourself. They're like family. They've sworn some sort of secret oath to stick around despite your hideous faults. Melody even hugged me when she left, and we both laughed together. I think she called me a mouthy, cranky nuisance, or something like that. But she loves me anyway. She's seen my better days. I'm pretty certain I've had better days.

After she left I put Zach in one of his slings and walked him around the block. I told him about the trees and the new buds and the coming leaves, about sunlight and rain and dirt and photosynthesis. When we got back to the house, Drew was just pulling up.

"You're way early," I told him. "We usually don't see you until well after midnight. Like a werewolf." Of course this hadn't started with Zach. Drew worked like a dog long before. When he took the job at Clarkville, he'd only had four years of *teaching* high school, which meant there was a lot of catching up to do if he wanted to make it as the lead administrator.

It's true the school was falling apart; that's why they wanted him. They'd been doing so badly for so many years, their reputation was on the line. Financially, they couldn't continue. Where once they enrolled four hundred students, they were down to less than two hundred. The board discussed either closing the school or allowing girls. They unanimously decided to close the school. No one could stand the thought of girls coming into the all-male playground. (Must be that vagina thing again.) Then one of the members had the bright idea of firing the headmaster, some guy named Luke Lampheter, who was about one hundred and fifty years old. They'd hired him years back because he was supposedly an expert at saving schools in financial ruin. He came with a price tag of more than four hundred grand a year. I think it's fair to call such an occurrence ironic. Normally, I don't use the word, but there is no better word for Luke Lampheter's brand of school saving.

Firing Dr. Lampheter and hiring a total nobody—my husband—enabled the place to stay alive. They pay Drew a more modest salary, for which he works tirelessly almost all year long. What they didn't expect is the revival that's begun to happen under his leadership. Drew's the unlikely candidate; he looks like the boys at Clarkville. He's as Anglo as they come—blond, blue eyes, pale, fit and articulate. Yet he came from almost nothing. Most of the kids at Clarkville have allowances the size of my yearly income back when I was editing. They all have summer homes on Nantucket or Martha's Vineyard. They sail and play tennis. I couldn't imagine Drew identifying with these spoiled, opinionated, entitled kids. But he'd managed to save the day. He'd increased the enrollment, kept the place financially viable for three years (after a year spent dragging it out of its hole), and managed to ensure that maxi pad dispensers would never have to insult the bathroom walls of Clarkville Academy, Private Preparatory School for Boys. I think "No Girls Allowed" would be a catchy byline for them; Drew just won't go for it. Oh, well. Their loss.

"Thought you might like some company," he said, getting out of his Audi.

"Maybe." I squinted at him. He ignored the comment.

"How's our little guy?" He peered over the edge of the sling. Zach's eyes were wide open. He looked away from the sky and toward his father's face. Then he smiled.

"Did you see that! That's the first time I've ever seen him smile for real! That was way more than the gas smiles!" Tears started to well in my eyes.

"You happy to see your pop, little guy? Huh? You got another smile for me?" He reached a hand in and gently tickled the baby's belly. Another smile, this one even bigger.

"I can't believe it," I said. "Where's the camera?"

And that's how the night went. The two of us, camera at the ready, staring and staring, waiting and waiting for the next smile. We wanted it preserved forever. Or maybe we just wanted a moment that would never end, a happy moment. I don't know what I thought, that he would never smile again? That we needed proof? Don't all babies smile, eventually? But he wasn't all babies. He was *our* baby, and for the evening we were joined in our mutual delight. We had done something right. By the time I made it to bed, I felt so thoroughly proud of our shared accomplishment—we'd managed to produce a baby functional enough to smile—that I reached over and hugged Drew.

"What was that about?"

"Don't be so shocked. It's not like I never touch you."

"Just wondered if there was a reason. I've been persona non grata around here."

"You know the reason for that, and I doubt you want to get into it again," I muttered. "And *when* are you around here?"

"What?"

"You're never here, Drew. Let's face it. I've been doing this parenting thing almost completely alone for the past two months. I feel like a single mother."

"I can't help that," he said defensively. "You *knew* when I took the job at Clarkville that I'd be working long hours. You wanted me to take this job. It means we have this house. It means we get to live in Clarkville."

"I don't care about the house, or the town."

"You did when we got it."

"Well, I don't anymore. I want help, Drew. I want *your* help."

"Joy. You know the deal. My taking the position of headmaster at Clarkville means you don't have to work. That's what you wanted. That's what we both wanted, right?"

"Right," I said, rolling over and giving Drew the cold shoulder. "Right." But it didn't feel right. It didn't feel right at all.

Three

ON MAY 8 BETH ARRIVED FROM LONDON. I'D BEEN SIT-ting on the back deck with my mother, who'd paid me an unannounced visit, *sans* Donny (thank God), in the hopes of recruiting me for some new project. A secret project. She wouldn't reveal the details. She demanded I agree beforehand. I told her it was ridiculous, and she'd raised me to have enough brains not to fall for that one. Besides, it made me nervous. Ever since she'd brought Donny over to meet me, I'd started biting my nails again. Don't ask me to psychoanalyze myself on this one. I'd probably have to go back to when she first took up with my stepfather. If not, I'd probably have to go back to life in the womb, and since I've recently given birth, I'd rather *not* think about wombs at all. Something about Donny creeped me out. The balding head? Couldn't be that. The heavy southern drawl? Maybe. Or was it the way his stomach hung over his pants? I simply could not, for the life of me, imagine why my mother would be attracted to an overweight man. This is my *mother,* after all. Madeline Steeley, president of AllBeauty. She's as well preserved as an

Egyptian mummy. Until I met Donny, I thought fat men gave her hives.

Instead of revealing her secret plan to me, she asked me about my bladder, and if I peed when I sneezed. Was I Kegeling on a regular basis, she wanted to know, and when did I hope to have a second child? I honestly began wondering, as she talked, whether Valium would mix well with breastfeeding. Frankly, it was too much to take on: preserving the elasticity of my vagina, planning my future and improving my bladder control. How much free time did she think I had?

"It's just the sweatpants, sweetie," she was saying when I finally returned from my fantasy in pharmaceutical land.

"What about my sweatpants?" I looked down at my favorite pair of pants in all the world, brown—or what the catalog cheerfully dubbed "sparrow"—going on ten years old, stained here and there, a little baggy in the butt, but hey, Zach never complained.

"Joy, I need you to be honest with me."

"I never lie to you, Mom."

"Honey, do you ever take them off?"

"Do I ever take what off?"

"The sweatpants, Joy. We're talking about your pants. It looks like you might have given birth in those pants."

"What are you implying?"

"I don't need to imply, sweetie. I'm asking point blank. Do you ever take those pants off?"

I looked at my mother with her wide brown-doe eyes. Wearing a tan soft brim hat that covered some of her fiery red thick hair (dyed, naturally and in a bob), a loosely tied pale pink scarf around her neck and a knee-length pale pink skirt with a flounce, she looked, as always, perfectly put together. Her legs were crossed at the ankles. Lipstick: frosted pink.

Because she'd been using her own magic serum for thirty years she looked half her age. Except at her neck. She had the neck of an endangered turtle. Or maybe I was just being feisty and offended. Who cares if I wear the same pants every day?

"Mom, I like these pants."

"Have you washed them, Joy?"

She spoke gently, as to an asylum patient. For a moment I wanted to curl up in her lap and cry like a baby. Okay, so I hadn't glided smoothly into this motherhood thing. Lumpkin still weighed me down. In fact, when I would lie in bed on my side, my whole belly sank down to mattress level, pulled by gravity, forming a loose ball of random, irrelevant flesh. How long would this last?

"I'll take them off. I promise," I told her. And I meant it. Zach was nearing three months. I certainly did my fair share of laundry. No, revise that statement: I did *all* the laundry in the house. Drew has a thing about laundry, like a phobia. A severe phobia, like the people who can't get on planes without taking horse tranquilizers. He could really do it, drop dead of a heart attack upon setting eyes on the washing machine. And what a sad way to go.

But that's beside the point. In fact, the whole conversation with my mother wouldn't merit any attention if it weren't for the fact that right at that moment, as I made my promise to eventually remove my fading, stained and, let's admit it, slightly smelly sweatpants, Beth appeared. And behind Beth a tall, beautiful, curly-headed man. More specifically, Jake.

I'd mentioned to Diana, my mommy friend, my new favorite person in all the world, about the imminent arrival of hunk-college-boyfriend-who-dumped-me-for-being-too-boring.

42 □ *Samantha Wilde*

"Too good to be true?" she said.

I described Jake to Diana, the silken blond curls, round blue eyes, wide shoulders, muscled arms, long legs with sexy thick calves. "More than too good to be true. He was perfect. He was everything I'd ever wanted. I couldn't believe my luck. I always wanted him to marry me. And the sex was also too good to be true. It was like doing it with an underwear model. I used to get up in the middle of the night and reapply my makeup so when we woke up and had morning sex I'd be more on his level."

Diana laughed. "I've never had too-good-to-be-true sex."

"Believe me, I paid my dues before Jake came along. My first college boyfriend, Noah, left a lot to be desired. Generally speaking, he had an orgasm *before* he even got inside me."

"You're kidding?!" Diana looked like she didn't know if she should laugh or blush.

"And then there was Ralph. We had about seven one-night stands. We kept ending up at the same parties and going home with each other. It was all very random. Finally, the last time, I woke up and told him that we had to stop accidentally falling into bed with each other. It's not as if I even enjoyed it. It was kind of something to do . . . to not feel lonely."

"I know how that goes," Diana said. "Sometimes I sleep with Jeff"—that's her husband—"just so *he* won't be lonely. I don't get lonely anymore, with Addicus around."

"I wish I could get lonely," I said.

"What will you do, when he comes?"

"Who?"

"Jake? Do you think it will be hard to see him?"

"After he dumped me, we were friends for quite a while. I'm sure it will be fine. It's so long ago now. I don't even know what he's up to, romantically, that is. He moved to London when his brother offered him a position at his publishing company. He's worked there as an editor for the past six years. Last time I talked to him I wasn't even pregnant."

"So you're not worried?" she asked me, staring down at Addicus and Zach who lay side by side on a large blue blanket spread out on my living room floor.

"I'm not worried at all. Why would I be worried?"

True to my word, I wasn't thinking about Jake's Adonis-like body when he showed up that day with Beth while my mother sat poised like a china doll in the sun on the porch and Zach snoozed in the bouncy chair at my feet, looking nothing short of completely angelic.

No, I was not thinking about how I snagged the sexiest man in college then lost him a few years later for lacking the "you know, spark." I wasn't wondering when my mother would reveal her latest secret, nor was I, for the moment, even dreading it. I was not, as I should have been, filled with joy at seeing my best friend. I was not full of pride to show off my newborn son.

I had one thing on my mind.

My sweatpants.

I couldn't believe that I would greet Jake, after years and years, in my old, raggedy, stinky sweats. I promptly stood up and shuffled into the house, dragging Lumpkin and my ten-foot long perineum with me. I felt like the Elephant Man. Only I was the Elephant *Woman* because all my deformities met around my still-swollen belly. I didn't even stop to say hello. I made a mad dash for the bedroom and dug through a pile of clothes, thigh deep, on the floor. I found a baby-blue knee-length skirt, wrinkled but apparently clean. I ripped off the old sweats, tore off the old underwear, collected some new white granny panties from the drawer and pulled on my skirt. Then I went back outside and smiled at my old friends.

It didn't occur to me until much later that day, when we'd said good-bye to Jake and I'd said good night to Beth (tucked away in our guest room), and Drew had begun his symphonic snoring, that that act of vanity, the small ego-driven desire to be presentable for an old flame, meant I had not been completely motherized. On closer inspection, my antics seemed almost hopeful, as if one day my womanhood would be restored to me. More simply put, it seemed like there was a chance that eventually I'd care about something other than Zach. Like hygiene.

"He's so beautiful," Beth said the next day.

"We think so."

"No, really, Joy. He's a beautiful baby."

"We think he's gorgeous, but you worry, you know, that maybe love has blinded you and maybe you've actually given birth to the only ugly baby on the planet. Motherhood totally lacks perspective."

"Okay. That's deeply neurotic thinking. Just to give you some perspective." She snorted. I'd had a similar conversation the other day with Diana. She'd nodded her head in ferocious agreement.

"You have a way with words," Diana had said. "You know how to say what I'm feeling."

"Seriously, Joy," Beth was saying. "He's perfect. I mean it. Now let's get going. We've got some shopping to do."

"I don't want to." I sat facing Beth, both of us on my bed, Zach lying between us, gazing interestedly at our faces. He'd reached a new milestone in his development. He could "play," which consisted of looking at colorful toys, gurgling at the ceiling fan, and smiling.

"I've seen your closet, honey. We've got to get you something that fits for the reunion."

"No, I mean, I don't want to go to the reunion."

"It's only a few hours' drive. You'll be fine."

"It's not the drive."

"What?" Beth looked at me tenderly, or as tenderly as a career woman with a twenty-four-inch waist can look at a jellified, mommified old friend. "Are you worried what people will think?"

"Actually"—I sighed and picked up my little guy—"I think it's that I don't care. I'm happy to see you and . . . Jake, of course. I just don't want to see anyone else. Reunions are a lot of drinking and melancholy reminiscing anyway. I don't have enough active memory to reminisce about anything. This is my life," I said, kissing the baby and pressing him up to my cheek.

"Joy McGuire, don't be such a pathetic soccer mom. Your life is a lot bigger than that baby. It'd be good for you to see some old friends—and get away from Drew for the day. He needs to miss you, see how good you are for him."

"He won't notice I'm gone. He's always working. That school consumes him. Before Zach I hardly noticed how much he worked. I'd work late nights too, or go out with a friend. I never realized how much time Clarkville takes up. Not to mention the fact that I'm still pissed about the birth, and I'm not forgiving him until he makes a formal apology."

"What can you do?" Beth said. "Don't go looking for problems. I wish I had someone, anyone, half as good as Drew. You're lucky. Not that I want kids—you know that's not my thing. I'm too selfish to clean up someone else's shit...but I wouldn't mind my own Drew." She stood up abruptly and smoothed her khakis. "This place smells." She wiggled her nose and giggled. "Let's put some clean sheets on the bed, whaddya say? Then we'll hop in the car and hit the mall."

I pouted.

"Do it for my sake, Joy. I don't want to go to the reunion alone."

"Jake will be with you. You won't be alone."

"It won't be the same," she said. "Besides, he probably came for you—"

"What?" My heart started to pump just that teensy weensy bit faster. "What do you mean?"

"You've always been closer, that's all. And he's seen me a few times over the years. We do live in the same city. He hasn't seen you in forever."

"Oh, right." Of course. What had I thought?

"Just come, all right? Don't make me bribe you." Beth sat back down on the bed. "He looks good though, doesn't he? Maybe I should go for him." She laughed, as if the whole thing meant nothing.

But he did. He did look good. He looked delectable. He looked so good it surprised me to realize I had a lusty molecule left in my body. Don't they all come out with the afterbirth? Isn't placenta code for: your brain, your libido and your looks?

Here's what I remember for details, because I don't remember many of the little things.

Jake and I got our own apartment senior year. We adopted a small gray dog aptly named Toto. Jake would wake up early in the morning with the sun. He'd take Toto out for a long walk. He walked with him rain or shine, in snow and sleet and impossible humidity. What I remember best of those days is this: Jake always came back to bed and kissed me after his walks. In the late fall and winter his cheeks would be so cold, he would even smell like the cold. But his lips were always warm against mine.

Later that day Drew came home and asked me, with Beth sitting right at the table, "What do you do all day?" as if it had only just occurred to him that I might have something to do. Or perhaps he asked because it occurred to him that I didn't appear to have anything worth doing at all. Or maybe it's because he knows I spend my days taking care of our son and somehow taking care of a baby doesn't qualify as "doing" anything. Like it's still pregnancy and I just carry him around all day. Like it's just life as normal around here.

Okay, to be fair—and I'm not sure I even want to be fair about Drew anymore—but I'm a good person so I'm going to try. To be fair . . . to the sniveling little toad he's become . . . he phrased it this way: "What did you do all day?" and he might have only meant this one day, but he had a look in his eyes, a tone in his voice. I mean, I know I'm over all that hormonal stuff. I'm not just reacting in rages or in tears anymore. I can't be making this all up. I honestly think the guy didn't mean a nice thing with that question.

Right. You're thinking the same thing that Beth thought, that maybe I didn't need to get up from the table in a huff and do all the dishes before anyone had had a chance to eat. Maybe I didn't need to empty out the last of the milk into the sink, claiming it was old when it wasn't, so that Drew couldn't have his favorite cup of tea with milk and sugar. Maybe I could have been slightly more gracious when he came into the kitchen to make it right, spouting enough feminist rhetoric to make Gloria Steinem jealous and promising me he didn't mean anything by his comment.

But I bet you would be wrong. I know the guy too well. Drew and I go back almost ten years now. I've been married to him for six of them. When I stood in front of that judge, I knew what I was getting into. I knew he wore smelly leather shoes in the summer. I knew he snored all night. I knew he didn't do laundry, rarely cooked and once on the couch had the particular habit of staying there. Still, we had so much in common on account of both having dead fathers. Being half orphans is something you can explain to people with two living parents, but they won't ever understand. Drew and I had an understanding about our sadness. Only we did entirely opposite things with it. In order to survive I became angry and funny. (I'm not saying this because I figured that out about myself on my own through astute powers of self-observation. Drew actually summarized the situation that way. "You dealt with your father's death pretty well. You got to be angrier and funnier." If I had to analyze myself I would have simply stated I was more fucked up.) Drew, meanwhile, became quieter and more remote. Basically, not funny.

I guess I just didn't bargain for this—this sense of being so different from him when I'd always felt like we were mostly alike. Since Zach's birth, or now that I thought of it, since the pregnancy, it seemed we didn't even live in the same world. I hadn't bargained for his I-want-to-save-the-world complex (one of the first things I loved about him) to turn into 2 a.m. nights at Clarkville Academy, phone calls from trustees during dinner and the general inability to think about anything other than his total responsibility to the school. Like, for example, his wife. And child. I never noticed how bad things had gotten, until Zach came along.

"What do you know about taking care of a baby?" I asked him later that night as we fought in hushed whispers, trying not to wake Beth.

"Look, Joy. Just let it go, okay? I didn't mean anything by it."

"I'm not so sure about that, Drew. If I thought you meant that I'd forgive you in an instant."

"There's nothing to forgive. I didn't do anything wrong."

"Innocent, as usual."

He sighed. Huffed. Puffed. Would he blow the house down? Would I? All of a sudden I had to sleep in bed with a stranger, and not just my gelatinous belly. My husband. The man who was supposed to be my best friend. My lover.

He rolled over and showed me his back. It seemed one of us was always turning away lately. Then the phone rang. My heart leapt as I picked it up. Who would call after ten? Everyone knew we had a baby, that we went to bed early. Could it be Diana? We'd told each other to call at any time, day or night, if crises set in.

Drew grabbed the phone. "Hello," he said. "Not at all. Of course."

I could tell by the tone of his voice, it was a trustee.

"Why don't you two get a room," I said grumpily, and heaved myself out of bed in search of some chocolate.

The next day, on two segments of three hours' sleep each, I had to face my ten-year college reunion. Here is a concise summary.

Al Barton drank until he slurred. Mary Clare Muggins, née Clark, talked about her real estate investments. John Downy came with his wife, Marigold, and their newborn daughter, Siesta. (Yes, you heard me right. Siesta.) I didn't ask if the next one would be Fiesta. Abby Kornfield, née Jones, told us about converting to Judaism after marrying a rabbi. And we heard, though we didn't talk to him, that Bruce Tate converted to Mormonism. I kept looking at him from a distance to see if I could tell, like he might look different somehow, somehow more Mormon. (I've heard they have secret underwear; *I* want secret underwear too. I debated pulling Bruce Tate's pants off. It seemed like a good sign that sanity was returning to find, at the end of the night, that I had not even made an attempt at it.) I was relieved to see that my old pal Ralph hadn't made it. Overall, everyone had put on weight. Except maybe Mary Bloom, who we always called "the slenderizer" anyway. She told us about her divorce. I couldn't help feeling secretly happy to hear of her misfortune; she'd always been so . . . smug, the way only naturally skinny people can be.

They served more drinks than I've ever seen in my life, probably to make up for the fact that the food stank. Had college food always been so bad? Beth sat to my right, occasionally taking Zach for me. We'd dressed him in baby blue pinstripes. (Drew stayed home. He had work to do, what else? It wasn't his college and he wanted to give me a chance to bond with people, he said, to cover his ass.) Jake sat to my left. Every time he moved, I could smell him. The smell aroused me. I wore black. At the store, Beth had insisted I go for something patterned. She thought the zebra stripes flattered my figure. I wanted black. It went with my postmortem attitude. "This is a funeral for our youth," I told her. "Don't let the melodrama kill you," she said in reply.

As the dinner wore on I became desperate to nurse but equally afraid of nursing in front of all my old classmates. Zach seemed to be holding up all right; meanwhile my breasts had morphed into two enormous whiteheads just begging to be popped. (Not a pleasant thought but neither are engorged breasts.) I could have turned to Jake and said, Please, nurse me! but that might have been a bit strange. Instead I turned to Beth.

"I'm ready to go."

"We just got here."

I looked at my watch.

"You're right. We just got here four hours ago! I've got to find a private place; I'm dying to breastfeed. Do they look any bigger? You should feel them. They're hard as rocks. Here, feel them, you won't believe it."

"Now, there's a good idea! I can feel you up at our ten-year reunion. That way everyone will know we've become lesbian lovers." Beth laughed. "I'll have to pass. I have my sights on someone else."

"Who?" Her intrigue instantly drew me away from the drama of my breasts. She made googly eyes in the direction of David Martin, a tall, rather thin, elegantly dressed man with all his hair still intact. I could almost draw up a memory of him as a geeky college student playing Ultimate Frisbee on the quad at dusk.

"Didn't he used to have long hair?"

"Not anymore," she said, smacking her lips. He did look pretty handsome, even to me. "I'm going to see what his life's all about," she said, getting up from the table. That left me in the awkward position of having to make small talk with people I never wanted to talk to in the first place while I desperately wracked my brain trying to remember if there was a good, comfortable chair somewhere nearby to sit in and nurse. As it happened, small talk at your ten-year reunion does not cover the topic of where to breastfeed. Instead, it revolves around one issue: work. Apparently career and career planning is the only appropriate discourse in the real world. I hadn't realized this until I didn't have one.

"And what are you doing now?" everyone asked.

"Staying at home full time with Zach."

Up the eyebrows would go.

"He's not even three months," I'd mutter apologetically, which lowered the eyebrows about a quarter inch, but they never did return to normal. Either that or everyone had acquired a face-lift since last I'd seen them—the eye-lift variety that makes you look constantly startled. Who thought that one up? "Besides, I like staying home. They're young for such a short period of time." I truly appreciated the jaw-dropping response to that comment. I could see the double-income mommies imagining in horror life without power lunches or cash for pedicures.

I guess I could have said that I'm a baby professional. That might have been a more impressive translation of my occupation. What is the right word for one who cleans shit out of cloth? (Yes, that's right, we're using cloth diapers. Drew insisted. He has a deep bond with landfills everywhere. It's part of his desire to save the world and everything on it. I did, by the way, admire this quality in him for a time. Unfortunately, I'd begun to see it as deeply pathological and dangerous to my health. At least cloth diapers are much better than they used to be. No sticky pins. However, poop is poop, and when I rinse them out in the sink I occasionally have to use my nails to get out all the goo. Glamour? I've never had it so good.)

"It doesn't matter," Beth told me when I pathetically complained about feeling joblessly inadequate. "None of them were being honest anyway," she said. At least that part was true. Laura Carton, for example, seemed awfully impressive, already into her pediatric residency and with two children out of diapers (early potty training, naturally). But I did watch her down about ten glasses of wine with such aplomb that I am quite certain she makes a regular habit of it.

So we didn't talk about hemorrhoids and impossible husbands and alcohol problems and postmortem insanity. It was a party, after all. Instead we stuck to the safe stuff and talked work and politics until my head was about as ready to burst as my breasts. I finally (it seemed like an eternity but it was only ten minutes) excused myself from the table and found a couch in the student lounge where I gratefully breastfed Zach for half an hour.

I couldn't get my mind off my mother and Donny. It was a bit of a pastime of mine; running her beaus through my amateur psychologist bullshit-o-meter. Only because I don't have anything else to do, obviously. And because the man is a freak. Overzealous for one thing, which is always suspicious. Tickling isn't quite the right way to interact with a three-week-old. They don't even know they have bodies, which gets in the way slightly when you're expecting some kind of reaction. God knows what he'd do with a three-month-old—teach him to drive? Maybe it was just naïveté on his part. And I had to wonder if he'd made up his thick southern accent. He said he'd been living in New Haven for thirty years; that's hardly y'all territory. I didn't ask, though I felt a touch suspicious, about how the two of them met. My mother generally meets men "in the industry" (beauty or fashion or television) in places like Paris and Milan. Donny struck me as someone you'd meet from a newspaper personals section. When I asked what he did for a living, my mother had laughed and said, "Donny's a renaissance man." Renaissance indeed. He called my mother "my lady" every time he talked to her. It all made me feel rather morning sick. He shook my hand when he left, and it was sweaty.

In an effort not to think about how weird all of *that* was, I allowed myself to think of Jake. It was an excellent reprieve from every other disappointing thought coming my way. It was also slightly unavoidable. Everywhere Jake went, my eyes followed, even though I willed them not to. I told Beth later it felt as if I'd become a marionette. "Uh-huh," she said. "Or maybe a poltergeist took possession of my body." "Uh-huh," she said. I didn't let myself think too much of it. What's a little involuntary eye movement, after all? I enjoyed it. All this time, I'd thought my desire had gone to the grave along with my size five underwear—replaced by wholesome mothering, high-waisted size eights. Was I wrong? I couldn't be wrong. So Jake reached over for the bottle of white wine and accidentally brushed his arm against the front of my shirt and it made me feel hungry in a way I hadn't been hungry for a long time. Reunions are like that. They make you feel young, maybe even beautiful.

No, it couldn't be lust. I knew my libido had safely gone into retirement. I get reassurance of this all the time at home, where I generally feel like Medusa. Whenever I enter a room, Drew jumps. "God, you scared me," he keeps saying. Really, it's insulting. It's not like I'm still prone in bed bleeding profusely and begging for narcotics. I've made great strides in three months. I can do laundry and make dinner most nights. I've even devised a leg-shaving strategy. I place Zach on his play mat then rush to the bathroom to fill up my sitz bath with water, grab a razor and gel and then head back on the double. For as long as he'll lie there cooing, I can shave. Generally, I can accomplish one leg and then get to the other one at least by the next afternoon. For nonmothers this incredible feat of ingenuity may go unnoticed, but let me assure you, shaving legs is more time consuming and involving than writing an email. And I still haven't been able to write an email and send it off on the same day.

"It's disgusting," Beth said as we drove home. It was so late that we were the only ones on the highway. Zach, totally depleted from the excitement of the evening, had fallen immediately asleep when I put him in his car seat. Talk about overstimulation; he hadn't been able to take his eyes off the enormous ceiling fans in the cafeteria.

"What's disgusting? My body? Look, it happens—"

"For heaven's sake, not your body, Joy. You look much better than you think you do, anyway."

"Thank you."

"You're welcome."

"So what's disgusting?" I leaned against the cool window, relieved to be heading home.

"The men at the reunion."

"Say more."

"Did you notice that most of the women in our class have already made something of themselves? They've either gotten married or had a kid or have a real job. The guys? Bachelors. Still farting around their parents' houses."

"Is that so bad?"

"Not technically bad, not like evil bad, but it's an emotional disaster. I once dated a man who still lived with his mother, and I will never, ever do that again. He was like a Freudian time bomb waiting to explode."

"It can't have been that bad."

"She fed him food off of her spoon! I mean, yuck, yuck, ick, gross. It's too weird, that whole mother-son thing. There wasn't space for me in his bed, his mother took up so much room. What is it, anyway, with mothers and their sons? Scary, is all I can say . . . Joy?"

She looked over quickly. She'd agreed to do the two-hour drive home. I didn't have enough energy to keep my eyes open. On the other hand, her little tirade on the mother-son relationship woke me up a bit.

"Oh, honey," she went on quickly. "I wasn't talking about you and Zach. You'll be a wonderful mother for him. I'm sure you won't smother him and make him unfit for married life. No, no, there are some good mothers out there. And some good men, still." She patted my arm. (What is it with all the patting? Just because I look like an éclair stuffed in a black sack isn't any reason to patronize me.) "Don't take it to heart. You're doing a wonderful job."

"Thank you," I muttered. "I think I'm going to try to sleep."

"Okay," she said cheerily.

"By the way, on the topic of men, what was with you and David Martin? I could barely break you two apart."

"Just getting to know each other again."

"You never knew him before."

"Details, my friend, just details."

"He doesn't live with his mother, does he?" I giggled.

"Very funny. Of course not. He even does his own laundry."

I couldn't keep myself from laughing. "You asked, did you?

You asked him about his laundry? I'd like to know how that came up."

"I've been in the field a long time," she said, quite seriously. "A lot longer than you. You've been married your whole adult life. You don't know what it's like. It's one of the first things I ask—right up there with 'What do you do?' and 'who do you live with?' I've learned how to weed them out. If they don't do laundry, I don't date 'em."

"Well, I wish I was there. I wish I was single."

"You do not."

"I'd date Jake."

"You're crazy."

"Am I? When he looks at me, I feel like I'm twenty and everything is still in front of me."

"Don't get cheesy on me."

"I'm serious. You know that feeling when you're driving in the car and a song you really love comes on the radio and the window is down and you can go a little faster than you should and you feel like everything is yours and the world is beautiful and you're free? That's how I feel when he looks at me."

"Uh-oh," she said.

Uh-oh, indeed.

THE NEXT MORNING, I WOKE UP IN A VERY BAD MOOD.
Or should I say a very bad mood woke me up?

"He's in the shower, Priscilla. I can have him call you
back."

"Oh, I don't need Drew. I just thought I'd let you know
that I'm on the way over."

"You're on the way over?"

"I'm just dying to see my little grandson. Drew said you
had him out until all hours last night."

I looked over at Zach, who'd gone down for an early
morning nap.

"He's sleeping right now, Priscilla. Maybe later."

"They never sleep long, newborns. I bet he'll be up before
I get there."

"Actually . . . we have company now. My friend Beth from—"

"You can just ask Drew to wait until I get there. I want to
see him too. I love seeing my boys. My Walter always believed
in putting family first, you know."

"Priscilla, I was up so late—"

"Oh, Joy, I think you're breaking up. I'll see you in a few minutes."

Hmm. Drew's bad idea to get his mother a cell phone. "She's old," he reasoned. "For safety." The woman, instead, used the thing like a weapon, and I was her favorite target.

"Your mother's coming right now," I said when Drew walked in naked from the bathroom. It wasn't quite seven. He had an early meeting, as he always did on Tuesdays. I watched him get dressed. It amazed me. I felt nothing. Not a single thing. He hadn't gained a pound in all the years I knew him. He still went to the gym three times a week—the school had some state-of-the-art equipment—and he played volleyball whenever he got the chance. Yet, even with his firm, slender body, looking healthy and vigorous, I didn't have a single grain of desire for him. He seemed distracted. Too tied up with more important matters. Everyone knows, anyhow, that the sexiest person is someone who pays *attention* to you.

"What are you doing, honey?" he asked.

"Watching you."

"You look upset."

"I'm exhausted. That was a long trip. I'm not sure it was the right thing to do."

"To go to the reunion?"

"It was nice to see people, but the only people I really care about are Jake and Beth. It took a lot of effort, I guess. I'm tired."

"You'd be tired anyway, right? Seems like it. Seems like you're always tired these days." I watched Drew knot a tie, then he sat down beside me on the bed. "Hey, have a good day, okay?" I made a face, like the opposite of the face-lift face. I narrowed my eyebrows and puckered my lips and probably looked ten years older. I guess one would call it a sneer.

"What now?"

"Nothing." I reached down and patted my flubby belly. I'd woken up feeling even more like a jellyroll than the night before.

"I've got to go."

"And?" Now I did the eyebrow raise. Like: Tell Me Something I Don't Know. I'd been through Tuesdays with Drew for four years ever since he took the job at Clarkville Academy. I knew his schedule so well I could set my libido by it. For example, we only had sex in the mornings on Monday or Friday, because Tuesday, Wednesday and Thursday he couldn't spare the time or the energy. At least that was the case back when we had sex. Back when we had mornings that weren't interrupted by loud squawks. Back when we liked each other.

"You never asked about the reunion," I muttered.

"Didn't you just tell me about it?"

I sighed. "Does one comment count as telling you anything about it?"

"Fine," he said grumpily. "How was it?" I could tell he was just itching to get out the door, and not just because he had a meeting.

I wanted to open my mouth and tell him that Jake had involuntarily touched me and I got aroused for the first time in thirteen months. Would that make him stay? Would that make him interested in me again? Not likely. He looked downright hostile. I stared him down. I debated telling him his nose had gotten smaller and his jowls larger and not just to be mean, even though I did want to be mean. I really did think his nose had gotten smaller. Or maybe, and this is the worst possibility of all, his nose had always been small and I'd never noticed. Maybe I'd loved him so much I'd overlooked the way it sort of pinched in the middle. Can you trust a man with nostrils that small? I'd never thought of it before but all of a sudden it seemed troubling, the size of his nose, like a sign. I scanned my memory bank for an image of Jake's nose. If I remembered correctly, he had a hearty nose, a manly nose, a nose he probably stuck paper airplanes up when he was a child. Meanwhile, this man, my husband, well, it seems he didn't have a normal childhood at all. It seems nothing could have been stuck up that nose.

"Joy? I'm going. You can glare at me later."

"You can't leave."

"Look, I have—"

"Not me," I said with the appropriate amount of disgust. "Your mother. She's coming over. She wanted you to stay."

"Well, I can't. You'll have to talk to her for me."

"Great."

"Great."

"Great."

Why didn't anyone ever tell me how like third grade married life really is?

I tried not to spend the day pondering the size of Drew's nose. After all, I had to deal with Priscilla, who came in and woke the baby then stayed to watch her television programs while I brought her food and drinks while she lectured me on the dangers of breastfeeding. I had Beth to deal with, who wanted to go out shopping since it was her last day in the States. I had to deal with Zach, who hadn't quite learned the word "wait." Then I had to deal with Jake, who came up from his sister's in Mystic for the day to spend time with Beth and me.

"This is terrific," Beth said when Jake arrived. "We can all go out for dinner."

"I couldn't—" I started, terrified by the prospect of leaving Zach alone with Priscilla. Sure, she could keep him *alive*. I wasn't worried about that. But what about permanent damage? What about Zach sitting on a therapist's couch trying to recall his early experiences of motherly desertion?

"That's perfect, dear" came a squeak from the High Priestess of Annoyance. "I can watch Zachary. You go on out. You probably have so much catching up to do. I'll give the baby a bottle."

"You know he doesn't really get bottles when he breast-feeds so easily. I really couldn't leave him." With you, you nasty old witch. "I can bring him."

"I don't mind," Priscilla said firmly. "It seems like he might have a tummyache, anyhow. Your milk doesn't seem to agree with him."

"It's best if he comes," I said, and then I gave *her* the eyebrow raise. I lifted them up to the top of my scalp and gave her my best look of complete disdain.

"I'd prefer if he came," Jake said, as if he'd intuited my fears. "We'll make it a party." He gave Priscilla a generous smile. "In fact, I was hoping Drew would be able to come too." Drew and Jake had become buddies around the same time that Drew and I started dating, although I knew they'd lost touch, just like I had with Jake.

"Drew won't be able to make it," I told Jake. "He's got a meeting he can't miss." Jake looked disappointed.

"He's got a very important job," Priscilla said.

"Well, then Zach will have to take his place," Jake said.

"Saved the day, didn't he?" Beth said a few minutes later while we changed in my bedroom into dinner clothes.

"Was he always so charming? So in tune? He was, wasn't he?" I asked, running my hands through my hair in an effort to tame it. Brushes don't work with my hair. Nothing works with my hair. It's highly antisocial.

"He should be on that bachelor show. He's that kind of guy. Tall, rich and good-looking."

"If he were the bachelor, I'd go on the show—and I can't even stand to watch reality TV." Beth peered at me from behind her compact. She was standing at the full-length mirror.

"Don't worry," I said in response to her gaze. "Drew and I are like a barnacle and a rock."

"That's romantic."

"Actually, there's nothing romantic about marriage, and there's even less that's romantic about having a child with the person you effectively have no romance with."

"That's why I'm single," she said breezily.

"I'm jealous."

"No, you're not. You're just tired. A few good nights of sleep and you'll realize how lucky you are."

"I don't feel lucky. I feel like Drew has a small nose."

"He does. So what?"

"Don't you think men with small noses are...untrustworthy? They're like weasels."

"Weasels don't have small noses."

"Well, then what animal has a small nose?"

"Bunny rabbits," Beth said, quite pleased with herself. "You don't have anything against bunny rabbits, do you?"

"Why does everyone defend Drew?"

"I'm not trying to defend him. I just think you're a little— overwrought."

"I know you mean that nicely."

"No, I really do, Joy. I really mean it nicely. Besides, it's not personal. I think every new mother is overwrought. You've got to deal with crying and throw-up and stretch marks and the total life change from woman to mother. You're in a new category now. You're officially the kind of person that some men will never sleep with on principle. I've dated a number of men who just can't go there. They can't hop into bed with a mother."

"Thanks, Beth. You always cheer me up." I looked out the window into the backyard feeling a touch dismal. I loved Beth; she was like a sister—someone permanent, irritating, but reliable in the story of my life. It wasn't her fault. Motherhood made the differences between us seem even greater than they were before. She'd never wanted any of what I had: the marriage, the motherhood thing, the house, the domestic chores. Beth was constitutionally opposed to marriage. She'd lived through her parents' harrowing divorce and sworn never to get herself into a similar mess. I could remember her saying almost daily in college that she'd never repeat that mistake. "Marriage is for morons" was, if I recall correctly, her favorite tagline. I couldn't help feeling that she pitied me just the littlest bit. Not that she would ever be the kind to say "I told you so." But she told me so.

"It's not all bad," I finally said. "Most of our marriage has been great—until the birth." I held up my hand to stop her. "And I don't want to talk about it, okay?"

"Okay, okay." She turned to look at herself from the back. "Your life isn't so bad. I might die skinnier, but you'll probably die happy and not alone." She turned toward me, her auburn curls (curling iron) framing her face. She was pretty, as pretty as any woman, slender, with full lips and high cheekbones. But she had funny toes. Toes that run at odd angles to one another. Asymmetrical toes. They are also long and square at the tips and quite manly. She hated them, naturally, but I loved them. They were so totally human. I'd always loved her because of her toes. They evened the playing field. No matter how fat, boring or unfashionable I became, she would always have ugly toes. She would never be able to wear flip-flops or sexy open-toed sandals. And I would.

She reached over and put her hands on my face, one on each cheek. She looked me dead in the eye. "I am a little jealous," she said quietly. "You're pretty lucky. Even with all the poop and a husband with a small nose." I raised my eyebrows again, innocently this time. A question. "No," she said. "I am not jealous enough to do anything about it. I won't get married and no way am I going through childbirth. It's meant for horses, not humans." We laughed. It was quite possibly a perfect moment. Then the baby sang out in a shrieking cry. The bell tolling for me. I felt my breasts respond; before I knew it, two small wet spots, the size of dimes, appeared on my shirt.

"Horses, huh? Try cows," I said, getting up to fetch the baby.

After I nursed Zach, I shuttled Priscilla out the door.

"I've got to call Drew before we go," I told my friends. "It won't take any time." They happily headed out to the deck with wineglasses in hand. I overheard Beth telling Jake that my important phone call had something to do with laundry.

Indeed it did. The dryer had stopped working. I wanted to see about getting a new one. Drew bristled at the irrelevance of my phone call. He assumes he's got more important things to do than consult on dryers. He's in charge of a school of two hundred and twelve teenage boys. It's more than a man his age should have to control. But he's totally immersed in their world. It's like he left me to join the Cult of Adolescent Testosterone. He knows each of the students at the school by name. By *name*. Can you imagine the kind of brain you need to know the name of each kid and match it with his face? It's like that memory game we used to play as kids. I bet Drew won it every time. If I'm honest, I'll admit that it's just this sort of thing I used to love in Drew. Before I realized that the more he gave to other people, the less I'd get.

So what that the man doesn't care about the heaping pile of piss-stained cloth diapers sitting in a pile on the basement floor? The only reason I do laundry every other hour is because of his deep concern for the Earth. Some days I have wished he would have an equally deep concern for the Wife. However, all things wifely are of no interest to him whatsoever. It's like he's forgotten this world entirely. Diana told me her husband developed a serious back problem about the time her son was born. The doctors can't find anything wrong and yet he is in constant pain. Curious, isn't it? Is mothering that horrifying? Is it too much like birth? Does everyone need to leave the room when the vagina makes an appearance? Does everyone need to leave the room when spit-up enters the conversation? Okay, maybe I'm not quite as interesting as I used to be, but it *is* his kid. And it's his EARTH. I figured he'd be interested in the dryer problem.

"Hang them outside. It's nice out now. They'll dry perfectly well."

Of course, they'd probably dry even better outside with the sun to whiten them. I knew that. I just didn't want to DO the work to get them there.

"I want a new dryer."

"Let me look at it first. I may be able to fix it."

"When will you have time to look at it?"

"This weekend."

"This weekend?" I could feel myself getting angrier. I looked down at Zach, who was lying on his play mat staring up at me, or maybe he was looking at the ceiling, or the fan, or the edge of my nose. I couldn't tell.

Beth trotted in to grab the wine bottle. She gave me a questioning look. I suppose I looked rather dire. I held up one finger to motion her to stay.

"Yes, Joy. You can survive until then," Drew was saying.

"That's easy for you to say—"

"I have a lot to do. You know the end of the year is a busy time."

"It's always a busy time."

"That's because I have a job."

He said the words slowly, as if to a disobedient puppy.

"You're going to be sorry you said that."

"I didn't mean it that way, Joy. For God's sake. You're so testy. Don't take it personally."

But how could I not? It appears that everyone and his mother assumes that I have no job, that I am, in fact, busy with the activity of eating bonbons. I will concede that it's easier than it was in the first month. Easier than the second month. But I still can't sit down and eat a meal. Zach has some sort of internal timer that goes off the second my butt hits a chair. As soon as I want to sit, he wants to be held and he wants to be walked. I finally figured out how to wear the ergonomically correct baby carrier I got as a shower gift. The thing is genius—except for the fact that it takes me twenty-five minutes to put it on and tighten all the right straps and place Zach in as carefully as a raw egg. Once he's in there, though, freedom! Two hands! I can wash dishes. I can chop vegetables. I can floss my teeth. I can do almost anything, except I can't sit. The second my rear end touches down, all hell breaks loose. All that effort, all the energy expended walking around and around the block, around and around the kitchen table, up and down the stairs, does not, apparently, constitute a JOB.

I decided to let it go.

"You know what you remind me of?" Beth said when I got off the phone. "One time, years ago, I was at the beach. I'd unthinkingly placed my towel down next to a family. I think there were two kids, maybe even three. They were pretty kids, blond and doughy, old enough to walk but still looking like babies. The mother had on a slimming black bathing suit and a wide-brimmed hat. Occasionally she'd read her book, but mostly she ran after one child or another. The father was a little paunchy but stylish. He still had those nice man thighs. You know what I mean?" I nodded.

"Anyhow, that's not the point. The point is, every time the mother talked to her children, she would say 'Okay, honey, let's not do this.' She used a nice voice, like I'm using with you now. Every time she spoke to her husband, it was like 'What? What's the matter with you? Get it yourself!' " She stopped her story and looked at me expectantly.

"What's your point?"

"You're loving when you talk to Zach."

"He's a baby."

"It's just funny, that's all. Typical, I guess."

"It's not my fault Zach has better manners than his father."

"Just an observation."

"You know he's on probation with me," I said.

"You've got to make up some time."

I didn't want to, but I *could* see her point. If I cared, I might even have done something about it. It reminds me of my father's parents. They had a wide porch where they'd sit together. My grandfather would sit me down beside him and teach me card games. He was a mean poker player. My grandmother still thought of gambling as sinful. I don't think she made her way into the modern world. She wore two braids twisted and knotted high on the top of her head. She called my grandfather Pop and he called her Ma and they would shout at each other across the dinner table.

"What did you put in this, Ma?"

"Not good enough for you, then?"

They bickered about food, too much salt, too little, not enough meat, not enough vegetables. I don't think my father thought anything of it. I asked him once. "That's just how they are. They love each other; they drive each other crazy." They apparently also drove their children crazy because my father's sister, Hilda, lives in some kind of a special group home for crazy people. I've never met her in my life. She's more of a legend than a person. I once saw a picture of her as a girl, and she was mystically beautiful staring out at the camera with a shy smile.

I could tell Beth that I grew up with the working assumption that hating your spouse was the stuff marriages are made of. But then, she knew it already; she's single for a reason.

Jake sauntered in to join us. He looked appropriately casual, his blue button-down shirt hanging over a pair of khaki shorts.

"Ladies," he said.

Just the sight of him made me more self-conscious. I hadn't counted on him coming for the day. My hand immediately flew to my chin, where I could feel one short, spiky hair poking out. I'd noticed it first thing that morning but hadn't, with all the Priscilla/laundry/breastfeeding and infant commotion, found the time to take care of it.

"Excuse me. I'll be right back." I put Zach into Beth's lap and headed for the bathroom where I proceeded to make a copious, fervent search for the hair. I brought out the magnifying mirror and sent out a search party; even with the bright lights and my pores blown up to a hundred times their size, I couldn't find it.

Then I found it.

It was white.

A white chin hair.

You know what that means? It means I will grow up to be an old lady with whiskers. I will sit in a nursing home and no one will tweeze me and I will look like a half-plucked chicken and my grandchildren will be afraid of me and they will ask: We won't look like that when we're old, right, Daddy? And their daddy will say: Be nice. Old people can't help it.

I swear if I didn't have a date with my college sweetheart, and if he didn't smell so good and act so charming, I would retire from life altogether. I am clearly not fit for human consumption.

We went to Louay's. I lugged Zach in his travel seat, which I consider one of the worst inventions of modern parenting. The thing weighs about twenty pounds empty. It's impossible to carry gracefully. When you walk you have to hold it far away from you until your shoulder aches or else it will bump against your leg and give you bruises. It has only one practical purpose as far as I can tell: You can transport a sleeping baby in it without waking him up.

I had too much misplaced pride to let Jake carry it, though he offered a dozen times.

"For heaven's sake," Beth said. "What are you trying to prove? Let the man carry the baby thing."

"I do it all the time," I said. In the back of my mind I worried that if I handed the carrier over to Jake, our arms might touch. Arm touching, in my current state, seemed dangerous indeed.

I put my sleeping baby on the floor by my feet. Jake sat across from me, Beth to my right.

"This is better," Beth said, settling her napkin in her lap. "Like old times. Now we can really talk. I want all the dirt, Jake. And from you too, Joykins."

"You know all my dirt. Actually, it's not dirt. It's more like baby poo."

"Motherhood seems to suit you," Jake said.

"Are you being serious?"

"I'm being honest," he said.

"You do look good, Joy," Beth said.

"What are you two buttering me up for, huh? What do you want? All my money? You want Zach to sell him into the illegal adoption trade?" They laughed, which made me inanely happy. I loved that I could still make people laugh.

"You're all rosy and mothery," Beth said.

"Like something in bloom," finished Jake, and though he was looking at his menu when he said this, I got a flutter, somewhere in the vicinity of my heart.

I started to drool when Beth's margarita arrived. I would have killed for a drink.

"You're too pure," Beth said. "One drink isn't going to ruin Zach for life."

"It goes right into the breast milk."

"What are you afraid of? That it will make him dumb? Stupid people are happier anyway," she said, toasting Jake.

I lifted my water glass. "I'll have to remember that. You might be right. I know a stupid person, and he seems very happy."

"Who's this?" asked Jake.

"My mother's new boyfriend."

"That woman has stamina," Beth said. "I want to be like her when I grow up."

"Me too, only I've realized I'm far too ordinary."

"I always liked your mother," Jake said.

"Yeah, but she has terrible taste in men."

Beth wanted to know what was wrong with him so I proceeded to give a full account of Donny's Texan faults. "I cannot imagine what she sees in him. For one thing, he's a lot older than her. For another, he's a lot fatter. For another, he has no discernible vocation. Or chin, for that matter."

"That's love for you," Beth said.

"I can't believe you of all people would say that! You don't even believe in love."

"I do so," Beth protested. "Just not marriage."

"It doesn't sound like they've dated for very long," Jake said.

"My point exactly. I don't know who he is. I don't know what he's all about."

"Did you Google him?" Jake asked.

"I hadn't thought of it." All of a sudden, I thought of it! What a genius idea. I could Google the guy, find out what he was all about, if he had a criminal record or something, find out if he belonged to the Texan mob.

"I Google every guy I date," Beth said. "You wouldn't believe what I find."

"I Google the women I date," Jake said. "And I don't find anything out!"

"Then they must not be interesting," Beth said.

Jake laughed heartily. I couldn't help gazing at his face, his open mouth, his full lips. I remembered how nice it was to kiss him. For a flash, that's what I wanted, to kiss him, but not just to kiss him, but to be young again, to be alone in the world, that kind of free I would never be again. Just as I had this wickedly selfish, unmotherly thought, Zach, as if he could read my mind, began to holler, a gut-wrenching cry, pure agony on the ears. I scurried to get him out of his seat. I could see the heads turning in alarm, the unspoken words: "Shut that baby up."

By the time I got my son with his emergency siren vocal cords settled in my lap, I had returned to my normal self. I no longer felt like leaping into Jake's lap, thank God. Besides embarrassing myself terribly, I'm sure I wouldn't have fit.

I'm not regretful. Really, none of my friends would use that word to describe me. I have plenty of other bad qualities. I'm sarcastic, moody, maybe even temperamental, but not regretful or melancholic or depressive. There's only one thing in my life I've regretted, and that's what happened when Jake broke things off with me, and only a teensy bit.

"Water under the bridge," I muttered to myself, trying to clear my head.

"What?" Jake asked.

"Nothing. Nothing. Let's talk about you guys for a while. Tell me about the wild, English single life. Go ahead, make me jealous."

"Jake's not so single, are you, Jake?"

"Not so much, lately." He grinned.

"And you know how it goes with me," Beth said, before I could break in and find out about Jake's girlfriend. "HIV tests, condom supplies, dark bars..." She laughed at her own joke just as Zach began to scream again. "Give that baby a drink," she said. "Preferably alcoholic."

I wrestled with my nursing shirt and finally managed to get Zach latched on. I could feel beads of sweat on my nose and my upper lip. Nothing like a crying baby to make a woman feel completely inadequate. I felt awkward and starving. Where was our food? When I looked up from my breast, I met Jake's eyes. He'd been staring at us.

"That's pretty cool," he said, nodding at the baby suckling away. I blushed. Of course I didn't know I'd blushed, I only found out later when Beth kindly pointed it out by saying "You really do still have a thing for Jake, don't you? You blushed throughout the meal like a Catholic schoolgirl in health class."

But at the moment I couldn't deal with my own foolish reactions to Jake's sweetness because my cell phone rang and it was Drew and Drew wanted to know what I had done to his mother to make her so angry and why hadn't it occurred to me that she might like to join us for our meal out.

"At least she could have watched Zach then," he said rather plaintively.

"Right. She would have felt right at home with us while we reminisce about college."

"That's not the point," he said.

"What is the point? You're *friends* with Jake and you didn't even come. Why would I invite her?"

"You hurt her feelings," he said.

"What about *my* feelings?" I said.

"I told her you'd apologize."

"You did what?" Jake and Beth were gazing at me intently. "We'll have to talk about this later," I hissed, then I gently pressed the End button without saying good-bye.

Five

HAVE I MENTIONED MY NARCOLEPSY? IT'S JUST A LITTLE problem I have. Like the little problem of peeing when I sneeze. It goes like this: Whenever I sit down for more than sixty seconds, I fall asleep. I've even mastered the art of sleeping in my armchair with the baby nursing or simply resting in my arms. Drew swears I fell asleep during dinner the other night. I'd gone to the huge effort of making food from scratch—you know, not previously frozen, not delivered by a teenager with pimples and not falling under the category of "easily microwavable." We were supposed to spend time together while the baby slept, since he'd routinely being going down for "the night" (which is merely a euphemism for a few hours before he wakes me out of a dead sleep and demands the boob) at about nine o'clock. The only problem is, nine o'clock is pretty damn late in my book.

About a month after Beth and Jake returned to London, leaving me relieved and melancholy over my college years, Drew suggested that, in honor of Zach's four-month-birthday, we watch a movie together.

"A movie?"

"Yeah. I brought one home for us."

"So that's why you're home so early."

"Nothing wrong with that, is there?"

"Do you know how long a movie runs?"

He stared at me like I was sprouting wings. I wasn't sprouting anything. In fact, I'd been losing more than I'd been gaining, and I don't mean weight. I'd been losing hair. The kind on my head. I'd rediscovered the shower after many months of neglect. I'd figured out how to place Zach down on a clean towel and play peek-a-boo around the shower curtain in an entertaining enough way that he could last almost ten minutes without demanding to be picked up. It's not like I hadn't noticed my hair falling out before that moment. It's just that in the shower the gobs of hair seemed even more disgusting. They'd lie like miniature hamsters on the floor of the shower. I started buying volumizing shampoo. Why do they have to say it right on the bottle? "For thin or thinning hair." I tried to grab one without attracting too much attention. It's one thing for a man to be thinning. It's another thing for a woman. I kept searching the top of my head for an impending bald spot. I asked Melody and Diana if this had happened to them. They both reassured me it was a totally normal part of the postmortem experience. Just like flatulence, indigestion and hemorrhoids are a normal part of pregnancy. Isn't nature a wonderful thing?

Drew swears by nature. It's part of his rabid environmentalism. He's done everything in his power to turn Clarkville into a "green" school. Actually, he's pulled off an impressive number of changes, enough to get written up in the *New York Times.* Clarkville is now *the* model of how to do it. I'm proud of him. I just don't have the same affinity for nature. I mean, nature isn't just 100 percent organic T-shirts and canvas bags at the grocery store. Nature is mosquitoes and ticks and weeds and poison ivy. It's tornadoes and volcanoes and landslides.

I can remember the first time Drew took me camping. We'd been dating for almost a year and were crazy for each other, the way you can be when you're having sex twenty times a week. Drew took me for my birthday up to Massachusetts to Mount Greylock because he thought it would be fun to climb to the top and then spend the night in the campground listening to the sounds of the wild. And just think of all those trees to look at!

He thoughtfully remembered a cake—chocolate with white frosting, my favorite kind. But no utensils. In the dead of the night, I woke up to the sounds of some very hungry animals. I don't know if they were bears or raccoons or over-grown squirrels, but they were big and they terrified the shit out of me. I'm not just saying that either; as soon as the sounds died down, I grabbed the flashlight and ran the fastest I've ever run all the way to the horrifically smelly outhouse, where I emptied myself of every last bite of cake Drew had so romantically fed me with his fingers (as well as everything else I'd eaten for days).

Now that Zach is four months, Drew has decided to take us on a camping trip. It's summer; he's on vacation. He figures the baby can snuggle up with us on the ground. It sounds like a form of punishment to me. I keep asking him what I've done to deserve such cruelty. I mean, I know I've got enough padding to qualify as a feather bed, but that doesn't mean I want to sleep on the ground. Drew doesn't find any of this funny. He wants his vacation in the great outdoors. He wants to make a fire from downed trees. I asked him if there was a spa at the campground. "Yes," he said. "It's called fresh air."

Fresh air is fine if you're looking for fresh air, but I'd been thinking more along the lines of a massage. I know I'll need one after a night on the cold, hard earth with an infant wailing beside me.

Zach has reached a whole new level. If I surround him with pillows and blankets, he can sit quite comfortably for long periods of time. I act out puppet shows for him, nibbling on his toes with the puppet mouths until I get a toothless smile. We have also devoted ourselves to "tummy time." After all, we've got to keep up with the Joneses. No slacking for my little soldier. Every day I get him down on his belly, while he whimpers and generally complains. "This is good for you," I tell him. When he's had enough he puts his head down on the floor and cries to break your heart.

Diana and I compare notes on the progress we're making in our new careers. We get together for our business lunches, and it's all about who napped when, and how many times someone woke up in the night, and what soothes them during the cocktail hour. She's also the only one I'd been confiding in about my feelings for Jake. Diana and I could joke about it, like we joke about the mess our lives have become since we gave birth, like we joke about being homicidal. (You can't joke with just anyone about being homicidal. Some people would not find it very funny.)

Diana, however, listened with a flattering level of interest. She wanted every detail, every line of the conversation. She was such an appreciative audience that when I talked to her, I felt like I belonged on the cover of a magazine in the checkout aisle of the grocery store. Being attracted to Jake was about the most interesting thing I'd done since giving birth.

"I can't blame you," Diana said. "If I had a handsome ex-boyfriend come to visit, I'm sure I'd feel the same."

"They're just feelings," I said.

"It's probably healthy to have sexual feelings. It's a sign that things are working normally."

"I guess it might be better to have them for my husband."

"It's hard to have them for our husbands. After all, they're the ones that got us into this situation in the first place."

"Good point," I said. "Jake never knocked me up. That makes him a lot sexier. But then the feelings aren't just sexual. Sometimes I imagine what it would have been like if I'd married him instead."

"And what would have happened?" she asked, all ears.

"It's not *what,* it's just the feelings. I imagine I would be feeling love, if I were with him. Not this, this pale, domestic sense of joint responsibility."

"I know how you feel," she said. But I wondered if she really did.

My mother called late in the evening.

"Sweetheart?" she said.

"Mom? What's going on? You scared me, calling so late."

"Have you guessed yet?" she said, ignoring me.

"What are you talking about?"

"My secret. Have you guessed the secret? Oh, honey. I'm so excited."

I hadn't guessed her secret. I'd forgotten about her secret, as a matter of fact. I suppose it hadn't occurred to her that I had other things on my mind. "Mom, it's late. I'm super tired."

She didn't say a word but I could hear her disappointment. Before the baby came along, we often talked at night, back when sleep wasn't an exotic country I dreamed of visiting. You *know*, back in my other life. Why hadn't she noticed that things—everything—had changed?

"Okay," I muttered, trying to put some heart into it. "I'll play along. Umm . . . what could it be? You're moving to Paris?"

"No."

"Ah. They're doing another write-up about your company in the *New York Times*."

"No."

"Come on, Mom. How can I know? You're pregnant?" We both laughed.

"That would be a miracle," she said.

"Or a disaster. You'd barely live to see him out of diapers."

"I'm not that old, thank you very much. I've got a lot of life in me."

"I give up, Mom. Just tell me. I'm exhausted." I wanted to say so tired of everything, particularly my husband who'd managed to fall asleep despite the conversation. His ability to fall asleep the instant his head hit the pillow was a particularly annoying habit; he might as well have been lying next to me laughing and saying "I sleep more than you! Nanny nanny boo hoo!"

"I'm getting married!" She paused. "That's it! That's the big news! Can you believe it? Donny asked me and we're going to do it, we really are. And you are going to be my matron of honor. We're having a winter wedding. I've set the date for December twenty-second. Picture white muffs, white fur trim on the collar of my dress. We'll have to think about the flowers. I think all red. What do you think about that? Isn't it wonderful, Joy? This is going to be so much fun. There's so much planning to do. You know I never thought I'd get to do this again. It's so exciting! Joy? Joy?"

"Excuse me just a moment." I put the phone down on the bed, got up, walked into the bathroom, shut the door, screamed as loudly as I could into a pile of towels, something along the lines of "AAAAAHHHHH," and then opened the door, walked back to the bed, sat down and picked up the phone.

"Honey? Are you okay?"

"Just fine, Mom. Never better."

"Isn't it wonderful?"

"Wonderful. It's just that your timing isn't great."

"My timing?"

"Never mind." How long had she known this southern charmer, anyway? Five, six months? Whereas I had been in her life forever. Didn't my needs come first? I *needed* her. I needed my mommy. That's right, me, a grown woman, a mother myself, with a house and a husband and the kind of life most people would kill for. And all I wanted was to curl up in my mother's lap. Except, of course, I wouldn't fit there. I doubt I'd be able to fit one butt cheek on her petite lap. "I'm really . . . happy for you. I guess I'll have to get to know Donny better." I wanted to do this about as much as I wanted to go through labor again.

"Oh, you will, darling. Soon enough you'll love him as much as I do." This I doubted very, very much. "This is going to be so fun! But we don't have much time so we're going to have to work fast. Let's shop for dresses next week. Keep your calendar open. Or maybe that isn't the best thing to do first. How about securing the location? Can you help me find a place? Should it be country or city? Maybe, since it's winter, we could have a sleigh, that's if it's in the country. Wouldn't that be romantic?"

"I'd say."

"Don't plan anything big," she said. "I'm going to need you."

At least that part wasn't going to be hard.

I had every reason, naturally, to be dour the next day, and Drew's absence, some meeting about school uniforms followed by a trip to the garden store, didn't do anything to help my mood. (Technically, Drew had the summer free, although that meant planning and meeting with someone almost every day. Funny how this quality I fell in love with, his compulsive responsibility, had turned into the thing I hated most about him.) Not that his presence would have done anything for me. In fact, I determined that nothing would make me feel better. Still, after I nursed Zach to sleep for his afternoon nap, I sat down at the computer to contemplate my email in-box. What exactly was I hoping for? I hadn't received an interesting email since I'd sent one (about five months). I weeded through the advertisements for sexual products, sexual favors and sexual pharmaceuticals (promising myself the whole while to get a better spam filter), which pretty much left me with nothing.

I shot a quick email off to Beth saying hello.

Then I chewed on a nail.

I went to the bathroom, checked on Zach (still sleeping), came back, searched my address folder and chewed on another nail.

Then I quickly wrote:

Great to see you. Isn't it amazing how time has changed all of us? I can't believe it's been ten years. That reunion

made me feel OLD. Anything new since you left the
States? —Joy

I sent it off to jakephilips@lunerpress.com.

I went to the bathroom. I got myself a glass of water. I flipped the television on, watched the weather (sunny, humid), flipped it off. I checked on Zach (still sleeping). I went to the bathroom again and looked at myself in the mirror, grunted, then returned to my seat at the computer.

I took a deep breath. I hit the refresh button.

One new email. He'd written me back almost immediately. My mood instantly improved.

Great to hear from you, Joy. It was great to see you too—
motherhood seems to be treating you well. I've been
meaning to send off an email. Things are in a buzz here.
Luke—you remember my brother—runs the press. He's
keen on taking over another small publishing house—
constant negotiations now. It's always about the
almighty dollar. BTW—did you ever check out your
mother's new boyfriend? I've been wondering what
happened with that. J.

I'd forgotten about his advice. He was right. I *did* need to look into Donny's history. What if he led some kind of a double life with another family in another state? What if he was wanted by the law for being part of a child prostitution ring? It could happen. I knew it could happen. I've watched television; I knew the world. These things happen all the time. You can never be too careful. It was the perfect antidote to the terrible nuptial news. I wrote Jake back, explaining the status change from boyfriend to fiancé. He would get what a disaster this was. If Zach hadn't woken up right then, I would have begun my search in earnest. It was the perfect cure for what ailed me, a little old-fashioned snooping—in my mother's best interests, of course. If there was something wrong with Donny, I'd find out.

Six

"ESTELLE'S, SWEETIE, TOMORROW AT FOUR," SHE SAID when I picked up the phone. "And I can't wait to see that little treasure of a boy."

"Hello to you too. And I thought we weren't doing dresses first."

"It's going to be the hardest, so I thought I'd make it the first thing we do. Donny suggested a renaissance theme—"

"Tell me you're kidding."

"Don't be so quick to judge. I look good in an empire waist."

"Mom."

"You're right, honey. It's a bit over the top. Let's just take a look and see what we see, get some good ideas of what's out there. Now tell me how my little grandson is."

"You wouldn't believe how much he's changed. I swear every day he does something new. You can hand him a rattle now; he loves it. He'll shake it and gurgle. It's like he's singing."

"I remember those days, honey. I really do. I always loved having babies."

"Well, that's good, since you had so many."

"Is five so many?" my mother said, laughing girlishly. "If I could, I'd have another."

"Oh, please, don't. Drew already thinks you've single-handedly ruined the world by overpopulating it."

"How many children does Drew want?"

"Two."

"Hmmm." She was quiet for a moment. "Anyway, sweetheart, it's a date for tomorrow, right? I can't believe how soon it is. December twenty-second. How many months is that? Six? My goodness, we're going to have to work quickly. Do you know what size you are now?"

"Oh, God. Do we have to do it by size? Can't I just try things on and see what fits?"

"We'll see, honey."

"What's the color anyhow? What hideous pastel are you going to stick me in? For your second wedding, what did I wear? Oh, yeah, it was that light blue thing with the puffy sleeves: very eighties. I think even *your* dress had puffy sleeves. And then when you married Steve? That was yellow, wasn't it, but strapless. Please, please, tell me you're moving away from the pastels."

"I'm open," she said. "I want to go look and see what's pretty. You're the only person in my wedding party, you know. The kids are going to contribute in some other way, and Danny is boycotting the whole thing." The kids are my mother's three middle children from her second marriage: Marcus, Aden, and Trevor. Danny is, of course, her extra-credit baby, who's almost fifteen. He spends a lot of time with his father, Steve, in part because Steve leads travel tours all over the world, and Danny would rather travel than go to school. That's pretty much his only normal teenage quality.

He spends his free time playing cello and researching wine—but he won't drink the stuff. He's what my mother lovingly refers to as "unique."

You may have noticed I'm the only girl in the family. Thank God. Otherwise I might have gotten lost in the masses without a single distinguishing characteristic. Or I would have resorted to peculiar tendencies like Danny. Maybe I could have taken up canasta at thirteen.

"I'll be there," I tell my mother. "In fact, I'm kind of looking forward to it. It's better for Zach if we get out. He takes longer naps if he's had some excitement."

"I'm just the same, sweetie," she said seriously. "He must get it from me."

I didn't say anything about my plot to pick her brain and find out just what this Donny—give me a renaissance wedding—was all about.

That night I tried to explain to Drew why my mother's fourth marriage was enough to drive me back into my postmortem blues. Or maybe just lead me to eat a super-size bag of M&M's. He didn't get it.

"I'm happy for her. From what you've said, Donny is a great guy."

"What do you mean, 'great guy'? We don't know anything about him. He could be a criminal. He could be a child molester." Drew raised his eyebrows at me. "It happens all the time on TV," I said.

"This is not TV. This is your mother we're talking about. She's an adult. She knows what she's doing."

"Exactly. It's my mother we're talking about. That's what makes me suspicious. He's not her type."

"Not everybody has a type," Drew said, shifting his leg off of mine. We were lying in bed together while Zach nuzzled against us. Every time I got a whiff of his little baby head, I felt swoony with love. I was finally beginning to understand why my mother went through labor five times.

"I don't mean type like tall, dark and handsome. I mean type like normal human being."

"Come on, Joy. Now you're not being fair. He seems like a normal person, just because he's southern—"

"What if he just wants her money?"

"This really isn't a prime-time drama, honey. Besides, your mother isn't stupid. If she were stupid she wouldn't be so rich."

"She's not *so* rich," I said defensively.

"Relatively speaking." Drew closed his eyes. He looked tired, older. I could see a few silvery hairs mixed in with the blond. His skin gleamed fair as porcelain. I'd been hoping our baby would inherit it, instead of taking after me. I'm a "winter" according to a color analyst my mother once forced me to visit. I don't wish this on Zach. Winters look best in hot pink. Poor kid, he's doomed to a life of either looking sallow or being beat-up on the playground.

Drew reminds me of my Ken doll. He always has. As a child I had one Ken and ten Barbies. Ken would have to go away on business trips so he could come back and pretend to be someone else's husband. I tried to share him equally among my Barbies. He had sex with each of them once a week. That seemed pretty fair to my ten-year-old mind. I knew about sex, of course. My mother was into the biological model. When she got pregnant with Marcus I had just turned ten years old, and I got the full story—egg, sperm, embryo. When my Barbies had sex, Ken would lie beside the woman and say: "Now I am going to give you my sperm." I guess I missed out on a few of the details.

"I just feel like she's stealing my thunder," I said, trying again to get Drew's sympathy. "It should be all about the baby, but now it's about her."

"Your mother has always been about herself, Joy."

"How can you say that?"

"Because it's true." He reached over and lazily stroked my shoulder. "Is he asleep?" he asked, nodding to Zach. Then he opened his blue eyes and there was my Ken doll, ready for action. Where did he get the energy?

"I think so. But I'm not having sex with you until you apologize."

"For what? You've even said it to me before yourself. Your mother's self-consumed."

"She's busy," I said angrily. "Not self-consumed. The woman's done nothing but work like a dog and raise kids all her life."

"Selling beauty products is hardly manual labor."

"Drew! She runs a company. Don't be so petty. I could start in on your mother, you know. She's done nothing but live off of *us* for years."

"Okay, okay," he said, rolling onto his back. "We're even now. No more mother bashing."

I looked down at Zach, who lay flat on his back with his legs pulled up tightly below him, feet touching, like a frog.

"Is he going to talk like this about me?" I asked.

"You can count on it."

I sighed and lifted him gently off the bed and into the bassinet. We'd thought about moving him into the crib in the nursery but neither Drew nor I could bear to part with him.

We liked seeing his face first thing in the morning. We liked listening to his breath late at night. I liked not having to walk down the hall to soothe him when he cried. Most nights he only spent a few hours in his cradle anyway. Why torture myself further by having to get up in the night and sit in a rocking chair? I'll admit he's a little too into my all-night buffet, but who can blame him? If I had a soft-serve ice-cream machine in bed, I'd take advantage of it too.

"Mothers get a bad rap," I said, curling back up into bed.

"I'll give you a bad rap." Drew reached over and pulled me in. He kissed me. I thought of my Ken doll returning from a business trip every day to find a new wife, a wife with pointed feet and pointed breasts. I guess he had it pretty good. I, however, did not feel like Barbie.

"Another time? I'm really not up for it."

"You're never up for it."

"I'm sorry, I guess."

"You've changed," he said.

"You're a deserter," I said.

"Jesus, Joy," he said.

"Is that your foreplay?" I said.

"Good night," he said.

"Yeah, *good* night."

I intended to do some research on Donny before I met my mother the next day. Two things got in the way. My child, for one thing, and an hour-long screaming fit that left me dangling by a toenail on the cliff of sanity, and second, the fact that I had no idea what Donny's last name was. At least one of them was only a minor obstacle.

When I got to Estelle's in the city, I hugged my mother.

"Hey, sweet cheeks," she said, kissing Zach on the nose. "Let's get moving. I've got a dinner date with Donny at six."

"Oh, about Donny," I said. I could feel her tense up. I did have a bit of a history of disliking her boyfriends and husbands. Actually, it's a touch more than a history. I made some serious attempts to end her previous weddings. When I was ten, right before her second marriage, she found me looking through a book on witchcraft I'd taken out of the library. I was in deep contemplation of the poppet doll (think voodoo doll, big needles in various body parts) page when she caught me. What can I say? I was just a kid. My father had died. (Not like a poppet doll would have worked anyway.) "Nothing bad," I said. "I just didn't know his last name."

"Oh," she brightened. "Macnamara."

In five minutes flat, she had me loaded down with dresses and tucked into a dressing room.

"I'm coming in," she announced, as she threw open the dressing room door.

We both stared at my reflection in the mirror. I had on a handkerchief-style dress, the only problem was I actually looked like a handkerchief, which I don't think was the intention.

"No. Absolutely not." I shook my head vehemently. "This is not right for me."

"Well . . ." My mother trailed off. She put her hands on my hips and turned me this way and that. "I guess you're right."

"This is just depressing, Mom. You're almost sixty and you look better than me."

"Honey, be nice to yourself. You just had a baby." She ruffled through the dresses hanging on the wall. "Try this one." She held up an ankle-length burgundy A-line dress.

"I've never looked good in that style. I need something to hide my Lumpkin." She frowned and then walked out of the dressing room. I sat down on the floor next to Zach's travel seat. He was fascinated by the whole process, gurgling and giggling every time I put a new dress on. He always behaved better when he was out. My mother came back with a forest green empire-waist dress that looked to fall just below the knees. I pulled off the rag dress and stepped into this one. Again we looked at my reflection. Green works well with my dark hair. (Color analysts don't know everything.) This one had long sleeves and a square neckline. It accentuated my bosom and fell over my waist in the most merciful way.

"Oh, that's lovely," she said. "Let's go with this one, sweetie."

"What color are you wearing, anyway? Will this work with it?"

"I wanted to get your dress first," she said, "and go from there. I decided I'd match with you rather than the other way around." She pressed her check up against mine. "You're my girl," she said softly. "You're my little girl."

I called Melody on the way home.

"It wasn't as bad as I thought," I told her as I drove. I had on my fancy earpiece. It made me feel like an old-time phone operator. I loved the thing. "I actually found something that fits me. A miracle."

"You look good in everything," she said.

"That's a lie. What's everybody buttering me up for? Is there something going on I don't know about? Is it like the end of the world?

"Don't be so suspicious, you! Besides, where are all the

compliments coming from, anyway? Has Drew finally stepped up to the plate?"

"Drew, God, no. He's more absent than when he was at school full time. He can't seem to tear himself away from the garden. He's got about twenty different vegetables going now. I was thinking of Jake."

"Jake?"

"Oh, right. I never did tell you about this, did I?"

"I can't believe you're keeping a secret from me!"

It's true. I have had a history of telling Melody everything. She was the first one to know when I was engaged and the first to know when I was pregnant. Every bad thought I've ever had, she's heard about. But then I haven't had that many bad thoughts. Okay, that's not exactly true. I've had hundreds of millions of bad thoughts, especially about Priscilla, they're just not bad enough to cause any problems.

"Don't get so excited. It's really not that interesting. I just sent Jake an email and he wrote me back."

"Well what did he say? What was the great compliment?"

"It's not a big deal. Something about motherhood suiting me. Anyhow, it made me feel good, coming from him. He still looks like he's twenty."

"And? You want to kiss him, that's it, isn't it?"

"No! What do you take me for? I'm a mother, for God's sake. The only man I want to kiss is Zach."

"Come on, Joy. I've known you a long time."

"What's that supposed to mean?"

"It means, I *know* you. I know what Jake does to you. I have been your friend forever, you know."

"Oh, please. I don't even have the energy to *imagine* having an affair, let alone to actually have one. I lust after sleep. Zach's been taking so long to get back down. He'll wake up in the middle of the night sometimes and be up for an hour or more. I'm still not doing much most days except napping when he naps and folding laundry."

"I know, I know. Sarah had a phase like that. Can't you nurse him back to sleep?"

"I *do* nurse him back to sleep. It just takes an hour."

"Wow. He's got an appetite."

"It's like gassing up a Hummer."

"I'm sorry. That sucks."

"Thanks, Melody. I need the sympathy," I said, pulling into our drive. I looked up at the house, a large gray colonial. We'd chosen it together, Drew and I, when he got the job at Clarkville. It was our celebration house, bigger than we'd thought we could afford, and nicer. I looked at it objectively for a moment, trying to imagine—if I didn't already know it—what kind of people would live in it. Happy, I thought. Lucky, I thought. And I got out of the car.

Once again I had it in my mind to Google Donny Macnamara, but when I walked into the house, the disaster that stared me down stopped me short. I don't want to be the kind of person who complains about everything, it's just that I have a lot to complain about. My life has turned into some kind of retro-reality television show. It's like I've got myself trapped in a Donna Reed episode and I can't get out. I always thought Drew had a working pair of arms and functional legs, but no longer. He also used to know where the dishwasher was. The other day I literally had to take his hand and lead him there. "It's not lost, honey," I told him gently. "It's just been a really, really long time since you've looked at it."

Was it just that I never noticed before Drew's inability to

close drawers? Or his tendency to leave his socks on the kitchen table? This one is definitely a mystery to me. *Why* are they there? What purpose could they possibly serve? I know he can't be dusting with them, and I doubt he's eating with them. And since they're still there for me to clean up, I know he isn't eating them for breakfast. What could it be? It makes me wish they were still airing that *Unsolved Mysteries* program. But then they didn't really deal with domestic mysteries, did they? Like why objects dropped on the floor stay on the floor, or how men who for years managed to feed and clothe themselves suddenly lose all control of their limbs and must constantly lie horizontal on the couch when they acquire a wife. Could it be a strange case of possession, alien invasion, a poltergeist?

The other day I asked Drew if he could put a new diaper on the baby because I was in the bathroom enjoying a magazine, something I haven't done for a long time. And yes, it's true, I was done for the most part with my business, but I couldn't bring myself to leave the sacred quietness of that place. After I called out to him, I heard this reply: "Where are they?"

I sat for a moment in stunned silence. I even shook my head as if I had heard him incorrectly. It couldn't be possible that he didn't know where the diapers are kept. (Never mind that they are kept in plain sight in a basket beside the changing table.) Had it been that long, really, since he'd changed a diaper himself?

"In the nursery," I called back in a weak voice. And then the unthinkable, the unimaginable, the unforgivable:

"I'll just wait until you get out of the bathroom," he replied casually, as if it hadn't dawned on him how totally unbelievable he was being.

"DO I HAVE TO DO EVERYTHING AROUND HERE! NEXT THING YOU KNOW I'LL BE WIPING YOUR ASS TOO! OR MAYBE *YOU'D* LIKE TO WEAR DIAPERS SO YOU DON'T HAVE TO WALK TO THE BATHROOM, IS THAT IT? JESUS, YOU MAKE ME ANGRY!" I flushed the toilet with a violent push, washed my hands in a hurry and stormed out into the living room where Drew sat speechless, holding the baby in his arms.

"You must be under a lot of stress," he said calmly. I peeled the baby away from him and in a fit of frustration stuck out my tongue as I walked away. "Really adult, Joy," he said as he picked up the remote and flicked on the TV. "Maybe you should consider some anger management courses. It's not going to be healthy for Zach to grow up with a mother who acts like that."

I stopped dead in my tracks. I had thought in our many years together that I had heard it all. Drew and I had fought our way up one tree and down the other. We'd never hit each other, but we'd dragged out every name in the book to beat each other over the head with. But nothing like this before, nothing so low as insulting my mothering skills, my character, my ability to take care of my son. Oh, no, this was bad. This was very bad. This was war.

I turned around. If I hadn't been holding the baby, I would have throttled Drew. Anger management? I wanted to give him *real* cause for concern. Instead I said: "I hate you, Drew McGuire. I don't know who you've become. But if you'd acted like this when I met you, I never, ever would have married you."

I could feel my pulse racing and the sound of blood whooshing in my ears. I walked away slowly and purposefully because I was afraid I would do something crazy. When I lay Zach down on the changing table, he cooed and smiled at me. I smiled back. "Good boy," I said, loud enough for Drew to hear. "You're Mama's good little boy."

I whipped the socks off the table and threw them on the stairs. Then I put my blinders on and headed into the office with Zach. I set him up on his favorite blanket on the floor and set to work.

Donny Macnamara, I typed into the keyboard.

I'd never Googled anyone before. I'm not quite sure what that says about me. Does that mean I *do* have a life or I *don't* have a life?

I wasn't prepared for the million plus references that came up on the computer. How many Donny Macnamaras could there be?

I scrolled through the first page. My eyes landed on one blurb that contained his name and the word "Connecticut." I clicked on the link and a bright blue and purple page flashed open with the words "Coach Donny Macnamara says Dream Bigger than Big" writ large across the top like a banner. I almost immediately shut the window to continue my search. Whoever this guy was, it couldn't be the same Donny that my mother would consider marrying. Then I noticed, with a terrible sinking that started in my belly and landed in my toes, a picture.

How could I have overlooked the picture? There in front of my very eyes was a snapshot of my mother's Donny wearing a bow tie and an enormous grin. I couldn't believe it. A coach? I didn't even know we *had* coaches in Clarkville. Clarkville is sophisticated. Clarkville is the next stop after

NYC. Clarkville children wear Hanna Andersson. We don't need to "dream bigger than big," because everyone in the town already has a big house, a big car, a big job and a big, fat bank account.

"Why be mediocre when the world calls you to be grand?" a paragraph in the middle of the page said. "Life Coach Donny Macnamara is the man whose vision can make your life plan a reality. Founder of MacCoaching" (oh, yes, that's when I noticed I had landed at MacCoaching.com), "and originator of the affirguestion, no one but Donny can get you there."

"Oh, God, Zach," I called out in utter horror. "How can this be happening?" In a fluster I picked up my precious son and treated him to a monologue on the dangers of pop psychology. "And what is an 'affirguestion'?" I demanded of Zach and the computer. "Where did my mother find this man?!"

I scrolled down the page, my stomach rolling over as I did so. There was a picture of Donny giving someone a high-five. And there was a picture of Donny cheering someone on, hands caught in the motion of a clap. And there was Donny wagging a finger in my direction. "Bigger!" the screen shouted at me in bright red letters. I swear, if I hadn't been holding that baby, I would have fainted dead on the spot. The man was obviously completely, totally and utterly off his rocker, like six miles off his rocker. Of course, I realized, sitting back down at the desk, my mother couldn't know about this "profession" of his. My mother's the kind of person who makes fun of people like coaches. My mother needs a life coach like a woman needs a man—if I can borrow from a famous phrase. I would have to tell her. I would have to break it to her gently. Surely, Coach Donny Macnamara, "the man who can make your dreams reality and kick your reality to the curb" (and no, I'm not making this stuff up), in addition to being eerily exuberant, could not possibly make money at his work. I mean, what kind of person would *go* for this stuff? (Actually, I *know* what kind of person would go for it, I just don't personally *know* anyone who would.) It wasn't simply that he was a life coach, it was the excessiveness of the website— almost like a parody of a coaching site.

"Just like I thought," I told Zach, closing down the window. "He's in it for the money."

I opened up my email account and sent off a quick note to Diana with a link to Donny's website. I wrote the subject line "HELP!" Then I scanned through my in-box for an email from Jake. But there wasn't one. Of course there wasn't one. Why would there be?

Seven

DIANA SHOWED UP AT ABOUT TWO IN THE AFTERNOON with Addicus in tow. We'd decided to meet at my house because she lived in a dinosaur-age antique Cape Cod that only had fans. We, thank God, had central air, which, despite Drew's obsessive love for the intangible "environment," got used with some frequency, at least by me.

We placed the babies on the living room floor where they proceeded to ignore each other, cycling their legs and arms in the air. They were about the same height, only Addicus's hair was golden blond and he already had two bottom teeth. They shot up like August corn one day, surprising Diana completely.

Diana normally looked a little raggedy. Since I didn't know her before she had the baby, I have no idea what she used to look like. She's always clean—it wasn't that bad. It was more an air about her, just like when I met her in the grocery store. Sometimes she seemed like a person who'd fallen down a well, and would require some work to get back up to the surface.

That day, she seemed particularly quiet. She wore her

brown hair in a ponytail. She had on a sweet summer dress, lemony yellow, that flattered her figure. She was smaller than me in every way—which I'd decided to forgive her for a long time ago.

The first topic of the day, far more pressing even than our mutual sleep deprivation and lack of functional brain cells, had to be Donny.

"Did you see the website?" I asked her. "I can't get over it."

"Where did she meet him?" Diana asked.

"That's my question! How could they possibly have anything in common? I'm thinking he might be after her money. No way is he successful at coaching. His website looks like it belongs on a *Saturday Night Live* skit. For one thing, what in the world is an affirguestion?"

"A cross between an affirmation and a suggestion," Diana said matter-of-factly. "I read all about it."

"You did? I got so upset I had to close it down. Tell me everything. Unless something's really, really bad. Then don't tell me."

"The bio page is under construction, I noticed that. It said to come back later."

"Oh." Even more suspicious.

"But it does say on the 'Getting to Know You' page that he's had a variety of careers but his favorite has been being an uncle."

"Okay. That's completely not reassuring. Uncle is not a career. It's the happy result of someone else's family planning."

"He does seem a bit...like a novice?" Diana has a tendency to be generous.

"I know. It's embarrassing. I'm going to have to tell my mother."

"Don't you think she must know already?"

"Maybe. But it's hard to believe. If she knew, how could she *marry* him? Besides, she doesn't search the Internet. And when I asked her about his work, she didn't mention coaching. She said he was a renaissance man, but as far as I can tell the only thing that means is that he wants to wear a sword for the wedding."

"Oh, dear," Diana said, and then she burst into tears.

"Oh, God, did I say something wrong?" I knelt down beside her. Both of the boys looked our way and then Addicus began to wail. Diana picked him up, stood and swayed side to side.

"It's not you," she said, but she didn't stop crying.

"Oh, dear. Let me get you a tissue. Will you keep an eye on him?" I gestured to Zach, although the chances of him going anywhere were pretty slim. Addicus had already started rolling over, but Zach had couch potato written all over him. I tried not to worry too much about how this would affect his chances of getting an Ivy League education; I have so many more years to be neurotic about that, why get ahead of myself?

When I came back, Diana was nursing the baby on the couch. She looked like she was in pain.

"It hurts so much," she said. "I don't know how much longer I'll be able to nurse him."

"Oh, no. Is it his teeth?"

She shook her head then started bawling seriously again.

"Is it Jeff?" I asked. She was married to a contractor, a man I'd only met once. They'd married three years prior and spent their whole married life trying to have a child. Addicus was the surprise who came just when Diana was heading for fertility treatments.

"No, it's not Jeff."

"Is the baby okay? Is he healthy?"

"Oh, yes. Look at him. He's almost seventeen pounds." He was a large baby, round and a bright pink. I would never have said it to Diana but he reminded me distinctly of a pig. Of course, I like pigs and think they're cute, but I doubt she'd appreciate the similarity.

"It's me," she finally said. She wiped her tears away with the tissue and blew her nose one-handed with the baby still in her arms. "I just found out. I'm pregnant." The announcement set off another cycle of sobs. I hardly knew what to say or do.

When she'd quieted down, I said, "Really? How can that be? I mean, you're breastfeeding. I haven't even had my period yet. I'm practically still bleeding from Zach. Are you sure it's not a mistake? I mean, our hormones might be crazy now. Who knows what's going on?"

"It's not a mistake. I had one period. I figured we didn't need anything. It took so long to get Addicus, how could I know I'd get pregnant again so quickly? Jeff and I both figured it would be at least another year even if we were trying." She started to cry again. "I'm so tired. How am I going to do this?" She put Addicus back down on the floor on his tummy, and I rolled Zach over to join him.

All of a sudden, a host of unsavory, unhelpful thoughts came to mind and ran out of my mouth so quickly I couldn't censor them.

"Oh, my God. You're going to have to go through labor again! And so soon! All that pain, when you've barely even healed! And what if you're having twins? What if this one has colic? How can you even carry two babies? And they'll both be in diapers, just the thought of it. It's almost like Irish twins. Are you Catholic? No, I know you're not Catholic. Oh my

God. I can't believe it." And then it hit me. "Diana." Diana was
sitting on the couch looking calmer, which surprised me.
"Diana. This means that you've been having sex. Sex! How
can that be? I don't think Drew and I have had sex in at least a
month, or maybe we did, I can't remember. But it was only
once."

A smile broke across her face and then she threw back her
head and laughed. She genuinely roared. It scared me a bit, I
mean, I wasn't *that* funny. "Oh, man, my belly hurts. Oh, Joy,
you always make me laugh. That's what's so great about you.
You don't have any tact, but you're very funny. Thank you."
She reached over and took my hand. "I feel better now."

"Really? That's great. I probably shouldn't have said anything—"

"You do have a way with words."

"Drew says I need anger management classes."

"We probably all do," she said kindly. She sighed and sank
deeper into the couch. "I do want another baby. I just didn't
think it would happen so quickly. I am a little bit excited." A
small smile spread over her face. That was the Diana I'd
started to know, small smiles and gestures and laughs. Not
hysterical sobbing and wild laughing. Frankly, it was a little
offputting. All the time we'd known each other, Diana had
been the calm one. If I called her crazy with exhaustion, she'd
hold the line steady with comforting words. "This will pass"
was her favorite phrase. How could I trade in a rational, stable
friend for a hormonally psychotic pregnant lady?

"How do you feel?" I asked.

"Good. Nothing like with Addicus. I wouldn't even have
noticed if the breastfeeding hadn't become so uncomfortable.
I'm already a month into it." Then she got quiet again. "Do
you think I can do it?"

"Look. My mother had five children. The middle three she had one right after the other. She also had a business, a husband, and probably a couple of lovers. You can do it. And if you have any questions you can call her, she's a veteran, a mommy emeritus." Zach started fussing and I picked him up to hold him in my lap. He smiled at Diana. "Seriously, though, you *will* get through. I know some people who plan to have their children closer together. They say it's easier."

"You know what they say? If you want to make God laugh, tell him your plans."

"You know what I say? If you want to make me laugh, tell me there's a God." That got another good chuckle out of Diana. I couldn't help feeling a little proud of myself for making her feel better—even if her hormones helped me seem especially funny. "I'm allowed to say that; we weren't religious in my family. My father was a nonpracticing Jew and my mother was a nonpracticing atheist."

"Did your father help?"

"What do you mean? Help my mother with her atheism?"

"Oops. Sorry. Switched to a different topic. I'm having a hard time focusing lately. I *meant* did your father help with all your siblings?"

"My father only had one child—me. He had the bad taste to die in the middle of my childhood. I've already used the money he left me for therapy." I smiled sincerely. I'd been using these lines for a long time to describe my father's death, and they still worked for me. Although truthfully, he never left me any money and I certainly never spent any time in therapy. At any rate, my father, the quintessential joker, wouldn't have wanted me tearing up two decades down the line. "My mother remarried when I turned ten. My stepfather? What did he do? I can't remember if he helped with the babies. I helped with them, I remember that. By the time the youngest was born, I could have had him myself. Besides, I adored my mother. I felt such loyalty to her, like we were the original family who got caught up in some bad *Brady Bunch* masquerade. I never could figure the other kids into the permanent picture."

Diana laughed again (I was beginning to feel like I should go into stand-up.) Then she looked serious. "I'm sorry about your dad. I had no idea."

"It was a long time ago."

"Oooh." Diana jumped up. "Can you hold Addicus a minute? I've got to pee." She plopped her little piggy in my arms and dashed off. With Addicus curled into one arm and Zach in the other I felt like the mommy of twins, an idea that in the first weeks after giving birth seemed like a fate worse than death. Funny how in that moment it didn't seem so bad. I didn't tell Diana, but pregnancy seemed like a better problem to have than an aging male cheerleader after my mother's money. Oh, and a disintegrating marriage, I don't want to forget that problem. All jokes aside, my marriage had begun to feel like an adolescent with a drinking problem and a fast truck; I wasn't sure it was going to make it to adulthood alive.

Eight

ZACH AND I HAVE A BAD HABIT. IT BEGAN AS A SUR-vival mechanism. In the first few weeks of his life, I felt at a complete loss as to what one *does* with a baby. I'd nurse him and walk him, hold him and let him sleep. But I can't say that that limited variety of activities did much for *me*. So I did what mothers have done through the decades: I turned on the television. I'm not proud, and I'd never tell Priscilla. She relates to the TV. She knows the people on it by name. She might even have a name for the television itself. The thing is family to her, and I've always thought that anyone who has to turn on the television to get someone to talk to her, well, let's just say the word "pathetic" comes to mind. I don't mean just watching a few shows now and then or having a favorite show. I mean, if you don't watch the thing you don't relate to any other life-forms that day except your plants.

We watch *Oprah*. There, I said it. But I won't let myself watch anything else. Zach doesn't pay any attention to it whatsoever, but I wouldn't be surprised if his first word turns out to be "Oprah." If not that, then "Viagra." There are enough commercials for that stuff to get every male of every species on the drug. (And did you ever notice all the men in the commercials are old and the women are thirty?)

Most afternoons I can spend almost the whole program with Zach nursing in my arms. I sit in the family room, not the living room, even though our living room has a television in it too. The living room has the enormous TV. It's a man-size television. Whereas the family room has the antique variety—you know, the kind you measure in inches instead of feet. It also has my favorite chair, a fabric rocking chair that I bought just out of college at a yard sale. It has an ottoman and cushioned armrests. It's blue. Every time Priscilla comes over she says, "You *still* have that chair?" I think it embarrasses her because it looks like the kind of furniture she has and she knows we can afford better now.

I suppose I could have worse habits, like caffeine, Internet porn, scratch tickets or crack; still, Oprah has her down sides. For one thing, she's setting the bar too high. In the past month alone, she's aired programs on how to be thin, be young, be rich, give away your money, be kinder, be more successful, and in general be more like her. I started to follow her advice. I tried not to eat for two hours before bed. I started drinking more water for my pores. I gave up saying negative things about my upper thighs. I brainstormed ways to make money while staying at home so we could pay off the house and get rid of all our debt. I gave ten dollars to the fundraiser for the VFW at the grocery store—even though I didn't want to (That's even better, right?). And one day I even attempted to hug Priscilla, but she just stood there like an artificial ficus tree, all leathery and dry.

All I can say is, Oprah is bringing me to my knees. I thought I was going to have a real mental collapse from all the effort it takes to keep up with her. I finally broke down and told Drew. I told him how worried I was about the size of my ass and the size of our mortgage and the hour we eat dinner at, and the starving people everywhere, and the lack of thoughtfulness and civic interest in America, and how I've finally started developing crow's feet and need to put an end to it. This is the year! To put an end to the madness of my life! I need to start helping victims and stop being one. Right?

It was a shining hour for Drew anyway. He rubbed my shoulders lazily while he watched the baseball game over the top of my head. "Relax," he said. "Oprah's not talking to you personally."

"Really?"

"She's never even seen your ass."

Sometime he really is a very good person to have around.

That day the program pretty much centered on how cool Oprah is and how cool I am not; I had to turn it off. At least she's not emaciated. If she were, I don't think I'd be able to take it. I'd have to switch my allegiance. I'd have to start watching the shopping channel again, waiting for my mother to make an appearance. She's gearing up to launch a new product. A neck cream.

"That's wonderful," I told her, when she called to announce the new product. "Granny necks everywhere will thank you."

"Of course it's meant for younger women, sweetie. To help *prevent* unnecessary signs of aging. Women your age."

"Right," I said, searching for the hidden meaning. Was she trying to tell me something about my neck? And if wrinkles around the neck are unnecessary signs of aging, I want to know what the necessary ones are. As far as I can tell, aging isn't *necessary,* it's just inevitable.

"Honey pie, I've got even better news."

"Actually, Mom, I've been wanting to talk to you. I have some news too. Some things I found out—"

"Well, sweets, yours better wait, because this is some exciting stuff. Are you sitting down?"

"I will be as soon as I get back out to Zach." I'd left Zach playing on the floor in the family room, i.e., lying on his back staring at the ceiling fan. (How could it be that for the sixty or so seconds it took me to grab the phone and come back I'd been anxiously concerned over Zach's well-being and the possibility that during my brief time away he, a baby who could not walk or crawl or roll over, had managed to entangle himself in the media cords and had strangled to death— without a sound—or in a freak accident the ceiling fan had fallen on him and somehow I'd managed not to hear it colliding with his tiny body? I've called my pediatrician about dry skin patches, morning sneezes, ear wax—I mean, no one ever tells you how much is too much—a back of the knee rash and how in the world to successfully use a nose bulb to extract snot. She politely reminds me that my new job in life is to worry. "You think this is bad? Wait until he's driving." What a bedside manner.)

"You remember Aunt Hilda," my mother said as I retrieved a perfectly alive and perfectly content Zach from his blanket. I sat down with him.

"*The* Aunt Hilda, you mean? Dad's crazy sister? The one I've never met who's been locked up in a loony bin her whole life?" Aunt Hilda is also my father's only living relative.

"A group home," my mother said. "She's been in a group home."

"A locked group home, right?"

"It's for her own safety," my mother protested. "She's harmless."

"We're talking about the same Aunt Hilda then."

"Of course we are! She's the only one! And she's coming to town. Apparently, they've finally found an excellent medication for her, and she's had so many years of therapy now. She's ready to live on her own—with the help of an aide, that is. Honey, I am so happy, I can't tell you. Aunt Hilda was your father's favorite person in all the world."

"You're telling me she's been released?"

"Joy, don't be so mean, sweetie. This is *good* news. She might even stay with me in the city while she looks for a place to live."

"She's got to be ancient."

"Let's see. She was about nine years older than your father and your father was about six years older than me. That makes her something like seventy-four."

"I can't believe it," I said. And I really couldn't. I never thought I'd see Aunt Hilda. All these years, I've barely even believed she existed.

"You'll love her," my mother said. "She's unique. I've given her all your contact information. She's just dying to meet you."

"Wow. The mysterious Aunt Hilda." Now that I thought about it, this was good news. My aunt Hilda, free at last.

"I've got to run, honey," she said. "Let's catch up real soon."

"But, Mom, I've got to talk to you about—"

"Kiss yourself for me," she said, and then the phone line went dead. So much for a heart-to-heart about Donny MacCoaching himself.

*   *   *

When I think about Aunt Hilda, I'm not sure how I ended up with the life I have. My life is so normal, so excessively not like the life of a crazy person—speaking relatively here, of course. I live in suburban southern Connecticut, home to more money than seventeen other nations put together. As a child, all I'd ever wanted to be when I grew up was mysterious. Until I understood Aunt Hilda's exact condition (which I gathered to be schizophrenia but my mother's never been certain and she's also not big on labels. "It limits people, honey," she says), I wanted to be like her. In my child's mind, someone talked about but never seen constituted a very mysterious person indeed. Then I imagined I would become an intriguing, beguiling woman, maybe someone who wrote poetry and lived on wine. Someone rich and well known like my mother. Instead, I've landed myself in a hotbed of commonality, performing the one profession (if motherhood can be called that) that holds no mystery whatsoever. I have in fact succeeded in the goal of being entirely mediocre. Frankly, I'm not as upset about this as I should be. What does that say about me? Was Donna Reed hiding under my childhood petticoats just waiting to come out? I thought as soon as I gave birth I'd run into the city for any decent job they could throw at me. I hadn't planned on going back to work when Zach was born, but that's a lot different from finding out that, bored as I may be, I don't *want* to go back to work. I might as well be honest: I'm not mysterious, I'm as provincial as they come, but because of Zach, every now and then I get glimmers of true happiness.

It is a bit shocking to grow up and find out that (a) you are

not, thank God, your mother and (b) you are not, unfortunately, your mother. My mother lives in New York City
(where else?), although I grew up in New Haven where my
father was a professor and my stepfather an administrator
at the "local" university, as we loved to call it. I generally end
up in the city only once a year for my mother's enormous
Christmas bash. She invites everyone she's ever known *and* all
her ex-husbands too. She calls them her wasbands. On a regular basis she giggles like a schoolgirl. Occasionally she takes a
ballet class. She doesn't go to the opera because she finds it
stuffy and overdone. She likes rock concerts and exotic wines.
I don't know how she managed to give birth so many times
and maintain such glamour. I did not receive that gene, and I
am bitter. I am bitter and common. I am loath to admit it, but
if you set me up against my mother and Priscilla, in terms of
glamour and domesticity, I'm a heck of a lot more like
Priscilla. (Now that I've said that, give me a paper bag to wear
over my head.)

Drew returned home that evening with She of Catholic
Widow Torture in tow. She lives in Clarkville too. She lives
wherever Drew lives, naturally, and has, since he left her
house. She's a few years younger than my mother, but she
looks ten years older, which is why I never like to put the two
women in the same room together. I think this is kind of me;
Drew doesn't agree. Priscilla is gray and frail and old when
she shouldn't be. Is anyone under eighty old anymore? From
what I've gathered from *Oprah,* ninety is the new fifty—
especially if you can afford a few rounds of plastic surgery. By
that point the work is easy; they simply attach your eyebrows
to your forehead. Then you look deeply troubled. Young, but
deeply troubled.

Priscilla also smells. It's not a bad smell. It's an old-people smell. Not mothballs, but one of those cheap perfumes. I can't tell if she always has the same cheap perfume on or if she's simply using samples that she gets from recycled magazines nabbed in the doctor's office. At any rate, I'm a bit sensitive to smells and if I get too close to her, I get hives. Drew isn't a big fan of that little problem of mine either.

When I first met her, I wanted to love her. You know how it is. I loved her son, I wanted him to love me, and the quickest way to a son is through his mother. To be fair, it also took me a long time to dislike her. Some people you grow to love over time; some people you grow to dislike. Priscilla was like the slow-growing plantar's wart variety. I had no idea at first what trouble she would be. Then she started to be subtly annoying, so I couldn't quite tell what was wrong. Now I've got a wart about three inches deep that hurts every time I step on it. I have never shared this metaphor with Drew. Call me smart, but finally I learned my lesson.

She insists on calling the baby Zachary. We did name him Zachary. We named him Zachary with the intention of calling him Zach. No one uses his or her proper name. It's like saying "Thus and So," and meaning it. Or calling people "madam" when you aren't in France. I guess I've turned into a mean, lumpy grump. And here I'd thought motherhood would make me all gooey and lovey and bleary-eyed. That would make number 999 of the mommy myths that have exploded for me since the day sperm met egg in my body all those months ago.

The latest battle turns out to be baptism. Priscilla has her heart—no, I take that back, her whole being—set on having Zach baptized in the Catholic Church. There's no way I'm raising a Catholic child, so I can't really see the point. Technically, I'm Jewish. Okay, that's an overstatement. I'm about as Jewish as an Easter egg, but I am more Jewish than I am Catholic. My father was the son of a Jewish father—just no Jewish mothers in the bunch, which makes me officially a non-Jewish Jew. (My mother comes from a long line of agnostics who once were vaguely Methodist. She's an atheist, she told me once, "until God comes back into fashion.") Still, Priscilla can't tell the difference. It's really the only point she can't seem to argue.

"You were baptized," she said to Drew over dinner that night. "I can't see how it's done anything but good. My Walter would never let a grandson of his go without baptism. It's akin to sending him straight to hell." She looked pointedly at me.

Generally I set the bar at homicide; if I manage to eat dinner with her without killing her, I've done a great deed. That night I gave myself an even greater challenge. I decided I wouldn't even open my mouth. I just sat there looking as neutral as I could.

Actually, I lost myself in a fantasy about Jake. Since he so clearly didn't count as a real option, he seemed like a safe outlet for my hibernating libido. (And I do mean outlet, like those great shopping outlets near every good ski resort that hook you on their sales like a dope fiend with his dealer. You know that's the case when whole families go on vacations to places that have natural scenery to die for yet spend entire days lost inside a building without windows. Not that I've ever done that.) Anyhow, I spent dinner imagining moving to London to be with Jake. We would have wild sex every day, just like we did the first year we dated. Never mind that the sex eventually waned; I focused on the good details, like his ability to nibble ears, and the way he looked when his eyes closed in pleasure. I could do London. It would help me acquire some of that mysteriousness I'd never managed to attain. Everything European is mysterious, isn't it? Just because it's not American?

My fantasy turned out to be the perfect antidote for Priscilla's particular brand of annoyance. I got so far into the fantasy, I even smiled at her a few times. I think she took this as agreement.

"I'll talk to Father Michael," she said.

I looked over at Drew, who seemed confused by the whole situation. I don't know how I missed seeing this spineless quality of his. He'd turned into a gummy worm, loose and pliable. I left the table, grabbing up all the dishes and whisking them into the kitchen.

The kitchen was meant to be the best room in the house; it was the room Drew fell in love with, a real chef's kitchen with no detail spared. We had two ovens and a beautiful six-burner gas stove. Every drawer rolled out. The island had a sink just for washing vegetables. It even had a rotating bookshelf built into it for cookbooks. Every time I go into the kitchen, I immediately want to leave. Who lives here? I think. Certainly not me. I went into catering to make a buck, not because I had any special talents with food preparation. Sometimes I wish I loved cooking. Like I wish I wanted to be a doctor or a lawyer or something specific and useful like that. Alas. I've always been me. And you know what I'd like to find in my house instead of a designer kitchen? A restaurant with a full-time chef. Now that beats marble counters any day.

When I got back out with the pie in one hand and several dessert plates in the other, Drew and Priscilla were deep in conversation. They looked up startled. I felt like an intruder on their gorgeous little love affair, which frankly I felt most of the time when I saw them together. Cozy little unit of two. Vomit.

"I'm feeling a bit tired," I said. "Do you mind if I just miss out on dessert? I'm going to go up and lie down."

"That's a good idea," Priscilla said. "You don't look well. Are you gaining weight? You'll never lose your pregnancy weight if you keep breastfeeding." Then she actually smiled at me. I smiled back. Why bother explaining to her that breast-feeding actually helps you to lose your pregnancy weight faster (unless of course you have a serious problem with chocolate consumption)? Her insults couldn't touch me that night. I'd disappeared into a fantasy life with Jake. So, I thought, trudging up the stairs alone (Priscilla held the sleeping Zach in a death grip), what harm could it do to send off an email to an old friend?

To: jakephilips@lunerpress.com
From: jmcguire@fanfare.com
Just hello. Wanted to tell you that I finally Googled my
mother's fiancé. Turns out he's one of these "life coaches"!
And amateur is the best thing I can say about his
website. I'm freaking out. I'm sure my mother has no
idea. How could she? He's so not like her. Any more
helpful advice? Anyhow, hope you're well. Joy

After I sent off my email, I Googled Donny again, just to see if I could find anything else on him—a criminal record maybe? The same million hits came up, and after about ten minutes of reading innocuous references to Donny Macnamaras I checked my email again just in case Jake had written back. This time he hadn't. What did I think? That he sat around staring at his computer all day and night just waiting for an email from me? The man has a life. I'm sure he was sleeping. I went to lie down.

Instead of falling asleep, I lay there for a long time, wide awake, listening for the sound of the baby's breath and then reminding myself over and over again that he was downstairs. It was simply another manifestation of my momsomnia. I'd read about it in all the books, and at last, I'd caught it. Anticipating Zach's frequent night wakings, I won't let myself sleep. Instead, I stare at the clock. I count the hours and the minutes until he'll wake up. This is very bad on my nerves (not to mention my looks. The whites of my eyes look like candy canes. Nice touch at Christmas, I suppose, but not in June.) Every little snuffle of breath has me leaping up to get him. And when he's quiet? He must be dead. Leaping up to get him ensues again. Never mind that at *that* moment he wasn't actually in the room with me. That's the thing about momsomnia. It essentially turns you from a normal night-sleeping mammal into a nocturnal subhuman, not unlike a vampire—minus the blood-sucking, of course.

Why, I wondered, as I stared at the red numbers on the clock, isn't there a game show for neurotics? I'd win it.

I needed a plan. Counting sheep doesn't cut it.

Then it hit me. I was under too much stress. How could I not be? I had a new baby, my mother was getting married for the fourth time instead of helping me with my new baby (to a sketchy character with a dismal career no less), my college sweetheart stirred up feelings I should have been feeling for my husband, my best friend had gone prego on me, my mother-in-law was going to kidnap my child and force him into a lifetime of crucifixes and guilt, and I was fat.

I clearly needed some help.

I would go to yoga class. That's what I would do. Melody had mentioned one the other day. She'd started to attend a class just for mothers and babies. She'd even suggested that I come. She said it was a good way to meet other mothers. She also said the teacher Carol had a way with abdominals. She could even help mine. So what that I'd never had any interest in yoga? I'd assumed yoga involved a lot of thinking about your forehead and chanting until you pass out. But now that it had been Americanized, maybe even I could attend a class. It would be like touchy-feely aerobics, sculpting class with a spiritual twist, stretching to Enya. I could do that.

I even had the right clothes. Melody said you could wear sweats if you want.

nine

ARE YOU FAMILIAR WITH THE SMELL OF BABY VOMIT? Not spit-up, that barely has a smell. I mean the real stuff, the stuff that's gone all the way down, wrestled with a few intestinal bacteria, and then come back up.

I am.

In fact, I wore it one day as a fashion accessory.

On the beach.

But when else would be the perfect time for vomit except at the one moment when you have no immediate access to a sink, a paper towel or soap?

There also happened to be a lot of other people at the beach, so any washing of vomit into the water would have to be done on the sly. Meanwhile, I am not subtle. Nor is there anything subtle about my son, who managed to scream so terrifyingly after his copious puke-fest that I actually heard one woman (who I ran by on my way to the bathrooms) ask if there was a shark. In the bathroom I made some progress toward removing the vomit from the crevices between Zach's thighs where it had managed to lodge. It was a little hard, though, to effectively remove it from my own hair. Eau de vomit, anyone? I decided to go home instead. It was July, and it was Zach's first trip to the beach. Drew had, at the last minute, decided he didn't want to come. He doesn't like the beach. He doesn't like sand. And he doesn't like the sun. (There are no trees.) I think he gets paler in the summer with all the clothes and hats he wears in a desperate attempt to ward off the negative effects of ozone depletion.

Suffice it to say, our trip to the shore turned out to be a complete disaster. Zach projectile-vomited the whole way home. (We only discovered later that this was a "normal" re-action to a routine vaccination. Okay . . . you know your life is special when projectile vomiting is a "normal" response to *anything*.) When I walked into the house I shouted up to Drew, "We need a new car," then I stripped off our bathing suits and got us both in the tub for a super scrub down. At least Zach loved his bath.

"Drew," I called out again. No reply.

When I got out of the tub, I dressed Zach, nursed him and put him down for a nap in his crib. I'd recently gotten orga-nized enough to give him a regular nap every day at about eleven. Generally, because I did something good in a past life, he slept for two hours. I coveted the time. I didn't want any-one to call me during that time. It was mine, mine, mine. In fact, I preferred when Drew left so that I could be totally alone without any interruptions. Diana and I had made a pact that if we ever called each other during this sacred time, we would not take a quick good-bye personally.

I searched the house for him that day and didn't turn up any evidence. Then I headed out to the garden, but he was gone. I figured he must have gone for a walk because his car was still there.

As I headed back into the house, a figure caught my eye, which at first I mistook for a cardinal—a flash of red by the driveway. That flash turned out to be a long silk scarf wrapped about six times around the frail, petite body of an older woman who stood leaning on a cane staring at my house.

"Can I help you?" I noticed a car idling on the road. A teenager sat at the wheel. He bobbed his head in time to some music I couldn't recognize.

"Maybe I can help you," the woman said, and then she cackled, showing off a set of very yellow teeth. Despite this, she was remarkably beautiful, more like a fairy godmother than a witch.

"Oh," I said, realizing, all of a sudden, just who I was talking with. "You're Aunt Hilda."

"The one and only." She smiled from her toes to her forehead.

"Wow." I couldn't believe she stood there before me. My aunt Hilda. The mythological figure herself. The crazy lady I'd never met. My father's only sibling. She tottled over and hugged me pretty strongly for someone five feet tall. In other words, she all but jumped into my arms. "Aunt Hilda," I said again.

"I've been in the loony bin, honey," she said with a smirk. "I just got out. You're the first person I wanted to see. Now what do you think of that?" She wore her silvery white hair on top of her head in a braided bun. "I said to myself, I've got to see my Paulie's girl, that's who I want to set eyes on. That's the one who counts. See what Paulie made for himself."

"You've been in a"—I desperately tried to remember my mother's language,—"a group home, right?"

"It's the modern-day institution. Now they've got me on the modern drugs, and don't I feel fine!" She brought a hand up and smoothed down some of her hair. "But, honey, I *wanted* to be locked in there most of the time. The world just scares the shivers out of me." She clapped her hands. Something about her reminded me distinctly of an elf. "But now? Now I get to see you." She gathered me up in her arms again.

"I'm sorry I haven't been in touch," she continued.

"No problem," I said, rather inanely. Wasn't it *me* who should have been in touch with her?

"You're the spitting image of your father."

"Really? You think so?"

"Oh, yes. He was built like you too, strong, with good legs."

I noticed her leaning heavily on her cane. "Would you like to sit down? Come in and sit down? Have a drink?"

"Paulie," she said, looking off toward the backyard. "He was my favorite brother."

"You mean I have an uncle I don't know about?"

"No," she said giggling. "He was just my favorite. Until Lulu came along."

"Who's Lulu?" I asked, imagining another crazy aunt no one had told me about.

"Our secret sister," she said, humming now a bit in between each word.

I wasn't quite sure what to say. When you meet a crazy person who knows that she's crazy, should you point out the crazy things, or ignore them and pretend everything is normal? Then she looked me dead in the eye. Her blue eyes shimmered in the sunlight. Old and crazy, she was still very beautiful, just as she had been in the one picture of her I'd seen.

"I read fortunes, you know I'm very good at it. Would you like me to read yours?"

"Um," I said. I hadn't had my fortune read since high

school, when friends and I would play with the Ouija board or borrow someone's Tarot cards and alternately doom one another to lives of spinsterhood or predict futures of indescribable wealth and fame. Since I'd entered the adult world, I didn't *do* fortunes. I'm a firm believer in logic and reason, not lightning and tea leaves.

I looked over at the car where the teenager continued to obliviously rock to the beat.

"My boyfriend," she said, and then she winked at me, daring me, I supposed, to believe it. Didn't seem so impossible. I've seen *Harold and Maude.* The only thing stranger than movies is life.

"Can I take a rain check on the fortune?"

"I'll check the rain," she said, smiling and wrinkling her nose up to her eyes. Then she looked up at the sky. "It's a beautiful day, isn't it?"

"Can you stay awhile? We can sit on the deck?"

"What time is it?" She stared on her wrist, where there wasn't a watch. Instead, she wore five or six bangles that plinked together when she moved. "Oh, I forgot! I've got all the time in the world."

"What about . . . him?" I gestured to the boy in the car.

"He gets paid by the hour. Not bad work, is it?"

"Then you'll stay for a bit?"

"Life's nice," she said. Was this intended to be a response? I couldn't tell. She began to walk toward the house. She sort of teetered and limped and swaggered all at once. "Life's hard," she called from in front of me. She began to waddle up the stairs to the deck. "Life's nice," she said.

I got her a glass of lemonade. She stayed for exactly sixteen minutes. I only knew this because she told me. Then she kissed me and went back to her driver/boyfriend.

In those sixteen minutes, I didn't find out that I was the illegitimate child of my father and Jackie Onassis (oh, well—another childhood dream dies) or that he'd been a government spy or that he hadn't really died and now lived on some tropical island as part of the witness protection program (my last impossible hope). I didn't turn up any extra siblings or any deep family secrets, but Aunt Hilda was a treasure of wisdom just the same. Somehow, listening to her stories of my father finger painting and keeping frogs and acting in the third-grade play, put me in a very fine mood. I even impressed myself by remaining calm when Zach woke up and puked right down the front of my shirt.

If Aunt Hilda had arrived during the immediate postmortem period, I may have mistaken her for a figment of my imagination. As it was, though, I'd made some moderate strides away from my Medusa-esque early days—which meant Aunt Hilda, as strange and rather wonderful as she seemed to be, had to exist. (I half wished, after I met her that first time, that *I* could go crazy; it seemed pretty enjoyable.) I knew this because I had, in fact, been doing a not-half-bad job of mothering. Zach's five-month birthday came and went as the summer heated up. I'd take him walking around the neighborhood in the early mornings. We'd walk as fast as possible. In this way I had managed to reduce Lumpkin slightly. I now had a petite Lumpkin. It wasn't so jellified either, though it still held on to its bubble shape. Drew, not so nicely I might add, poked it one day when I was sitting down and said: "Pregnant?"

"Obviously not," I said, since we both knew, given our current rate of intercourse (about equal to the rate that happy news is reported in the media), that the chances of conception were 1 in 5 zillion and that's only if you believe in the virgin birth. "But thank you for being an asshole," I said.

"It was just a joke," he said. Because I'm next in line for sainthood, I didn't slap him in the face. We did have sex once in recent history. We ended up doing it on the floor of the living room. When I came over and kissed him, trying to be sexy while I unzipped his pants, he looked mortified. "What are you doing?" he asked. I put my mouth on his belly and kissed it seductively, although it was hard to pull off with the *The Simpsons* playing on the TV. When I sat up to kiss his mouth, I hit my head against his elbow and fell. He didn't even ask if I was okay. But you know how the old saying goes, Try, try again. I got back up and attempted some nonchalance. "Let's just do it on the floor," he said, switching off the television. "Good idea," I said. Well, it might have been a good idea if someone had vacuumed the rug in the past half century. Drew didn't seem to mind, but then he was on top. He didn't have to spend the rest of the night picking bits of lint out of his hair. I'm so over sex anyway. I am the living, walking proof of the kind of trouble it will get you into. Everyone just wants to have sex, but sex makes babies. And babies stop sex. This is nature's idea of a practical joke. Maybe that's why I'm not so keen on nature.

But instead of planning Drew's imminent demise, I plotted a way to get to a yoga class with some fantastical hope that going would transform me into a beautific Stepford wife. I hadn't actually gotten to a class yet, but I'd tried. One time the baby had a poopy diaper just as we were leaving, and it took so long to get him clean—it was the explosive variety—that I missed my opportunity. The next time Melody called to cancel, and I couldn't bring myself to go alone. What if I didn't do it right?

The point is, I was being about as good as I knew how, given my limited resources, and I think this was pretty gracious of me, as Drew still hadn't gone to the trouble of apologizing to me for being a total screw-up. Priscilla also presented a major obstacle on my path to sainthood. She'd gone on a shopping frenzy at the outlets, bringing back piles of clothes for Zach. How thoughtful, right? Well, every single one of them was baby blue, every shirt, every pair of shorts, every sweater, every pair of overalls, every hat, every sock. If I don't use my ESP and dress him in one of those outfits on the days she surprises us with her presence, she'll say, "What's wrong with the clothes I bought?"

I lied once to get her off my case and said they were all in the wash.

"That can't be possible. I gave you so many. You must not do the wash very often. I did my Walter's wash every third day, like clockwork." Tell me, please, why does this woman still think about the dirty laundry of a man who's been dead for two decades?

In a magnificent effort to be kind, I explained that I preferred a variety of colors in his wardrobe.

"He's a baby boy," she said defensively.

"That's true. But baby boys can wear all different colors."

"I've always known baby boys to wear baby blue. That's the way it's always been done. Walter's favorite color was blue." Now, why didn't that surprise me? I imagine if she'd bought all green clothes, Walter's favorite color would have magically become green.

She's also insisting that Zach switch to formula and begin

eating solid foods. Naturally, she means *cookies*. I'm following my doctor's orders and sticking with breastfeeding only
until six months. Do you think that stops her? Absolutely not.
She is the unstoppable, unreasonable grandmother of all. The
other day she simply put a cookie in his mouth despite the
fact that I had mentioned about seventeen times that I did
not want her to feed him cookies. It was a sugar cookie coated
in chocolate. You heard me. Chocolate. My baby has no teeth.
He's never had a Cheerio in his life, and there she was giving
him chocolate.

However, I did not throw her out of the house. I smiled at
her and walked away.

These are the facts, then. I'd been on my best behavior. I'd
minimized my inner she-devil. And that's how I knew, beyond a shadow of a doubt, that Aunt Hilda was not a symptom of my hormonal state but the genuine article.

I could hardly wait to meet my mother on Friday and fill her
in on my visit with Aunt Hilda. We had a date back at Estelle's
to find something she could wear for the wedding. For a bride
on her fourth marriage there aren't that many choices. I think
the first time she wore white, and the second time she wore
white. The third time she wore lilac. She promised me that
this time she would branch out. She would go modern, something that would match well with my deep green dress.

I had not anticipated a special guest star: Donny. Who in
their right mind brings her fiancé to the bridal shop? Still, my
mother's strange taste would be my good luck. I'd been waiting for an opportunity to spy on Donny and figure out exactly
what he was up to. Apparently, despite the fact that he's more
English than Scottish (my mother says) his latest thing is

wearing a kilt to the wedding. Frankly even if he didn't have the world's most embarrassing profession, that alone would give me pause to consider his intentions.

"He's here to watch the baby, so you don't have to feel divided," my mother said after the founder of MacCoaching.com gave me an uninvited hug.

"Oh." Oh, no, he's not, I thought, looking Donny up and down. He's short, so it didn't take very long. I wanted to spy on him; I certainly didn't want him babysitting.

"My grandson," he said, attempting to give Zach a squeeze. "I've come to help with my new grandson."

God, if I had a dollar for every man who'd been welcomed into our big, happy family. . . . Not to be unkind, but how exactly does Donny get to be my kid's grandfather if he marries my mother *after* the fact?

Donny leaned over to Zach, who lay sleepily in his travel chair.

"He might just sleep," I said quickly, hoping he wouldn't wake him up.

"No problem. I can do sleep."

My mother squeezed me into a hug. She glowed with joyfulness. As we walked over to the dresses I said: "Whatever happened to 'A woman needs a man like a fish needs a bicycle'?"

My mother just laughed. She has an annoying habit of laughing all the time. Sometimes I like it; sometimes I find it dismissive. It's an easy out. But then she said: "Hey, honey, even Gloria Steinem got married eventually, although the poor thing lost her husband to cancer." My mother shook her head in genuine understanding; she had a bond with every widow she met, barring Priscilla. "Grumpy," my mother said, the first time she met Priscilla.

"But why get married?" I pressed, hoping to get some dirt on Donny. "Marriage isn't that great."

"Neither is being single."

"Most people only get married once."

"I don't know about that. Look at Elizabeth Taylor." She'd started to shuffle through the cream-colored dresses.

"You said no white."

"It's cream, sweetie. And don't worry, I'm still getting a sense of things."

"I'm serious, though. It's pretty unusual to have four husbands."

"Well, then I'm lucky, sweets, aren't I?"

"How is it luck to have one guy die on you and divorce the other two?"

"You could look at it another way. I've had four men want to marry me; I'm pretty popular."

"I think you were born with an optimism gene that I lack. How can you know it won't end in divorce? How can you *really* know who you're marrying? People change, you know. Or sometimes they aren't who they first appear to be."

"I've had my hard times, honey. You know that. Life's about making the most of things. You deal with what life gives you because you don't have a choice. But you do have a choice about *how* to deal with it. That's my philosophy, sweets. You need to take risks for love, that's what makes love so desirable. Having it is like getting to the mountaintop. It's a long way up and a sharp fall down, but what a view."

"So you love Donny?"

"Oh, yes. I do."

"Do you *really* love him?" I wanted to get to the bottom of this bizarre state of affairs, but I couldn't risk alienating my mother. I knew from past experience that if I probed too much, she'd close herself off to me. One time, right after my twenty-fifth birthday (and I point this out to prove that I wasn't merely being childish—I *was* an adult), I told her exactly what I thought of my number-two stepfather, Steve. At the end of our very unpleasant heart-to-heart, she said: "Unless he's beating you up or molesting you, I don't want to hear it." Okay, so that wasn't a very hard message to decipher. Which meant I needed to proceed with utmost caution on the Donny front. I decided to go in with my best question: "Do you love him as much as you loved my father?"

She stopped where she was, in front of a large rack of mauve dresses. They dwarfed her. I couldn't imagine her in a single one. My mother's like an aging beauty queen, only somewhere along the way she picked up these strange qualities of patience, compassion and kindness. I don't think I have any of those. I am feisty, fiery, impatient, unkind and irritable. You can see why my mother can drive me crazy then. Instead of having shortcomings, she gave birth to me, a living blob of all the shortcomings she lacks.

"Your father was special. My once-in-a-lifetime love. But love comes in many different forms, right, sweetie? Not all of it will knock you off your feet. Some kinds of love are more like overhead lights than fireworks." She giggled. "Light is light, honey. You can still see by it, read by it; besides, overhead lights last longer; they're more useful too." She pulled out a hammock of a dress. "What about this?"

"I'll boycott."

"You're so picky."

"Thank you. Someone has to make up for all your generosity of spirit."

"Be easy on yourself. New motherhood is rough. I can almost remember it with you. Almost...." Just then Donny came up behind us, so quietly I jumped. He held Zach, deeply asleep, in his arms. "See," she said. "He's got the magic touch." It was all I could do not to peel the two of them apart.

"Right," I said. Then I realized it was my perfect opportunity. "You must work with children?"

"I've worked with all kinds of people," he said. With his drawl, "people" came out sounding like peephole. "Young adults, mostly."

"Donny is an incredible artist," my mother chimed in. "He has a real eye for color."

"Really?" Then I was right. My mother *didn't* know his true profession. "What's your medium?"

"I work with watercolors, but I've only had one show."

"They're incredible," my mother said. "Full of feeling."

"Uh-huh." I couldn't believe my luck. He was like putty in my hands. "Can't make much money from that, can you?"

"What's money," he said, "when you've got love?" He wrapped an arm around my mother and kissed her noisily on the cheek. My heart seized up. I was right! I could just feel it. I was right about him!

"What did you think of Aunt Hilda, honey?" my mother said, changing the topic of conversation before I could rephrase my question and get to the truth.

"How did you know?"

"I told you she was staying with me for a while." My mother laughed. "What a lady she is."

"I'll say. Is that teenager really her boyfriend?"

"Boyfriend?" My mother really loved that one. "He's a hired driver. Aunt Hilda doesn't know how to drive, of course. I'm so glad she's around. She'll be able to come to the

wedding. That will make it all the more meaningful." She began to tear up, nestling into Donny who still had an arm
wrapped around her.

"I better nurse him," I said, breaking up the love triangle.

"He's sleeping," my mother protested.

"It's his time," I said, pulling him out of Donny's arms. "I'll
be back in a jiffy to help you." I needed a break from all the
love talk. I sat on the floor in the dressing room, leaning
against the wall. I left a message for Melody while I nursed
Zach. I needed some backup. I needed some ideas about how
to get my mother out of this mess.

"Down to work," my mother said, when I found her
again, tucked into a dressing room. "Off with you," she said to
Donny, shooing him away. "Girl time."

"I'll keep the baby," I snapped protectively. "He's fine."

"Whatever you say, Mama." He smiled at me, the big,
cheesy, I'm-a-life-coach smile. "I'll see you in a bit, my lady,"
he said to my mother. I couldn't help rolling my eyes.

I spent the rest of the day putting my foot down; no bright
purple, no white with lavender flowers, no royal blue, no
business-style suits, no medieval costumes, and nothing with
a petticoat. I was the voice of reason in a sea of satin.

Since I'd made the mistake of leaving a detailed message on
Melody's answering machine about the suspicious Donny
Macnamara, I got the pleasure of receiving a return call from
her on my way home during which she berated me and ques-
tioned my sanity. Now, I know we live in the modern age, and
the modern age means talk therapy. This whole thing people
call modernity comes down to one thing: how Freud ruined
the world with his own deeply troubling neurosis. Why would

anyone think it was a good idea to sit around and talk about yourself, or, worse, sit down and say everything that comes to your mind? The whole point of the mind is that it's full of random, unnecessary, unpleasant thoughts that Don't Mean Anything. Call me the Grinch of Therapy, I don't care. It's just so self-obsessed. Everyone has weird thoughts about sex. Everyone has weird thoughts about their parents. Everyone wants to kill everyone else—sometimes. Maybe the guys who actually *do* that stuff need a little conversation with a professional, but why does that mean that the rest of the world has to be forced into routine psychoanalysis?

Here's my point. Telling Melody about my Internet spying was a big mistake. She's a therapist. She gets paid to dig up people's disturbing thoughts. I love her but she also has a habit of chiming in on *my* unconscious. I thought the point of an unconscious is that it stays unconscious. "Let's bring it back to you," she said on the phone. She wanted to help me with Jake and Drew and Zach and Donny all at once by grouping them into one category and calling it: my issue with men dating back to the death of my father. As far as she can tell, this is putting a round peg in a round hole. I, however, am not a round peg. I am octagonal.

I think my problems are pretty simple. I can't stand my husband and for good reason; he's impossible and hasn't even bothered to give me a proper apology for what he's done wrong; my baby has recently regressed to newborn status by refusing to sleep more than two hours in a row; my mother plans to marry a fraud; and I keep dreaming about Jake. Does anyone need an advanced degree to figure this stuff out? It's not rocket science. I need sleep. Zach needs to sleep so I can sleep. Drew needs to wake up. My mother needs to read that book about women who love too much. And Jake? Well, he's

not really that much of a problem, is he? He hasn't even bothered to return my email. No dangers there.

Point being, when Melody suggested some counseling, I
had to pull a code orange.

"You're dangerously close to getting on my hit list," I told
her.

"It's perfectly normal. Most people at one time or another
go for counseling. You've just got so much going on. A third
party might be able to sort things out for you."

"I don't want to be sorted. I'm not a pile of dirty clothes."

"It's just a suggestion, not a diagnosis."

"Well, I'm willing to do the yoga thing. That's enough
branching out for me for right now."

"Right. I almost forgot. I can come by tomorrow before
class so you can follow me to the studio. It's the last class of the
summer." I could hear Sarah in the background babbling. At
eight months she sat, crawled, ate, and played patty-cake.
Babyhood is the only time when three months can make such
an incredible difference; or is time usually like that, and I'd
just never noticed before? Without babies, days and months
seem to merge like gummy bears that have melted into one
large gummy mound. This happened to me one time when I
left a bag in the car. Drew and I ate them anyway, biting off
large chunks from the gummy ball. In case you're interested, it
didn't taste the same. They are much better eaten one by one.

"Okay," I said. "I'll suit up in my sweats and be ready for
you, at what, quarter of twelve?"

"That sounds perfect. You'll love Carol too, the teacher.
She kind of reminds me of you. She's got a good sense of
humor."

"Oh, that's good. I thought you were going to say she has
dimply thighs or something."

"I've known you so long I don't identify you by your current thighs. I remember when your thighs were size four."

"When I was fourteen."

"Exactly. When you were fourteen."

"I never did like being fourteen."

"It's a trade-off. Would you rather have dimply thighs or be a perpetual teenager?"

"Ah, you always ask the hard questions. I guess that's why you get paid the big bucks. I'll see you tomorrow."

"Wait," she said. "You've got to answer my question."

"Well, what would *you* prefer?"

"I'd take my cellulite any day over the torture of adolescence," she said.

"Wise woman. I guess I'd do the same, but only so I could be with you. It wouldn't be any fun to be fourteen without my best friend."

"You're sweet, Mama," she said. "We'll see you tomorrow."

That night I told Priscilla that she wouldn't be able to spend Saturday afternoon with Zach, as she often did, because I had a mommy-baby yoga class.

"Oh, good. I can watch him for you," she said.

"But that's the point, Priscilla. It's meant for mommies and their babies. He's supposed to come along." Not like I would leave him with Mrs. Formula Is Best even if it wasn't.

"Oh." She raised her eyebrows. "I've never heard of that. How can a baby even do yoga? He can't follow instructions. Wouldn't you prefer the time alone?"

She was sitting with me in the living room. We were watching Zach wiggle around on his tummy. He seemed to be days away from crawling. We were like the cheerleading squad, applauding and praising every time he'd scoot forward an inch.

"The point is to take him," I said emphatically.

"I can't see what good it will do you." She swooped down and picked Zach up, sitting him on her knees. She bounced him up and down and sang the pony song, loud enough to rule out any response from me. "My Walter didn't trust those Oriental ideas, not one bit." I sighed. Not that I doubt that Walter didn't trust them. I'm sure he didn't. I just don't give a damn.

And where was Drew, my international man of mystery? Lately, I'd been thinking of publishing my own series of books. Instead of *Where's Waldo?* they'd all be called *Where's Drew?* I'd draw pictures of our house and garden and the local Clarkville neighborhood and on each page somewhere there would be a Drew, only it would be almost impossible to find him without a magnifying glass and Newtonian determination.

I got up in search of him. I found him in the basement by his worktable. He was gazing intensely at a power tool the name of which I will never know, will never want to know and yet I will be told its name, over and over again.

"Want to come up and join us?"

"I didn't hear you come down," he said.

"Please don't leave me up there with your mother."

"Is it so bad?"

"I'm just saying, she's *your* mother. Besides, Zach is awake and full of energy. You'd enjoy him."

"Let me just finish down here." I have learned over the years the translation for this phrase, which can best be summed up as: no.

I ought to have simply resigned myself to a lifetime of Catholic Widow Torture. Some days I saw more of Priscilla than I did of Drew. It was as if I'd married her. I often wondered what kind of person would have married her. When Drew was twelve, his father died of a heart attack. I secretly think he must have died to get away from Priscilla. That's what I would have done. That's not a nice thought, I know. Some of my thoughts aren't nice, but they are just thoughts. That's why I'm not going to go have my brain picked by some social worker just to be reassured that I'm totally normal and everyone fantasizes about getting away from their mother-in-law. I think it's healthy to be offended by Priscilla. The person who isn't would be the one who needs therapy.

In one way, I feel sorry for Priscilla. I don't think she's had sex in almost twenty years. She's never had another lover, boyfriend or even close friend since Walter died. And she certainly hasn't had a vibrating friend of any kind. Imagine going twenty years without having an orgasm. It's quite possible, in her case, that she's never had one. I don't know the rules of the Catholic Church, but it might even be a sin for a woman to have an orgasm; at any rate she's not supposed to enjoy sex, it's meant to be exclusively practical, like flossing one's teeth. When I'm in a generous mood, I think about this fact. I imagine what I would act like if I hadn't had any loving in all that time. I guess I would be a nasty, brittle crank too. And that thought makes me feel a little bit warmer toward Priscilla. A little.

"I'm not really in to this," I told Drew, turning to walk back up the stairs.

"What is it now?"

"You. Being unavailable. You, being busy with other things.

It's either Clarkville or the garden or some other selfish endeavor, like inspecting your tools." I prepared to give the basement door a dramatic and profound slam, but Drew beat me to the chase. He turned on a power tool—God only knows which one—and drowned me out.

Ten

MELODY DIDN'T GIVE ME MUCH PREPARATION FOR mommy-and-baby yoga class, besides, of course, letting me know that it was one place where my sweatpants would be welcome. I expected some place eerily quiet, like a convent, with candles everywhere, like a church, and with a teacher dressed in white, like a health spa in some European country. I didn't expect the chaos of six small babies, or the brightly lit entrance with a mural of people in various states of flexibility. And I most certainly did not expect Oliver.

My mother does yoga; did I mention that? She started doing it before it got regular write-ups in the *New York Times,* before every ad for cars, footwear and soy milk had a picture of a woman in a yoga pose on it. Back when she started, classes were mostly empty and the people who attended them were practically certifiable. They'd chant in Sanskrit like the guys in the orange robes you're always told to stay away from. But I'd never practiced with my mother. She'd never asked me to and I'd never been interested. When I was a teenager, it was sort of like her secret place, or the place she went so she could pretend she belonged to a cult. She'd leave me with the kids for an hour some weekend mornings, disappearing into her room to do "the yoga," as we called it. I couldn't even make fun of her about it because I couldn't imagine what she actually *did*. A few times I saw books about yoga that consisted of old pictures of Indian men pouring water into their noses, or putting their feet behind their head. I knew my mother didn't do *that*: Her yoga had to be different. She was always a dignified person. It's hard to imagine she would have made a habit out of looking so ridiculous.

In New York City, yoga studios are now second only to Starbucks for being situated on almost every street corner. It's still been about as appealing to me as having my bikini area waxed, which is something I have sworn I would never, ever do. Beth worked at a spa during college. She was just the receptionist, but the horror stories she told about how all the wax girls talked would make a prostitute blush. I couldn't bear to have my pubic region discussed in such minute detail. Beth told me they even had different names for the variety of, and I quote directly here, "pussy smells." As far as I'm concerned, the only person who should know what your vagina smells like is your husband, and that will happen only if you are very lucky.

There I was, in the middle of a room of strangers. The room itself was just like I'd imagined. All the walls were white, except one painted in a drowsy shade of blue. I heard tinkles and waterfalls and birdcalls over the stereo—when I heard anything over the cries and coos of babies and the prattle of mothers. We sat in two lines facing a row of wide windows overlooking a small tree-lined yard. In front of us sat a man.

And not an ordinary man at that. He had skin the shade of creamy coffee, bright round, dark eyes like seventy percent cocoa—my favorite—and a short, tidy beard. I had to imagine there was some mistake. This man couldn't be the lovely Carol that Melody had told me about. That Carol had been a woman. This person was clearly a man. He wore black shorts and a tight black T-shirt. He was older, older than me by quite a bit, but slender and muscled and vigorous in his looks. That's right. Vigorous.

As you can imagine, this man put me very much on edge. After all, I'd come in my sweatpants. My hair stuck up in uncombed sections all over my head. Zach only wanted to nurse, and I hadn't gone to the trouble of wearing a nursing shirt so my Lumpkin flub hung out for the entire world to see.

"Wow," I said to Melody.

"I don't know who this guy is. Carol must be sick."

"Lucky us."

"You like him?" She raised her eyebrows. "Yummy, huh? He's got that exotic thing going for him. Although I don't go for older men." We were in the back row and didn't even need to whisper since the room was so noisy.

"You can't tell his age from his body. He looks so strong. And calm."

"He's got the rope necklace going on," Melody pointed out. "And the facial hair. Kind of hippie, free spirit. I guess you should expect that in a yoga class, but Carol is very hip."

"I like him," I said.

"He's not your type. You like blonds."

"I know," I said, smiling foolishly. "I just like the looks of him. He looks edible."

"Hello," he said in what seemed to be a Canadian accent, with the emphasis on the vowels. "Welcome. Carol couldn't be here today. I'm going to try to fill her shoes." He smiled at us revealing large, white teeth. I checked out his nose, which passed my small-nose exam with flying colors. It was a squat nose, close to his face, but wide and fat. "Let's begin by getting comfortable. You can hold on to your babies, or allow them to lie on the floor right in front of you. We'll begin in a sitting position today."

I managed to extricate Zach from my right breast. My breasts had begun to look like long-nosed fish, the poor things. I felt genuinely sorry for my nipples; they used to be so normal. Now they were flatter and longer and far less cosmopolitan. My career in adult movies was over before I had a chance to even consider it. Is there a lot of money in nipple modeling? I will never know.

Then the man said: "Let's pick up the flesh of the buttocks and move it out of the way."

Uh-huh.

I can't say this is a command I'd been given that often.

I looked at Melody, who disinterestedly readjusted her fanny on the yoga mat by lifting up one butt cheek and then the other. The teacher offered us all a demonstration by moving his own backside around with his hands. Truly I did not want to touch my hiney. I wiggled into the floor instead, glad no one was behind me. What can he do anyway? I thought. As far as I knew we wouldn't be graded, and we couldn't be kicked out. And I had to assume he wasn't going to come over and check to see if I'd done it right. What would that look like anyway? Would he personally pry my buttocks apart in search of my butt bones? Given the state of my derriere, this seemed quite unlikely.

"How hands-on is this class?" I asked Melody.

"I don't know about this guy, but Carol often gives assists."

"I think I'd like an assist."

"I just bet you would. You be good, Joy McGuire. No making me laugh in the middle of class. Yoga is serious."

"What do you expect when someone who looks like the bad guy in a cheap romance asks me to rearrange my body parts?"

"Do as you're told," she said in her best therapist voice. "And don't read cheap romances. They'll give you bad ideas."

I can't say it was the most dignified hour I've spent in my life. We rolled around on the floor quite a bit. The mother next to me let out a huge fart during our standing leg stretches. Normally I would have used this opportunity to make gagging faces at Melody and have a good laugh, but with Oliver walking around the class I almost died with embarrassment. Would he think it was me? I felt a desperate urge to make a good impression; I doubted the sweatpants would do it; nor would, for that matter, my inability to perform any of the poses.

We spent a lot of time pretending we didn't have any bones, and when we finally got to standing (which took about three-fourths of the class), we held our babies and stood on one leg—some ancient martial arts posture, perhaps? During the abdominal poses I quickly collapsed onto the floor in a ball of maternal ooze. Melody laughed at me.

"It gets easier," she said.

"I thought this was supposed to be yoga."

"It *is* yoga."

"I thought yoga was easy. I thought it was breathing."

"It is breathing."

"No," I said. "Breathing is easy. I do it all the time. This is not easy. This is like calisthenics as directed by a retired gymnast with sadomasochistic tendencies."

"Don't make me laugh," Melody said. "I'll pee." She heaved Sarah onto her knees and then straightened her legs skyward. She balanced on her butt bones.

"Upward boat pose," Oliver said, coming toward us. I lay immovable on the floor like a dead jellyfish.

The teacher, the leader of our training in self-flagellation, knelt down beside me. "Are you okay?"

"Just taking a break." I didn't want to imagine what I looked like. I tried to remember if I'd washed my sweatpants before I'd retired them to my closet. Could I smell as bad as I looked?

"I'll just give you a press," he said. He was so close I could almost feel his knee against my waist.

"A press?"

"Let's all come into child's pose," he said to the group. He stood up and looked at the other women. If I'd stared straight up and to the left I could have copped a look up his shorts. Does anyone do that, look up a man's shorts? Maybe teenage girls. But not grown women. I wouldn't let myself do it. I focused on the ceiling.

"Would you like to join us?" he said finally, still beside me. I looked over at Melody, who had turned over and curled up on her knees.

"Oh." I pulled myself around and rearranged Zach beside me. He was enraptured with the ceiling fan.

"Just breathe," he said. I felt two warm hands at the top of my butt pressing down gently. It felt so good; it took me by surprise. Nothing had felt good yet. Everything had been like a kind of torture. His hands slid down a quarter inch. Really, they were on my lower back, but his fingers lay gently on the top of my rump. I took in a breath and let it go the way he had instructed at the beginning of class.

"Good," I heard him say.

When he took his hands away, my body felt hot.

Zach fell asleep in the car on the ride home. It took Herculean efforts not to disturb him as I moved him into the house and gently put his car seat on the floor in the living room. The house was quiet. I snuck into the office to check on email. Despite the fact that I never get anything exciting, checking on it helps me to feel involved in the world, like I have an "office," and a "computer," and some urgent matters that need attending to.

Like Jake.

I clicked his email open.

Hey, Joy. Sorry it took me a while to get back to you. I told you about the buyout, right? Crazy busy here. So your mother's marrying a life coach? Did she go to him for coaching, maybe? I guess that's a bit odd, knowing your mother. Why don't you just ask her if she knows what he does for a living? Can't imagine she wouldn't.

Thought I'd mention that my grandmother just passed. I remember how much you two liked each other. That ruby ring you gave her for her 80th birthday—do you remember that? She never took it off. She always asked after you. I don't think anyone else would sit and listen to her stories for hours at a time! Man, could she talk. Good luck with your coach problems. —J

I wrote him back instantly. Was that really uncool to write back immediately? It's not like we're dating or anything. He knows I'm a bored housewife.

I'm so sorry to hear about your grandmother. I really did love her and loved spending time with her. She had the best sense of humor. Give your family my condolences, okay?

Sorry to pick your brain when you're so busy, but any suggestions on what to do about Donny? Your idea to talk to my mother about it—I've tried. She thinks he's an "artist," that's the latest. Before that it was "Renaissance man." Also, I have a bit of a bad history talking to her about her husbands. In other words, she doesn't listen to my opinion because I haven't always been, let's say, neutral. But this time, it's really in her best interest. Go to his website (maccoaching.com), if you get a second. You'll wet yourself laughing. Joy

I read my email ten times before I sent it off to make sure there weren't any signs of my teensy-weensy crush on him. It wasn't really a crush anyway. It was more of a distraction. Thinking about Jake was something akin to watching a soap opera—a total fiction. It was like imagining a fantasy life.

Meanwhile real life consisted of my mother's imminent demise. I had to save her. I went on to Donny's website again. On second glance it didn't seem quite so utterly terrible, but that didn't stop me from copying down the information for an upcoming "open house" he would be holding at his office. Maybe I could figure out a way to stop in and see what it was all about.

When I heard the muffled sounds of Zach's cry from the living room, I stood up. But before I left the computer, I checked my email one more time, just in case. Just in case Jake was online and had responded. No luck. I ignored the feeling of my heart falling into my shoes and shuffled out to take up mother duty once again.

Eleven

THE NEXT DAY, DIANA CAME FOR A PLAYDATE, HEAV-
ing the ever-growing piggy baby with her. She set
Addicus down beside Zach. Both boys were becoming expert
at sitting up. You forget how hard it is to be a human being
until you get to raise one. If you consider the challenges we
go through, even eating with a spoon is cause for celebration. But who has time to congratulate themselves and those
around them on the effective use of the potty? Yet it's these little successes that life is made of.

"I want to know everything," she said. She stood up and
smoothed out her summer dress, pausing briefly at her belly.
She didn't have a bump yet. In fact, it seemed that her belly
was a tad concave, a condition I personally find rude. If you
have to have a belly that's so small it actually doesn't exist,
then you ought to be kind enough to quarantine yourself until you've eaten enough cookies to rectify the situation.

"About yoga?"

"No. Donny. What did your mother say when you told
her?"

"Um."

"I showed his site to Jeff. He got a good laugh out of it. Did your mother already know about it?"

"Well. I tried to bring it up. I have to be a bit delicate with her. I didn't exactly get it out, about the coaching business, but I did learn something new."

"I'm all ears."

"She thinks he's an artist. Apparently he does watercolors. I think he's scamming her. He probably met her at a society party—maybe some client of his gifted him an invitation—and dollar signs went off in his head. It wouldn't be the first time."

"Are you saying your stepfathers were only in it for the money?"

"I don't know. I don't think so. Just some boyfriends. Maybe. God, I don't know anything. I just think he's creepy." I looked at Diana. She didn't look so hot herself. "Can I get you something?"

"I'm fine. Actually, I'd love some water. I'll watch the babies."

"Of course."

I came back with water and some plain crackers. She smiled thinly.

"I don't know about those."

"I'll eat them if you don't want them. I have to keep feeding my butt."

"You're silly. You look fine. You're too hard on yourself, Joy."

"I guess." I sat down next to Diana on the couch. "I've just never had weight I couldn't get off. This postpregnancy belly is like a leech. And it's not normal fat, you know. It's like a special kind of fat. Like loose-skin fat."

"Well, you're beautiful anyway."

"You're pathologically kind. Anyway, I'm planning on going to Donny's open house for his coaching business. What do you think of that?"

"It's perfect. You'll be able to get a sense of how well he's doing."

"Exactly. That's the plan. Then I can casually mention it to my mother. See how she responds. That way at least I'll have more to go on."

"You're a schemer." She smiled and took a tiny bite from one of the crackers. "I feel like I've been so out of commission. Tell me what else I've missed. What's going on with Jake?"

The boys started to fuss. "You stay there," I said, getting up from the couch and sitting down with them on the floor. I showed them some blocks, which they instantly took and shoved into their mouths.

"Nothing's going on, of course. We've emailed back and forth a few times. Maybe we'll be friends again. You know we all got to be friends for a few years, Jake, Drew and me. Jake and Drew watched ball games together. Anything that bounced, they'd watch it."

"Not still having feelings for him, then?"

"Depends on what you mean by feelings."

"Don't talk like a politician," Diana said gently with a smile. "I'm your friend."

"Same as before. Imagining what my life would have been like if I'd married him instead, but that's just a symptom of not getting along with Drew. It's silly. It's a mindless kind of thing, an escape."

"Why didn't you marry him?"

"He wouldn't have married me. I wanted to marry him. We talked about it, but we were just out of college. When

Drew asked me to marry him, I did hope it would be a wake-up call to Jake. Make him realize what he was losing, make him change his mind and take me back. But then I did fall for Drew, and we connected in ways I never had with Jake. No sense in debating what would have been. And this is enough about me." I got back up and sat on the couch. "You're the pregnant one. Tell me about your life. Are you coping?"

"It's hard," she said. I saw her bottom lip tremble.

"Oh, Diana."

"I'm so tired. I can hardly enjoy Addicus. All I want to do is sleep."

I put my arm around her and gave her a squeeze. We sat like that for a few minutes, watching the babies wiggle around on the floor. Zach looked days away from crawling. It was such a sweet sight that I forgot, for a moment, to feel sorry for myself. I can't tell you what a relief it was.

I may be grumpy, sloppy, disorganized and slightly adulterous (if you count the daydreams with Jake), but I am not insane. Drew, however, is. It's official. I've been holding off on giving him the diagnosis for a while now. I thought perhaps he'd make a recovery and join me in the small world of normal family life. Instead, he's gone over the deep end; he's decided he wants a dog.

"A dog? You want a dog?" This is how our conversation went late on Wednesday night. "Is a baby not enough for you? Or maybe you want a dog because you don't *do* anything for the baby. You don't have any diapers to change; you don't have any laundry to do; you don't have fifteen pounds to lug with you to the grocery store...that must be it. You're bored!" While I gave my monologue, Drew looked insulted and slightly disinterested, which wasn't the effect I'd been going for.

"You know I've been wanting a dog for a long time, Joy." He was lying on the couch in the living room.

"Well, you now have the version of a dog that adults get. It's called a baby. His name is Zach. I know it may seem to you like he sleeps all the time, but actually, he's awake quite a lot. You might enjoy him if you ever got to spending time with him. And like a puppy, he needs regular training, petting and grooming. Best of all, he's already here, so you don't need to go buy him or adopt him from some pound."

"Very funny."

"I'm not trying to be funny."

"Neither am I. I'd like to get a dog. I'm not asking for your permission."

"You're absolutely unbelievable. Who is going to take care of this dog?"

"I am. And stop treating me like a child."

"Then stop acting like one. Start acting like a father."

"How about you stop acting like your life is so hard. As far as I can tell, you've got it pretty easy. What is it, exactly"—and here he sat up—"that you do all day? Because as far as I can tell, all you do is nap and hang out with the baby."

I have to pause here for a moment to point out that if I were someone who actually *did* need anger management classes, I would have slugged Drew at this point. However, because I have about a cup and a half more self-control than that, I didn't. I said:

"I don't know when I started hating you so much. Oh, yeah, maybe February sixteenth."

"Yeah, yeah. I've already heard that one, Joy." Drew leaned against the back of the couch. He didn't look so tired that day, but he did look older. He looked much older than when I'd met and married him. "We've had this fight too many times now. I'm tired of it."

"And what? I enjoy it? I'm sick of it too. But you're the one who needs to change around here. I can't make things better if you're just going to keep acting the same way. You're hopeless."

"You can name-call all you want. Or you could be an adult about this and have a conversation with me about getting a dog. I don't see that it's such a big deal. You make it about the past. This is about my getting a dog."

"You don't see that it's such a big deal! Drew, my God, we have an infant son. I'm exhausted from figuring out how to cook and shop and take care of myself and take care of him. How do you expect me to take care of a dog?"

"I didn't ask you to take care of it. I'll do that."

I was standing in the middle of the room. At some point, I'd put my hands on my hips. I felt like an enraged schoolmistress shouting down a disobedient student, except I also felt like Alice who'd fallen down the rabbit hole. It was impossible for me to imagine how he'd missed the fact of our son so completely. When I'd imagined how our life would be with a child, it was just like the television commercials—a daddy throwing a giggling baby high in the air. I thought, like I'd been taught to think, that Drew and I would manage child care equitably, that even if I stayed home full time, Drew would be there every night for baths and every morning for breakfast. Was it my fault this hadn't happened? I didn't think so. In fact, I was pretty darn sure it was Drew's. But I took a deep breath anyway. Boy, I hope someone somewhere gives me points for this.

"Look," I said, trying to calm myself down. "How about next year?"

"I think it will be nice for Zach to grow up with a dog. I did."

"By next year he'll only be a little more than a year. As far as I can tell, that leaves a lot of growing up to do with a dog."

Drew sighed. "I'm going to look at dogs at the shelter on Saturday. You can come or not." He picked up the remote control. And, yes, that's right, he turned on the television and turned me off. I walked away full of disgust; how dare he? Then a strange whisper of memory came to mind, some conversation from sometime years ago about a dog he wanted. And what had I said? Had I said when we had a family we'd get one? I couldn't remember. Even if I had, why would Drew pick that exact moment to make good on our dream of a happy family—dog included? Didn't he get how maxed out I was? I was just about to storm in and give Drew another piece of my mind when the phone rang.

"Yes," I answered irritably.

"Honey, it's your one and only—"

"Mom," I responded.

"You got it."

"You don't need to say who you are. I know your voice."

"And I know yours. What's the trouble in paradise?"

"Drew is insane, that's all. Is this how things fall apart? Is this the lead-up to divorce?"

"How about you try forgiving him? You can't hold a grudge forever."

"You bet I can. Especially when he's not doing anything to make it up to me."

"Well, honey, things don't always work the way we want them to."

I stopped short of yelling at her. I was in no mood for trite advice. "Did you need something?"

"Sorry, sweets, I almost forgot. Aunt Hilda and I would like to come by for tea on Saturday. We'll bring treats along, of course. I want to go over some wedding plans with you. Show you pictures of the wedding site we might use, the Temple of Divine Light and Energy. What do you say?"

What did I say? I say, where does my mother find these things?

"Great idea. I'd love to see Aunt Hilda again. She's awesome. But what's the deal with this temple thing?"

"Oh, it's not religious. It's spiritual, honey."

"That helps me how?"

"You'll love the building, all shimmery and silvery. So we're on for tea, then? Aunt Hilda and I will bring all the fixings. We'll see you around noon, sweetie. Can't wait. We'll catch up then. I've got this pedicure coming up and it just ruins it if I talk on the phone." She made a kissing noise and then hung up the phone.

I sat down heavily in my rocking chair. Clearly I needed another yoga class. Oliver, the yoga teacher, had said over and over again "Breathe into things just as they are without trying to change them," which seemed as impossible to me as visualizing myself into a pair of size four pants. But I tried.

Twelve

I DECIDED I WANTED TO GO TO A YOGA CLASS WITH Oliver. No baby involved. I checked the studio's website and saw that they had a midmorning class on Saturdays. I called Melody just to check. She knows everything. She probably has the yoga schedule memorized.

"I thought you hated the class."

"I did hate it. Except the last part when you lie on the floor. That was great."

"Corpse pose? Everybody loves that."

"And I liked the teacher."

"You and every other housewife."

"That's not it; he made me feel at ease."

"That's the way it is in yoga. That's why it's so wonderful. You get to be yourself."

"Well, that's how I felt. I felt like I could be myself."

"Good for you," Melody said. "It's great that you're doing something just for you. I think you're overdue for a little personal care time."

"Oh, no! It's therapy talk!"

"Personal care time is not therapy talk. Plenty of people use it."

"People who are in therapy."

The only problem with my Saturday morning "personal care" plan was that it required I leave Zach. Who could I leave him with? I'd hardly left him for more than ten minutes to take a shower. Drew had taken to jogging on Saturday mornings since the summer began. Not that I would have asked him anyway. In addition to his usual allergy to Zach, he hadn't said a word to me since our fight over the dog. It was the cold war all over again. The silence was almost unbearable. *Almost.* Clearly I was bearing it. That left Priscilla. Or my mother.

"Could you come early on Saturday?" I begged my mother over the phone. "And watch Zach? Bring Aunt Hilda. You two could make a whole day of it."

"Well—"

"It's just a few hours earlier than you'd planned on coming for tea anyhow."

"I don't even know if Aunt Hilda likes children."

"What are you suggesting? Is she like the witch in 'Hansel and Gretel'? Is she going to eat him or something?"

"Very funny, honey. I simply mean I hope it won't be hard on her nerves."

"She can stay in the living room. You two can hang out in the family room. It's just a few hours. It's just one day. I'm desperate for a little time to myself."

"Let me ask her." I heard my mother calling to Aunt Hilda followed by a long silence. "Honey? She says she loves babies. She'd be happy to do it."

"Mom! I don't want Aunt Hilda babysitting. That scares me. For all we know she *escaped.* I want you to babysit."

"Don't worry, sweets, I understand. But we don't want Aunt Hilda to feel left out."

"Please don't do anything crazy like leave him with her while you go to the bathroom. I'll be so nervous."

"Joy, sweetie, I am so glad you're taking this yoga class. You know how long I've been doing yoga? About forty years now. It will do you a world of good."

"But Aunt—"

"And, honey, your Aunt Hilda likes to sleep a lot. I imagine that's just what she'll be doing. Okay? Now you go take care of yourself and we'll see you on Saturday."

I took a good look at myself in the mirror the Friday night before my class. I wanted to understand my arms. Why did they need to become so intimately involved in the pregnancy? I get why your butt would grow—it's near your belly. But why had my *arms* put on weight? It was another sign of my ultimate end. Not only would I be an old lady in a nursing home with long white braidable whiskers, I would be one of those old women with swinging triceps. You know the kind. They remind you of sails blowing in the wind. They shimmy. They drape themselves by your sides. They are horrific and inevitable.

When I used to work out at a gym—sometime back when I had free time, disposable income and a healthy level of personal vanity—I would see all the women in the dressing room with their sagging arms and fleshy hips and cottage cheese thighs and I would wonder. I didn't know how it happened. I thought it took years of McDonald's and daytime television. I had no idea that one baby, one pregnancy, could bring my body into such unsavory womanhood.

I looked myself up and down. At least I had a few good spots left. Like my eyebrows. I'd returned to a regular habit of plucking; they looked pretty good. My breasts, minus the Olympic-size nipples, were also a plus. Because I was still nursing they continued to stay in the middle of the alphabet in terms of bra size. And my knees. My knees didn't look too fat. Eyebrows, boobs and knees. That's not bad, is it?

When I got into bed, Drew didn't move. He was lying on his side reading. Zach had been sleeping for an hour already in his bassinet. He was beginning to outgrow it. Drew still didn't want Zach to sleep in his nursery at night. I think it was his strange way of making up for not spending much time with him, like fatherhood could be caught just by sleeping in the same room for as long as possible.

"I'm going to a class tomorrow morning," I told him. "My mother is coming to babysit."

"Why didn't you ask my mom? You know she wants to come and help you."

"I've never left him before. It feels better to have my mother this first time." Of course, this was not true. I asked my mother because his mother frightened me, and I worried that if I left Zach in her care for any length of time she would get him addicted to cookies, dress him in his newborn layette set and take him on a permanent vacation to the Vatican.

"Whatever."

"Excuse me?"

"That's just a line you're feeding me. You don't like my mother and you know it."

I didn't answer. I lay on the bed and stared at the ceiling for a while. I calculated how much sleep I would get if I only had to get up with Zach twice that night to nurse him. One night that week, he'd slept for seven hours in a row. I'd woken up feeling like Shirley Temple, I was so happy.

I needed my sleep, and I had more important things to worry about than my constant bickering with Drew or, for that matter, my overgrown upper arms. I had big plans ahead of me. Not only would I be leaving Zach for a few hours to brave another yoga class, but I had Donny's open house marked on the calendar for Sunday afternoon and I needed to prepare.

When the phone rang an hour later, I heard the telltale tone of Drew's professional voice. I knew what it meant. It meant: trustee calling. He didn't say much, and when he hung up the phone, he sighed heavily, heartily, so that I almost reached for him. But I'm stubborn. I stuck to my side of the bed.

Oliver had dressed again in his black shorts and his sleeveless black T. Maybe it was his yoga teaching uniform. I positioned myself securely in the back. The class was called: "Moderate level I." I didn't know what to expect. I'd switched out of my worn sweatpants (I mean, this yoga teacher is *sexy*) and into a pair of loose black cotton ones. I looked around at the mix of people, glad to see a few other mother-looking people who'd been kind enough to bring their thighs with them to class. I noticed one man, youngish, painfully good looking. I almost let myself be attracted to him, but the thought that I could be at least a decade older stopped me dead in my tracks. Joy, I said to myself. Move on.

"Let's begin by settling in, closing our eyes and taking a long breath." Oliver closed his eyes and imitated a breath for us. We all followed along. "Today, we are going to work on being gentle with ourselves."

I opened my eyes when he said this, sure he had been reading my mind and was saying it right to me. His eyes were still closed, though, and he looked peaceful on his purple mat. One could even say he looked gentle.

That day, I did everything as instructed. I managed to attempt every posture or, as Oliver called them, *asanas*. I still didn't like any of them. I kept watching the clock and waiting for the time when we would lie down. We spent a very long time in the dog pose, which killed my legs, made my arms ache and brought so much blood to my head that I thought I *had* reached enlightenment and that it was something akin to dizziness.

"Would you like a press?" Oliver said. I could see his toes by the edge of my mat.

"Uh, I think I need to sit down."

"Just rest in child pose for a minute."

I dropped my knees to the floor and sat up on my heels. My left knee cracked loudly. I let out a self-conscious giggle.

"Want to try again?" Oliver said. He had firm, shapely legs, almost like a woman, but quite hairy. Now that I thought about it, he did have the slightest hint of femininity to him, or perhaps it was just the yoga teaching. Teaching yoga is a rather girly thing to do, with all the talk about loving yourself and breathing into your belly. You can't talk that way and go hunting on Sundays, can you? You can't talk that way to your buddies over beer and not expect to be dragged into the parking lot and left for dead. So who was this gentle Oliver man with his beard and his deep eyes and his yoga uniform?

I pulled myself back up and pushed into the dog pose, my ever-widening fanny lifting into the air. Oliver put his hands on my back. His knees brushed against my upper arms. It gave me a shiver down my legs. Then he pressed me so firmly my hands lifted up off the floor. I laughed and fell down.

"That's what's supposed to happen," he said. "Makes it easier, doesn't it?"

"Yeah. Could you stand there the whole time?" He got the joke and laughed in a low chuckle.

"Partner yoga," he said. "You should try it sometime." Then he walked away, toward the front of the classroom.

When my favorite part finally arrived—lying on the floor— my whole body felt like the goo inside a lava lamp, except very, very trembly. Every part of me shook as I lay down. Then came the soft music with the birds and whales and crickets singing. That's the kind of nature I like: on audio. Because when you're really with the birds, you're also with the bees and wasps. When you're really with the whales, you're with the sharks and crabs. And when you're really with the crickets, you're with the ants and mosquitos. Oliver did his version of the voiceover, talking softly about something impossible and ridiculous. I think it was self-love. It didn't matter, though. I felt dreamy. I felt like I was floating. Then I felt the urge to fart. I spent the rest of my peaceful relaxation with my buttocks squeezed to within an inch of their lives.

"He's not keen on the bottle," my mother said when I got home. She handed me a red-faced, tearstained, hiccuping baby. "You sit and nurse him, sweetie. Let me get you something to drink."

"Where's Aunt Hilda?"

"Sleeping, honey. Just like I told you. I said she could use the guest bedroom."

"That's fine." I sat down with a wailing Zach and started to nurse.

Despite Zach's obvious state of despair, my mother seemed unfazed. She had on a pair of toothpick-thin, white capri pants and a pink gingham top. Her bright red hair was piled on top of her head and pinned with barrettes covered in rhinestones. She looked twenty-five.

"Did you have a good time, honey?" she said, handing me a glass of bubbling water.

"Some parts. Was he upset the whole time?"

"Not really. Nothing to worry about. I think he might have cried for ten minutes, not a second more. He just fussed about the bottle. He realized it wasn't the real thing."

"I honestly don't know who could mistake a bottle for a breast. They don't even try to imitate the human nipple. Mine don't look like rubber bullets; they look like raspberries." I looked down at Zach, who'd progressed from an insistent, military sucking to a more leisurely, sleepy pace. "Where's Drew?"

"He came in for a shower after his run. When he headed out again, he said he was going to the pound to look at dogs."

"Again?"

"You're too hard on him, sweetie." My mother sat on the sofa opposite me. I'd gone, naturally, to my favorite rocker in the family room so I could put my feet up.

"Am I? Can you be too hard on a man who has a new baby he ignores and then wants to get a dog? He's acting like a child."

"He says he's always wanted a dog." She threw her legs up on the sofa and reclined back. I noticed that even curled up, her stomach did not move. How had that happened? What woman who's given birth five times looks like that? You'd think I had Madonna (not the one in the Bible) for a mother, someone who trains every day at five a.m. for a marathon she will never run in. "I think you might want to be more gentle with him; have you forgiven him yet? And another thing, honey, you need to let him in, help him get involved. Did you ask him to watch Zach?"

"Ask him? Are you serious?! Next thing you'll want to know if I pay him when he 'babysits.' It's *his* kid. I shouldn't have to ask him. He should *offer*."

"New fatherhood can be as hard as new motherhood."

"That may be true, but I'm still pulling my weight, and I'm a new mother. Do you know what he did the other day?" My mother shook her head. "I'd had a terrible day with Zach. I don't think he'd slept at all for something like ten hours. He'd cried and fussed every time I'd put him down. I couldn't do a single thing other than take care of him. When Drew came in from the garden, I asked him if he could take the baby for an hour so I could lie down. What do you think he said?"

"No," my mother said and laughed.

"Right. He said no, but he said it like this. He said, 'Why are you asking me to do that?' Like it isn't his kid! Who am I supposed to ask? The neighbors across the street who we don't even know? I swear, I never understood before how people end up in a divorce or for that matter an affair, but now I do."

My mother sighed quietly. "It sounds bad, sweetie. I don't know why he's not being more involved, but, honestly, it doesn't seem like Drew. I'm sure he'll come around. Why don't you try talking to him? You two have always been so connected."

"Have we?" I could barely remember anymore. It had been nothing but sailing down the white waters in different rafts for several months.

My mother nodded toward the baby. "Asleep?"

Zach had, in fact, fallen fast asleep. I felt moderately bad for shouting over his sleeping head. I also felt like eating a chocolate cake.

"Marriage is really, really hard, honey," my mother said. "Everyone knows that children stress a marriage. You just need to live through it. Maybe Drew can't be the great daddy that you hoped for. But he's a good provider."

"Jesus, Mom, you sound like you're from the 1950s."

"Sweetie, I'm a working woman. And work counts for something no matter who does it, a man or a woman."

"It's not fair. I've never seen him so busy in the summer. I'm practically a single mother."

"I can promise you one thing, my sweet. This will all pass. It will pass before you know it, and you will be sorry it's gone."

"I've heard that one before. I just don't believe it. The years may go by quickly, but my days are like a century long. You know why they don't have a reality TV show about mothers of babies? They have everyone else, wives and cheaters and fat people and rock stars. But they don't have a reality mommy show because it would be so boring, so tedious, so repetitive that no one would watch it."

"Are you not enjoying him, honey?" My mother had closed her eyes at this point. She looked exceedingly relaxed, which annoyed me. I got a pinprick of memory back to the time when she wasn't so calm, so positive, so healthy. Then it faded out.

"No. I love him. And I actually love being with him. I never miss editing. I don't wish for a different job. As impossible as it seems, I think motherhood fits my temperament pretty well. It's just not always that interesting, that's all."

"Life's about more than interesting."

"You're one to talk." We sat for a moment in the silence. "Hey, Mom?"

"Yes?"

"Can you babysit next Saturday too? I'd like to go to that class again."

"Mmm," she said. And then she was quiet for a long while.

About a half hour later, I heard Aunt Hilda slowly descending the stairs. She teetered into the family room looking once again birdlike in a draping cape of red, turquoise and yellow that hung at her arms like wings. She greeted me with an enormously ferocious embrace.

"I didn't know she ever slept," Aunt Hilda said, gesturing toward my mother. "I haven't seen her rest for a minute."

It *was* a little unusual for my mother, but then she rarely spent time with infants. "I guess Zach wore her out. Babies have a way of doing that."

"What a sweet thing," she said, tapping Zach's fat thigh with a long finger.

"Let me just put him down in his crib. I think he'll sleep now."

"I'll read your fortune," Aunt Hilda said.

"Oh, no, no. No, that's fine. I'm fine. I mean, thank you, but I think we're having our tea soon."

"You'll enjoy it." She smiled at me. I found her at once comforting—after all, she was quite beautiful—and unnerving. What if she really did know something about my future?

"I'll be right back." I hurried upstairs to the nursery and tucked Zach into his crib, where he would sleep for naps but never at night. When I came back downstairs, Aunt Hilda wasn't in the family room. My mother still lay on the couch, gently snoring. I almost laughed out loud. The woman had enough energy to run a dynasty, but two hours with Zach left her depleted. Boy, wasn't that the truth.

"Aunt Hilda?" I called. I found her in the kitchen.

"Sit down." She pointed to a spot at our center island.

"I'm not really into fortune-telling, Aunt Hilda. I think I'd rather not know the future."

"Sit," she said again, this time firmly and the little bun pinned up on top of her head shook.

"If you insist." I sat down.

She flipped out a small deck of cards, the size of playing cards, from a deep pocket she had hidden somewhere in all her layers of clothing.

"Shuffle these." She was sitting next to me, on another high kitchen chair. She kept her eyes closed until I passed the cards back. Then they fluttered open and she giggled, in her young, wild way.

She laid out seven cards on the counter in front of us. They each held an image, meaningless to me, of symbols and people and animals. They were darkly colored, well used, and worn around the edges. She looked them over, one at a time, nodding and tapping each one with a long nail. If I didn't already know she was crazy, I definitely would have thought so then.

"Very good life," she said. "You're lucky." She smiled, rather sadly, I thought. Maybe she was jealous? Had she read her own fortune? Had she known she was going to spend decades in a facility? I shuddered to think. Although, quite honestly, I've never believed in psychics, and the ultimate proof that they don't know anything is the existence of the Psychic Friends Network, which served to confirm for me and every other intelligent person that the only goal of our so-called Friends was to make a buck off our total gullibility.

"This," she said, pointing to one card. "This trouble at the birth." She raised a single eyebrow. "What happened? What happened at the birth?" She looked pointedly into my eyes.

"What do you mean?"

"The baby's birth. It's right here. Plain as day. Something went wrong."

"What's my mother been telling you?" I asked.

"Your mother?" She closed her eyes for a moment as if I'd asked her a very challenging question. "She's very proud of you, she tells me that. But this, I see this trouble from the cards," she said finally. "This is your past." She pointed to the same card again. It had a black figure in the center. "This is the birth. What happened? I don't see medical problems, no, something else. See here? There's a hole in the middle. Some kind of injury took place."

I paused for a moment to recall the scene for the hundred millionth time. I'd thought of it so often in the first week after Zach was born, I had barely been able to enjoy his new baby company. The whole thing was imprinted so forcefully in my brain it felt like a cranial tattoo. The picture of me, alone, in the hospital. I'd called Drew when the contractions began. He'd gone to Atlanta with a group of Clarkville boys the day before. He insisted on going. We'd fought about it terribly. I'd worried that the baby might come early. He reasoned that, as the doctor had told us, first-time labors are long and usually late. He'd be able to make it back even if I did go into labor when he was gone. "What are the chances?" he said. "It will only be two days," he said. "It's only Atlanta," he said. "You're not due for two weeks," he said.

I'll tell you what the chances were, one hundred percent. The day he went to Atlanta, the contractions began. A false alarm, Drew suggested casually when I called, as if he'd dealt with birth so many times before. Besides, how could he get all the boys back? How could he leave just one chaperone? We'd fought again. I'd been furious. I needed him; he was my labor coach. And my husband. And the father of my child.

Zach, a statistical anomaly, decided to take the water slide out. The whole labor lasted six hours from first contraction to birth. This may seem a lot easier than twenty-four hours of contractions, but my perineum would argue with you on that one. He pretty much tore the whole thing up on his way out. Meanwhile, my obstetrician, the one I had conscientiously chosen and worked with for almost ten months, was at a wedding in Vermont. Talk about total desertion. I wanted to write in to *Lifetime* TV and sell my story so women all over the country could cry along with me. (I'm sure they've already made a movie about this, though.) I'd never felt more alone in my life than I did during labor. But when they gave Zach to me, I fell totally in love. Drew arrived ten hours later. Ten. And when he walked into my room, he tiptoed. It was like a stranger arriving. I'd gone through it all on my own. Priscilla and my mother met the baby before he did. I decided at some point during one of the contractions that almost knocked me unconscious from the pain that I would never forgive him. After all, I'd *warned* him. I'd told him not to go. And, because I'm so good at keeping promises, I hadn't.

"That's okay," Aunt Hilda said. "You don't need to tell me. I see it clearly enough." She giggled again. I heard Zach shifting in his crib upstairs through the baby monitor we always keep on in the kitchen. I wished he would wake up, or my mother would come in. This was silly. Of course my mother must have told Aunt Hilda about the birth and how angry I'd been at Drew for leaving me. I'd been so afraid to go through labor, and he knew it. I was afraid of the pain I would feel, afraid of all the things that could go wrong. Afraid, simply, to do it. But then I took basic geometry. You can't fit a big head through a small hole without a hell of a lot of trouble.

"Now, here," she said. "This is your future." She pointed that long index finger at a purplish card. "I have good news for you." She smiled up at me. "It won't happen again."

"What do you mean, *it*?"

"He'll be there," she said. "He'll be there for the next one. It's right here." She tapped her fingernail. "It won't happen again. He'll be there at the next birth."

"Drew?" I asked.

"I don't see a name."

She closed her eyes again for a long while. Then she looked down at the cards. "Oh, wait. There is something else." Her brow furrowed.

"What?"

"A conflict. Here," she tapped on another card. "That baby isn't certain. It's fading in and out. There will be a choice. A choice between men."

"Really?" Suddenly I thought of Jake. I didn't want to. I don't know why I did, but his face came to me, his strong nose, his head of curls. I hoped she couldn't read my mind.

"A decision. Deep trouble with love." She held the card up as if it would mean something to me. "You see? There's a choice, two roads, and very different ones." She paused, licked her lips, picked another card up and scrutinized it. "You need to forgive your husband for not coming to the baby's birth. If you don't, I see many complications." And then, as if she'd told me I would win the lottery, she smiled, giggled and swept all the cards back together into an even pile before I could ask another question.

* * *

I felt unsettled enough that tea proved to be an enormous relief. Listening to my mother's constant chatter about her social engagements and Aunt Hilda's bizarre replies ("And then Marcy Hamilton showed up," my mother says. "You can only walk a fine line for so long," Aunt Hilda responds), entertained me sufficiently enough to forget the uncomfortable truths of my "fortune." Damned if I would forgive Drew for being such a total asshole. I didn't have any intentions of it. I'd been waiting for months for a proper apology from him. Not that I believed in fortunes anyway. Especially from a mentally unstable old lady. I loved Aunt Hilda, but that didn't mean I had to believe her.

When my mother and Aunt Hilda started getting ready to go back to the city, I went to the garden, half in search of Drew, whom I was so certain was at that very moment choosing a dog in order to terrorize me further. Like I needed more shit in my life to clean up.

I put Zach in his new favorite carrier, the Baby Björn. I love his little baby body, his fat toes and smooth, cream-green skin. I find myself stroking his head often, running my fingers through his thick dark hair. I like to shape it, to pull it upward so he resembles a rooster or flatten it to one side so he looks more like a seventies rocker. A baby satisfies in a way few things do; obviously they're more satisfying asleep, but still. Still. Even with all the trouble he caused, taking care of him had become my favorite job. Would I trade it for some time with a two-hundred-page manuscript about the habits of feral rabbits? (I really did edit a book like that.) Never.

Zach and I walked the perimeter of Drew's garden. In his spare time, he tended the garden. It gave him another focal

point for his savior complex; or maybe it soothed his soul. I
don't know. But for whatever reason he did it, the thing became more beautiful each year. That summer he'd outdone
himself. The vegetable rows were off to a healthy beginning,
and they lined up with perfect symmetry, the tomatoes, the
lettuce—which was already at its end—green beans, squash,
peppers. Then in a smaller garden, edged with rock, he'd
made an herb patch, about the size of a large car. He had rows
of basil, cilantro, thyme, chives, parsley, rosemary, garlic root
(which was just ready for the harvest), mint, tarragon and
sage. The man had a green thumb the size of Vermont. I'm
sure I would have appreciated it more if I'd had any interest in
the great outdoors. As far as I'm concerned, tomatoes come
from the grocery store. I know this is very un-PC of me, very
archaic and postmodern. But what's the point of modern life
if it doesn't remove you from the drudgery of growing your
own dinner? I'm going to be first in line for the space age food
you can keep for twenty years and heat up in two seconds in
the microwave. Okay, I'll admit it, despite myself and my awful politics. Drew's garden was fantastic—vibrant, alive, incredible. It made me wish I were one of the plants he tended
with such backbreaking care.

But I was not a plant. And Drew hadn't had much to do
with me lately. And something I couldn't quite put my finger
on was bugging me. Oh, many things were bothering me that
were readily accessible—Drew's absence, my mother's wedding, and sympathy for Diana's new compromised hormonal
state. (I felt for her. I really did. If I got pregnant now I'm
sure I would have to surrender myself to a locked mental
ward for twenty-four-hour care.) I went back into the house
and got an old picnic blanket, slightly wooly and motheaten,
as if Drew and I hadn't had a picnic since the dark ages (we

hadn't). I spread it out at the back of the lawn beneath the shade of our biggest maple tree where Drew edged the perennial garden with such exactness we could have qualified for a Martha Stewart award. I lay the baby on the blanket so he could talk to the trees and the sky and the few passing clouds. I lay down next to Zach, foraging through my mental file cabinet searching for the one thought I had wanted to think.

Then I found it. Aunt Hilda's fortune didn't sit right with me, not just because I couldn't believe it, but because, worse still, I could. Or, at least, I could agree with her basic premise. If something didn't happen soon with Drew and me, real trouble would ensue. Since Zach's birth I'd been satisfied with the thought that *I'd* been the one ignoring Drew, angry at him, frustrated by his inadequacies, but it had never dawned on me to question *why* he'd missed the birth. I'd been so consumed thinking of myself, it hadn't occurred to me that maybe *Drew* had a reason to ignore *me*. I'd chalked it up to a stupid, unforgivable mistake, but what if it was more?

I instantly plummeted into a spin cycle of irrelevant insecurities. Could it be Lumpkin? Could my postmortem body be so fleshy and maternal that it could alter the course of our married life? Maybe this mother thing went so deep that I'd become someone else, some revirginized Sandra Dee, a sexless, Madonna-esque (and I mean the one you read about it in the Bible) matron. But that didn't make any sense. Drew's desertion came before our sexless-we-have-a-baby-now life.

Or maybe Drew had taken up with someone else. It's true that I didn't know where he was most of the time. Would I blame him? I pondered this thought for the blink of an eye.

Of course I would blame him. I would also sentence him to death at the gallows. Just the thought of him cheating made me sick with anger. And to cheat on a poor, disoriented new mother! What could be worse than that? I couldn't help the effects of childbirth. I'd been working on my vaginal muscle tone as hard as I could.

Zach cried to nurse and I rolled over and lifted my shirt, pulling him in tight to my side. Drew would never have an affair. I couldn't imagine it. But even without another woman, it seemed we had a problem—not just problems like everyone else on the planet—but a PROBLEM, like the kind you call a marriage counselor for.

Could I be that ugly? Could I be that different? I'd sworn off the sweatpants. They hadn't seen the light of day in weeks. I'd started showering more often. I'd even painted my toes. Once. So now the paint was chipping and made my feet look like long-forgotten relics of the punk era.

If I wanted to be rational, I could reason that Drew felt just the same as I did, tired and busy and grumpy, that we weren't getting along and that it would pass. We'd been together long enough to have gone through a few bad times. And maybe Clarkville really did require all of his energy, and all these problems and his ongoing absence had nothing to do with some deep, growing crack in the foundation of our marriage. Maybe?

Zach murmured and guzzled with pure satisfaction. He'd turned out to be a very contented baby; really, we were lucky. *I* was lucky. Drew was a talented teacher, a genius administrator, a *Better Homes and Gardens* gardener. I didn't have to work (thanks in no small part to a big gift from my mother when we bought the house, since there's no way Drew's salary could keep pace with a Fairfield County mortgage), but his good job made it possible. I'd accepted the job of housewife, hadn't I? I didn't have any right to complain about socks on the kitchen table or plates left on the living room floor? Or his need to work late. Did I?

I'd take my aunt's advice. I'd forgive him. That way I'd at least be able to see if *I* was the problem, or if something bigger was going on.

When I got back to the house, I found Drew in the kitchen popping open a beer.

"I didn't hear you come in."

"Just got here. Did you have a nice time with Hilda and your mom?" In a wordless dance, more familiar than intimate, we moved around the kitchen and then headed to the deck. It leads off the side of the kitchen with gorgeous French doors.

"A blast. Those two are good housemates for each other. I'm not sure who's more crazy. You know my mother has decided to have her wedding at a place called the Temple of Divine Light and Energy."

"Far out."

"It belongs to a congregation of twenty people. I guess their numbers have been declining. They had their heyday in the sixties. They believe eating pansies is the key to immortality."

"I'll remember that, on the off chance that it's true."

I noticed Zach had fallen asleep in my arms. "I think I'll leave Zach in the house," I said. "Bugs." I went back into the kitchen and found his bouncy seat, which he'd finally grown in to. For the first few months every time I put him down in it, he'd scream like I was chopping off a limb. Or maybe that was just *every* time I put him down.

"So," I said, joining him outside. "Aunt Hilda read my fortune." He lifted his chin slightly. "She gave me some good advice."

"Oh?"

"I've been officially told to forgive you. The fates demand it." I looked up at the blue sky. A few stray clouds lingered overhead. Oh, what the hell, I told myself. I was going to have to do it sometime. And for all I knew, Aunt Hilda *could* see the future. "So I forgive you. For not coming to the birth. Let's just call that one over. I guess it wasn't the end of the world. He came out healthy and wonderful. At least I was there!" I laughed at my own joke. Drew had a confused expression on his face.

"You forgive me?"

"Sure, I forgive you."

"You know that I'm sorry. You know I wanted to be there with you."

"Well—" I stopped myself. I could have said a few things, but then I suppose I already had. About six hundred times. "Let's not get into it. It was what it was."

"I *am* sorry, Joy."

"Better luck next time?" He laughed cautiously. I laughed. For a moment we were friends.

"She gave me a little reading too."

"What? When?"

"I was just coming in when they were leaving. She offered, and I accepted. I've been dying to know my future, anyway." He smirked.

"What did she tell you?" I asked, with bated breath. This was going to be *good*.

"The usual kind of thing they tell you—changes in my

future, a long life, that sort of standard psychic stuff." Then he started to laugh, really laugh. It was so contagious it got me going too.

"What? What?" I said finally.

"Your mother must have had a hand in all this. I'm sure she put her up to it, probably filled your aunt in on all the dirt about us."

"Why? What did she say? What's so funny?"

"Oh, nothing big. She just told me to be careful because my wife was in love with another man. But then psychics always have to make things up just to seem dramatic."

"Haha," I said.

"Like that would happen," he said through his laughter.

"Impossible," I said, not laughing. And then he laughed some more.

Thirteen

I COULDN'T HAVE BEEN MORE GRATEFUL THAT DONNY'S open house fell the next day. I desperately needed a distraction.

"Where are you off to?" Drew called out. He'd been acting very chummy since our forgiveness conversation. He even volunteered for bath duty with Zach on Saturday night. I, on the other hand, was putting the "um" back in chummy. As in "Um, honey, why would you find it so damn funny that I could fall in love with another man! You small-nosed turd brain."

"Off to a playdate," I called pleasantly.

"Diana?"

"Um. No—a new mommy friend."

"Have fun," he said from his position on the couch.

Well, I wasn't going to spend the afternoon enjoying the benefits of horizontal living, but at least I'd finally get the goods on Donny. He was holding his open house at an office in downtown Clarkville, but off of the Main Street, toward the edge of town, where businesses tend to come and go quickly. Clarkville has a high-end market, and nothing survives that doesn't make the grade.

That Sunday afternoon, I had about sixteen mental arguments while I drove on how exactly to spy on Donny without seeming like I was spying. This is much harder than it might first appear. In the first place, he knows who I am. In the second place, I have an infant. No quietly hiding behind doors and eavesdropping for me. Given the time, I finally decided that I would pretend I'd had a meeting in another part of the building. I'd act surprised to see that Donny had an office there too and would stop in to remark on the coincidence.

What a relief to find that all the names of all the businesses were listed on the glass entrance door of the building. The only trouble? I couldn't quite tell what any of them were. CC Enterprises—that could be anything. Dr. Adrian Walker, okay, but what *kind* of doctor was he? Details, LTD. I could use some details right about then. MacCoaching—of course I knew what that was. And last but not least, The Honoree Group. Perfect. If I said I was at any of those places, Donny would make small talk about it. He was bound to know what the other businesses were all about.

I leaned against the outside wall. Zach seemed to be enjoying himself. I had him in my front carrier, facing out. He loved an adventure.

"Let's just do this," I said to him. I opened the front door. A wash of cold air welcomed us in. Whoever ran the AC had turned it on high.

The lobby was simple and empty. Two gray elevators sat off to the right. Next to them a piece of paper, taped to the wall, listed the businesses once again, this time with floor and room numbers. I noticed that MacCoaching was on the third floor along with Dr. Adrian Walker. The doctor it was then;

I'd have to say I'd had a doctor's appointment. I could stop in the office and ask them what he specialized in. That wouldn't seem too strange, would it?

I took the elevator up, though I debated taking the stairs. They'd be better for my backside and slightly more discreet. Don't all private detectives use the stairs?

When I got off at the third floor, I realized why the AC had been on high. The hallway was stuffy and humid and stifling hot. It was a short, narrow hallway with two doors leading off to the left. I stepped up to the first one. Dr. Adrian Walker, it read on the door. I knocked and then turned the knob. It was locked. Shit. I guess doctors don't work on Sundays.

While I stood there asphyxiating in the heat, the door to MacCoaching opened and a small, fat, middle-age woman came out. She looked extremely uncomfortable in the heat.

"Oh," I said.

She looked at me with something akin to a sneer. This was not fair. I had brushed my hair before I left the house and Zach was being adorable. She kept walking toward the elevator.

"Can I . . . ask you a question?" When she heard my voice, she stopped in her tracks.

"I'm sorry." She walked straight up to me until we were practically kissing. Now this was very awkward indeed. "What did you say?" she bellowed into my face. Her breath smelled like stale cat food. "I'm hard of hearing."

"Oh," I said, backing up a step. Maybe she wasn't the best candidate for getting information about MacCoaching.

"Speak up," she yelled. I began to worry that all her noise would make Donny rush out into the hallway to see who'd died.

"Nothing," I said loudly. She shook her head at me, in a

rather disgusted way, then pressed the down button for the elevator. When she stepped on, lightning-quick thinking led
me to hop on with her. I was impressed to find that I could
still have a good idea.

"Excuse me," I shouted as we headed down the two flights
to the ground floor. "Can you tell me what the open house
was like?"

"The open house?" She looked at me sideways. I stood
about a foot taller than her. "A scam," she said, shaking her
head. "My husband told me not to bother. I should have listened. All these new-age gurus just want your money."

When the elevator landed she huffed off without another
word. I rode it up again. I felt a swirl of excitement in my
belly. I was really on to something. My mother was going to
thank me for this.

When I finally left the office and got back in the car, my knees
trembled with nervous energy. I couldn't stop thinking about
what had happened. I got the AC running as fast as I could
and sat right there in the parking lot nursing Zach, who was
just on the precipice of total hysterics on account of being ignored for so long. As soon as his eyes closed, I used my free
hand to uncover my cell phone from my purse. The only
question, who to call first? Not Melody, of course. She'd
proven to be a total party pooper where my spying was concerned. I wished I had Jake's phone number because I knew
he'd appreciate my findings. I didn't want to bother Diana, as
she'd taken to napping whenever Jeff was home, which essentially meant all weekend long (picture me dinosaur green
with smoke coming out of my nostrils). When I flipped the

phone open, I noticed I'd missed a call from Beth. Bingo. She was my girl. I put Zach in his seat and drove off.

"Well, hello, stranger," she said. "Zach enrolled in Harvard yet?"

"We'll never afford Harvard."

"Please. You people live in the richest county of the richest country in the world."

"Maybe he'll get a scholarship. He seems to have some incredible chewing skills. There isn't anything he won't chew. That's got to be useful somehow."

"Professional eating competitions." I heard the telltale clicking of her keyboard in the background. Beth lived on her computer.

"Do you see Jake often?" I blurted because I seem to have a teensy-weensy problem keeping my mouth closed. Most people spend all their time gossiping about other people; I spend most of mine gossiping about myself.

"We met once for lunch after the reunion. That was fun. You'll be happy to know we talked a lot about you."

"You did?" Was I getting breathless?

"Sure. You're the only married one. You're the only parent. We had to do our comparison thing. You know ... what life would be like 'if.' "

"Right."

"Then I see him every now and then at a party or something. He's got some leggy blond girlfriend now. She's a model or something."

"A model?" My heart dropped into my Lumpkin.

"Maybe I'm remembering it wrong. Maybe she's the next great literary talent. A poet or something and she just looks like a model. Whatever. I have too much to think about to keep track of Jake's love life. Anyway, why do you ask? Not still nostalgic for the past, are you?"

"Me? Never."

"But?"

"We've been emailing. He's helping me with this whole Donny debacle."

"He has, has he? Well, don't withhold the dirt. I want to know too. What's up with the new Mr. Madeline Steeley?"

"That's not funny."

"Sorry. Tell me anyway."

"I just got out of his open house." I realized I was whispering, as if someone could overhear.

"Oh, right. I think I remember getting a message about that. For his coaching business. What did you do? Dress in drag and spy on him?"

"Not exactly. I have to be myself, Beth. Zach's always with me."

"Forgot about that detail." Oh, to be single and childless when babies are only a *detail* in someone's life. "What happened?"

"Well, I hung out in the hallway outside his office for a while. Two people came out during the whole time I stood there."

"And?"

"There's no and. That's the scoop. *Two* people! That's the first big news."

"I don't get it."

"Well, he's obviously not doing well if only two people came to his open house."

"Maybe more people came earlier."

"Maybe, but it's unlikely." I found it a bit disappointing

that Beth could not follow along with me. "Also, and this is the biggest news of all, I saw Donny."

"Why is that big news? It's not as though you haven't seen him many times before."

"Right, right. But I met him in the hallway coming out of his office. He seemed very surprised to see me. In fact, he looked worried, as though he'd been found out."

"Oh. Well, what did you say?"

"He asked what I was up to. Don't you think that's suspicious?"

"I guess. Except if I found you in the hallway outside my office, I would ask what you were up to too."

"Okay. You're raining a little bit here on my great revelation parade."

"I'm sorry, Joy. You know I love a mystery. Hell, that's why I pick men up in bars, so I can ask myself in the morning how I got into a stranger's bed and try to unravel the plot." She laughed. "But seriously, I don't see the big deal."

"You had to be there. It was his expression. I could just tell that he felt guilty. I don't think my mother knows what he does. And I don't think he's telling her because then she'd know that he's not some artist but a failed new-age businessman."

"All right. I'm following now. Your mother *has* attracted some major losers."

"Right."

"So tell me what he said. Did he ask you not to tell your mother?"

"No, nothing like that. He asked what I was doing and I told him, and then I asked what he was doing and he told me, but the whole thing felt extremely awkward."

"Oh." I could tell Beth wasn't impressed. "So what was your cover? What did you say you were doing in his building?"

"Visiting the doctor next door."

"Good thinking. Who's the doctor?"

"I don't know. The office wasn't even open, but he seemed to buy it. The door to the office just said Adrian Walker. Maybe it was a therapist or something." Beth was silent for a minute or so. I could hear her typing again. "Hey, Beth? You know it drives me crazy when you email while we're talking. I need your help here. This is a big deal. I have to find a way to stop the wedding."

"Don't get ahead of yourself," she said. I could hear the smile in her voice. "I think I may have solved your mystery."

"Really?"

"Really. Your Dr. Adrian Walker, your cover?"

"Yes. Yes. But that's not the point. The point is how nervous Donny acted."

"Well, maybe he was acting strange because of you, sister, because it seems that Dr. Adrian Walker is a urologist who works exclusively in the field of erectile dysfunction." She broke into peals of laughter.

"What?"

"It says right here, on his web page. Boy, is that funny. I think you need some Detective 101 classes."

"Oh, no." If I wasn't so upset, I'm sure I would have been laughing. "But that doesn't rule out the possibility that—"

"Honey, you know I love you, but that must be why he acted so strange, wouldn't you think?"

"Okay." Now I started laughing. "You may be right. But that doesn't explain why only two people attended his open house. Even if he wasn't acting weird, he doesn't seem to be very popular."

"Fine," she said, settling down from her laughing frenzy. "I'll give you that."

"Let's talk about *you* for a while," I said, feeling a touch depressed from her findings. I really thought I'd been on to something. "What kind of crazy guy have you started dating? You mentioned someone in your last message."

"You won't believe it," she said excitedly.

"I'm sure I won't."

"David Martin. Remember how I saw him at the reunion, and we had such a good time talking. Well, he's come to London a few times on business—he's in exports—and we've had a little bit of the wham-bam-thank-you-sir."

"Were you always this crude?"

"Actually," she said, "you and I were neck and neck in college for the crudeness competition, if I remember correctly. Motherhood's just softened you around the edges."

"David Martin, huh? I guess he's not that bad. Little bit of a geek."

"Not that bad! He's so good I'd cruise on *The Love Boat* with him."

Beth and I had watched our fair share of *Love Boat* reruns in college. Actually, we shared an obsession. She had a thing for the captain. I had a thing for Gofer. Then in real life he ended up being some kind of politician. It broke my heart. I don't know why people can't just stay superficial. Everyone's got to get all worldly on me.

After we reminisced for a while about our *Love Boat* days, Beth said, "I just want you to know that I do think Donny's a weird guy, if it's any consolation. I've been to his website, just like you told me to, and all I can say is 'affirguestion' sounds like a disease."

"Thanks," I said. "I guess that's better than nothing."

"A *venereal* disease."

"Ha-ha. I get it. Thanks for your support."

"You're welcome."

My conversation with Beth did nothing to improve my mood. I drove right by Finney Hill (our road) on the way home and let my stomach lead me to the grocery store. I didn't have the heart to go home and face my adoring spouse, especially since I had to make up a few white lies to cover my misadventuring ass. I realized, as I grabbed the shopping cart, that chocolate, though it seems truly therapeutic, will not cure me of these troubles. But it would certainly make them more tolerable. If my mother was going to marry this impossibly strange dweeb of a man, I would need a very large supply of treats.

I filled the cart with the week's groceries as well as the staples in my life: M&M's, Italian bread and diaper wipes. When I got to the checkout counter, an older man stood waiting patiently. He looked nice enough, round, rosy cheeked, with the unfortunate condition of Man-Boobs that I have expressly forbidden Drew from ever acquiring. Not that he's in any danger; he's as firm as a lifeguard.

There I was, then, putting everything on the conveyor belt, when Zach began to howl. Up until that point he'd been wedged happily in my front baby carrier, which he normally loved. I had the distinct feeling he was letting me know that he had had all he could take of being carried around. I jiggled him and shushed him and spoke to him sweetly. I searched in vain in my purse for his pacifier. I knew there was one in there, but it had gotten lost in my version of the Bermuda Triangle. There really is a place in a purse where things will go, out of reach, out of sight. Then days later they will show up, as if they'd never left. I find this both reassuring in its consistency and hair-pullingly frustrating.

As the clerk rang up my bill, beads of sweat began to form on my forehead. I wanted to get out quickly so I could nurse Zach. There didn't seem to be much point in doing it right there when we were seconds away from leaving. Yet the clerk took his time. He inspected everything I bought. Then he looked up and said, not to me but to Zach:

"Why don't you just shut up, baby? What's your problem?"

I want to begin by saying, for the benefit of those who do not have children, that when you have a child, you develop the raw protectiveness of a mother polar bear. You are prepared to eat anyone who so much as hints at your baby's lack of motor coordination or funny-shaped head or who suggests, even sympathetically, that you might want to buy a different baby soap because the little sucker stinks. All of those are minor infractions compared to actually talking unkindly directly to your precious offspring.

Never one to mince words, I said:

"Are you serious? Are you seriously trying to tell my baby to shut up? Do you think that will work? Because if that sort of thing worked, mothers everywhere would be doing it. But we don't say that to them, do we? We soothe them quietly. We hold them and rock them. What does that tell you?" By this point, Zach had stopped crying, intrigued no doubt by my rising voice. The clerk looked dumbfounded. He stood motionless. A box of panty liners in his right hand hovered just above the scanner.

"And I'll tell you what his problem is. His problem is that he wants to go home. We both want to go home. So, if you don't mind, would you please hurry it up." I whipped out my credit card and held it expectantly. I lowered my eyebrows and stared a hole right through the man. I didn't pay any attention to the young woman who stood behind me. I didn't notice her look of alarm. I didn't notice her belly button piercing, I didn't notice the carrots and V-8 and natural spring water in her cart. And I didn't turn around and tell her that the expensive water she'd be buying in a few short minutes was simply tap water. I stared straight ahead until he was done. Then I smiled.

"Thank you," I said.

He grunted.

When I arrived home, Drew didn't say a word. He didn't question my whereabouts, he didn't criticize the hundred-dollar supply of chocolate I'd procured at the grocery store. He didn't look at me suspiciously or argue with me about anything. He said, "Do you want me to give Zach a bath?"

"Fine," I said, grabbing a few bags of chocolate. It would be my turn to lie on the couch. I flipped through our thousand useless channels, settling finally on a reality show about brides, which gave me ample opportunity to contemplate my failed spying adventure. If only affirguestion *were* a venereal disease.

Fourteen

THEN MY LIFE CHANGED.

An old era ended. A new era arrived. I thought I could stall it somehow, or that somehow we weren't so close to it happening. Yet it's true. The baby started crawling. And boy, is he fast. He's skinny and quick. His new favorite game is chase. I get down on my hands and knees and crawl after him while he giggles hysterically. Zach has begun to look like a gangly teenager, all limbs and accidents. If he didn't still poop in his diapers, I'd swear he was five years old.

In two days, on August 16, he'll turn six months. I feel such triumph; it's almost embarrassing. It's like those egg races we used to play at family picnics when I was a kid. You'd have to make it across the whole lawn running with an egg on a spoon. And you were six so you didn't have much coordination. I feel like that. I feel like I've made it to the finish line with my egg intact.

And to think that all of the people you see, at the post office and the grocery store and the gas station, had a mother who did a good enough job that she got them to adulthood alive; it's amazing. Sure, a lot of us are walking around with guilt complexes, and deep, mysterious neuroses that will never be healed, and we can't ever wear a size two because we eat to make up for profound feelings of inadequacy—but we *are* alive. I never knew how hard it was. I could have dropped Zach down the stairs, or smothered him with my breast while we slept side by side in bed. I could have forgotten him one day in his traveling car seat, and left him at the pizza shop to be adopted by the bubbly teenage waitresses. But I hadn't done any of these things. I had managed to successfully care for the smallest, most helpless creature I'd ever known. I felt pretty damn good. I felt almost like forgiving myself for the fact that Lumpkin had returned to its previous monstrous size or letting myself off the hook for my recent comment to Priscilla to "leave me alone." Her eyes swelled with tears when I said it, so I added "please," which made no difference whatsoever. Drew had a talk with me that night. He wanted to know why I had to be so mean to his mother. I asked him why she has to be so mean to me. It was the next logical question, which he, needless to say, didn't appreciate.

At any rate, for all my shortcomings, I'd done pretty well so far with mommyhood. I hadn't had a full night's sleep in more than six months, since you have to include the end of pregnancy—and who can sleep with a belly the size of a camel hump? Slowly, however, I'd learned to go without. Now if I managed to get five hours in a row, I could make it through the day without wanting to strangle anybody—except Priscilla, of course, and Drew. (But that goes without saying.) I'm talking about having enough patience to be nice to the people that it's not okay to dislike. You can get away with hating your family as long as you still love them. That may even be the definition of family. You can't, however, get away with hating innocent people, such as the clerk at the grocery store, who, by the way, I now make a habit of avoiding.

I had an appointment that day at the home of one of my old catering buddies who'd started her own business. This is because, in addition to my usual variety of domestic chores and my active-duty mothering, I have another full-time job: being my mother's matron of honor. This is unfair in principle since I don't approve of her future husband. It is also unfair because it requires a great deal of work. For example, I am meant to throw her a bridal shower. She doesn't want a traditional gift-giving party (I think it may also be proper etiquette not to expect your friends to buy you gifts for all four weddings—they'd go broke), so she directed me instead to throw her a dinner party. At my house. (She wants me to feel *involved.*) For her favorite twenty-five friends. Not until November, of course, but that doesn't mean that, given her requirements, I don't have to immediately begin planning.

I've also gone with her for every catering tasting, to listen to various possible bands, to interview the harpist, to purchase the tent, and to shoe-shop. My mother wanted two pairs of shoes. One for the wedding and one for the reception. I suggested she go barefoot and solve the problem of finding the perfect shoe, because the perfect shoe does not exist. Cinderella took it with her to her grave. We walked around and around every shoe store in Manhattan; we looked at thousand-dollar shoes and ten-dollar shoes. My mother didn't like a single one. Neither, I should say, did Zach.

As if I didn't have enough of attending to other people's needs, Drew gave me direct orders to make sure that his mother felt involved with the baby's life. That's just the way he phrased it too: "She needs to feel involved with the baby's life."

I suggested changing diapers was a good way to begin. "That's not what I mean," Drew said. Priscilla wanted quality time with Zach. Just like Drew. They both wanted the baby—but only when he was dry, fed, slept and happy. At all other times, he was mine. How generous of them.

On top of all this, Drew had planned for us to be away the last week of August for a vacation in Vermont. We'd compromised on a rustic cabin—the midpoint between a tent and an actual room—after I pointed out that if nobody slept, hiking for ten hours wouldn't be a very fun experience. Drew found the cabins, but I upgraded them. Staying in a shack with a dirt floor wasn't very appealing to me. I paid for the cabin with electricity and a working toilet, the one at the base of the mountain, close to civilization. I tried to cheer Drew up by reminding him that if we were at the base of the mountain, we would have a great time getting to the top. He likes climbing things. I think this is a very male trait. He can conquer the Green Mountains; I don't mind, as long as I get my running water. At any rate, since my great act of forgiveness (thanks to Aunt Hilda), my domestic life has taken on the qualities of a Doris Day movie. If I'm willing to overlook how much time Drew spends away from us and generally ignore our total lack of deep connection (but then who needs *that,* this is marriage!), life goes along quite well.

He did surprise me the other week. I'd mentioned to him that my diet seemed to be working because I'd lost three pounds, and he said: "You've been so cranky and miserable since you went on that diet that I'd rather you were twenty pounds overweight your whole life and died early." I laughed until I peed. (Doesn't take much.) I found it a very funny thing to say, especially for Drew. He was grateful that I got the joke. He knows I can be a little touchy about my body.

* * *

I ruminated while I drove to Susan the caterer's house (*I* certainly wasn't doing the cooking for twenty-five people), and checked on Zach in the rearview mirror every ten seconds, a habit I'd developed when he was newborn that I still couldn't shake. (Thanks in no small part to a genius invention supporting paranoid mothers everywhere: a special mirror that attaches to the back seat and allows you to watch the baby through the rearview mirror.) I was checking, of course, to see if he was still *alive*—like maybe the seat belt had come to life and wrapped itself around his neck or he'd managed to smother himself by turning his head sideways against the car seat. If you've never had children and someone told you about this helpless, neurotic tick (checking on him constantly), you would not understand. But this is the thing no one can prepare you for. This is the thing other mothers and fathers *won't* tell you when you're thinking about having a baby, when you're pregnant, when you're heading into labor. I'm going to tell you, because I'm that kind of person. I'll consider it my civic duty. My small contribution to world peace. You will never be free again. There, I said it. Sure, one day, say twenty years hence, you'll sleep through the night and you'll probably have an hour or two to yourself. You'll eat when you want, and you'll be able to take showers. But from the moment that baby, that person, emerges in a mess of blood and goo, your heart lives in another body. You will long to escape; you will long for free time, but even when you get it, you will feel strange, like a person with a missing limb, you will wonder what is missing, and then you will remember that you are not just you anymore. Your heart is not your own. Some little person carries it with them everywhere. This is wonderful if you're, say, supremely sentimental, but if you're not, it's a bit of hell.

I'm not being dramatic. I don't think I am at least. Maybe other people have their opinions. I'm being realistic. The other night I sat up reading and rereading an article about a toddler who'd been killed in a head-on collision. (I don't make a habit of reading the newspaper. It's not news they print, it's *bad* news. Why don't they have any articles like this: "Grandmother Enjoys Her 1,009,678th Chocolate Bar," "Businessman Gives Away All His Money and Moves in with the Monks," "Life Is Fun, Here's Why"?) The younger baby survived the accident. I could not put the paper down. I could not stop thinking about the mother of that dead toddler. Then, when Drew finally turned the light out, I lay awake for the longest time thinking about what I would do if something happened to Zach. Of course, I would have to go insane or jump off a bridge. Then I decided I would keep him safe by never letting him leave the house. I would never drive again. I would never carry him up the stairs in a hurry. We would childproof until the only things touching the floor were the sofa and the bed.

That is what they won't tell you. That you will be a neurotic, paranoid lunatic, but you will still have to live in the world. This is a dangerous proposition. It means your heart is that egg being carried across the lawn in the race, and you will kill any other racer who knocks you over. I just did it myself, as a matter of fact. This morning I went outside onto the deck and slaughtered a wasp's nest. It was filled with babies. The nest fell to the ground and I obliterated it with my pink Ralph Lauren sandal. I didn't want Zach to be bitten by a wasp. Ever. I can't get rid of all the traffic on the highways or dry up all the oceans, ponds, pools and puddles, remove every staircase and force him to wear a bike helmet every day of his life, but I can certainly kill a few wasps.

When I finally got home after my meeting with Susan, who, thank God, agreed to cook the dinner for my mother's party, I dragged myself into the house bleary-eyed. Zach, however, was having a revival. He was up for some serious baby exercise, so I gated him in the office and let him motor around in search of objects to chew on. I left a few chew toys in strategic places. I included his latest favorite toy, a strap from one of my expensive baby carriers. At least it was serving a purpose.

After an initial slump into spying-letdown-induced depression, brought on by my conversation with Beth, I'd rallied, more determined than ever to prove what I'd been suspecting about Donny. I just had a hunch. Call it mother's intuition. I wanted to do a more thorough search on the Internet, but first I had to check my email. I'd been waiting for an email from Jake. He felt a little bit like my partner in crime. And there it was, at last, in my in-box.

To: jmcguire@fanfare.com
From: jakephilips@lunerpress.com
*Hey joy. Thanks for the comic relief. I've been a little low
lately. I got a kick out of Donny's website. I've known
some life coaches who are really cool people, but this guy
seems like he's out there. I can't remember if I asked
you—did you talk to your mother directly about him?
That would be my advice. Or you could spend some
quality time on the Internet seeing where else his name*

comes up. Does he own a house? Real estate records are public information. It might make you feel better to know if he's got his own digs.

You know what this whole thing reminds me of? That time in college when Angela Brockman locked herself in her dorm room freshman year and refused to come out until all prisoners of war were released and you stood outside her door for about three hours talking to her until she changed her mind. Don't ask me why. Another crazy moment when you got to be heroic. Hope it happens again. —J

I sat for the longest time staring at the screen. I nearly let Zach eat a power cord I got so lost in reading the email over and over. What did it mean that he'd been thinking of me? And that he wrote such a long email? And that he thought me *heroic*? Now, there's a word I haven't used to describe myself in eons. On the average day I feel as heroic as *Beavis and Butthead*.

I grabbed Zach off the floor and propped him on my lap. I pumped my leg quickly to keep him happy while I sent off a reply to Jake. Of course I had to fill him in on my great adventure in Donny's office and also the embarrassing but true news that Beth had found out about Dr. Adrian Walker. I could just picture Jake breaking out in laughter, the way his Adam's apple would tremble just a bit as he threw his head back. I felt delighted writing the email, alive, fun, free. God, I felt like a person, a bona fide person. I felt so good, in fact, that I totally forgot to snoop on Donny. Instead I went and danced with Zach in the living room to an old Eurythmics album. Why not? I'm a child of the eighties. A little outdated rock music never hurt anybody.

* * *

On my third Saturday at yoga I went early just to sit in the quiet of the room. I sat in the back row, of course. I tried not to watch the other women coming in. I tried not to watch Oliver walking around and chatting. I tried to focus on my breath. I was lying down with my hands on my belly breathing as deeply as I could.

"Joy." Oliver stood beside me, looking down. Then he knelt down, the way he does, into a full squat. It's a position I never knew men could accomplish, and I refused to think about its many uses.

"Hi."

"Nice to see you again."

"Um, thanks." I found myself searching for a wedding ring on his left hand.

"How's it going for you?"

"The class?"

"Yeah. What do you think? Is it serving you? Are you getting what you need? Is it working at the heart level?" He tapped his chest.

I laughed, and he smiled deeply, his cheeks dimpling up just above the top line of his beard.

"What's so funny?" he said.

"I'm just not used to that kind of language, I guess. I don't even know what it means. I understand goo-goo, ga-ga much better these days."

"How old is your little one?"

"Six months. I brought him to my first class with you." He shook his head, not understanding. "When you were subbing for Carol."

"Ah, Carol," he said, putting his hands on my shoulders. "I

remember. You have a little boy, right?" I could barely think to speak. I just knew I didn't want him to leave my side. "That's beautiful." Oliver tended to say the word "beautiful" a lot, I'd noticed. He'd walk around the room—while we hung out in some impossible position, focusing all of our energy on our left toe, or our right groin, or world peace—and say "That's beautiful. That's beautiful" to no one in particular. I knew enough to understand that he didn't mean it literally. I could not look beautiful doing the things he made us do. I know I looked like Elaine from *Seinfield* doing her dance, only imagine her drunk, in sweatpants, doing it to music picked out of the new-age section. (In an act of pure vanity, I'd thrown all my gross old sweatpants in the trash so I would never be tempted to wear them to yoga class. I mean, Oliver is a hunk. I wear lip gloss to class.)

He left me then, stood up and called us all to sit up so we could begin class. I spent much of the class following his left hand, thinking I saw a ring, then thinking I didn't. Finally I got a good look. No ring. I didn't know why it would matter to me anyhow, although I was strangely relieved to see that he wasn't married. Maybe I just imagined that yoga teachers didn't marry. They're kind of like monks, aren't they?

But this was a completely stupid line of thought. There was no way Oliver could be celibate. I'm-good-in-bed is probably his middle name. A line from a song flashed into my mind, unbidden, I might add, from the band Nine Inch Nails. Something about having sex like animals—that's what Oliver makes me think of, not pure-minded men wrapped in white robes. (I'd actually like to start my *own* band, a screaming, angry punk mommy band. I'd call it Nine Inch Nipples.)

That day he wanted to "lead us through an experience of inversions, to explore the idea of turning things on their heads." This means he wanted us to put our feet in the air and our heads on the floor, a headstand—otherwise known as the thing you haven't done since you were ten. Since I'd already forced my body to accomplish the impossible—pushing out a seven-pound baby through a hole the size of a grapefruit—I felt up for the challenge. If I could do childbirth, I could do anything, right?

How can I describe it? How can I do justice to the experience? Can you imagine an elephant standing on its head? Or a cat? You know those very fat cats, with bellies that sway back and forth and graze the floor when they walk? That's the kind of stomach I have. Naturally, on my first attempt, my T-shirt fell over my eyes, so I couldn't see anything, and my belly, pulled by gravity, hung down toward my chin. I came out of the starting position and tucked my shirt in, determined to get my feet up in the air.

On my second attempt, Oliver stopped me in my tracks. He nudged me gently back to the floor and pulled my arms closer together. "You want to keep your elbows under your shoulders," he said softly, but his touch was firm and exact. I could tell he knew precisely what he was doing. He stayed behind me as I tried again to kick my feet up toward the ceiling. He grabbed my legs and lifted me up as if I were feather-light. For the moment that he held me there, in my headstand, I did feel rearranged. I did feel free. Then he let me go and I thudded like a rhino back to the sticky mat. "Beautiful," he said. And it felt like he meant it.

Even though it's a hip, new fad—and I hate hip fads—and even though it's strange, uncomfortable and awkward, I've liked the yoga classes. Just being around Oliver has been good for me. It gives me enough presence of mind to be nice to everyone I see for at least three hours after the class ends. I'd say that's a pretty good return on my twenty-dollar investment.

I can't say I've achieved Dalai Lama status, though. Drew told me his mother was coming on Monday for dinner, yet again. Only this time she was bringing her friend, otherwise known as Father Michael, the local priest of St. Katherine's Church, so that he could meet us and help us with Zach's baptism. I asked Drew what he thought of this plan.

"It will make my mother very happy. And I can't see how it will hurt Zach."

"If we baptize him in the Catholic Church, I will have to raise him in that church, and there's no way in hell or purgatory, or heaven, for that matter, that I am raising a Catholic child. If I'd have known I was having a Catholic kid, I would have had an abortion."

"That's not funny."

"But you have to admit it is clever. Besides, you used to like my bad humor."

"You go too far."

"I don't want to do this."

"I don't see that we have any choice," he said.

"Of course we have a choice! Tell your mother no."

"I can't do that. It means too much to her."

"Let me help you out here, Drew. You're married to *me*, not to your mother. You don't have to make her happy all the time. She's not going to disown you. She's not going to stop loving you."

"I've thought about it a lot. I think it's the right thing to do."

"What does that mean: the right thing to do? All of a sudden you're a moralist? I always thought we were on the same page about the religion business. You've never liked being Catholic, not for a second of your life. We always had this in common," I pleaded, because we had. We'd bonded on our total lack of religious life.

"It's not about morality, Joy. It's about my mother. She doesn't have much in her life. You could show a little compassion. This will mean the world to her."

"How about showing a little compassion toward me, or toward Zach for that matter. Don't you care about him?"

"Joy." I could hear him trying. We'd both been trying to keep the peace. We needed to be kind to each other. We'd never had to make these decisions before. We'd never had a third person to take care of. We'd never even raised a dog or a cat or a fish together. We'd *forgiven* each other. We were officially "working on it."

"Drew. I'm serious. I'm not still mad about the labor. This isn't arbitrary anger. I don't want my son's life to be dictated by your mother. It's not healthy."

"You won't lose anything if he gets baptized, Joy, except a little pride. She'll lose a whole lot more than that. She doesn't have any other family."

"When is she ever going to move on?" I said. "Her whole life has been about your father's death and poor, poor Priscilla. I mean, my God, can she even start a sentence without saying 'my Walter'? He's been dead for decades! She's got to have more to think about than what Walter did twenty years ago. The world is bigger than that. My mother lost a husband too—"

"Your mother is a different person. Besides, she almost lost her mind."

"That's not true," I said, taken aback by the accusation.

Drew frowned at me. "Anyway, that's not the point. The

point is, they're coming for dinner and I want you to at least be open to talking about it. It will make her very happy, and she deserves some happiness."

"But that's just my point, Drew! Why should she get her happiness at our expense? Can't she find some way to get happy without controlling other people? And since when is it our job to make her happy?" Drew sighed deeply. He finally admitted defeat recently in the dog disagreement. He brought home two separate mutts from the pound on two separate occasions. I didn't throw arrows at him or anything. I simply said they would need to be housebroken in order to stay. Now we're three rugs fewer, but dog free. I've never been more grateful for dog pee before; I doubt I ever will be again. But somehow, knowing that he hadn't gotten what he wanted made me feel tenderly toward him. So I relented.

"Okay," I said. "I'll talk to him, but please try and see my side of things."

"Fine," he said. He brightened a bit. The man who gets happy thinking about having his kid baptized is not the man I married, that's all I'll say. Not by a long shot.

When I went to Zach's six-month checkup, I mentioned to the pediatrician that the baby still slept in the bed with us most nights. We have a king-size bed. It's always made more sense than letting him sleep in his own designer-decorated nursery. She looked very troubled when I said this.

"I can't recommend that," she said, shaking her head and pursing her lips. "I think it's really bad for the marriage."

"The baby's really bad for the marriage," I said. "Any-one who has a baby knows that." She gave a half laugh then dropped the issue, making some sort of notation in her folder, probably to the effect of "crazy hippie."

Could it be me? Could it all be my fault? Could I be so fundamentally dysfunctional, so rudimentally hard to get along with, so hormonally off-kilter that I can't see the good a little religion would do for my son? Or worse, am I so off-balance that *I'm* the cause of the ever-widening chasm between Drew and me? It's not fair to blame it on the baby. Sure, he cries all night now that he's teething, and he's spit up on all of my clothes, and when I wear him in his baby carrier I look like I'm going out to hoe the fields, but that's not his fault. He's just a baby.

It must be Drew's fault. He's the only one left. Oh, right. It's not supposed to be his fault anymore. In that case, it's Priscilla's fault. It's got to be. Everyone knows the mother is always to blame.

Melody told me on the phone that she thinks I lack introspection, which I believe is her way of saying I ought to figure out what I'm doing wrong and change it. It may also be code for: I'm tired of hearing about your problems. In my defense, I mentioned my attendance in yoga classes. Then she pointed out the whole Donny issue. What had I done with that, for example? Had I stopped prying into my mother's affairs?

"You aren't fair when it comes to her and men," she told me. "You aren't rational."

"That's not true! I'm looking out for her best interests."

"Joy. You tried to boycott her previous marriages."

"Unsuccessfully."

"Still. I've seen the pictures. You refused to take your coat off during the ceremony. In July."

"I was cold."

"Uh-huh. Just temper your feelings with a little reality, okay? *Think* about things."

I don't like the thought of looking at my life through a magnifying glass. Magnifying mirrors should be outlawed anyway. Every time I look in mine, I spiral into a deep depression that can only be fixed by chocolate. Who would ever need to look at you that closely anyway? It's been to my advantage that all of my lovers have had bad eyesight. Jake used to see triplicates of me whenever we got close enough to kiss, and Drew is practically blind without his contacts in. All I can say is, the times I've inspected my face in one of those mirrors, I've seen things I didn't want to see, I've seen things no woman should be subjected to.

See, there's an example of a time I *was* introspective. And, as I told Melody, I *have* been thinking about what to do about Donny. I haven't searched my soul over him, but I don't think I need to.

"Maybe you should try soul-searching about Drew."

"And how exactly does one go about doing that?"

"Well, tell me, for example, how would it feel if Drew died?"

"If Drew died, I'd marry Jake," I told her, before I thought even a second. "But that's not going to happen, so what's the use of asking such a silly question?"

How do I know Drew isn't going to die? He's far too annoying to die. It's the people you adore who kick the bucket early. Like my father. Drew and I may make fun of each other's mothers, but our fathers are completely off limits. Unless you consider the fact that Walter, Drew's father, ate too much fried chicken, which may have contributed to his heart attack. Oh, and never exercised. And apparently drank every night. (But we don't talk about his "faults." It's too upsetting. Dead people aren't allowed to have faults, anyway. Like Marilyn Monroe, they get to be preserved perfectly in time.)

My father, had he lived long enough, would have received the Nobel Prize for kindness. This is not an exaggeration. He made a profession out of it. He remembered birthdays and anniversaries—but more than that, whoever you were, however he knew you, he'd also remember the day your grandma died, or your dog, or the day ten years ago you lost your job, or he'd remember your favorite kind of fruit and bring you a bag full of it just because. On the down side, he didn't think much of working. Instead he cultivated friendships and took care of people, my mother and me included, and sang songs and sent cards and smiled at everyone. Most of all, he loved me. He was best at that.

Fifteen

ZACH IS AN ACROBATIC NURSER. HE FLINGS HIMSELF back and forth and circles his free arm wildly in the air behind him. He's managed to roll over all the way onto his back while keeping my nipple in his mouth. Luckily, my nipples are like giraffe necks and can extend quite nicely. Diana has completely given up nursing. She couldn't tolerate the pain. She also insisted she'd only ever intended to nurse for six months. I never thought I'd say this, because I'm not a crazy breastfeeding Amazon, but I hope to nurse for as long as possible. Where Zach is concerned, my nipple is like the mute button. How could I give that up?

I got to nurse him through the whole wedding catering meeting I had with my mother. She's finally chosen an old friend of mine who runs a huge company, someone I'd never directly worked for but who I respect a great deal, Bob Ferris. Apparently, Zach didn't care much for Bob because he wouldn't come off the breast during our visit. Bob, happily enough, only seemed mildly offended by the activity. My mother loved that I nursed so freely. She'd nursed all of her children—for a short time. She had so much time on the road and in the office that she couldn't be around full time. God knows I took care of the kids enough, but I wasn't up to breastfeeding in those early teenage years. I barely had breasts.

My mother was ever so slowly becoming bridezilla, if you can imagine a fifty-eight-year-old bridezilla on her fourth marriage. She felt pretty confident that it would be her last, so she wanted to do everything right. She wanted to do everything she hadn't done before, and she wanted to correct the mistakes from her other weddings. She told Bob that she wanted the food to be good, but not too good. If it was too good, it would distract the guests from one another and the real meaning of the day; if it weren't good enough, ditto—distraction. The catering meeting was one moment when I felt truly glad not to have had a wedding myself. What would I have been like? I shudder to think of it.

When I got home, I felt completely exhausted. The energy it took to act happy about my mother's wedding left me completely depleted. So far I hadn't been able to drop the Donny bomb, although I fully intended to. Just not until I knew for absolute certain. I had to design another fact-gathering mission, but I'd had about as much access to spare time as I have to alone time, and that would be none.

My whole day had been taken up with meetings for her wedding, including my usual noontime nap with Zach. He'd slept in the car, but I hadn't. I couldn't. I was driving. My mother found it essential to find the one caterer who lives in East Angolia, Connecticut, out in the country, where suburbanites fear to tread. I swear a bear crossed the road in front of me on my way there, and a moose on my way back. At any rate, feeling about as energetic as a slug, I brought Zach into the family room and hooked up the gate across the wide entryway from the hall so he couldn't get out of my sight.

When I heard the voices in the kitchen, I barely registered them. I had my feet up on the ottoman. I was staring cross-eyed with tiredness as Zach crawled toward the television.

"Joy." The voice. That voice. The voice of the wicked witch of Connecticut.

"Priscilla?" Damn. I'd totally forgotten. This was the night. This was the night for Father Michael.

"Joy." That was Drew, sounding slightly hysterical and completely angry.

"Oh, hi, honey." I smiled weakly. "I just got in. I was with my mother all day. We had to go to the caterers and to visit half a dozen spas—"

"Your mother's very lucky to be so popular," Priscilla said with disgust. What she meant was: Your mother is a nasty little whore who'll go straight to hell. I wish people would just say what they mean. I do.

"Joy." Drew again. "I thought you knew we were having dinner."

"I'm sorry, honey. I must have spaced it. There's been so much going on."

"Well, what will we eat?" He sounded so pathetic, I could barely believe I had ever agreed to bear his children. Would I be carrying on the gene of patheticness? Would all my children be as equally unable to help themselves as their father?

"It's not like we're in the middle of a national disaster. There *is* food in the fridge. And the store is just ten minutes away."

"I'll take a look, Andrew." There she goes again with proper names. It's a shame she insists on a no-nickname policy. If she liked them, I could call her Pris—boy, would that give me a sense of satisfaction. "I can whip something together in no time," she said, sounding only too happy to be the one to save the day. But I didn't want her to cook. Her idea of food was pasta with a can of creamed soup. She did to vegetables what five hours in the bathtub does to your skin. Still, her food seemed better than getting out of my chair.

"Joy," Drew said again, this time hissing under his breath. They both stood stiffly on the other side of the gate like it was some kind of picket line they would not cross.

"How's my baby?" Priscilla finally said, stepping heavily over the gate. She swooped Zach up in her arms. "My little Zachary," she said.

"You better come in the kitchen," Drew said.

Oooh. The kitchen. I love to be reprimanded in the kitchen. What kind of punishment could he give me? Maybe a spanking with a wooden spoon.

"I'm watching the baby," I said.

"I can stay with him," Priscilla said. She walked him over to the window, as far away from me as she could get. "He shouldn't see you two fighting. My Walter never raised his voice in front of Andrew." Okay, this I knew to be a lie, yet she said it with masterful conviction. Perhaps she could have made it in the theater?

"Fine." I stood up and followed Drew into our state-of-the-art kitchen, undoubtedly my least favorite place in the house.

"I can't believe you forgot," he said.

"God, Drew, you'd think the Pope himself was coming for dinner. Just relax. Just because it's not made yet doesn't mean we'll all go hungry."

"It's just so typical of you, Joy. This is what it's been like with you all the time lately. You're so self-consumed. You never used to forget things. You were thoughtful."

"*I'm* self-consumed? Oh, that's pretty—coming from the man who spends all day doing exactly what he wants. Hey, Drew, when's the last time that you got up in the morning and took care of your baby? As far as I can remember, every time you get up in the morning you take a long run and a shower. What do I do? I take care of the baby. If I even want to take a long shower, I have to ask your *permission*. Now, which of us is more selfish?"

He banged a cupboard closed.

"I don't want to have this argument with you," he said. "Let's just make do. I thought we were working on things. Aren't we working on it, Joy? Maybe the stress of your mother's wedding is getting to you."

"Sure," I said. "I'm sure that's it."

Father Michael enjoyed his macaroni and cheese. He loved the salad with apples and almonds. He also drank a whole bottle of wine by himself. He was a quiet, mousy man. If he hadn't gone into the priesthood, I'm certain he would have become some man's sex slave. He had BOTTOM written all over him. (If you don't know what a bottom is, find someone more interesting to have sex with and ask them.)

He watched Drew and I bicker back and forth about possible dates for the baptism. Then he said:

"Are you both in agreement about wanting to baptize?"

"No, we aren't," I said firmly.

He looked from one to the other of us and then over at Priscilla.

"They're coming round to how important it is," Priscilla said. I think if she could have reached, she would have kicked me under the table.

"I'm more Jewish than Catholic," I told Father Michael. "Or I would be if I weren't a complete atheist." There it was again, the telltale eyebrow raise. "We haven't been to church in what, ten or twenty years, right, Drew?"

"This isn't about you," Priscilla said. "This is about Zachary." She was holding the baby in her arms, despite the fact that it was two hours past his usual bedtime. He'd fallen asleep. His lips opened slightly with each breath, giving him the distinct look of a fish.

"I thought you both wanted to have the baby baptized," Father Michael said quietly. He'd begun to look a little uneasy.

"I definitely do not want that," I said. It felt like my duty to be honest. After all, I was talking to a man of the cloth. How could I lie to him? Drew gave me his most intense evil eye. "Ah . . . I'd love to make Priscilla—happy." I choked on the word. I'd never seen the woman happy a day in her life, and I'm not sure, given all my choices, that I would put making her happy on my list of things to accomplish in my lifetime. At any rate, I could see I would be in for hell with Drew if I didn't make some effort. "It just goes against all my values."

"What about you?" Father Michael gestured to Drew. For fun, since we weren't having much of it at this point, I imagined Father Michael dressed like Cher doing a drag show. He kind of had a Cher nose.

"I'm open," Drew said in a very noncommittal way.

This is not the Drew I remember. You have to keep in mind that this man took over the running of an entire school at the tender age of twenty-eight. This is the man who asked me to marry him on the third date. Drew's bold and strong and direct. He's not a wilted old lettuce leaf.

But whoever that guy was, the one who saved the school he runs every day, he wasn't the grasshopper sitting at my dining room table.

I wouldn't have it.

At the very least we ought to make joint decisions.

"Maybe we ought to talk further," Father Michael said. "I wouldn't feel comfortable baptizing Zachary at this point." Priscilla sighed loudly. Father Michael patted her hand gently. I got up to take in the dishes, and Drew coughed deeply into his hand, which meant: You are in so much trouble with me.

The next morning, momsomnia came on strong. I couldn't sleep. I slipped out of bed at 5 a.m. before even Zach was awake and tiptoed down to the computer, slinking along like a robber in my own house. I didn't want to wake anyone up. The sense of being alone thrilled me.

But not as much as the email from Jake I found in my inbox.

> *Just a quick note to tell you that I did a little research on your behalf. Isn't the Internet cool! I wonder who's snooping on me . . . Here's a link to a site that mentioned a Donny Macnamara. Seems like your guy, only he's writing to a gay online site about gay people in the military. So what do you make of that? Take a look and tell me what you think but I'm guessing your Donny might pinch-hit for the other team, occasionally anyway. Ciao, J*

Wow. Now we were on to something. If Donny wasn't just poor but gay and poor, certainly my mother would listen to me. It did seem a bit far-fetched, but I checked the website just the same and there was a posting on the chat page of a gay online magazine from a Donny Macnamara in southern Connecticut.

Okay. I had some head-clearing to do. I got up from the office chair and headed to the bedroom, where I wrestled a peacefully sleeping Zach out of the warm sheets of our bed. I stuffed him in his stroller, then headed out for a walk. Even though it'd been sweltering hot, a miserable August, Zach and I have taken daily walks. He loves his stroller. He begs to get in it. When he sits in it, he draws his foot up to his mouth and sucks on his toes. We walk in town. We walk to the playground. We walk our neighborhood.

I saw a woman the other day coming out of a coffee shop. She was carrying a teeny tiny baby, probably not more than a few weeks old. She looked stunned, alarmed, lost. It made me realize just how far I've come. I could even see in this woman's walk the remains of birth pains. She carried herself gingerly back to the car. I watched her the whole way, mesmerized. I knew exactly what she was feeling. It's like being the person time has forgotten. You don't think you'll ever belong in the world again—or if the world will ever matter. And the answer is...

It doesn't. It still doesn't matter. Zach and I live outside of time. It's cool. It's like being on *Star Trek* or something. We're just visitors to the world of business meetings and power lunches and places you have to be at a certain time. On our planet, we nap and cry and crawl. We can spend whole days without seeing the outside world. We play with blades of grass and the cardboard roll left from the toilet paper. Our favorite toy is the nose bulb the hospital gave us for cleaning out snot. It's the best teething toy we have. It goes with us everywhere.

At the end of our neighborhood stroll, I still didn't have a perfect plan for discerning Donny's actual sexual preferences. Thank God I had a playdate planned with Diana at ten. I needed some sage advice. Nothing like a pregnant woman to dispense wisdom.

Diana's like every television mom I ever saw. She answers the door. She smiles. She even owns an apron. And she *wears* it. In other words, she really gets into the whole stay-at-home mother thing. But when I got there, no happy homemaker opened the door.

"Diana," I called into the house. "Diana." I let myself in. I could hear Addicus babbling. He hadn't started crawling yet, though he still outdid Zach in his ability to flip over. "Diana, it's Joy."

"In here" came a faint voice. I followed it into the living room.

"Are you okay?" I plopped Zach on the ground and hurried over to Diana's side. She was lying on the floor in a little ball, looking more like one of those roly-poly bugs than like my good friend.

"Is it the heat?" I asked. The humidity had been wretched. Although hands down the worst part of summer now consisted of the daily application of baby sunblock. Now that Zach was officially six months, I had the nerve-racking job of making sure every inch of exposed skin got routinely slathered before we went out into the light of day. I read a new report every other day about how we're all going to die from skin cancer. Of course, if I managed to get Zach through childhood without a sunburn, I would have bigger worries, like lung cancer, and if not that then breast cancer (yes, men can get it), and if not that then colon cancer, and if not that, then prostate cancer, and if he got free of the cancers, it could still be diabetes or obesity or a heart attack, and if not that, a bus could run over him when he runs into the street after a ball. I was beginning to wonder why I'd dared leave the house at all, when poor Diana broke through the thick fog of my maternal paranoia and said:

"I'm so sick. I never had this before. I've thrown up four times already." I reached over and stroked her back. "Please don't touch me," she said. "I'm sorry. I don't mean to be rude. It just makes me feel sicker."

"Oh, no, I'm sorry." I took my hand away and thought for a moment. I'd never vomited during my pregnancy, but I had eight months of perpetual nausea that for some reason could only be stopped by watching MTV rockers telling their life stories.

"Diana. Why don't you go upstairs and lie down?"

"I wanted Addicus to play. It isn't fair for him to be deprived because I'm pregnant. I want him to have everything Zach has."

"Well, that's an easy problem to fix. You go upstairs and rest and let me watch the boys. Then he'll get all my attention. Just like Zach."

"Really?" She finally lifted her head off the floor and looked at me. She looked like death, but she smelled liked something else, like the stuff you find in the back of your refrigerator from 1995.

"Really. I've always wanted twins." About as much as I've wanted a lobotomy. "As a matter of fact, I want to come over at least once a week and watch the boys for you. If not more often. I'll clear my calendar."

"That's too much."

"It's not enough," I protested. "I'd be over here anyway." Zach crawled over to me and wailed. I picked him up and tapped his back. Then Addicus let out a howl, and I quickly gathered him up in my arms too. "See," I said, balancing one baby on each leg. "I'm made for this."

"If you really think it's okay."

"Diana. I insist."

"I feel so guilty. I want to be mothering him more, and better. Sometimes I wish I wasn't pregnant, and then I only feel worse because I feel like all those bad thoughts will get to the new baby and he'll come out thinking I didn't really want him."

"Diana, you've been reading too many attachment parenting books. In the old days children were slaves, okay? Addicus has the good life, and he has the best mother I know. He's lucky. No, go upstairs and brush your teeth and take a nap. I've got it covered."

She smiled weakly. But she took my orders and went upstairs.

When she came down an hour later, she looked slightly more appetizing, but she still smelled.

"We're having a wonderful time," I pointed out. The boys had, in fact, been very good during her nap.

"I'm so grateful."

"Don't be. It gives me something to do. And I'm coming again next week. How's Tuesday?"

"Okay. Thank you. I can't make it up to you, though. I won't be able to return the favor."

"Yes you will. I need your advice."

"Of course! You can get that any time, for free."

I told her what Jake found on the Internet about Donny. Her jaw dropped, literally. But that's the great thing about Diana. She's so *good*, it's easy to amaze her.

"What are you going to do?" she asked.

"That's why I'm talking to you. I have to figure it out. What would you do?"

"Oh, gee," she said, rubbing her belly. She had just begun to show. "I suppose I'd want to tell my mother. But if you tell her, she'll find out that you've been snooping."

"That would be bad. Very bad. You know I have a bit of a history of disliking her husbands. I'm not exactly the most reliable source of information for her."

"How about an anonymous note?"

"Too ABC after-school special."

"Right," she said. "Maybe you could talk to Donny, mention that you saw his name."

"That could work." I started to picture our conversation. Maybe if I told him what I knew, he'd graciously back out of the marriage. No harm done. "Would it be so terrible, to ruin it for my mother if in the end I was saving her from a disastrous marriage?"

"Pretty terrible. But I still wish I had your problem. I'd rather have a Donny in my life than morning sickness."

"Pregnancy is so a disease, I don't care what anyone says."

"You make it better," she said. "You've got a very entertaining life." She smiled sweetly.

"Thanks. Nice to know since I feel so totally boring. The

only way I don't feel boring is working on this problem with Donny. And when Jake emails me, I feel like a human being again. Actually, more than that, I feel like I used to feel, like someone involved in the world, doing something worthwhile. That's how it felt in college, at least."

"You *are* doing something worthwhile."

"Am I?"

"What's more important than raising a child?"

"Ha. Right. I get it. But the world doesn't." We sat for a moment, looking at our two boys. They'd been relatively peaceful that morning, not too much crying, not too much drooling.

"Does it feel like you're still in love with Jake?" she asked.

I stood up. "I don't want to think about that. Life is better—not perfect, but better—with Drew now that we made up over the whole labor thing. I've tried to put those feelings out of my mind. If I am in love with him, you're the only one who knows it. So do me a favor and don't remind me, okay?"

"I don't know what I'd do without you," she said, coming over and hugging me.

"I know what I'd do without you. I'd be lost. And very lonely."

"Let's take hold of the inside of the left foot, with the palm facing out." Oliver stood sideways, showing us how to get into the dancer pose. "On the in breath, raise up your right arm and then hinging forward, kick back with your left leg." I stood on two feet watching him turn his body into a beautiful design, almost a circle. His chest puffed up. His left foot was within inches of his head. I could hardly believe his body could make such a shape, and if it hadn't been so totally bizarre and a little like looking at someone double jointed, I would have enjoyed it a whole lot more.

"You look like one of us," another woman said to him, "and then you do something like that and I know you definitely are not one of us." She laughed. He laughed too. He came out of the pose slowly and turned to watch the class. I hadn't moved yet. He looked over at me, the only one in the class not trying the pose. He raised his eyebrows slightly and smiled curiously. Then he came over.

"Not in the mood?" he asked. He was close enough to me that I could smell his breath. It was minty and earthy at the same time. It made my heart beat faster, which was not supposed to happen. As far as I knew, Oliver was taken. For all I knew, he had ten girlfriends. And I was not one of them.

I shook my head. "Just zoned out," I said. "Not sleeping much."

"We're almost done," he said. "Why don't you take an early *savasana*." *Savasana* is the yogic version of naptime. I love it most of all. The only thing that would make it better is a snack beforehand and recess afterward.

"Really?"

"Go ahead and lie down," he said. Then he turned and began leading everyone through the second side of the posture. He started talking about the "gifts of balance." I felt foolish not doing the posture, but it seemed insulting not to take his directions. He was the teacher, after all. If he thought I needed to lie down, why argue? I sat down, then rolled onto my back. I picked up the eye bag I'd recently acquired. You put it over your eyes during relaxation to block out the light. I bought one filled with lavender. It and my mat made up my entire collection of yoga paraphernalia. I didn't want anything else. I certainly didn't want the spandex unitards or the clinging yoga pants with their OM symbols or the groovy yoga bags that carry your mat and water bottle and probably improve your karma. I simply would not let myself be that cool. I wanted the comfort of my old clothes. The minute I started wearing those yoga pants, I'd be expected to *do* all the poses, and call them *asanas* too. I didn't want that. I didn't come to class to learn yoga. I came . . . What did I come for? I came for the quiet. I came for the last ten minutes of sleep I got each time. I came for the sound of Oliver's voice. And for his touch. That's probably wrong for so many different reasons, like lusting after Mr. Rogers. Still, it's the truth.

At the beginning of *savasana,* he came back over to me. He did his squat thing behind my head. He picked my head up in his two hands, his fingers reaching down to the base of my neck. He pulled his fingers along either side of my neck up to the top of my skull while holding my head off the floor. It gave me tingles in my toes. All the while, I could hear him breathing, and it was so nice, so sweet, I could have cried. Luckily, I did not.

I thought this story meant something, but when I told Melody she said: "Everyone falls in love with their yoga teacher."

"In the first place, I didn't say I was in love with him. And in the second place, why do you have to rain on my parade?"

"Sorry. It sounds like a crush, though."

"No. It was . . . a really nice moment, and I don't have many of those these days outside of Zach."

"It's true, though. It's classic, to have a crush on your yoga teacher. That's because yoga teachers are people you only see in one context. You only see their best sides, their most loving sides. He probably goes home and drinks beer and yells at his cat."

"Melody, that's terrible."

"See? You *do* have a thing for him. All I can say is, be careful. He's not a real person yet. You don't know him. He's just creating feelings in you that you've been missing. But you know what? Those are feelings you can re-create by yourself. You don't need him for—"

"Okay with the therapy talk. If you're going to give me advice, why don't you help me with my mother-in-law, who's hell-bent on saving Zach's soul, or my mother and her soon to be scam-artist husband?"

"Your mother's easy; stop meddling in her business and you won't need to worry about her. As far as Priscilla goes, that woman needs some Prozac."

"Thanks for the words of wisdom," I said grumpily.

"Anytime."

"I'm not worried about my mother, by the way." I could hear Sarah start to wail in the background.

"That's okay, honey. Why don't you play with a soft toy?"

"Are you talking to me? That's more therapy talk, isn't it? You want me to role-play my relationship with my mother using a stuffed animal?"

She ignored my joke and said, "You always worry about your mother."

"That's not true. It's been a long time since I worried about her seriously. I just hate her timing. She should be helping me with Zach. Instead, I'm spending all my time running around taking care of her, helping her with the wedding and protecting her backside with Donny. I wish she'd just take care of me for a while."

"If I had a penny for every time I'd heard that."

"I doubt I say it that often."

"Don't forget that I knew you way back when. I knew you

224 □ Samantha Wilde

when she was just getting back on her feet after the hospital. I knew you when the kids were babies—"

"I know. I know all that, Melody. Don't patronize me."

"Hey, not so touchy. I'm just trying to be helpful."

"I'm sorry. I'm like the dragon lady. I think I've got PMS again."

"You've got life, honey. We've all got it. And speaking of, Sarah's got a poopy diaper. Can we talk later?"

"Let's try to see each other before we go away for vacation," I said.

"You got it."

Then I was alone again with the baby—the alone that I'd come to think of as the permanent condition of my life. The alone that I hadn't put into my fairy-tale vision of married life. There are days when I get so claustrophobic I could eat my own hair in frustration. Okay, maybe not my hair. That's pretty disgusting. Besides, I don't have much of it these days. The feeling, though, of entrapment, is terrible. Those are the days I'll pray Diana's well enough for a visit or I'll drive to the park or take a really long time in the grocery store hoping someone I know will be shopping and will stop and have one of those grocery cart conversations with me.

I don't want to confess this because it might make me look bad. Under normal circumstances, I'm a very consistent person. Motherhood, however, doesn't have a single normal thing about it. Unless you think it's normal to lock an adult woman up every day in a house with a person who has the temperament of an unhousebroken orangutan.

This is my confession. Every now and then, when I have absolutely no one else to play with and absolutely nowhere else to go, I'll call Priscilla. For one thing, she never goes anywhere, so she's a sure bet. For another thing, she loves Zach almost as much as I do—albeit in a sort of psychotic, compulsive way. She's also extremely easy to be with. That may contradict everything I've ever said about her. But she is easy to get along with—as long as she doesn't open her mouth. If I put on the TV for her, or if she watches Zach while I cook, she's perfect company. For some reason, she can't open her mouth without saying something offensive. For the longest time, I thought it must be me, that I must be so awful she couldn't help but insult me. Then I realized, with a little help from Melody, and on the basis of a few stories from Drew, that she acted like that with every girlfriend he'd ever had. She simply did not want to share him; she wanted to kill the competition. Very Freudian. And I don't like Freud at all.

I'm not proud. I have called her a few times. But sometimes even Priscilla is out, though I can't imagine where she could possibly go, other than church. This means that every now and then I will have a day like today, when Drew is in his office planning for the fall semester and my mother can't visit because she has to look at leopard-print scarves to sell with her neck serum, and Sarah is sick so Melody can't go anywhere, and Diana has another friend over (traitor), when I will find myself alone in the house for hours at a time.

These days mean something else: They give me time to think. Thinking is overrated. What can come from it? Can you think your way out of your life and into another one? I don't think so. It's a popular idea now. They've got all these books out about how you can think your way rich and think your way healthy and think your way into a marriage with a sexy god of a man. These books are written by aliens who are trying to take over our planet by slowly making us into ludicrously gullible people. These books are written by people like Donny. In fact, I wouldn't be surprised if he's got one in the works. I have only read about ten of them, and I didn't like a single one. I guess other people have more mind control. I can't get my brain to think a bunch of hokey thoughts. It just does what it wants. Which means that on these lonely days when Zach and I aren't in perfect tune with each other and all the planets, I wonder who invented all those yoga poses and why. I wonder if I will ever have another baby. I wonder if I will ever be a good enough person to love Priscilla. I wonder if my mother's fourth marriage will last and for how long. I wonder why she would pick such a loser to marry. I wonder why my labor went the way it did. I wonder why my father had to die. I wonder what my life would have been like if he'd lived. I wonder if I really have a crush on Oliver. I wonder what my marriage is built on. I wonder if I do love Jake. I wonder if Aunt Hilda really knows what she's talking about.

You can see why I try to avoid these days at all cost.

Sixteen

I HAD SEX! YES, IT'S TRUE! I HAD ACTUAL, BONA FIDE, penis enters vagina sex. And it lasted almost ten minutes. We didn't have much time. Zach was lying in the bed in our vacation cabin in Vermont having his morning nap. We went into the bathroom to do it. I didn't want him to wake up and see his mommy's ass in the air, or his daddy's for that matter. I ended up on my back on the floor with my head wedged between the toilet and the standing shower. I know, the romance is unbearable. I couldn't have cared less. I was just so happy it was finally happening. Did it mean I wasn't as hideously ugly as I felt postmortem? Did it mean Drew and I loved each other again, that all was fine and forgotten? Did it mean I spent the rest of the day trying to gracefully remove beads of sand (left from our bathing suits on the bathroom floor) from my butt crack? At least I can answer one of those questions in the affirmative. Yes, there was a lot of sand in my ass.

We did have a pretty good time together, the three of us. We went swimming and hiking every day. Drew cooked for us in the miniature kitchen area of the cabin. After Zach fell asleep, we played card games outside at our very own picnic table. Then we'd drink wine and watch the stars, saturated in bug spray.

At any rate, the sex put me in a good mood. We only had it that one time, at the beginning of the trip, but it was enough for me to remember that once, in a galaxy far, far away, my breasts had been suckled by grown men who weren't looking to fill their hungry tummies.

It also rained for three days. That was a bit hellish since Drew thinks rain is just as good to hike in as sun. He just whips out his mountain of hiking rain gear. We suited the baby up and did what we could. After I slid down about thirty feet of trail on my backside because the whole thing had become a mudslide, he was kind enough to suggest we turn around. Zach cried for most of the hike, but it was pouring so heavily we could barely hear him. Then when it stopped, the mosquitoes came out. And I mean came out. It was like the 1970s gay liberation movement when everyone came out of the closet at once and suddenly everyone was gay including you. Or at least that's what they told us in history class. I wore diapers for most of the seventies. After the mosquitoes came out, we sprayed ourselves within an inch of our lives and then ran the rest of the way back. Finally an activity that Zach liked. He laughed hysterically while he bounced in the backpack Drew had on.

When we got back from Vermont, life seemed a little better. For one thing, I'd gone a whole week without seeing Priscilla. For another thing, I'd had more sleep than I'd gotten since Zach was born. Some magical fairy must have tapped Drew with her wand, because he took a real shine to Zach on vacation, going so far as to watch him for an hour in the morning while I snoozed. So maybe that hour was 6 to 7 a.m., and I refused to get out of bed. But still. It was a nice moment, my hero.

I hadn't had much of Drew's help for the summer, but I was about to get even less of it. The new school year had begun. With it came more meetings with more people than even God has to attend. He'd already gone with the freshmen for their orientation and kayaking trip (meant to induce male bonding). This week he'd be meeting with the new teachers for their orientation, which included three nights of dinner out—in a row. He would write a talk for convocation. He would write an essay for the school magazine. He would be everywhere, with everyone, and at the same time.

Only he wouldn't be with us.

I won't go so far as to say something got rekindled during our vacation. I'm not a hopeless romantic, after all. One orgasm isn't enough for me to forgive all the arguments, disrespect and celibacy of the past six months, even if I had forgiven him out of some silly fear that Aunt Hilda knew what she was talking about. But when we came back from vacation and the school year started, I felt for a moment that I would miss him. Or maybe I realized that I had been missing him all along.

To: jmcguire @fanfare.com
From: jakephilips@lunerpress.com
Haven't heard from you in a while. I'm wondering
what's going on with your mother's fiancé. Did you
manage to talk to him yet? I had a great idea, if you
want to use it. You could have a friend go to him for a
coaching session, see what he's all about. Or, I suppose,

*you could go yourself. Just ideas. Or you could always do
the honest approach and just mention that you saw his
posting on that website, see how he responds.*

*I'm swamped with work. My girlfriend, Angela, just
lost her dog, Hambone. He died of old age, but it's still
upsetting. Do you remember Toto? Whatever happened
to him? I still think of the time when we found that dog
in the road, the one who'd been hit by a car. I don't think
I'll ever forget the sight of you lifting him and putting
him in the backseat while I directed traffic. Do you
remember what you said to me, when I offered to move
him? You said, "I just have a feeling that if I hold him,
it will be all right." And it was. Magic touch, you. J*

You know that song with the line "take my breath away"?
That's what Jake does, every time. Takes my breath away. But
we all know what happens if you lose your breath for too
long. You die. I'm not interested in dying. At least not anytime
soon. Still, I don't mind a little flattery. I don't mind thinking
of a time when I was magic, or even better than that, a time
when even if I wasn't magic, someone thought that I was.

The third Saturday in September, I nestled into what had become "my spot," in the back right-hand corner of the yoga
room. I saw no sign of Oliver. Every time someone walked
into the room, my head whipped around to see if it was him.
It was like I didn't have any control of my head. It wanted to
find him. It wanted to be reassured that we wouldn't have
some anorexic teenager teaching the class. I wanted Oliver,
with his huge brown eyes, his dimples, his subtle Canadian
accent. I wanted Oliver to touch my head again. But that's not

the kind of thing you can just *ask* for. Maybe if I looked pathetic and tired enough, he would do it?

He did come, but late, which I'd never known him to do. He tripped on the rug on his way to the front of the room. It made me laugh. Normally, he had such poise. When he heard me laughing, he looked up and smiled right at me. He lifted just one eyebrow but said nothing.

I hadn't forgotten anything since my last class. I could still get into my version of the dog pose and the host of other animal poses like lion and seal and cow and rabbit. I had forgotten, though, how much I enjoyed his endless chatter, the sound of his voice talking, talking, guiding, suggesting. The way he said "beautiful" over and over, but each time with meaning. I realized, maybe for the first time, that he seemed sincere. Now, how often do I say that?

I suppose one has to be sincere if one is going to teach people how to put their legs behind their heads. Or how to roll around on the floor, or how to properly practice the "wind-relieving pose." How could one be anything but genuine about that? Yoga class is a pretty serious place. It's like a library or a hospital; you have to be quiet when you enter. I hear that they used to have their teachers practice on raised platforms, like kings. If I can get some royalty in my blood by learning to massage my intestines with my breath, fart freely in public and make friends with my hamstrings, I'll take it. I'm not going to get to be Queen Joy McGuire any other way.

Oliver seemed particularly talkative that day. He went into a long explanation on the spine and cerebral spinal fluid during which I had a lengthy and unexpected fantasy about what his boyfriend must look like and why it's such a shame that he's gay. Or at any rate, I told myself he was gay so I wouldn't feel so bad every time he touched me. Because every time he touched me I got aroused. I'm no expert on yoga, but I'm pretty sure that's not what he's going for when he offers to "give me a press." If that were the case, classes would cost a whole lot more, but they'd still be filled with middle-age women and mothers.

I didn't get an assist of any kind that day. Then the class ended with a singsong OM—that's when we all chant together like the good people we are pretending to be. That's also the time when we wish peace for every living creature. I find this a bit challenging considering the fact that I'm occasionally a bitter, resentful person. You may have noticed this. So I wish peace for every living creature that's never done anything against me. That seems to work just fine. That way I can continue to be irritated with my husband, with Priscilla, with the grocery store clerk, with my mother, with my father for that matter and with life in general. Honestly, I can't understand where all this peace and love will get us. In the first place, when people are happy, they have nothing to talk about with one another. The only times I have really good conversations with my friends are when they're down in the dumps. Would I give that up for world peace?

Oliver, on the other hand, probably means everything he says. I can just see it on his face. It fascinates me, actually. He's like someone you see in the circus who you can't stop looking at. That day, he came up to me after class, probably because I was taking about twenty-five minutes to roll up my mat and get out of the room.

"Joy," he said, smiling broadly. He smelled minty again.

"Great class," I said, because I couldn't think of anything else to say.

"You're a real natural."

"I am?"

"Absolutely. Your body has really taken to the *asanas.* Are you sure you've never done yoga before?"

"Now you're just buttering me up." And unnerving me, I wanted to say, but didn't. He was standing so close to me that I could almost feel the heat of his body, and if I wasn't mistaken it was having the nicest effect on me. If I hadn't absolutely known that he was taken and that I was a wet blanket, I would have sworn that I was getting turned on. Really. I felt, warm, happy, sexy, tingly all over.

"No, I mean it." He smiled again. It was disarming. I still couldn't quite put my finger on how old he was—although I could tell he outnumbered me by at least a decade.

"Oh, well...then, thank you." I didn't know what to say, for once at a loss for words, which is not a quality I like in other people and can't stand in myself. So I said the first thing that came to mind: "Are you married?"

Oliver laughed freely. "That's a funny question," he said.

"Oh, just curious. I thought maybe yoga teachers had to be...like monks maybe." Not a bad save if you consider the other places I could have gone with it.

"Not at all." He smiled again.

"You mean you're not at all married?" I figure this comment pretty much took me over to the land of flirtation, a place I avoid at all costs and haven't visited for a decade. I'd like to say it horrified me to be acting like a schoolgirl in front of my yoga teacher, but it didn't. After all, he'd seen my butt in the air in every position it can get in the air.

"Not married at all," he said. "And yoga teachers don't have to be celibate—which is what I meant. Not in America. Not unless you're taking all of the principles of the tradition literally. Then you practice what's called *bramacharya.*"

"Oh." Then I was stumped. What else could I say? Surely

we didn't have anything in common. For example, only one of us could speak Sanskrit. "So no kids then?"

"No kids. I wish I had, though. I love children. How's yours?"

"Zach's fantastic. He's seven months. He is absolutely the reason I get out of bed every morning."

"That must be so powerful, so immediate, having a little one."

"I don't know if I speak your language. I guess sometimes it's fun. Sometimes it's hard. Sometimes it's lonely. Sometimes it's boring. Sometimes it's mind blowing. I'll tell you one thing, though, there isn't a person I'd rather be with in all the world than Zach."

Oliver reached over and cupped my cheek. He must have meant it in a fatherly way, right? He held my cheek in his hand and said, "You're very lucky, then. That's the serious yoga, motherhood. It's beautiful." His brown eyes caught the sunlight and sparkled at me. I didn't want him to take his hand away. If I believed in the yoga stuff, which I don't, I would have thought he was a magic person, and his touch was a magic touch. However, I gave up the idea of magic a long time ago—like when I was eight and realized that life just happens the way it happens even when you are praying with all your might to all the fairies and elves and warlocks (not to mention God who needs a replacement hearing aid) to make it different.

Then Oliver walked back toward the stereo and started to gather his CDs. I felt in my whole body an emotion I could hardly name it had been so long since I'd felt it. It wasn't love, which I knew now in the touch of my son's body against mine, the sweet look on his face while he nurses. No, this wasn't innocent in that way or peaceful. In fact, I felt a bit like a wild animal. I wanted to go to him and press myself against him and simply forget everything else. It was lust. That was it. Old friend of my adolescence. A youthful desire, purely sexual, washed over me. I wanted Oliver.

So naturally I felt disgusted with myself. To be a cliché! I could never tell Melody. Lusting after my yoga teacher. How...ordinary!

"Did you have a wonderful time?" my mother asked when I arrived home. She'd agreed to watch Zach that morning in return for some more wedding planning.

"I have a good teacher."

"That's excellent, honey. Listen, I need you to look over the final copy of the menu with me. And how's everything looking for the big bridal dinner? We're less than two months away now."

"It's going to be a bang-up time, I promise." As if I could ever forget her party at *my* house. In the first place, the house would have to be cleaned. Not "cleaned" the way I'd been doing it for months—dragging the vacuum over the rugs once every week or so and wiping down the toilets and the sinks with some clean toilet paper when they had accrued the look of total neglect. You know that look, with pubic hairs clinging to the toilet rim (Drew's, of course) and water spots all over the sink and some ten-day-old blob of toothpaste stuck to the side of the sink faucet.

Second, I would have to find something to wear that fit me without making me look like (a) a bowl of marmalade or (b) somebody's mother. Naturally, I did not want to shop. Shopping brings out the worst in me. It is not fair to be forced to look at my half-naked body under fluorescent lights. Also, shopping with Zach isn't the most peaceful experience I can think of. Neither, for that matter, is shopping with my mother, who is thinner, more fashionable and nicer than me. Which meant I might have to enlist Priscilla as a babysitter. Except that would leave open the possibility of her driving him down to the local church and throwing him headfirst into the baptismal font.

And last, I would have to formulate a plan of action on how to tell my mother the news about Donny.

I sat down next to my mother on the sofa at the same moment that Zach, tuckered out from a great crawling spree, lay down on my shoes and scream-cried. I've already discovered that crawling is a very, very bad idea. Who thought young babies, who want to eat everything, who understand the dangers of nothing, who can't speak or hear properly, should be mobile? I would call this a very bad idea. On the positive side, he's old enough to sit in a high chair and eat baby food. This is a euphemism for expensive mush. After I bought a few bottles from the store, I started to make it myself; I may not have many gifts in the kitchen, but I can mash a banana as well as the next person.

"By the way, how's Donny?"

"The best. He is *so* much fun to be around. I don't think I've ever known anybody so carefree."

"*Really?*"

"We enjoy each other, honey, we really do. I'm always laughing with him."

"Sounds like he's a good friend to you."

"The best."

"The guys I knew who were the best friends like that, back in college at least, were always gay."

"Well, not my Donny, sweets. We have as much fun in the bed as out of it."

"Gross, Mom."

"Not gross at all, daughter of mine. I hope the same for you."

"Thanks, Mom, that's really kind of you. But seriously, you don't ever wonder about Donny?" She looked at me. "I mean, because he's so easy to get along with?"

"Are you trying to tell me something?"

"No, no! Of course not."

"Are you worried about Drew, honey? Is that it? Do you think he's gay?"

"Geez, Mom, that's ridiculous. He's as gay as I am." She raised her eyebrows. "Not gay at all, obviously."

"Good. That's good, honey. It's nice to want to sleep with the gender you've married. Now, look this over. I need your final input. I've got to get this in to the caterer, and then I've got to scoot. I'm meeting Donny for dance class."

"Dance class?"

"We're learning the two-step."

Now, if that's not gay, I don't know what is.

Seventeen

AS WE MOVED INTO OCTOBER, CLARKVILLE ACADEMY'S demands increased, and Drew went from hardly around to never around. When he was around he'd bore me with tales of Mark and David and Justin and Caleb and Henry. There were so many of them I couldn't remember who was who and who had what drug problem and who'd been kicked out of his other boarding school ten times and which one kept smoking in the woods. You have to feel a little bad for the children of the extremely wealthy. Nothing creates an ache in the soul quite like having everything you want. If you always get what you want, you find out sooner than most of us that life isn't about what you have. But then you're left wondering what it *is* about. So you think it's about getting high or having sex or killing yourself for shock value. Better to be poor. Better to spend your whole life thinking that if you only had more of this or that, then you'd be happy. The rich know you don't ever get happy. I wonder, does that make them smarter?

I didn't think it was possible to feel worse than I had in the first few weeks after Zach's birth when my hormones were like terrorists knocking down all my sense and rationality and logic—the things I'd spent a lifetime building. I did, however, in October, reach an all-time new low. If I could've blamed it on someone, I would have, but it doesn't seem very nice to blame your psychosis on a baby. Zach had begun teething in earnest. He went from mostly sleeping through the night (in the bed with us), to nursing his way through the night to ease the pain in his gums. I very definitely know what it's like to be a cow, forced to lactate and be constantly milked. I'd also forgotten how to sleep through the nursings like I did when he was little, so I lie awake at night and try not to hate the baby. I know there are a few people out there who can live on twenty minutes of sleep a night, but I am not one of them. It brings out the she-devil in me.

It's not Zach's fault. It's nature's fault. Whose idea was it to have a baby come out with no teeth and then immediately go through a period of intense physical anguish to get them? Is this what those people call "intelligent design"? Because I have a bone to pick with the designer. What did they do before Tylenol, those poor mothers? I bet they really did bring out the whiskey and drank half the bottle themselves before they shared it with the baby. I've made it through by doling out baby Tylenol and freezing wet washcloths for him to chew on. Melody, sensible as ever, gave me a lecture on how Tylenol can cause liver damage, which terrified me enough to come up with some creative alternatives, like offering my own fingers for sacrifice on his hard gums.

I don't feel up to much creativity these days. I feel like a prisoner of war. I've never had Chinese water torture, but I can guarantee that this is worse. I just know it. It doesn't help that Drew's gone to sleep in the guest bedroom now. He's taken himself out of the situation completely. He can't afford not to get his sleep. Who can blame him? He's got a whole school to run. What do I have?

I have Priscilla. Or at least that's what he keeps telling me whenever I complain about not having his help. *Call my mother, call my mother, call my mother* is his new mantra. I have had her over a few times while I've napped. Those were the worst days, when the momsomnia got so bad I'd see not just every hour but every minute on the clock. Zach would fall asleep. I'd get him off my nipple. I'd curl up and drift off, and he'd begin whimpering again and rooting. A few times he'd miss and start suckling on my arm. I tried the pacifier. It worked now and then.

I have one respite for which I feel cargo-ships full of guilt. I have yoga or, more specifically, I have Oliver. The other day he was saying that yoga is the thing that cracks you open, that we are all like eggs with hard shells, and the yoga practice can crack that shell to reveal a soft, pliable, flexible and vulnerable interior. I wanted to go up to him after class and let him know that I had already been cracked. That my belly was my egg yolk falling out. That I'd lost my brains and my kindness when the shell broke. That I'm not sure all this being open stuff is a good idea.

Of course, I still had the task of being matron of honor to fill my endless days. I filled my endless nights wondering how I could get rid of Donny. I'm afraid to say he'd begun to take on some of the qualities of my nighttime momsomnia. I'd started dreaming of him doing terrible things to my mother postwedding, like stealing all of her money and running off with his gay lover. Or chopping her into little pieces—but that one only when I was very tired and had watched too much bad TV the night before.

When I met my mother at the flower shop the other day, she gave me a definite looking over.

"Sweetie, you look very tired."

"You think so? Do you think it may be because I never sleep?"

She put an arm around me and an arm around Zach, who was sitting happily on my hip. Almost 8 months, he pretty much fit there.

"Group hug, darlings," she said.

Sometimes a group hug does the trick. Sometimes it doesn't. Sometimes you resort to unthinkable activities, like compulsively emailing your college sweetheart.

To: jmcguire@fanfare.com
From: jakephilips@lunerpress.com
Hey private I. Have you got up to any more spying? Or have you made peace with the fact that your mother has a thing for a trendy, new-age bisexual? ☺

Life here is grand again. Just got back from three weeks in the south of France. I'm thinking of visiting my sister in Mystic again. She's planning a trip to India, maybe even a move there. Thought I'd visit her in the States before she heads off. Will you be around all fall? I might pop in on you.

To: jakephilips@lunerpress.com
From: jmcguire@fanfare.com
I can barely focus my bleary eyes to read your email but I don't intend to make peace with anything right now, I'm far too cantankerous. If you won't begrudge me a sentimental moment, I like to think of my college day heroics. I feel hideously suburban these days and

*b-o-r-i-n-g. I think I might take your advice and visit
Donny myself, or enlist my friend Diana to have a
session with him. Have I just gone crazy, or does he seem
like a really bad match for my glamorous mother? God,
love must truly be blind. Joy*

To: jmcguire@fanfare.com
From: jakephilips@lunerpress.com
*You haven't been boring a day in your life, missy. I love
to tell the story of how we met. It's still one of my most
impressive tales. "She dropped out of a tree?" people say
incredulously. "Yes," I tell them. "She was climbing a tree,
swinging from a branch like a monkey and she fell right
in front of me." But college was fun, wasn't it? Hanging
out with Beth and listening to her off-humored jokes.
And you, the funniest woman around. So I don't know
if love is blind. You always looked good to me and I've
always seen very well with my glasses on. Keep me posted
on the drama. It makes my day. —J*

Drew came into the bedroom (from his peaceful night of
sleeping in the guest room *sans* baby—otherwise known as
Nipple Leech) Saturday morning and said: "I'll watch him if
you want to go to yoga."

"Feeling bad for neglecting us?"

"Don't be so sour, Joy." He came and sat down on the bed.
On Zach's side. "Did it ever occur to you that I *wish* I could be
around more? That I *wish* this job didn't take up so much of
my time?" Actually, it hadn't.

"Really?"

"Of course."

"Okay. That makes me feel a bit better. So how did you sleep without a baby attached to your nipple?"

"Pretty well. How about you?"

"Sleep is a foreign concept. It's something other people do. I'm beyond sleep."

"I'm sorry," he said.

"Well, you could do something about it."

"Could I?" He looked helpless.

"Yes, you could. You could get up with him sometimes and let me sleep."

"I can't nurse him."

"You could give him a bottle."

"But I thought you didn't want him having bottles?"

"I'm almost tired enough to change my mind. Besides, it's no fun being a purist."

"You're doing a good job," he said, looking at Zach.

"This is much harder than I thought. And I had some stupid notion that gender equity would play out in my life. Like you would be around to help me."

"I'm sorry."

"I like how it used to be," I said plaintively. I didn't even like the sound of my own voice.

"Hey, by the way. I forgot to tell you. Jake sent me an email the other day. It was great to hear from him. Remember when we all used to hang out together and watch baseball and drink—what was it? Red Dog?"

"When he and I still lived together?" I laughed. "I haven't had a beer in forever." *Oh, and Jake and I are emailing all the time, honey. Hope that's okay.*

"You could get away with drinking just one."

"It gets into the breast milk."

244 □ Samantha Wilde

"There you go. A purist again. You could probably cut yourself some slack. You've made a very healthy baby." We both turned our attention toward Zach, who'd started to wiggle wildly on the bed. Drew put his hand on my arm.

I can remember back before I got pregnant, when we were deciding if it was the right time, Drew and I both said we didn't want to be like our parents. I didn't want to have more than one marriage; as happy as my mother is, I just didn't want her life. I couldn't have her life. She'd learned to take things and roll with them. I didn't roll, if you hadn't noticed. Drew didn't want us to be like his parents. I guess his mother used to wait on his father hand and foot. She called him "Daddy." Now she's a Vampire of Life, sucking everyone dry—and he certainly doesn't want to be like that. He never wanted to be like his father either, who went to work and came home, but didn't do much else but complain and drink, or drink and complain; I can't remember which came first. At any rate, he wanted equality for us. Something real. Friendship.

I think we used to be equals. We also used to have romance. He never did laugh at my jokes very often, but the times he did were wonderful. It was like winning at the slot machine and having streams of quarters run into your lap.

I spent the entire yoga class crying. Tears ran down my face and I couldn't stop them, though I tried in every way imaginable. I forced myself to think of happy things. I told myself knock-knock jokes. I pictured the other women in class naked. They weren't hysterical sobbing tears. It was more like leaking.

Thankfully, I'd sat in the back as usual so no one could see me, except Oliver. He kept us in triangle pose for an awfully long time. He adjusted me in the posture, gently pulling me backward over my leg. Then he carefully wiped a tear off my cheek. His hand felt like the brush of a butterfly. After it was over, I thought maybe I'd imagined it. Or maybe he'd touched me accidentally and I'd misinterpreted it.

Personally, I can't stand sentiment. I'm not much for tear-jerker movies. I'd prefer a comedy any day. And I'm not fond of crying in part because it makes me feel sad, and I'm not fond of feeling sad. I also don't look good when I cry. I get instant puffy-blotchy-hivey face.

After class, I made a beeline for the door, keeping my gaze on the ground. I've never had any problem getting out of there as quickly as I wanted. But that day, Oliver sought me out. He found me in the hallway slipping on my sneakers.

"Joy," he said. I liked the way he said my name. He said it with the same tone he used when he said "beautiful."

"Oh, no. What did I do wrong? Do I have to stay after class?" I smiled broadly, hoping I wouldn't look as upset as I felt. He laughed.

"Just checking in," he said. "Everything okay for you?"

Oliver often talked with students after class. I'd seen him in the hallway many times with different students, so I didn't think much of his asking me. He had a habit of checking in with people. He was that kind of person. He cared. He wanted to know. He was also more sexy than any yoga teacher has the right to be; he made me feel like a teenager talking to her rock-star crush.

"Oh, you mean because of the crying? It's nothing," I sniffled. "Very sleep deprived. That's all."

"You know in yoga, tears are considered the highest offering and crying the highest form of practice and praise."

"Really?" All right, so I guess I did care a little bit about this yoga thing, even though, and you can quote me, it's hokey.

"It's also considered a kind of purification, when you cry while you practice *asana*."

"Oh, boy, you're losing me now."

He laughed again. Then he reached out and put his hand on my arm. "Can you stay an extra while?"

I looked into his wide brown eyes, at his lovely wide brown nose. What could it hurt? I had a crush on an old man. "Sure."

"If you wait just a few minutes, I'd love to follow up with you." Then he took his hand off my arm and left, presumably to do all the teacherly things he does when he finishes a class.

There were a couple of amazing things that happened to me that Saturday. Oliver was only one of them, although hands down he wins the prize for the most amazing, if I were to rate them. Which I wouldn't. I don't like ratings. I don't know why so many people bother to rate things. I mean, it's great that they can tell you now what you're most likely to die from, if you want to know that sort of thing. I'd prefer to be surprised. They also rate the top ten worst foods and the top ten best vacation destinations and the top ten ways to stay thin and the top ten strategies that will doom your marriage to eternal hell. Again, I say, I'd prefer to be surprised. Wouldn't life be more interesting without all those graphs and statistics and averages? Honestly, if we didn't know that half of all marriages end in divorce, I don't think half of all marriages would end in divorce. Give a man or a woman an idea... and he or she will make it a reality.

Standing in the hallway of the yoga studio, I wasn't thinking about ratings. I was thinking about Oliver, which is not something I wanted to do. I wanted to be a better person. So I went outside to get some fresh air. The studio is downtown just off the main street. I strolled toward town, half thinking I wouldn't go back and find Oliver. I imagined Drew sitting at home on Zach duty; it made me feel liberated and guiltily pleased. Now he'd get a sense of what *my* life felt like.

When I got to Main Street, I noticed a couple walking down the sidewalk with what appeared to be about twenty children. When they got closer, I noticed they only had five. Three of them were walking, though they were quite young. The oldest couldn't have been more than seven. Then they had one of those baby carriages that can only mean one thing: twins. There was no room for anyone else within ten feet.

The parents were slender. The mother wore tight jeans. I tried to calculate, based on her perfect figure, the age of her babies, although my first thought was that she *had* to have adopted. The father had on dark jeans and a navy blue pea-coat. He was telling the older son why no one in the family eats ice cream for lunch.

As they neared me, I couldn't help but stare. I peered round the tops of the double carriage to see the babies. Two girls. They couldn't have been much older than three months, if I remembered accurately what three months looked like.

"Oh, my," I said. "They're beautiful."

Both parents were wearing sunglasses. They looked composed. Whereas I had just been weeping in a yoga class.

"How old?" The family came to an unexpected stop. In other words, I don't think they would have wanted to talk to me if given the choice.

"Sixteen weeks," the mother said. "I know they're quite small. They were tiny at birth."

Then I asked the obvious question:

"How do you do it? I just have one. I just had my first. He's eight months now. He's getting teeth; I'm not sleeping at all. You both look so . . . calm!" I tittered a bit. I could see the compliment pleased them because they both smiled. Then Daddy flipped his sunglasses to the top of his head.

The little boy said: "Daddy, why can't I have ice cream?" His younger sister said: "If he has ice cream cone, can I have ice cream cone?"

"I remember being where you are," the father said to me. "It's awful, that first one. This is much easier."

"Really?" I tried not to act completely and utterly stunned. Maybe they had a few nannies?

"Really," the mother said. "This is much easier. It just gets better. The first is the hardest—with the adjustments and everything." She smiled kindly. I wondered if it could be Prozac? Atavan? Morphine? What could possibly make these parents of five children so . . . happy?

Or could what they said be true? I headed back toward the studio, walking slowly and thinking as hard as I could (which I have to admit isn't very hard of late). How could those people, with their newborn twins and whiny preschoolers look at me, the mother of one fairly content baby, with pity? Was the transition to mommyhood really harder than feeding five screaming mouths? And if it was, didn't that make sense of my mood swings, my flubby body, my stinky marriage and my crush on my yoga teacher?

I walked back into the studio feeling a bit better, like the world—my world—made much more sense. Like maybe I wasn't just a bitter, resentful, irritable, fickle person. Maybe I was just a new mother. Apparently, they're the same thing.

*　*　*

Oliver and I sat down at Moonstar Café, which for Clarkville feels like a visit to Woodstock. All the alternative people for miles and miles around come out of the woodwork and congregate at Moonstar, where the ceiling is painted with stars and moons and planets, and they serve vegan fare with a capital V. It's the kind of place people who do yoga go to. Somehow, and the thought gave me chills, I'd become one of those alternative people. I'd never liked Clarkville's supersuburban, pearls-and-plaid attitude, but then I'd also never gone to all-night naked drum events during the Solstice. I guess I was somewhere in between.

Oliver fit in perfectly. He sat across from me drinking a fruit smoothie. I tried not to think about how handsome he looked or how he had touched my cheek. I tried not to think about my pulse racing or the fact that my hands had gone as clammy as a fifteen-year-old boy's at the school dance, which they have a habit of doing at such moments.

"This is nice," I said awkwardly.

"I love it here," he said.

"I haven't had much time for cafés lately, although Zach is pretty good when we go out to eat."

"That's your son, right?" I nodded. "He must be good company."

"If you're into nonverbal communication." He chuckled.

I checked my watch. I began to tap my toes with anxiety. "Are you single?" I blurted out. Oliver laughed.

"I'm sorry. I've never been one for tact. Everyone tells me I should try not to say everything I think." Of course, I already knew he wasn't married; I wanted to know how *un*-married he was.

"Honesty is just fine with me," he said smoothly. I watched his full lips move as he spoke. "And yes."

"What do you mean 'yes'?"

"I mean, yes, I'm single."

"You're kidding!"

He laughed with delight. "Do I seem taken to you?"

I looked him over again. He'd put on a pair of khaki shorts and a blue button-down shirt. What, exactly, does a man who's seeing someone look like? Tired? Frumpy? Not trying very hard?

"Oh, God. I'm so ridiculous. You've got to forgive me. I've been having quite a year. And lately I haven't slept at all. I don't mean to be so silly, really. Or rude. Or both, depending on which you think I've been."

"You're adorable," he said, in his way, almost like a purr. "I take it as a compliment. I'm not bothered at all."

"Really?"

"Really."

Probably because you get asked that all the time is what I didn't say. "I love your class" is what I said, steering gently away from the danger zone, a.k.a. shameless flirting. What would I say next if we stayed on the topic of his sexual status? _Drop your pants now?_ I've never been known for subtlety, and motherhood hadn't done anything to improve my social graces.

"Thank you. Yoga is such a powerful practice. It really changed my life. I love being able to teach it. It beats my day job too." He laughed again. Whenever he laughed, his face opened up, yes, like a flower. I wouldn't say it if it weren't true.

"Oh. What's your day job?"

"I'm a carpenter."

"Oh." Immediately I began to sing _If I were a carpenter and you were a lady_ ... in my head. I'd never slept with a carpenter before. "Oh, dear," I said, to stop my evil thoughts. "What time is it? I probably should go home. I've got a son and a husband waiting for me." I put the emphasis on husband since I had the distinct impression that despite my state of terminal postmortem uncouthness, and my vain attempt not to, I *was* flirting with my yoga teacher.

"Of course." Oliver stood up with me. "I'll take this to go," he said of his smoothie. "Then I can walk with you."

He wasn't much taller than me, or at least not as tall as Drew. He strolled beside me easily. We walked for a while without speaking. Frankly, I couldn't speak. When we got to the studio, I fiddled in my bag for my keys and made a huge production of taking my cell phone out of my bag, just so he would know I really did have people to call, people who were waiting.

I'm not a romantic. I can't stand love songs. I don't like flowers, although I wouldn't refuse a box of chocolates even if it were given on a Hallmark occasion. Drew and I never spent hours looking into each other's eyes. For that matter, neither did Jake and I. I've always found intimacy a little bit questionable, like bad wine. So you can imagine how it felt when Oliver and I stood there for the longest time (okay, about sixty seconds, but when you are standing, looking at someone, saying nothing, seconds morph into an hour each), simply looking at each other. A smile crept over his face. I wanted him to touch me more than I wanted anything—more than I wanted my pre-baby freedom, my pre-baby body. I wanted him to wrap his arms around me and kiss me.

Father figure, father figure, father figure, I told myself as I headed home. That's all. Nothing more.

* * *

The third significant event of the day went something like this.

A stout, older man in a leather coat (very John Travolta *Saturday Night Fever* if you ask me) took the crosswalk in front of me on Main Street, seconds after I'd left Oliver. When he turned and waved at me, it took me about a minute to figure out what had happened. He was waving so spasmodically, I worried that perhaps I'd hit him somehow. Then I realized just who I was dealing with. Donny Macnamara himself. Mr. "Live Bigger than Big."

"Hey, Joy," he said, coming over to the car. "So good to see you. Where's my little grandson?"

I avoided slapping him on the basis of total presumption—Zach isn't his grandson, at the very least not *yet*—and smiled instead. "Hi, Donny. How are you?"

"Fantastic. Really great. On top of the world."

"Really? What's going on?" A car beeped behind us.

"Just being in love," he said. He had a tendency to remind me of this fact every time we met. This just deepened my suspicion.

"Yes, you've said that. Listen, I better get moving. But you know, I was thinking. I'd love to have a coaching session with you."

"You would?" There he went again, looking worried. I knew I had him.

"I'll call your office if that's okay?"

"Oh, okay," he faltered. I felt minutes away from triumph. "Talk to you soon."

I waved as I peeled away. He looked small in my rearview mirror and altogether harmless. But that's just what small objects look like, from far away, reflected in a mirror.

* * *

That night, after a very messy supper with Zach, who'd taken to throwing his food over his head, smearing it in his hair and breaking into hysterics of joy, I climbed into bed feeling like I deserved the scarlet letter on my chest. Drew hadn't asked why I'd come home late from class, and I hadn't told him, other than to say that I'd stayed to talk a little with my yoga teacher. He knew about Oliver, enough to know who I meant when I talked about him. So I crawled into bed feeling like the scum on the bottom of our bathtub (which no one had bothered to clean in quite some time), because now I really was keeping secrets from my husband.

Maybe it's time to admit to myself and anyone else who cares that I have a few problems with men. I didn't think I did, but it seems like I officially fall into that category. I'm going to have to head for the self-help section the next time I hit the bookstore so I can learn about women like me. In the meantime, I can't think of anything except Oliver—the color of his eyes, his warm face, what his trim beard would feel like against my cheek, how much I love to hear his voice and how whenever I set eyes on him I can only think of one thing: what his strong, healthy body would feel like against mine.

While I lay in bed sinking in my own corruption, guilt and fantasy, my husband, the actual man in my life, came into the room. He sat on the bed and proceeded to reach out and touch me. He put his hand on my shoulder and squeezed. It got my attention; being squeezed is a lot better than being patted.

"You know, Joy," he said in a husky voice, "I do love you. I don't want to lose you."

A suspended silence filled the room. Life wasn't so bad

with us, really, was it? A few bumps here and there, a few necessary apologies. Now that we'd gotten over Drew's labor desertion, everything would be fine, wouldn't it? Isn't that what Aunt Hilda promised? Why, then, did I close my eyes and think of other men? Three to be exact. Oliver, first. Then Jake. And finally, as he grunted beside me, Zach. The only man I was sleeping with and the true love of my life.

Eighteen

THE NEXT MORNING, A SUNDAY, I WOKE TO THE SOUNDS of Drew rustling through his closet. I rolled over to see him putting on a work shirt.

"We're having a breakfast meeting this morning."

"Who's we? And why on a Sunday? Zach and I want to spend time with you."

"I'm sorry," he said, pulling on a pair of khakis. "You know how it is at Clarkville. The meeting's already planned. There wasn't any time all week for us to get together—Sharon, Russ and Mike." Sharon is the assistant head of school, a terrifying six-foot-tall woman with a crew cut. She'd be the perfect lesbian if she weren't married to Morris, a small Jewish man with a lisp. Russ is the academic dean and Mike is the head of athletics. They've all been at Clarkville for years.

"What's the big secret?" Zach still slept beside me in the bed. Since he spent so much time nursing through the night, he'd taken to sleeping in most mornings until at least eight. "Planning a coup?"

"I've told you a hundred times by now."

"You have?" I searched the vacant in-box in my memory. Whoops. There goes the sieve again, losing things. "I guess I haven't been paying attention."

He looked at me with a touch of irritation. "Like I told you before, we've had a gang of kids causing problems; we've already had four parent calls this year, and we haven't been in session two months." Parent calls aren't when the parents call the school, they're when the school calls the parents. Drew usually had to do the ugly deed, and it was ugly. Bambi and Happy and Marigold and all the rest of the rich, spoiled, disinterested mothers do not want to hear that their sons are drinking and doing drugs on the campus. They just want Drew to do something about it. "I'm really worried about this one guy, Caleb. He reminds me of myself. Doesn't come from money. He's on a full scholarship, but he wants in with these guys so much, and he just doesn't have the system to handle it." Drew shook his head. He looked truly worried.

"I'm sorry," I said, feeling like a complete lame ass. I hadn't remembered him telling me anything specific about the school recently. Of course I knew all the usual stuff, the pressure from the parents, the pressure from the media. He had to make the place look not just good but perfect. After all, he had a few senators' sons.

Oh, to have the life of the rich and famous.

"See you later?" I asked. I reached over and brushed my hand against the sleeve of his jacket. Didn't I love him? Jake may be the one real love I had who got away, Oliver, the sexiest thing under the sun, but Drew was the man I'd promised my life to—and I'd been totally sober when I did it so I must have known what I was doing. Why then hadn't I responded to him the night before?

"I'll be back in a few hours." He walked to the door and

pulled it swiftly closed behind him; the sound woke Zach. It made me laugh. For a moment, I'd forgotten I was a mother. Silly me.

The Big Day, December 22 to be exact, was fast approaching, and my mother, the great goddess of fashion, she who wears no wrong, had still not found herself a wedding dress. She didn't know about my upcoming coaching date with Donny, but I had it in mind to tip her off on our next dress-seeking expedition. She called me on Monday in a desperate state of panic while I was having a food fight with Zach. I'd figured, if you can't beat 'em, join 'em could be my new parenting method. Zach and I took turns smearing sweet potato mush into his hair. It was actually giving me a good break from my serious life. Until the emergency call came from the matriarch herself. She needed me, and she needed me fast. There was hardly time to explain. "Bring the baby," she said as she hung up. As if I wouldn't, as if I'd just leave him at home watching Baby Einstein videos.

We met at Copa, Copa, a woman's bridal shop in Stamford. Copa, Copa is the kind of place only my mother could uncover. It's a warehouse building with more dresses than Imelda Marcus had shoes. It's been around a hundred million years, yet no one knows about it. My mother heard about it from Aunt Hilda (who's still shacking up with her in the city—"Thank God for my four bedrooms," my mother says), and now it will become the hottest place for wedding dresses. That's the kind of influence my mother has. Apparently Aunt Hilda bought her prom dress there all those eons ago. My mother also informed me that Aunt Hilda still has—and still wears—this exact dress. "At least she's kept her figure," she said.

For once, my mother looked like an average person. She was wearing jeans—designer, but they're still jeans—and a white button-down shirt. Despite the fact that she'd done her eyelashes à la Tammy Faye, she looked a touch disheveled. I love the woman, but it gave me a great deal of pleasure to see her looking so . . . realistic.

"You've joined the human race," I said.

"You're such a joy, my Joy," she said kissing me. "Hello, sweetie pea," she said, kissing Zach on the top of his head. I'd put him in his front carrier so he could help make the selection. I'd noticed he had very good taste in clothing. Whenever I asked him what I should wear, I swear he said the baby version of "sweatpants," which sounds something like "swopoot."

"You've got to help your mommy. She's getting desperate," my mother said as we both looked in horror at the sea of dresses in front of us. Right at that moment, a woman appeared from nowhere. She must have been about four feet tall and three hundred and seven years old. She looked exactly like a troll.

"Who's the bride?" she said, with a thick Polish accent. She looked from me, with baby attached, to my mother, with an expression of bewilderment.

"I am," my mother said proudly.

"Ah-ha. I'm Mary." At that moment, another woman appeared from the darkness. She was rotund, about three inches taller than the other woman, with short white hair and cheeks she must have stolen directly from Santa Claus.

"I'm Mary," the slightly taller woman said. "Which of you is the bride?"

"I am," my mother said again, this time with a little less enthusiasm.

I'd begun to think we'd entered the twilight zone. It's not just a movie, you know. It can really happen. Like when you go shopping at an upscale, unheard-of bridal barn.

"This is my mother, Mary," the younger Mary said.

"I've told them," the older Mary said stiffly. "Come with me," she barked at my mother. We made a train and followed her to an aisle filled with smart white suits.

"How many times you marry?" she asked my mother.

"Three."

"This your third?" Mary said.

"Fourth," my mother said.

The older Mary shook her head and made that small *tsk*-ing sound I thought only school teachers were allowed to make. My mother turned and whispered in my ear: "I got it directly from Aunt Hilda that these women are worth every bit of suffering they put you through."

I raised my eyebrows. "How old can they be?" I whispered. Then I turned to them and said, as kindly as possible, "Do you mind if we just take a look ourselves?"

Mary the junior caught up with us, huffing and puffing as if she'd climbed Mount Everest.

"They don't want our help," the older Mary said to her, looking very cross indeed.

"Actually," I said. "We'd just like to look around first, by ourselves. Then we'll come and find you. Or," I said, feeling extremely powerful given the extra foot I had on them, "we could go somewhere else."

"Of course you can look around," the young Mary said. She took her mother gently by the elbow and walked her away.

"They don't like us," my mother said.

"We don't like them," I said.

"I'm about to give up," my mother said. "You've got to be on your best behavior. They're my last hope."

"Don't give up yet. We haven't even started looking."

For a moment, my mother looked tired. I didn't see her looking that way very often. She'd looked tired for many years after my father died, but then I suppose she was. Later, with the kids and Danny and work, she'd stayed invigorated.

"Is something wrong?" I asked her. Maybe it was Donny. Maybe he'd finally revealed his true identity. "It isn't Donny, is it? You know, I saw him the other day."

"Oh, no." She brightened. "I'm just a little overwhelmed. I want to do this one right, sweetie. I want you to have a good Grandpa," she said to Zach, rubbing her nose against his.

"Oh, Mom." She turned away from me, scanning the rows of dresses. "About Donny being Grandpa..."

"Yes, honey."

"I guess I don't feel like I know him very well. You two haven't been dating for long. Do you feel like you know him? I mean, what is his work, anyway? You said he was an artist—"

"He does all kinds of things," she said, her head stuck between two lilac patterned gowns. "He's mostly retired."

"I've been to his office in town," I said defensively.

"Oh." She pulled a dress out, a purple polka-dotted dress. "That's nice. What do you think of this?"

"It's for a six-year-old. On Halloween. I wouldn't let you be caught dead in it." My mother giggled. "I worry about you."

"Don't worry about me, sweets. I'm fantastic. I feel like a new woman. You know how love makes you feel."

"That's my point, though. How can you really trust that feeling, or for that matter trust someone you don't know very well?" My mother carefully placed the dress back on the rack, smoothing down its satin, ruffled front. I could see her lips purse.

"How do we trust anything?" she said. She turned and looked directly at me. I couldn't make out her expression; anger or simply tiredness crossed her face quickly. My mother isn't one for battles. "Life leads us on, doesn't it?"

"But Donny—"

"Is a blessing. I didn't think I'd find this again, Joy."

"I just wonder—"

"I'm not so sure I want your exact opinion, sweetie," she said with an altogether not-sweetie tone. "Given your track record."

"I was young. My father died. You've got to cut me a little slack."

"What about this?" She pulled out a little pink number. I shook my head. "Give me your help. Show me what you like." She took my hand and gently pulled it as she walked through the aisle, a gentle way of ending the conversation. If I didn't love her so much, I would have been pretty upset with her evasive little ways. I had my backup plan, though. Once I confirmed what I knew with Donny, I'd talk to her again. She wouldn't be able to argue with the facts.

I thought my own life had become a terrifying place to be, filled with sleepless nights and 3 a.m. feedings, marital spats and intrigue. That is, until I turned on the television the other night while Drew was giving Zach a bath (his new thing—he actually *volunteered* for the job) and saw something no person should ever have to witness: a woman who'd given birth to sixteen children and, AND, was pregnant again.

Okay, so maybe I'm not the most open-minded person in

the entire world, and compared to Gandhi I'm a little judgmental, and lately I haven't been the best sort of person one could ever hope to be in the world. Given those circumstances, it seems like I shouldn't throw stones. In that case, I'll be as nice as possible when I say, maybe, and this is just a suggestion, anyone who has more than ten children should be sent to the mental ward or, at the very least, get daily counseling. I know I said I didn't think much of counseling, but then desperate times call for desperate measures.

In the first place, when does this woman have time to complain? She's got to be so busy, she may not even have time to think for herself, let alone shit or read or eat a box of chocolates. How do you even get seventeen children? Did they miss the class in sex ed? Did they get my mother's definition? Is she having a lot of deep communion with the stork?

In the second place, what can birth possibly be like for her? Wouldn't those babies just fall out? Or is she like the Grand Kegeling Master of All Time, with vaginal muscles that could core an apple? I shudder to think of it. I winced just watching the show. It didn't say whether she'd breastfed these sixteen children, but if she did, how long are those nipples? Do her breasts look like aging cow udders? And when do those two find time to have sex?

I think bodies should come with warning labels. Honestly. It takes about ten seconds to conceive a child. Ten seconds of pure pleasure. But a kid lasts for a really long time. They aren't like the cans you buy at the grocery store. They don't ever expire. If I'd had anything to do with this, I would have made sure that sex lasted at least as long as the time it takes to raise a toddler—just to balance things out. That way, you get to have an orgasm for a few years, then you raise a kid for a few years. Doesn't that seem fair?

I instantly had to call Diana to share my disgust and amazement. I hadn't seen her since our recent I'll-Come-to-Your-House-So-You-Can-Sleep date.

"I can't imagine," she said weakly. "I can barely do one."

"It's so hard. It's so much harder than anyone tells you it will be. And no one remembers! I ask mothers of older children how they did it, and they can't recall anything."

"I know. I know. But it's worth it, right?"

"Of course it's worth it. Or it will be, anyway, when we're old ladies in a retirement home and they're taking care of us. Speaking of old people, did I tell you I have an appointment with Donny next week?"

"No. Wow. You're really getting in to this."

"I have to. It's my mother. I have to know. Maybe, just maybe, there's some plausible explanation for all the stuff I've discovered, but I doubt it. I can't just let her marry some freak."

"You're a good daughter," she said. "And a good friend."

"I don't feel like a good anything lately. Everything is still so chaotic. You think once the baby is three months, it will get better, or six months, but they're eight months now, right? And I'm still not sleeping through the night. I don't think I've slept for more than five hours in a row since giving birth."

"It's the cumulative effect of the sleep loss that really does it."

"You said it. I try to explain that to other people who aren't actively mothering small children—they don't get it. One bad night is one thing. Eight months of bad nights is Guantanamo Bay torture. It messes with your coping methods."

"How is Jake, by the way?" she said.

"Very funny. He hardly qualifies as a coping mechanism. We're just emailing. We're *friends*. I've been friends with him forever, we'd just fallen out of touch. The reunion brought us together again. He's been emailing Drew too."

"Really?"

"Yup. So it doesn't mean anything. Now, Oliver is a different story."

"What happened?"

"He's definitely a coping method. He's like a sex god. I am so totally lusting after him it's embarrassing, and I think he feels bad for me or something. He was very nice to me the other day. Maybe he feels fatherly toward me."

"I shouldn't be hard on you," Diana said. "I've got my own bad habit."

"You? It's not possible. You're practically a saint."

"I can't turn off HGTV. I'm obsessed. I think I'm going to have our kitchen redone. And our bathroom. And the bedroom."

"That's hardly the same as emailing your old boyfriend."

"I have bought a few things."

"A few things?"

"A few thousands and thousands worth of things," she squeaked.

"Diana!" I was totally shocked and selfishly pleased. What a relief not to be the only crazy person in Clarkville.

Before Drew got home from his series of meetings, I set Zach in his Exersaucer and checked my email feeling like a horrible failure of a mother the whole time. I mean, I should have been looking at *him*, not the computer. His babyhood was happening right in front of my eyes, and here I couldn't take my eyes off some glowing screen. I cannot defend this sort of behavior. All I can say is, if you want to know how selfish you actually are, have a baby.

To: jakephilips@lunerpress.com
From: jmcguire@fanfare.com
I'm so glad to know that you still tell the "tree story." I haven't climbed a tree in the longest time. I'm sure I will again—once Zach starts doing it. And what's this business of my being the "the funniest woman around"? I hadn't heard that one before. Now you, on the other hand, had a campus-wide reputation: varsity lacrosse, swim team, starring role in every student-directed one-act play. I was just your shadow. But hey, I'm sure enjoying remembering how things used to be.

   BTW I've got an appointment with my mother's beau soon. I'm going to pick his brains, get some confirmation before I break the news to her. Internet evidence seems a little shaky. I'd like to have some indisputable facts to present to her. She won't take it well, though. I'm sure of that. But who would? Let me know if you discover anything else. But what else could there be? I guess he could be an illegal immigrant looking for a green card too. Nothing would surprise me after all this. Joy.

I sent the email off and then I sat around, staring at the screen, until his reply popped up. Every now and then I shook a toy in Zach's face.

To: jmcguire@fanfare.com
From: jakephilips@lunerpress.com
Right, I did things for me in college and you did things

*for other people. You were the volunteer Queen of the
universe. Weren't you a member of every club the college
had? I distinctly remember going to pick you up every
Thursday evening from Sunnyside LongTerm Care.
What did you do with all those old ladies?*

    *Don't be too hard on your mother. Maybe she's got a
thing for new-age men; she wouldn't be the first. There's
a lot we don't know about other people, especially family
members, especially mothers. You're a mother now. You
should know that.*

    *Still thinking of my visit to the States. Can I come see
you if I do?? —J*

Could he come see me? Shit, yes. God, yes. Please, yes.
Come see me. Pull me out of this chaos. Be my knight in shining armor. Take me on your white horse—

An explosive poop startled me from my daydreaming.
Zach glowed with pride.

"Oh, right. Mommy's got cloth-diaper poop duty. So
much for white horses." It was a good one too. I rinsed it out
in the sink for about ten minutes, bouncing Zach on my hip
and singing "Row, Row, Row Your Boat," in operatic alto to
keep him from crying.

That night Drew climbed into bed looking glum and serious
as ever.

"Not in the guest room tonight?"

"Thought I'd give this a go. I miss you."

"Guess what I saw on TV?" I said before his head hit the
pillow.

"The second coming," he said.

"Wow, honey, that's pretty funny. You're making a lot of jokes these days." He shot me a look.

"Aren't you at all curious?"

"Okay, I'm game," he said, putting down the newspaper he'd brought in with him. "What did you see?"

"A woman who's about to give birth to her seventeenth child. What do you think of that? You think we have it rough, imagine feeding sixteen hungry mouths. How much do you think she spends at the grocery store? Do you think they need to drive a school bus? I guess they don't worry about over-population either." This is one of Drew's biggest pet peeves. We've had many a conversation about the virtues of birth control.

"Here we go again."

"What?"

"Joy McGuire, critic at large. She's got an opinion about everything."

"Oh, come on, Drew. Are you honestly going to tell me you think it's normal to have that many children?"

"No. I'm honestly going to tell you it's none of your business."

"I thought you were an environmentalist."

"I am. I still think it's none of your business."

"You're being serious, aren't you? You used to love to talk like this about world events and local news. You used to cut out interesting articles for me from the paper, remember? So we could talk about them? You liked my criticism. You thought it was funny."

"Everyone has the right to try to live the best they know how. We all also have the right to make mistakes," he said seriously.

"Speaking from personal experience?"

268 □ *Samantha Wilde*

"As a matter of fact," he said, "I am. I have to reserve judgments on the kids I work with. If I judged them superficially, I wouldn't be able to help them. And who knows? Maybe those people are happy."

"When did you become such a wet blanket? It's not like I'm going to the woman's hospital and gunning down her doctor for allowing her to have so many children. I just wanted to talk about it. We used to have fun dishing on other people. And anyway, it's human nature to judge. I don't know anyone who doesn't judge. It's not as though my thoughts about them can hurt them. It's just talk."

He picked up his paper again. This was certainly not how life used to be. Life with us used to consist of enjoyable arguments full of sparring. We had fun talking. At least I remember that once upon a time we did. We'd already lost the sexual part of our marriage. If we lost the friendship, what would be left?

"Are you saying you want seventeen children?" I said, hoping to entice him back to a debate with me.

"Don't be crazy, Joy."

"Just curious. You seem to think it's a great way to live..."

"I don't think it's a great way to live. I just don't think it's fair to judge other people for their decisions. We don't know them. We don't know what's happened to them. We don't know anything. Most people have pretty good reasons for what they do."

"Even the big oil companies and the logging companies?"

There was a long silence.

"Got ya," I said, just before I turned off the light on my bedside table. I could see a hint of a smile on his face as I did it.

nineteen

"TODAY, I WANT YOU TO BRING SOMEONE YOU KNOW into your heart. Someone you're having problems with, someone who irritates or upsets you. I want you to see them sitting in the center of your heart." Oliver sat on his mat with his eyes closed and his two hands clasped over his heart. I kept one eye open so I could watch his face move, his mouth move.

"As you practice today, keep this person in your heart, so they can receive all the benefits of your practice, as if they were here with you."

I was having a hard time with his instructions. First, because I kept imagining what it would be like to kiss him, and second, because I couldn't choose just one person. I put Drew in my heart, but it didn't feel right. Then I put Priscilla in, but she didn't quite fit. I put the grocery store clerk in, whom I had continued to resent and avoid. Finally, I decided to put in my fourth-grade teacher, Lily Feinberg, who had always treated me poorly. She'd mess up my name all the time, calling me Jess and Jen. It's not like Joy is that hard to remember.

I figured the trauma she caused me was far enough away that I wouldn't explode if I inserted her into my heart.

"Our practice is for ourselves," Oliver said. "But it is also for all beings everywhere, because the truth is, on a fundamental level, we are all one."

I closed both of my eyes and took a deep breath with the class. If anyone else were up there saying such ridiculous things, I would have left a long time ago. I know for a fact I am not one with Lily Feinberg; I heard recently that she died. Can I be one with a dead person? I also know I am not one with Drew. If you are one with your husband, that means you connect. Our cold war was over, but I hardly felt united with him in any sense of the word. I wouldn't mind, however, being one with Oliver. I kept getting an image of this at-oneness, which entailed a partly naked Oliver pressing me up against the yoga wall. When I opened my eyes to peek at him, he was looking directly at me. He smiled. And I smiled back. I felt like the cat who'd eaten the canary.

I'd promised I'd meet my mother after yoga for tea and a final trip to Copa, Copa, where she would have a fitting with the two miserable, miracle-working Marys, as we'd come to call them—miracle-working because they claimed to have found the perfect dress for my mother. Zach, meanwhile, had developed a talent for screaming in public. It seemed like he'd gone from being a relatively normal infant, to a demented hyena with sensory integration problems. I wasn't so sure I wanted my hyena around the two Marys. It's possible, given their temperaments, Zach could get us thrown out. I needed a babysitter.

Drew had watched Zach during my morning yoga class,

but he had another round of meetings, this time with parents, in the afternoon. Diana had gone to visit her parents in Rhode Island; Priscilla had her basketweaving class (thank God almighty. I prayed she would make friends!). I called Melody and asked her if she could watch Zach the virtuoso for a few hours. They were skipping mommy-baby yoga that day so it would work perfectly. Baby Sarah had continued to be the world's best infant. She'd been sleeping twelve hours every night for four months and generally acted like a super laid-back Rastafarian child whose mommy had smoked too much ganja during pregnancy. Lucky Melody.

When I arrived at Melody's country estate—I call it that because it has a pond, two barns, a three-bedroom guest cottage, *and* the house that they live in—Melody was in the kitchen feeding Sarah some tofu.

"Hey, old friend," she said. "Long time no see."

"Sorry," I said. "I spend so much time keeping men at bay."

"Oh, really? Spill the beans." She came over and hugged me. I put Zach down on the floor.

"Is your floor clean enough for a baby?" I asked.

"Clean enough for my baby." Sarah smiled at Zach, who immediately crawled over to her high chair.

"Drew's a clean-floor fanatic."

"Really? I never knew that."

"Yeah. He thinks the floor should be washed every day with hot water and disinfecting soap—for the baby's health."

"Do you wash it every day?"

"No," I said, grinning. "But I leave out the bucket and mop so it looks like I do."

"That's terrible, Joy!"

"And I spray the kitchen with Lysol so it smells clean." I couldn't help but laugh at my own wicked ways. They gave me a tremendous amount of satisfaction. It was almost as good as eating chocolate. "He'll never know," I said. "And it doesn't actually make any difference. I mean, it's not like Zach's getting TB from my kitchen floor."

"You wily coyote," Melody said.

"How's life in Happyville with you and Eric?"

"It's okay." She took out a container of yogurt from the fridge. "You want this, baby?" she said to Sarah. "A little tiring. Are you trying to dodge the issue? I want to know about these men you're keeping at bay."

"Nothing. Just a crush."

"Oh, dear. Not Oliver."

"Yes. Oliver. I want his body. And strangely enough, I feel like he wants mine." She raised her eyebrows. "Don't worry. Nothing's going to happen. He's my yoga teacher, after all."

"Well, you might like to know what I heard." She smiled coyly.

"What did you hear?" I practically jumped out of my pants with excitement.

"A rumor going around the studio. But you wouldn't want to hear gossip, would you? A good upstanding citizen like you?"

"Oh, give me a break. I practically invented gossip."

"Okay then." She messed a bit with Sarah in her high chair. Just to keep me waiting, I'm sure.

"Come on!"

"He had an affair with a student."

"*No!*"

"Yes."

"Wow. Okay, I *so* want him."

"You said that already."

"Well, it's even truer now." Melody put her hands on her

hips. "You don't think it would really happen, do you? I'm a frumpy mommy, for heaven's sake. He probably had an affair with a twenty-year-old. I bet they had sex while doing the splits. Yoga postures must come in really handy then."

"Even better than that. Word is that he likes mommies. The word is he had an *affair* with a mommy. Easy prey and all that."

"Not Oliver! He's spiritual."

"Right, honey. Don't let the lingo fool you. A man on a yoga mat is still a man."

"I can't believe it. I mean, I can believe that he had an affair. He isn't married or even dating—he told me himself—so what does it matter?"

"Just be careful, that's all."

"I'm a married woman! It's only a fantasy. It's like eating chocolate and reading a good novel. It's filling a need. I would never do anything. I've got Drew."

"How is it with you two these days?"

"Better, not the best. Thanks to Aunt Hilda terrifying me into forgiving him. I'm beginning to think like Drew and wonder if my mother didn't put her up to it. That's the sort of thing she would do. Still, things have improved since we made up about the birth, only now, in the absence of all that fighting, there's simply a void. I don't feel in love with him. He's like a roommate. It's like living with a brother. But my marriage is so boring. Tell me about yours."

"Eric and I had a big fight the other day about when to have the next baby."

"You did?"

"Look at you! You're licking your chops! You're enjoying this!"

"Sorry." I tried to look bashful.

"Anyhow. He wants to wait. He wants to wait and see. But he doesn't know what he's waiting for. It infuriates me."

"I had no idea."

"Like I said," Melody said. "You just *think* no one else has problems. You think you're the only one who's got it hard. But it's hard, the whole thing, parenthood, marriage. We all go through our trials." She'd been spooning mouthful after mouthful of yogurt into Sarah's mouth. Sarah ate quickly. Maybe she thought Zach would snatch it away from her.

"You really want another baby?"

"Of course. I want a sibling for Sarah. And I've always thought it would be more fun to have a few kids and have them closer together. That way we can all do things together. They'll be into the same stuff at the same time."

"I'm so tired I can't even think about having another baby."

"Once you get sleep, it'll get better. Sarah's such a good sleeper. Aren't you, baby?" She wiped Sarah's face and pulled her out of her chair. At eleven months, she was a good inch taller than Zach, and much more agile, though Zach could beat her in a crawling race any day.

"I should go. I don't want to be late for my mother." I went over and hugged Melody again. "Thanks so much for doing this."

"My pleasure. It'll be good practice for whenever number two comes along."

"Hang in there."

"You hang in there too, Joy. We're all going to make it out alive."

What I wanted to say to Melody, but didn't, is that we don't all make it out alive, except that doesn't seem like a very friendly thing to say. Also, she's a therapist, so she might actually know more than I do. She might know that we're all going to make it out alive. The only trouble is, we die. I've known that for a long time. Maybe it's a morbid thing to say, in which case, dress me in black and give me a supporting role in the next *Addams Family* movie. As far as I can tell, people die. They don't make it out of their lives alive. Their lives kill them. One way or the other.

Okay, so that might qualify as slightly depressive thinking and normally I don't get into that. When my father died, it was early June. I'd been eight for almost half a year, and I knew it, because I liked celebrating my half birthday. My father had been a consummate gardener. He excelled at growing beautiful tomatoes in the backyard and filling the perennial beds with flowers that bloom in perfect rhythm with one another, creating a garden where something is blooming every week of the summer.

After he died, no one tended his garden. Once or twice I went out to weed, like I'd done when he was alive. But it only made me cry. What amazed me, though, was that those flowers all kept growing anyhow. They came up and bloomed just the same. It took years for the vines and weeds and grasses to completely overcome the hibiscus, the lilies, the beautiful purple butterfly bush.

My mother and I spent our tea discussing the exact order of events for her big night. The ceremony would take place at 5 p.m., followed by a cocktail hour, followed by dinner at 7, with dancing until midnight to a band she'd paid to have flown up from Houston. Despite my mother's fortune, she wasn't a spendthrift. Apparently, this act of extravagance was a gift for Donny. Donny loved country music. Help! is all I can say. Help me knock some sense into this mother of mine.

When we arrived at Copa, Copa, Mary the elder greeted us with a cross face and a curt nod. We followed her like two puppies after their mother. She led us back to the changing room. "On with the dress," she said. My mother rolled her eyes at me. Secretly, she'd confided that she liked Mary the elder because she reminded her of my father's grandmother, Nina.

"Was she that rude?" I'd asked her. I'd met Nina sometime before I learned how to control my bladder so naturally I don't remember her.

"She was a character," is all my mother said.

My mother slunk into the dressing room. After about five minutes, she emerged. She looked like a candle in that dark warehouse, like the only bright light those miserable Marys would ever see. The two Marys had uncovered a long golden gown for her with a matching cream and gold embroidered shawl.

"Mom, you look perfect." The dress gathered in gently at the waist. Since my mother had a waist the size of a chicken neck, the design fit exactly. She looked breathtaking. It almost made me wish I'd worn a wedding dress to my own wedding.

"Turn round," the old Mary barked, and my mother spun in a circle, then laughed, the way she does, like a child, like someone without a care in the world.

"You put on yours now," my mother said. I'd brought the green dress along so we could see them together and make sure they worked. If not, I suppose I would be headed down through the racks of dresses with Mother Mary in the lead, not something I would want to do while conscious.

I brought my plastic bag into the same dressing room and

shook out my dress. I slipped it over my head and gently tugged it down. And tugged it down. And tugged it down.

"Mom," I called.

"Come on out, sweets. Let's see."

"Mom," I said again, insistent, irritated.

"Don't be shy, honey. Let's see them together."

I groaned and opened the dressing room door to see the withered prune face of Mary the elder, and in the shadows Mary junior, looking displeased.

"Too tight!" the elder Mary squealed. "Where did you get that dress?"

"Oh, it fit when I got it," I said.

"Honey," my mother said. "We can have it let out. Maybe Mary could even do it." She looked winningly at Mary, who looked disgustedly at me.

"I don't know if it's possible." She came over and began pulling on the dress and pinching my waist.

"I knew I was getting fatter," I said to my mother.

"Are you having a baby?" Mary asked.

I looked down at her small white head. I wondered if we could bring her the gift of a Miss Manners book. Or did they not have etiquette in Poland?

"I just *had* a baby," I said angrily. "Don't you remember? He came with us the first time."

"Oh." She softened a bit. "How old?"

"Eight months," my mother exclaimed proudly.

The elder Mary raised her eyebrows and clucked her tongue.

"I like to eat," I said to her with disdain. "There's nothing wrong with that."

Nothing like sales clerks with attitudes. I could just see it now. Every bride in Manhattan would head to Copa, Copa in Stamford, Connecticut, for a taste of it. It's like fine dining. You only feel like you're getting your money's worth if the waiter has more attitude than you do.

Needless to say, this meeting put me in an entirely bad mood. If I didn't already feel so morbidly fat—which, by the way, for all my complaining, I am not—I would have gone and eaten a bag of M&M's. Instead, I stopped at the Moonstar Café on my way home for a chocolate chip cookie. What else could I do?

I didn't notice him at first. The place was full of people on laptops and women in black T-shirts and men with beards. I got my cookie and cup of tea and sat down alone to eat slowly and savor my last few minutes of freedom.

"So this is what you do when you're not in yoga," he said, all of a sudden next to me.

"It's you," I said, looking up at Oliver. He was wearing jeans, loafers, a dark red turtleneck. "Do you want to join me? I'm going to eat this cookie as fast as I can."

"Good idea." He sat down. I didn't know what to say to him. I am she who never lacks words, and yet over and over again Oliver left me speechless. Probably I should have been embarrassed. I should have been embarrassed to be a pudgy mommy eating a chocolate chip cookie in public while my son was being taken care of by someone else and my husband worked and the man whose clothes I wanted to rip off piece by piece looked at me . . . kindly, as if I wasn't a fat, cookie-eating, adulterous, evil mommy and bad wife.

"I think I have a problem," he said.

"Oh? Well, try me. I'll see what I can do."

"The thing is." He smiled, his dimple smile. "I think."

"Yes." He was making me very nervous. And aroused. Very aroused.

"I know that you're married?"

Oh, God, where was this going? "Yes. Quite married. Can't recommend it." I laughed. "No, seriously. I've been married for almost seven years. Drew's amazing. Head of Clarkville Academy. You know Clarkville?"

He nodded. "And there's Zach."

"Yes, indeed. Eight months ago I was giving birth. Not a pretty sight."

"No." He shook his head and tried to look serious but I could tell he was laughing. "I'd imagine it's got a bit of the gore. But life is a miracle. And women are the only ones to bring life in. That's an exceptional gift, isn't it?"

Was it? Okay, if he said so, I believed it. I would have believed anything he said. He could make perineum ripping sound sexy. Now, *that's* a real gift.

"I think I've got a bit of a crush on you." He looked sheepish while he said this. I must have looked incredulous. I started blithering away.

"Oh my goodness, I didn't expect that, I mean, I just lost some weight and then put it all back on and couldn't fit into my dress today when I tried it on. I'm the matron of honor, you know, at my mother's fourth wedding and she's marrying a man I'm afraid is going to steal all her money and desert her for some crazy utopian life-coaching we're-cheerful-all-the-time cult, but I love her so I'm trying not to interfere. I don't want to be interfering; my mother-in-law is the interfering one. She's trying to baptize Zach, that's my son, and he still isn't sleeping through the night, which means I haven't had a full night's sleep in a really long time so sometimes I mishear things, did you just say that you have a crush on me?"

He was grinning ear to ear. "Maybe I should put it another way. I want to kiss you."

"Oh. Like *that* kind of crush?" In a desperate act of awkwardness, I brought the last piece of cookie to my mouth. He stopped me just before it reached my lips. He reached across the table and put his hand on my hand. He took the cookie from me and he broke it into two pieces. He ate one. Then he took the other and fed it to me. My heart thudded like a stallion in an old Western. I got warm all over. When his thumb grazed my lip, I think I moaned. And for a moment the world stopped.

When the world started again, it brought me back to my son, back to my home, back to my husband, who wanted to know, since there was no dinner, should we just eat pizza, because he didn't mind. He was exhausted. The kids at school were wearing him out. He needed to talk about it. He needed to know if he was doing the right thing.

I sat on the toilet seat while he bathed Zach and listened to him go on and on about things I knew were important, but I had left myself behind. In my mind, I still sat at the café, across from Oliver, talking for hours and then, reaching toward him over the table, a kiss. A real kiss, the kind you see in the movies that reminds you of the very best moments in your life.

That's not what actually happened, not the kiss anyway. Of course not the kiss! I'm a decent married person. Instead, we talked. We talked about yoga and babies and marriage and life. Oliver, I found out, had just turned forty-four. He'd never been married, although he'd had two almost-ten-year relationships. He didn't mention any yoga student girlfriends, and neither did I. So what if he has the hots for suburban mothers? In fact, God bless him if he does. Maybe we aren't so bad after all. And how guilty did I feel, sitting there next to my husband who had no idea my yoga teacher had come on to me that very afternoon? Just the smallest bit, like a cookie crumb. After all, it's just a crush. A crush has nothing to do with reality. It's all hormones and fantasy and hope, right?

Twenty

DONNY'S OFFICE, AS I SAW IT ON TUESDAY, CONTRA-
dicted everything I'd assumed about the man. In the
first place, it was gorgeous. The possibility that Donny and I
could have the same taste in furniture simultaneously frightened me and comforted me. The whole feel of the waiting
room was ease and relaxation from the broad-back armchair
that I sank into immediately, to the long, deep-purple couch
piled with pillows. Whoever decorated the room didn't just
have taste, they had money, which led me to two conceivable
conclusions. First, that I somehow had it all wrong and
Donny actually did have money and managed to make an
enormous profit off the insecurities of the Clarkville popula-
tion, or second, that I was right and he was broke and had
earned his poverty by spending all his money carelessly on
things like ten-thousand-dollar couches.

I spied the bookshelf, in a dark wood finish. Since Donny
hadn't made an appearance yet, I set myself in front of the
books to see what I could uncover on my own. Self-help fa-
vorites from the past twenty years packed the shelves, each

with a more upbeat title than the one before; I could barely read them without feeling negative. There's nothing like someone trying to *make* you be positive to make *me* depressed. It just can't be real; no one can be happy all the time. And if you are happy all the time, how in the world can you possibly be *interesting*? If I didn't have problems, I probably wouldn't even talk. What would there be to talk about?

I waited another five minutes without hearing a single sound from the inner office. A door off the waiting room presumably led to the inner sanctum where, in just moments, I assumed, I would be on my way to "living bigger than big," by way of a few affirguestions.

Something in the corner of the room caught my eye, a piece of paper trapped underneath the edge of the sofa. I looked right and left before I crossed the room, either expecting traffic (unlikely) or because I knew, on some intuitive level, that getting caught searching under Donny's office couch wouldn't be the best way to start my coaching session.

I lay flat on my belly and reached my arm back toward the wall. I pulled out a hot pink flyer with the word "Pride" written in bold letters across the top and the image of a rainbow flag printed in the corner. Just at that moment, naturally, Donny appeared. Not from within his office, but from the hall door. He looked almost as mortified as I felt. I quickly returned the paper to its rightful place (back underneath the couch) and stood up.

"Donny," I said, for lack of a better explanation.

"Great to see you, Joy. This is so exciting." He reached out and pulled me into a bear hug. The feeling of his pot belly pressed against me forced a premature end to our warm embrace. God, what does my mother see in this man!

"So, coaching," I said.

"Where's the little man?"

"With a friend. We have a standing playdate on Tuesdays. Zach and her son Addicus are the same age. I trade baby-sitting time with her. She's going to get an extra long nap in return for today," I said.

Donny shook his head like he didn't quite understand—which I'm sure he didn't. Then he said, "Well, come on in." He unlocked the door to his office and led me into yet another delicious room, painted in a warm apricot with more gorgeous dark brown leather furniture. The rug shined with a golden ribbon threaded throughout. A small water fountain trickled in the corner of the room. He gestured for me to sit down in a cushioned rocking chair.

It was right about then that I began to feel ill. Had I finally been overcome with guilt for my spying, cheating ways? Did my conscience desperately want me to confess to Donny that I knew the truth about his business and his personal life?

"Tell me what led you to want a coaching session," he said, rather timidly I thought for someone interested in BIG living.

"Well, I guess I just wanted to see what you're all about."

"I'm afraid I won't be able to offer the best—" He stopped speaking abruptly and looked at me with concern. "Are you sweating?"

"Am I sweating?" I reached up and felt two lines of sweat dripping off my cheeks. "I guess I am. Is it hot in here?"

"Not so hot. Are you okay?"

"I don't know. All of a sudden I don't feel well." I pulled my sleeves up to reveal goose bumps. "Now I'm cold."

"You must be sick."

"I can't be sick. Or anyway I wasn't sick. Before I got here." It was happening then, some cosmic punishment for being an awful person.

"You must have a fever." Donny got up and walked out of the room without another word. When he returned he had a thermometer in his hand. "Here. I've cleaned it."

"Thank you. Where did it come from?"

"I have a first-aid kit in the bathroom."

"Oh."

"I like to be prepared." He sat down again, leaning forward on his stubby legs, as if he couldn't wait to find out the results.

"Here goes." I inserted the thermometer. We sat together in a deeply awkward silence waiting for the beep. I couldn't speak, obviously, and he clearly didn't know what to say. He jiggled his knee nervously. Either I make him nervous, or he's as guilty as I am. And since I haven't made anyone nervous in the past decade with my benign suburban existence, I had to assume it was the latter.

"Oh." I read the numbers. "I've got a fever of 103."

"Wow. That's high."

"I can't believe I'm really sick."

"Let me help you get home. Or maybe you should visit your doctor. Who's your primary?"

"Mullins."

"Do you have his number?"

"On my cell phone." I took it out of my bag.

"I'll call 'em," he drawled, taking the phone from me.

"No, really. That's okay." I stood up, reached for the phone, felt faint, then sat down. "I can't be sick. I wasn't sick five minutes ago." Then it occurred to me that Donny might have poisoned me somehow. Maybe he'd figured out what I knew; maybe he intended to get me out of the picture so he could have his way with my mother. It could happen, couldn't it? It happens all the time on television. Or maybe I was hallucinating on account of my fever. I could almost see a glint in his eye, a look of satisfaction. But then it dawned on me that I hadn't drunk anything he poured or inhaled any mysterious aromas. Maybe he'd sprayed a secret, poisonous spray into the room, and that's why he came in late for the appointment, so that only I would breathe it?

While my mind raced through all of these totally plausible explanations for my illness, Donny scrolled down my phone's call list. From my sweaty stupor I heard him requesting an urgent sick visit and I realized I really *didn't* have the energy to do it myself.

"Go on over," he said. "Oh, no, maybe I should drive you. Do you think you can drive? No, you shouldn't drive. That's quite a fever you've got."

"Really," I said. "Really, I'm okay." And then I vomited on his shoes and all over the delicate weave of his fiber rug.

By the time I was home, on antibiotics and in bed, I did feel disappointed that I should be struck by a severe case of mastitis at the exact moment when all my spying efforts ought to have culminated in finding out "the truth" of Donny's identity. If you don't know what mastitis is, then you are all the better for your ignorance. I can't recommend it. Technically, it's a blocked, infected breast duct. I would say more specifically it's a kind of torture reserved for breastfeeding mothers so that we don't get too comfortable with our lot in life and plan to nurse our children straight into early adulthood, tempting though that may be. The cure, in addition to the antibiotics that will cause a rash of other symptoms—like constipation, yeast infections and digestive problems (hey, pregnancy all over again!)—is to nurse the baby frequently on the infected breast. This feels something like I would

imagine nipple clamps might feel, if they were left on indefi-
nitely and came with sharp claws. (Unfortunately, I have not
yet tried nipple clamps. I doubt they're in my future. When
Drew and I have sex, it's the highly domesticated variety.)
Anyhow, that's how it feels every time Zach feeds.

I felt like the worst friend in the world when I had to call
Diana and explain not just why I was so late to pick up Zach,
but why I couldn't (my car was still at Donny's office). She
had a neighbor watch Addicus while she brought Zach to me.

"I'm supposed to be helping you!" I wailed from bed.

"Don't worry," she said kindly. "I'm sure I'll be pregnant
longer than you're sick."

My mother called concerned that I might not be well in
time for her bridal shower, scheduled at my house in two
weeks' time. I explained that while it was ever so nice of her to
be troubled over my condition, the doctor had projected a return to normal health in short order.

"He also said I was doing too much. You get mastitis when
you're worn down."

"Aren't all new mothers worn down?" my mother asked.

Priscilla came over to offer her brand of help, which consisted of a great deal of verbal arrows flung my way.

"I certainly never had mastitis," she said triumphantly.

"You didn't breastfeed," I pointed out.

"Exactly," she said, smiling. "My Walter wouldn't have allowed it."

I passed some of my sick hours scrolling through a zillion
web pages about life coaches in an attempt to ascertain exactly where things stood with Donny. As far as I could make
out, he didn't have any of the "official" credentials. I hadn't realized the world of coaching had so much to offer. Every other
website offered to make *me* a life coach, so that I too could

have a career helping people realize their full potential. And
to think that all along I'd thought *I* was doing it, only I've
been calling it motherhood.

At any rate, I decided that I knew what I needed to know; I
couldn't keep postponing the inevitable. I had, after all, found
that suspicious-looking pink paper that screamed "gay"
louder than the Village People. I can read fast. It's one of the
few abilities garnered through my years of taking English
classes. That paper advertised a meeting, some kind of private
"Pride" meeting. Whatever Donny was up to, it didn't jive
with what my mother knew of him. I had to tell my mother,
even if it meant risking our connection. Wouldn't she do the
same for me?

To: jakephilips@lunerpress.com
From: jmcguire@fanfare.com
*Aloha. I've come down with a booby disease. I've been
convalescing by reading weird websites about life
coaches. I barely got to meet with Donny before I puked
all over his shoes. (Don't ask.) He did have some kind of
a flyer for a weekly support meeting for gay people, so
does that confirm our suspicions?*

   You can come see me anytime. I would really love it.
—Joy

To: jmcguire@fanfare.com
From: jakephilips@lunerpress.com
*Hey, you. We're always on line at the same time. Think
it means something? ;-) The computer's my thing when
I've got insomnia. And of course it's on all day at work.
But I still think we've got some kind of psychic thing
going on. Anyway, yours are always the best emails I get.*

*I'm sorry to hear the news about your mother's fiancé.
Maybe there's some other explanation? Have you found
out if he makes any money? Some coaches do really well
and are completely legit. The gay thing—not sure where
to go with that one.*

*And so sorry about the boob trouble! I've got my own
version of it, girl trouble. Tell me, why did I ever break
up with you? I can't remember anymore. And to think I
could be sitting pretty in suburbia with you and a baby.
Boy, did I miss out.* ☺ *J*

Before I could think, before I could stop myself, I wrote
back. Isn't that the worst thing about email? A letter you can
pore over, you can write and rewrite. You can put it in your
home mailbox and then rip it out a few hours later when you
realize how *stupid* it would be to send it. Not so email. It's the
capricious person's communication method of choice.

To: jakephilips@lunerpress.com
From: jmcguire@fanfare.com
No, I missed out.
    *BTW, you left me because I was boring, or something
like that. Oh, no, wait. I remember. Because we didn't
have "the spark!" Joy*

To: jmcguire@fanfare.com
From: jakephilips@lunerpress.com
*I highly doubt that. You are the most spark-ly woman I
know. Remember when you wore that tiara to the Spring
Fling Senior year? And the huge yellow dress and the
dozen yellow roses in your hair?*
    I do.

Twenty-one

THERE HE WAS. DRINKING A MUG OF COFFEE AND reading a book—probably something complicated and spiritual—with his ankles crossed.

I'd only gone in for a cookie and a hot chocolate. And to make sure that other human beings exist. It was November and it was freezing. Drew had left, the day before, for Ohio, to a conference held annually just for headmasters of private boys' schools. I tried explaining that leaving me for a week alone with the baby wasn't very nice on his part. He pointed out, as he always does, that he *wasn't* leaving me alone; I had his mother. "Isn't that why we live so close together?" he asked. I'd forgotten. One big happy family. It was enough to make me want to move to outer Siberia.

But not at that moment. At that moment I wanted to be one big happy family. With Oliver. While my husband was somewhere in Ohio learning about the ins and outs of adolescent education, I stood at the Moonstar Café looking at the back of Oliver's head with lust circling in me like a tropical storm. I stood motionless for about three minutes and twenty-eight seconds waiting for him to notice me. (Yes, I counted.) Then I slung Zach onto my opposite hip and went over to say hi.

Earlier that day I had attempted my first postmastitis shower; how convenient that I can now date my life by another post-mortem event. Zach had entered a new phase that included short morning naps and long afternoon naps. I no longer planned anything big for his morning nap—like writing a novel or baking a pie or cleaning the house, all of which take more time than I will ever have again. Instead, I set the bar a little lower. Put in a load of wash. Take a shower. Pay a bill. Write an email. Do a sit-up. I'd long passed the days of putting Zach on the bathroom rug to stare in wonder at the ceiling while I showered. Now he had a mind of his own, and as we all know, a mind is a very dangerous thing to have. It can lead babies to open cupboards and eat entire packets of powdered bubble bath.

That day I arrived in the shower at about ten past ten. Since my leg hair had grown long enough to land me a starring role in *Hair, the Musical,* I went in search of my ladylike plastic razor, which had merged into the bar of Ivory soap. I honestly do not know how this sort of thing happens, unless razors and soap have some innate attraction to each other that I don't know about. It used to be a shower every day and every day a shave. My legs were like a skating rink you could slide smoothly across. At any rate, when I'd finally managed to extract the razor, the whole leg-shaving ordeal seemed much more grueling and exhausting than I remembered.

By the time I got to the actual shaving, I had a load of conditioner slicked into my hair and my right leg covered in thick green gel. (Drew's shaving gel, but I couldn't find anything else and would have to settle for smelling manly for the rest of the day.) It was at the exact moment when I had run the shaver up the length of my leg only once, that I heard the sounds of a baby. It took a moment for me to realize that the baby I heard crying belonged to me, that no one else was home, and that I would somehow have to find a way to get to him, to soothe him, and to get him back to sleep. I knew from experience that Zach wouldn't go back to sleep if I didn't reach him quickly enough; his own crying would wake him up. That meant I needed to get to him Superman fast, only I was naked, had shaving gel all over my leg, conditioner in my hair, and I was wet.

I threw a towel around my middle and ran down to the nursery, which we'd painted a Granny Smith green back before we knew whether it would be Jack or Jill popping out of my orifice. The only time Zach was in his carefully planned, exquisitely decorated nursery was for naps. He still slept with us at night. Drew had the great idea to let Zach sleep with us until *Zach* decided he didn't want to anymore. Like that will ever happen. Even adults prefer to sleep with someone else given the chance. If that weren't true we would all have a set of twin beds in the master bedroom like Lucy and Ricky Ricardo. And sex would be a four-letter word. And babies would pop out of petticoats.

I rushed to Zach's crib, but for some reason, his crying intensified. I looked over the crib's edge at his little gray eyes and shushed him; he turned red with wailing. He stared at me with curious horror for quite a while before I realized he couldn't recognize me with my hair glued to my head with conditioner and a blue towel wrapped around my middle. I tried to reassure him. I tried singing to him. Finally, I picked him up and rocked him. He would have none of it. He wanted his mother back. And he wasn't going to sleep, that much I could grasp.

This is the great drama of a mother's day: to let the baby cry or not to let the baby cry. I put Zach back in the crib, told him I would be right back, and raced to the bathroom where I stepped back into the shower, rinsed the conditioner out—mostly, since I later realized I missed a few spots—and sprayed off the shaving gel. Then I dried myself, threw back on my pajamas, and went to collect Zach, who was beside himself with sobbing, but at least knew who I was this time.

I thought of this as I stood before Oliver. I thought of it as I noticed his hair, and his smell, and the carefully trimmed shape of his beard. He was wearing brown corduroys and a red button-down flannel shirt.

"Joy. Wow. What a surprise." He stood up and embraced me. I started to remind myself that nothing had happened between us, that probably he didn't even like me anymore (can a crush be passing, like a twenty-four-hour flu?), and that certainly I did not like him any longer. I had been mistaken; it had just been the yoga classes, the sweet sound of his voice, a space away from the chaos of my life that had stirred my hormones into a flurry of desire.

"Oh, Oliver, it's great to see you."

"And this is the new soul, little man Zach." He looked at Zach who sat shyly on my left hip.

"Yes, and Zach, this is Oliver."

"Nice to meet you again. What do you think of the world? I love meeting people new to the world. They're always so

much smarter." Oliver laughed his laugh, a manly, deep reso-
nant chuckle, which made Zach giggle in response. "God, it's
great to see you. Do you want to sit down?" I sat. I gave Zach a
spoon off the table. I could feel Oliver looking at me. It was
like having the summer sun beating down on you. His gaze
felt hot, unmanageable.

"What are you up to?" I asked.

"I'm doing some planning for a yoga retreat I'm leading
up in Quebec, finding some good inspirational quotes to
share. I have a friend up there who runs a studio. I'll go up for
the week and lead a workshop for her students."

"Sounds fun."

"I love retreats. My heart is really there for them, for that
kind of sustained practice. It's a way to be powerfully present
for a long time, just everyone there together and awake."

"Hmmm," I murmured, not sure if I had an inkling what
any of it meant. Of course I'd never been on a yoga retreat.
Actually, it sounded terrible to me. I'd probably walk out a
permanent cripple; if I ever got my feet behind my head, I
know I wouldn't be able to get them back down.

"It's so great to see you," he said again. "I've been thinking
about you."

"Oh?"

"I'm sorry about what . . . what I said before. I was way out
of line."

"Don't—"

"It's just that I believe we all have to speak from our truth.
It's not healthy to keep things inside. You know, Joy, the universe has brought us together for a reason."

"It has?" I imagined myself in my mind's eye, conditioner
still in my hair, hairy ankles that I don't have time to shave,
my shirt stained with banana mush from Zach's breakfast.

"I've got this baby." I stood Zach up on my lap as if to prove it. "I have a husband!" I knocked my hand against my head as if this were something I had stupidly forgotten, like milk at the grocery store.

"Joy," Oliver said, in his calm way with all the vowels included, like the Canadians do.

The sound of his voice, his voice saying my name, caused a quivering in my loins—and I can say that. I've read enough novels from the 1800s to know what quivering loins are all about. I searched desperately for a way to change the course of the conversation. "Are you Canadian?" I finally asked.

"Yes. I was born in Toronto."

"I see."

"Where were you born?"

"New York," I said. "Manhattan. My mother's stomping grounds."

Zach started fussing in my arms. I knew he wanted to get down and explore the crumbs on the floor. Sometimes he would collect crumbs, make one big crumb pile, then show it to me with such pride in his eyes you'd think he'd just finished building the pyramids.

"I should probably go," I said, standing up.

"What are you up to later? We could grab a bite to eat."

"Are you asking me to have dinner with you?"

"I am."

"But you can't."

"Why can't I?"

"Because I'm married."

"So you can't have dinner with people?"

"Not with people like you."

"Like me?" He laughed. "People who find you charming, humorous, humble and sexy."

Oh, God. Gulp. "Yes, that kind of person could be a bad thing."

He stood up. "We won't do anything but talk."

"Of course not. I didn't think we would," I fumbled. We were standing facing each other. I had to close my eyes for a moment just to feel how good it was to be near him. "I'm so silly. I'm sorry. It's just that what you said made me think—"

"Joy," he said, grabbing my hand and holding it firmly. His firmness always took me by surprise because he had a gentleness about him in yoga class. "I'd love to eat dinner with you and talk, but only if you can, and only if you want to, only if it feels right for you. I want you to feel safety when you're with me, to feel held and provided for by the Universe because I just know there is something divine between us. Okay?" Let's forget the fact that his eyes were like pools of Lindt chocolate and his skin looked like it had been rubbed with olives and his hand holding mine made me feel stirrings in a region of my body I'd recently relegated solely for utility purposes, like giving birth. Let's not focus on all that. I wasn't in a breath mint commercial after all. I was a woman with one and three-quarters hairy legs. My hair hung limp around my ears, coated with a thin film of conditioner. Nothing was going to happen.

"Okay," I heard myself say.

Then I booked it out of the café double time and ran to the car. After I'd buckled Zach in, I dug for my cell phone and dialed up the Wicked Witch.

"Priscilla, I'm so glad you're there."

"Where would I be? Personally, I can't imagine what could be so compelling that you would go out when you're sick. Unless of course you're not sick." She paused for dramatic effect. "I suppose we can't all have social lives like yours." I know

she meant this as an insult, but coming from her, it felt like a
genuine compliment.

"Thank you," I said, as I backed out of my parking space. "I
have a huge favor to ask."

"Do you?" I could practically hear her rubbing her hands
together; the blackmail all but crackled over the phone line.

"Well, not huge, but big enough. I've got this dinner with a
friend tonight and Drew is out of town—"

"I know where Drew is. I just spoke with him."

"Great, great," I said, running a yellow light. I did a quick
mental scan of my closet to see if there were any clean clothes
I could change in to. I was wearing jeans and a pink sweater
that my mother had bought me about twenty years ago on a
trip to Mexico. That's right, a 1980s pink sweater from
Mexico. It wasn't going to dinner with me, that's for sure.
"How's he doing?" I said without waiting for a reply. "Do you
think you'd be able to come and give Zach his dinner and bottle and put him to bed?"

"For my little Zachary? I'd do anything."

"Oh, wonderful, thank you." I couldn't believe the kindness coming out of my mouth, except I really did feel grateful.
Who else could I have called and trusted? At least I knew she'd
keep him from climbing out a window or eating some vita-
mins out of the medicine cupboard. Drew and I still had
some babyproofing to do. Actually, I'd started to wonder if we
shouldn't buy a different house, one with padded walls and
no electrical outlets and no stairs. Already the house had begun to look like a strange asylum, with plastic toys littering
every hallway and everything pretty we'd ever been given or
purchased stashed on the top of the dining room hutch,
which at eight feet tall, Zach wouldn't reach until he learned
to use a ladder. I didn't doubt that would be soon enough.

"No," I heard Priscilla say, "thank *you*. I'm glad to do it."

And that was the first time she'd said "thank you" to me in six years.

Oliver and I met at Antonio's for dinner, which is somewhere between a pizza place and a white-tablecloth restaurant. I'd suggested it because I'd never been there with Drew. For years Drew and I had gone up and down the Connecticut coast finding every interesting restaurant to eat at. But Drew didn't like Italian. He said pasta gave him gas. Personally, I always doubted this. I think he secretly believed it would make him fat; he'd want to eat Japanese or at a fish house or find some vegetarian hole in the wall so he could put another notch on his saving-the-world belt.

I brought something special with me to Antonio's that I hadn't anticipated. I shudder even to remember it. My own personal tumor-size pimple. Where did it come from? How did it grow so quickly? I could have sworn that I didn't see it in the morning when I briefly looked at myself while brushing my teeth. Yet by five-thirty, a *Titanic* zit had emerged on my chin. Now, as everyone knows, if it had been a whitehead, I could have done something about it. I could have squirted the bastard clear across the room. But it wasn't. It was one of those big, red, throbbing kinds that lay in wait for the one significant night of your whole year to blossom. I became convinced that it would turn into a whitehead over the course of the dinner, that Oliver would reach over, saying "You have something on your chin," attempting to romantically brush it away. Then I would turn scarlet as he tried over and over to brush it off, the uncouthness of which would end the entire meal and all the mystical, illicit, yogic-style sex that would ensue. In which case, I would owe the salvation of my marriage to a zit.

I did what any reasonable person would do. I put on enough foundation to cover the faces of all the poor people in America who don't have makeup. Then I powdered it until it resembled a snowcapped mountain. I put on earrings, a necklace, a headband, and a tapestry shirt, so that Oliver's gaze would be pulled away from my chin. When I took a last look at myself before I left, I felt defeated. Lumpkin still required a girdle. I didn't look a bit like myself; the foundation made my face at least an inch thicker in every direction.

Priscilla, however, thought differently.

"You look pretty," she said, spooning a mouthful of oatmeal into Zach. "Just a friend?"

"Girls' night," I said. "Thought I might as well do it while Drew's away."

"That's good," she said as if she didn't mean it one bit. "That's a nice skirt." She hadn't seen me in a skirt in at least two years, and I knew that because I'd had to dig through a bag in the eaves of the attic to find the one I had on.

"Are you two okay?" I couldn't hide the anxiety in my voice.

"I've got it covered. Zachary and I always have a wonderful time together." She smiled at me, her thin-lipped, tight-faced smile, and for a moment, awash in the excitement of meeting Oliver, I felt generous enough to have some compassion for her. I don't think she was ever an attractive woman, even before her husband died, and it's not easy not to be pretty. Drew's good looks were nothing short of a miracle, maybe enough to make one believe in a god.

I did think about Drew all the way in Ohio while I sat down across the table from Oliver. I thought about him, then about Zach, then about my zit, and every now and then I thought about Aunt Hilda and the fortune she gave me and the fortune she gave Drew. On one hand, thinking about her had a tendency to make me happy, just genuinely happy. She was like a direct line to my father. And my father? He was a direct line to myself, that carefree little girl that, oh yes, I once was. On the other hand, she'd given Drew and me a rather ominous future forecast. Was I just about to make it a reality?

Oliver told me he didn't drink. He ordered sparkling water for both of us. He smiled at me warmly. I could feel my heart beating like the backbeat to some techno music.

"This is beautiful," he said. "I'm so glad it worked for you to meet me."

"Me too."

"Tell me something."

"Something?"

He smiled, giving me a probing look. "Yes, something. Tell me something real about you and your life. I want to know who this Joy is—is she joyful like her name?"

"Okay." I sat for a moment, thinking. I tried to capture the feelings I'd had with him in yoga class. With the birdcalls and the whale songs and all the other pudgy ladies with their bums up in the air doing a downward dog, it felt like things were okay, even though they weren't. Right at that moment, I felt anything but calm. I felt horny and I use that word purposefully; I felt like a pubescent teenage boy on a date with a Playboy Bunny. I'm just so sure there isn't anything remotely spiritual about that sensation.

"Tell me something most people don't know about you."

"Oh, you want *that* kind of thing?"

"I don't know," he said, smiling that dimpled smile again.

"I'd just love to get inside of you, know what makes Joy the lovely being in front of me."

He wanted to get inside of me? Boy, did I want that too, but I didn't gather that he was asking me to take his pants down. "Oh, let's see. My father died when I was eight. That's pretty much my standard secret."

"Wow," he said appreciatively. "What was that like?"

"Oh, it was nothing. Maybe like the far side of hell."

He laughed again. "You're funny. Such a wonderful sense of humor, a lightheartedness. I love that. How do you manage to be funny about your father's passing?"

"How can you not?" He nodded in agreement. "Oh, and after my father died, my mother went off the deep end. That's the part that's not standard sharing material."

"That's not as funny," he said, crinkling his nose and shaking his head. "You can drown in deep water."

"Exactly." It was like he *knew* me. "We don't talk about it, my mother and I."

"Why not?"

"Because my mother doesn't like to. She went off to that hospital in Boston—she got that deep—I always forget the name. Where Sylvia Plath went. Actually, it kind of fits with my mother's near-celebrity status. How can you be rich and famous without checking into a mental institution or rehab center at least once?"

"Oh, you definitely couldn't. It's a prerequisite," he said, and I laughed. When had that happened? Drew never made me laugh. *I* could barely make me laugh.

"I actually lived with the neighbors for eight months, if you can believe it. I felt like Little Orphan Annie. They didn't know if she would make it back alive. She apparently couldn't find a reason to live. I try not to take that part personally. After all, she really loved my father. She loved my father, like, like..." Here I searched around the room because I couldn't think of the words. When I looked at Oliver, his dark eyes met mine with so much compassion, I lost my breath. He knew how I felt. I remember when Drew and I first talked about our dead fathers. We were in the same club. We spoke the same language. But had it been like this, like this look of understanding that Oliver gave me? Or was it simply part of why I married him when I was still pining for Jake? Had we been two people paddling down the same river in different boats all along?

"More than life itself?" Oliver said.

"Yes. Much more." And I didn't care that the tears started to fall, slicing a pathway through my foundation and dribbling over my zit. I didn't care at all.

At home, there was a message from Drew on the machine.

"I couldn't get to the phone," Priscilla said. "He called right at Zachary's bedtime."

"He does that," I said, without thinking that this might seem like an insult against her son.

"Well, it takes men longer." She was standing by the door on her way out. "To get used to the whole thing. I remember that with my Walter. It just takes a while."

"I guess," I said, not sure what to say, since I hardly wanted to ruin the mood. Priscilla had literally never confided a single thing to me in all the years I had known her. She'd never acknowledged that Drew could be anything but the world's most perfect model human being.

"Don't stay up until all hours. My Walter always believed

in going to bed at a decent hour," she said. Then she left. Our time for gossiping and drinking tea ended before it started.

I went to check on Zach who, naturally, she'd put to sleep in his crib. Inevitably he'd wake up in a few hours and end up snuggled in bed with me. He still had his habit of nursing through the night, probably to ease his teething pain, or so I'd read in one of my many baby-rearing books. Although I'd improved over time in my ability to snooze through his prolonged nursing sessions, he'd become much more active in his sleep, which did nothing to help my lengthy bouts of momsomnia. If you'd ever told me before that sleeping straight through the night would come to seem as unlikely as winning the lottery, I wouldn't have believed it. Don't let anyone ever tell you differently; sanity has everything to do with sleep.

Drew had left a long message on the machine. I listened to it. He talked about how the meetings were going and the quality of the towels in his hotel room ("like super-duper plush"). Where did I go? he wanted to know. And oh, yes, he missed us, Zach and me. I listened to it twice. I couldn't tell if guilt made me do it, or an old whisper of love. It was nice to be missed, and it hadn't happened in quite a while.

Then Beth called. She'd come in from a late night of dancing. She still went out until all hours in the morning, like— my God!—a teenager. She rambled on for so long I went upstairs and brushed my teeth while she talked. She mentioned David Martin and how good his clothes smelled. You wouldn't believe how long one person can discuss the ins and outs of laundry detergents. I was just starting to fall asleep on the phone when she started in on Jake. Instantly, I perked up. Apparently, he'd broken up with his emaciated, gorgeous, blond-bombshell girlfriend (no doubt the one he referenced in his email), which meant I was actually in the running, or so I thought for one fleeting moment before reality dawned on me. I wasn't in the running. I was married. I was a mother. It wasn't ten years ago. It was now. And now was Drew.

Or at least it was supposed to be.

I curled into bed thinking of Oliver. I thought of him standing by me at my car before we said good night. We just held each other, in the sharp autumn air, close enough to the highway to hear the roar of trucks. He mumbled some sweet nothings in my ear, more stuff about karma and fate and the forces of goodness bringing us to each other. "Breathe with me," he'd said, and we'd matched our breathing paces. "Very tantric," he'd said. I'm not quite sure I know what tantra is, not quite sure that I care. But it was so good to be against him, sinfully good. I fell asleep with a smile on my face, and I can say with some confidence that it had been a long time since that had happened.

Twenty-two

THE NEXT MORNING I WOKE UP TO A KING KONG–size whitehead on my chin. My uber-pimple had made its transformation. Zach and I looked at it for a while in the mirror. Up close it could have stunt-doubled for some of the more interesting things you find on the Discovery Channel, although I couldn't quite place it as animal, vegetable or mineral. Finally, I put Zach down and had my way with it. When all that was left was a bit of a bloody hole, I pressed it with a cold cloth. I have to admit, it certainly put me in my place. To think I'd been feeling sexy and desirable and womanly. But I wasn't a teenager in love. I was She of the Cumulative Sleep Deprivation. At least my hair had stopped falling out in large chunks. And my stretch marks had turned from lobster red to a more subtle grapefruit pink.

I'd made plans to meet with Oliver again, but I felt the pimple situation might rule it out. Maybe it was even a sign from the universe, a chastity belt of sorts that would effectively keep me away from him until Drew's return. The only trouble was, I didn't want to be away from him, Drew or no Drew.

In the meantime, Zach and I had a date with Diana and Addicus. I'd come to enjoy my mornings of helping Diana; it made me feel more like Mother Teresa than I ever had in my life, excluding those times in college when I made weekly visits to the local nursing home to hang out with the old chicks. There was one woman, Verna, who I especially adored. When she died, I couldn't bear to go back. I had brought Verna lemon cupcakes, her favorite. She always started our conversation with the same opening line: "Who are you?" I'd say, "I'm the lemon cupcake girl," and then she'd nod her head with appreciation, point her finger at me, cackle and say, "I knew that!"

Addicus continued to resemble a butterball. He also knew four words in sign language. Occasionally when I went over to Diana's, I worried that Zach was underweight and maybe just a touch mentally challenged. After all, he was shy, and Addicus was outgoing. Zach needed time to adjust to new places and new people. And so far had refused to sign any words at all—including the all-time baby favorite, "cookie." Addicus could roar like a lion and sign the word "more" like he'd come out of the genius baby factory. Had I failed my son somehow? Would he ever even make it to preschool?

"You're a sight for sore eyes," Diana said when I came in.

"Look at me. Tell me what you see."

"My good friend Joy come to save the day."

"No. Look at my face."

"Okay." She squinted at me. "And?"

"Well, honestly, how can you miss it!" I pointed at the remains of my pimple. "My trophy pimple! Can't you see it?"

"Well, I guess I see it now. It's not that bad, Joy, really."

"You're just constitutionally unable to say anything unkind to anyone at any time."

"Oh, please." She sat down heavily on the kitchen floor where Addicus was undertaking an operation with his spatula and his teddy bear. Open-heart surgery? Or was he just trying to take the bear's rectal temperature? I couldn't tell. She said, "I feel like crap."

"Is that nasty little embryo giving you a hard time again?"

"I was never this sick with Addicus."

"Must be a girl then. They're the worst."

Diana smiled up at me. "Thanks. Can you take my mind off my suffering? Got any good stories?"

I put Zach down next to Addicus and handed him his nose bulb, the one from the hospital, the one that goes with us everywhere we go. "Actually," I said.

"Actually what?"

"I had dinner with Oliver."

"Oh my God!"

"Don't worry. I didn't sleep with him. Nothing that terrible."

"But what?"

"But we did do some kind of tantric breathing thing when we hugged. He's got a crush on me. I can hardly believe it. Of course nothing can happen, but it's so absolutely, totally, completely, lusciously wonderful to have his gorgeous attention. His skin is like caramel fudge—"

"Ugh," she said, holding up a hand to stop me. "Please don't talk about food."

"What would you do if your yoga teacher had a thing for you?"

She lay down on the floor on her side and rubbed her belly, like it was a magic ball ready to show us the answer. "You're asking the wrong person. My life is about my placenta right now."

"Of course. I know. I remember how it was. I was nauseous for at least eight months. At any rate, it's all hypothetical. I like to imagine things, though, what I would do if I were single for example. I've got plans to meet him later in the day, at the yoga studio. A private yoga class," I said, trying to gently wrench the spatula Zach had stolen from Addicus out of his hand.

"Aren't you tempting fate?"

"Well, according to Oliver, it's fate that's brought us together. I've got to get my mind off of him, though. My mother's party is in two days and I'm planning to break the news to her about Donny then. It won't be pretty."

"I'd love to be a fly on the wall."

"I promise I'll tell you everything, no detail left out."

"I'm counting on it. I'm living vicariously through you these days," she said.

"That's funny to me because I still feel like my life is a suburban hostage situation that I'm permanently trapped in."

"Isn't it funny? All your life you long for something, you long for a husband and a big house in a good neighborhood and babies. And when they come along, you..." She petered out. We both looked at our two boys playing. My heart burned with love for Zach. Still, we sat there in silence for a while like two schoolgirls, thinking about the lives we'd always imagined and never would have. You know that life, with endless supplies of money and flawless spouses and babies that don't cry. The kind where someone brings you flowers every week and tells you you're beautiful every day and vacations go on for months and months. The kind where nobody dies, nobody gets morning sickness and nobody falls in lust when they're already married. The kind with enough Ken dolls so that every Barbie gets her very own and never has to share. It's called make-believe, and someone would do little girls everywhere a really big favor if they broke the truth before puberty. Tell the poor things everywhere that Happily Ever After isn't the end of the story—it's the punch line to a joke.

What could I do? I had to meet Oliver. I couldn't stand him up. That would be rude, and I'm cranky, not rude. I debated putting a Band-Aid on my chin and telling Oliver that I'd sliced off a chunk of it in a freak accident while cutting carrots. I even tried the Band-Aid on for size. Zach took an instant fascination with it and couldn't keep from peeling it off. Another reason mommies shouldn't date. My mother called my cell phone as I was driving to the yoga studio. She wanted to make sure everything was in place for the big bridal dinner at my house. She insisted on going over her checklist with me line by line. I could barely get her off the phone in time to stop Oliver from leaving the studio. Luckily, Zach began to wail so loudly it made conversation impossible. "I'll call you later," I screamed into the phone.

When I walked in to the studio, Oliver was just putting his shoes back on.

"I thought maybe you got tied up," he said.

"I've been in the parking lot for a half hour. I couldn't get my mother off the phone."

"Would you still like to spend some time here?" he asked, one shoe in hand. "I have some powerful partner postures I could teach you."

"Yes."

Then we smiled at each other, and Zach said something in his yabba-dabba language.

"You're going to love it in here," Oliver said to Zach. "It's already babyproofed."

I took off my shoes and Oliver took off his one sneaker. We left our layers of sweaters and coats in the hallway and let Zach crawl by himself into the large room.

"This is a sacred space, little guy," Oliver said. "This is where we do yoga." Zach immediately crawled over to the stereo to investigate the cords.

"He might be a little young for that kind of thing," I said.

"Oh, they come out knowing more than us. We all do. Then we spend a lifetime unlearning everything we know about who we are and where we come from."

"I know one thing for sure," I said. "I know where he comes from. And it's no mystical place." Oliver laughed at me. I loved to hear him laugh. It made me feel funny and sexy, like I had something that somebody wanted.

We sat down on the floor and began our partner postures.

"Press your back into mine," he instructed as we sat back to back in a cross-legged position. "Now feel my breath. Catch my breath and breathe with me." After a few breaths, he said, "Very good, Joy. Beautiful."

Next we moved to face each other with our legs spread wide apart in two Vs, feet touching. He grabbed my arms and pulled me around in a circle. I might have been more aroused, as every few seconds my head circled within six inches of his crotch, but the searing pain in my inner thighs didn't leave room for other feelings.

"Mmmm," he whispered. "Feels good. Let's try this." He reached his hands out and pulled me straight down so that I was leaning in toward the floor. He pushed his hands against my back.

"Oh," I cried, sorry to break the moment. "I think that's too much—"

"Sensation?"

"Yes, too much sensation." I sat up quickly.

He reached out and cupped my chin. "You're too cute," he said.

"Oh, I don't feel cute. I feel tight." Normally the word "tight" uttered in a yoga studio comes out sounding illustrative—as in "my hamstrings are really tight." But as the word lingered in the air, it just smacked of sexuality. Oliver raised an eyebrow.

"We've got to open you up," he said. "Why don't you lie down?"

If Zach hadn't been in the room, eagerly attempting to unroll a pile of yoga mats or, at the very least, chew on each one, I would have definitely felt that something naughty was about to happen. I had to assume Oliver's intentions were good. He was a *yoga* teacher after all. He'd taken some kind of sacred vow to support my well-being.

"Okay." I lay on the floor and Oliver picked up my legs. He swung them gently side to side.

"Feel good?"

"Great on my lower back."

"Just let go, Joy. I'm holding you."

"Okay." I closed my eyes and for a moment surrendered into the bliss of his touch. Then I lost my breath as Zach crawled boisterously over my tummy.

When Oliver put my legs back on the floor he began to massage my feet. I couldn't help letting out an involuntary sigh. He gently made his way up to my calves and then began kneading my thighs. That's right, my thighs, those two fleshy trunks that just happen to be right next to the very vagina that may one day have its own monologue.

"Oh," I said, startled.

"We need to relax your muscles," Oliver said. He continued to knead me. It felt pretty damn good and pretty damn weird.

Then, with one hand still on my thigh, Oliver leaned in and kissed me. Not exactly the best moment as I'd started to drool, just the littlest bit, on account of the massage feeling so heavenly. The kiss wasn't half bad either. Oliver's mouth covered mine. It was warm and soft and wet. It went on and on. It consumed me so thoroughly that I didn't hear the sound of the studio door opening. When Oliver pulled away, it was to acknowledge that a woman had joined our little tantric party.

"Carrie," Oliver said.

"I'm here for my private," she said. 'Private' is yoga lingo for a one-on-one yoga session.

"Excellent," said Oliver. "I'll just finish up with Joy." He smiled at her, then he smiled at me. I couldn't quite tell if she'd seen us kissing or not. After all, yoga teachers do get themselves into all kinds of positions in order to help their students get into all kinds of positions. Maybe she thought we'd been doing a special pose?

Twenty-three

AND THEN, IT WAS NOVEMBER 12, THE DAY OF MY mother's wedding shower, and all I could think was thank God it was finally happening because I couldn't bear to plan for it any more. Diana, feeling moderately less nauseous, came over to help me get things ready. The caterer was scheduled to arrive at 5 p.m. In the meantime, I certainly couldn't prepare the house for twenty-five people with a baby strapped to my back. Drew, as usual, wouldn't be much help, but this time he had a good excuse. He'd rolled in from Ohio at three in the morning after a four-hour flight delay. Frankly, this was fine with me. This was good for me. I had a strange fear that he would take one look at me and be able to tell that I'd kissed another man.

When Diana arrived she put Addicus in one of our bouncy chairs for a long nap. It looked pretty inviting. I might have napped in one too if I'd been able to fit. Zach, meanwhile, took over a half hour of nursing to get down for his nap, but when both babies were finally asleep, Diana and I made quick work of cleaning up. I'm not insane—of course I'd had the place professionally cleaned earlier in the week. I wasn't going to invite my new *pregnant* best friend over and have her spray down the toilet with bleach and clean the sink with a toothbrush. But even with clean bathrooms, more needed doing than one mommy can do.

Diana was dying to know what my plan was re Donny, and if I felt mentally prepared to break my mother's heart.

"Do you think she's really in love with Donny?" Diana asked.

"I keep asking her. She keeps saying yes. *I* think she doesn't want to be alone," I finally said. "Ever since my father's death she's been hell-bent on living with someone. I even think she's enjoyed having Aunt Hilda around, as strange as she is. My mother isn't into being solo, if you hadn't noticed."

"Who is?"

"My mother-in-law. She's got a terrible condition: VCW."

"I've never heard of it," Diana said, following me up the stairs with a pile of towels in her arms.

"Vaginal cobwebs."

"You're too much," she said, laughing.

"Oh, I'm serious." I took the towels from her and loaded both of our armfuls into the upstairs closet. "Are you in love with *your* husband?" I asked, trying to sound casual, but what I really wanted to know was if I was the only one having a loveless relationship.

"In love? I don't know. I do love him very much. I'm not in love like fireworks and weak knees, though. But then I've never trusted those feelings. What about you?"

"You know how it is with Drew and me."

"You've got it hard. He works so much. He's got more than a full-time job and you're more than a full-time mother. That would dampen anyone's romance."

"Well, I can guarantee you my mother isn't having fire-works with Donny. He's got the personality of a sloth."

"What about your father? What was he like?"

"My father had more personality than all the late-night talk show hosts put together. And then some."

"What does everyone else know about him? Like your brothers, what do they think of Donny?" We headed back down the stairs to set the table in the dining room.

"I have no idea. They talk to me about once a year. Trevor's my favorite brother. He called me when Zach was born; the others just sent cards. The kids are all in college now, probably too busy learning about the female anatomy and alcohol poisoning to think about their mother. And Danny has Steve—that's his father, my mother's third husband, in case you're confused. The two of them are like twins. So I don't know what Danny thinks of Donny. I hope he's offended by my mother's lack of foresight. I mean, how does she plan to live in a house with a Danny and a Donny?"

Diana laughed, then she put a hand on her hip and said: "Seriously, though. Aren't you worried about upsetting your mother? If all the things you think are true, won't it break her heart?"

"Madeline Steeley can handle anything—that's been her whole M.O. since she recovered from my father's death, like nothing can hurt her now, not after that. And if all the things I think are true, a broken heart will be the least of her problems."

"But what if you're wrong? What if he isn't gay? It could have been someone else's flyer on the floor of his office. Maybe a client's."

"And some other Donny Macnamara writing in to discuss gay men in the military? What are the chances?"

"You have a point."

"And I do know absolutely that he's a life coach. And I do have proof that he didn't get a good turnout to his open house."

"True."

"Does it sound like flimsy evidence?"

Diana shrugged. "Maybe a little?"

"I've just got a hunch. He acts so weird around me. Call it mother's intuition. I think something's up. I'm tired of beating around the bush with my mother. The wedding will be here in no time, and I've got to talk to her before it gets any closer."

"Good luck, then," she said.

"I'm going to need it."

There was enough food and wine for a hundred people.

"Two for me," Aunt Hilda said, taking two glasses of champagne off the counter in the kitchen where we'd laid out an almost full bar. "Because I'm twice as old." She winked at me. The meal hadn't gotten under way yet. It was cocktail time. There were aging beauty queens in every downstairs room of the house. My mother sat in the living room chatting with a few cousins of hers who had driven down from Boston for the big event. I'd attached myself to Aunt Hilda's side. "And two of these." She grabbed at a passing platter of sushi rolls.

"Because you're twice as thin," I said.

"Posh! I'm decaying. I long for flesh like yours. Look at your bosom. I'd pay to have my breasts restored to their former glory."

"Actually, Aunt Hilda, you *could* pay to have them restored."

"Just a manner of speaking. Nobody touches this body. It's all mine." She giggled as I led her into the living room. The women in the room parted to make way for her. When she sat down in the wide armchair, champagne splashed out of the tops of both glasses.

"Overboard!" she called playfully. I knelt down on the floor beside her. My mother smiled over at us. She was at her finest, decked out in shimmery black with bangles glinting from every body part. She had on earrings, necklaces (three), bracelets, several gold rings, anklets and two toe rings. "Impressive," I'd said when she arrived, looking at her feet. "Keeps me limber," she said. "That way I make sure I touch my toes at least twice a day. Once to put the things on, and once to get them off."

"You didn't get married, did you?" I asked Aunt Hilda.

"Married? Why would I get married? I'll marry myself, how's that."

Right. What had I been thinking? For a moment I'd forgotten that Aunt Hilda had lived her whole life under a watchful eye. Then she sighed.

"I could have, you know. Paulie, your papa, had a friend, Morty. We had sex a few times." She says this blithely. "Long penis, skinny at the end. And he always wiped his nose with his hand." She looked away, as if she could see the memory floating above us. "But I loved him anyway. Or I think I did. Sometimes I can't remember." Then she turned and looked at me in her uncanny way, right into my eyes. She widened her own eyes until each one resembled my mother's large beaded necklace. "I didn't have to stay, you know. I didn't have to live in a special residence. I wanted to. For a long time the world scared me. I felt safer in there."

"Oh—"

"But now I don't mind it so much. And you." She bopped me on the head. "You're a pretty girl. Where's that baby of yours?"

"He's with my husband at his mother's house."

"Good." She curled her lips into a huge smile. "That's just what I wanted to hear. He's finally pulling his weight. The future is looking brighter," she said as she winked.

I debated long and hard the exact moment to break the Donny news to my mother. I didn't want to humiliate her in front of all her friends, so I encouraged her to stay the night— and Aunt Hilda too as they'd traveled together. As the party wound down, I suggested that Aunt Hilda read my mother's fortune. Certainly, if there were any truth to her cards, my mother's fortune would reveal Donny's intentions.

"She already has," my mother protested. "A lucky life, that's what they said."

"Very lucky," Aunt Hilda echoed. "Pink and shoelace lucky." My mother and I both looked at her quizzically but she simply took another sip of champagne.

"Maybe it's changed," I said. My mother frowned. "Oh, come on. It will be fun."

"I've already had so much fun tonight." My mother dabbed at her lips with her finger, wiping away the last of a shortbread cake. "I'm stuffed to the gills, happy as a clam, sitting pretty."

"Nature calls," Aunt Hilda said, pushing herself up and taking a slow walk to the bathroom.

I looked at my watch. It was almost eleven. Drew was set to bring Zach home at eleven. I wanted to talk to my mother before he arrived.

"Mom," I said.

"Oh, honey, what a wonderful party." She leaned over and smooched me loudly on the forehead. "You did a splendid job."

"Thank you. The thing is, I just wanted to talk to you about Donny."

"Darling Donny."

"It's just that I'm a little worried about him. I had the chance to go to his office. You know, his *coaching* office." I paused, waiting for some response. "You know, Mom, he isn't an artist, he's a life coach."

"He's many things, sweetie. And I know him better than you."

"I'm sorry. I'm just worried that he may not make a living on his work. Does that ever bother you?"

She took in a deep breath. "*You* bother me. Your prying—"

"Mom, I'm looking out for your best interests. You have a lot of money. People notice that—"

She let her breath out sharply. "Honestly, Joy, you surprise me."

"He's a *life coach*, Mom! That's not a job."

"Of course it's not a job! It's a hobby. And who are you to judge?" I could hear the sounds of Aunt Hilda shuffling down the hallway, making her way back to us.

"He can't have any money."

"He's a history professor emeritus. From *Yale*." She put her glass down heavily on the table and pushed herself to standing. "He's been doing some soul searching in his retirement, some exploration, trying out things he always wanted to but couldn't before. That's why he retired early."

"Oh." I looked down at my black dress shoes. "Are you sure?"

"For heaven's sake, Joy! We have a prenuptial agreement."

"Oh. That's good. That's great. I was so worried that maybe he was just in it for the money."

"I'm disappointed in you," my mother said. She was visibly upset. It takes a lot to upset her, I knew that better than anyone. "No, more than that. I'm embarrassed for you."

"There's another thing, Mom, that I think you need to know. As long as you're angry at me, I might as well say it."

"I doubt I want to hear it."

"Donny might be gay."

Then she started laughing. I wouldn't call it a happy laugh. It was more like the kind of laugh you can imagine the Wicked Witch having just before she puts Hansel and Gretel into the oven. I heard Drew pull into the driveway. I started to feel a little queasy. If I'd had sex any time in recent history, I would have thought I had another case of morning sickness.

"Okay, Joy. You've crossed a line, so I might as well cross one too." She sat back down and looked at me sternly. "I don't know what's going on with you. I don't know what's happened to you; I used to think you had a sunny disposition. I know your marriage isn't all you hoped it would be; nobody's is. But you have no right to pry into my affairs as a way of not dealing with your own. You're not a child anymore. In fact, you have your own child to take care of. And it's time that you grew up." Aunt Hilda appeared in the arched entryway to the dining room. She stood there with her head cocked to the side, listening to us. Her white hair seemed to float above her head. A few wisps even stood at attention. She looked slightly electric.

"It's time that you believed in love. It's time that you found your love, really *found* your love and started living it. Stop wallowing in what's lost and all the things that can't be. In so many ways, you're still a child, petulant, selfish, making choices for your ego. You need to take your eyes off of Donny and take a good, hard look at yourself. If I didn't know you better, I would think this was all caused by jealousy. You see what Donny and I have and you want that for yourself—"

"That's ridiculous!"

"Oh, Joy." She stood up again. "What's *wrong* with you?" She threw her napkin down on the table and walked away.

Drew walked in with a sleeping Zach on his shoulder. "What's going on?" he asked.

"The end of a party is always such a sad time," Aunt Hilda said.

"Joy?" Drew said.

"Excuse me," I said, walking out.

"You're crying," Drew said.

"A sad time," said Aunt Hilda, and then I couldn't hear them any longer. I took the stairs two at a time. Once in my bedroom, I peeled off my dark purple dress. I caught my reflection in the large dressing mirror.

"What *is* wrong with you?" I said to myself. And then I put on my pajamas and hurried back down to nurse Zach.

I met Drew on the stairs. He was bringing Zach up to me.

"What's going on?"

"You don't want to know."

"Of course I want to know."

"My mother's mad at me. Really mad at me."

"Why?"

I took the baby from him. "I'll just nurse him in bed."

"I'll come with you." When we settled in the bed, Drew asked me again. "Tell me what's up. Did something go wrong with the party? I thought you had it all set up."

"I did. It was great."

"Why is she angry at you?"

"I gave her some bad news, although it didn't turn out to be all that bad, or maybe it is, I can't tell." I wasn't quite sure what my mother's reaction to the whole gay thing meant. Did it mean she did know, or didn't? Or worse, that I'd had it all wrong?

"I'm not following."

"I told her some things I'd found out about Donny. Things I was pretty sure she didn't know."

"What? You're confusing me now. What about Donny? You've never said anything about Donny."

"I know. I just did a little Internet research—"

"Internet research?! On your mother's fiancé? Are you crazy?"

"Apparently."

"But the Internet is full of bullshit."

"I knew you would say that."

"It's true." Drew looked pretty upset.

"It seemed likely that he was a sketchy character, maybe even just in it for the money. I was looking out for her."

"Jesus, Joy. You go too far."

"You don't even care, do you? See, I knew I shouldn't have told you anything."

"I think you should get some counseling," he said.

"What? What does that have to do with anything?"

"You haven't been yourself lately."

"Of course I haven't! I don't even know who I am!"

The phone rang. We both startled. Drew picked it up.

"Yes," he said into the receiver. "I understand. No, please." He paused. A look of grave concern crossed his face. I gently pulled Zach off my nipple. He'd fallen back into a deep sleep while nursing. "Oh, no. Jesus. Okay. I'll be right there." He hung up the phone and got up from the bed without looking at me.

"What happened?"

"I don't know all the details. That was Sharon. Caleb is missing. Nobody's seen him since yesterday afternoon. And nobody bothered to call me until today."

"Caleb?"

"I've been talking to you for months about this kid."

"Oh."

"Don't you ever listen, Joy, or are you so wrapped up in your own world that you don't care about anyone else?"

"That's not fair—"

"I don't have time to fight with you. I've got to go."

"Now?"

"Yes, now. Someone is *missing*." He stormed out of the room.

"You're missing!" I screamed after him. "That's who's missing. You're who's missing from this family!" My screaming woke Zach up. I picked him up and sang his favorite song, the "Itsy Bitsy Spider," to soothe him. His eyelids shut. His head fell back. His mouth opened into a lovely pout.

I stopped singing. And then I wondered, when did the Itsy Bitsy Spider stop being enough to make everything better?

Twenty-four

FOR ANY NORMAL PERSON, THIS MIGHT HAVE BEEN A great moment for some reevaluation. If I had a life coach, perhaps I would have been encouraged to redeem myself in my mother's eyes or maybe even run out and join the search for the missing Caleb. Instead, I woke up with a throbbing headache. I'd slept all of six minutes. I'd spent the night feverishly thinking about Drew and Caleb, and then Oliver and his kiss, and then the look on my mother's face as she yelled at me. As far as this Caleb was concerned, part of me felt like *What's the big deal?* Teenagers run away all the time. He'd probably hidden in the woods somewhere so he could smoke a pack of Marlboros and drink a fifth of Scotch; he'd be back when he missed his *Hustler* magazines. I had bigger problems than teenage angst. I had a serious case of my own angst and about as much ability to unravel it as Zach has to type a letter.

When I finally made the descent downstairs, relief filled me. I'd been terrified of running into my mother, but it seemed she and Aunt Hilda had made an early morning getaway. No doubt my mother hadn't been too keen on seeing *me* either.

I put on a pot of coffee. When my backside finally hit the kitchen chair and my lips made contact with the warm coffee mug, all relief evaporated. The voice of torture filled the room.

"Good morning," it said. Clearly nothing good about it.

"Hi, Priscilla."

"I see you sleep in late as well as going to bed late. I can't say I approve."

"Bad night," I said.

"Oh, I know. It's such terrible news, I had to come over. I simply can't believe it. After all he's done for that boy, for all those boys, for all those trustees, taking care of everybody!"

"What?" It took me a moment to realize that Priscilla was talking about her own bad night—not mine. I heard a sharp intake of breath and realized my mistake. "Oh, right, sorry, of course. I'm just so tired. And so much is going on—isn't it?"

"We've got to do all that we can to help him," she said.

"Absolutely."

"I can't imagine the pressure. This might be the end for him, and he's given that place his heart and soul. If my Walter were alive, he'd know what to do."

"I hope it's not the end for Drew," I said without thinking. Then a lightbulb went off in my head. Could this be the end of Drew's marriage to Clarkville Academy? In which case, what could I do to hurry along the divorce proceedings? He could always get another job. He could go back to teaching. We could live on ramen noodles. I never had liked our big house in the suburbs anyway. It made me feel so, well, so sub-urban.

"Um, Priscilla?"

"Yes?"

326 □ Samantha Wilde

"Do you think you could watch Zach again? I, um... thought I could meet with someone who may be able to help... Drew?" I can't say I have a great history with lying. For a moment I felt sure Priscilla would find me out, but then she said:

"Of course. Thank goodness. One of his colleagues? That's great, Joy. Good for you. I didn't know you ever got involved with school business, but this is perfect. Come to your grandmother, little Zachary." She held out her arms for him.

"Thank you," I said, passing him over.

I had to go see Oliver. I hadn't seen him since the kiss. Sorting him out seemed like the first step to sorting out my life.

If I lived in a world of make-believe, or in Hollywood, all my problems would be erased by the arrival of my knight in shining armor, Oliver, who would save me from the Evil Prince, Drew, and his gruesome mother, the Evil Queen, who keeps coming around to tempt me with a poisoned apple. However, it did dawn on me, as I drove to the center of town, that Oliver, sexy and spiritual as he was, probably wasn't up for bailing me out of my own personal after-school special (not to mention the fact that I don't live in LA and the last time I checked I wasn't a princess of any kind). The real person to ask would have been Drew. He wasn't around to ask, and he wasn't the right person either. But Drew knew how to solve a moral dilemma better than a TV talk show host; I mean, he was good! He was moral. I have to confess that living with someone so virtuous weighed on me. I'd become dishonest and lazy just to balance him out. In fact, now that I thought of it, as I drove toward the Moonstar Café, Drew's perfectionism had forced me to become, well, myself. And I wasn't at all sure I liked who I'd become.

At this point, it may not appear that I have much of a good side, considering my close encounter with adultery, my total disinterest in my husband's problems and my general dislike for people who annoy me. I never thought I'd get the Nobel Peace Prize. In fact, growing up, all I ever wanted was to marry someone who would live. I'd call that setting the bar pretty damn low. Maybe it was time to raise the bar, or maybe it was time to change the bar. I didn't know. I also didn't know how to find Oliver (and I had no idea what I was going to do when I saw him). We'd never exchanged numbers. I decided to try the café first and then head over to the yoga studio.

I scrambled for my earpiece and speed-dialed Beth as I drove. She's known me forever. She's as close to a sister as I will ever get—now that my mother has safely moved past menopause without giving birth to a sixth child. Surely she could help me untangle my knotty life.

"This is Elizabeth DiVerino. I'm so sorry to miss your call. If you'll leave a detailed message, I will return your call at my earliest possible convenience."

"Love that message," I said into her voicemail. "So officious. Anyhow, I'm calling you back in the midst of extreme chaos, and I no longer mean baby puke, sleep deprivation and cranky mothers-in-law. We have moved into an orange alert over here. Drew's got someone missing at the school. I kissed my yoga teacher, or he kissed me, I don't know how it happened, but I wish it would happen again. I should be playing Wife of Clarkville Academy's Headmaster. Probably wouldn't be a good time to be caught kissing another man, would it? Have you seen Jake again? Is he still single? Don't ask me why I care. I care. God, after all these years, I still care. Pathetic.

Anyway, call on the cell phone. You can't breathe a word about any of this on the home phone. Priscilla is watching the baby. She's my new favorite babysitter, if you can believe it. That should tell you how bad it's become. Call soon. Okay, love you, bye."

I walked through Moonstar trying to appear calm. I didn't spot Oliver, but why should I have? It's not as though he lives at the café. I decided to walk to the studio. If I didn't find him there, I didn't know what I would do. If I *did* find him there, I didn't know what I would do. Would I kiss him again? Ever since our kiss, my mind kept flashing scenes of the two of us rolling around naked together in bed. I am a boring suburban mother, but I did wonder about his penis briefly, and naturally imagined it would be monstrous and chiseled like that of a Greek god.

Of course, I never truly believed I would have an opportunity to see said penis, even given my state of mommy-induced hysteria. Oh, how little did I know.

I pushed the door to the studio open. It took a great shove, which it doesn't normally, as if humidity had caused it to seal. It didn't occur to me that it might have been locked. It's a flimsy door and a flimsy lock. Besides, I was a woman on a mission.

"Oh."

"Joy."

"Wow."

"Joy."

"I'm sorry. The door. I didn't think—"

I stared for longer than I should have. There was a lot to stare at. Oliver, with his yoga shorts down around his ankles, and a really quite lovely penis throbbing with intensity at the mouth-level of a woman I'd often seen in class. In fact, if I wasn't mistaken, she had a daughter Zach's age and her name was Brenda and her bottom exceeded mine in every direction by several inches.

I wasn't sure if I wanted to laugh or cry, or neither or both.

"I'll come back later," I said politely. Brenda didn't look in my direction once. I can only imagine her humiliation. Blow job *asana* is not the posture you'd want to get caught doing.

As soon as I got out of the studio, I called Melody.

"You won't believe it."

"You kissed Oliver."

"What? What are you talking about? How did you know that?"

"A rumor. Going around the yoga studio."

"You're kidding!" I almost fell to the sidewalk with horror. "It can't be!"

"Well," she said calmly. "*Did* you kiss him?"

"I did kiss him, but I'm supposed to tell you that. You're my friend. You're not supposed to hear it through the grapevine."

"Well, my goodness. You've officially surprised me, and here I'd been upholding your reputation."

"It was *one* kiss. And I enjoyed it tremendously. But it's not going to happen again."

"How can you be so sure?"

"Because I just walked in on some other woman giving Oliver a pelvic kiss."

"This is no time to have manners, Joy, besides the fact that I've never known you to be modest in the slightest! Are you telling me that you just walked in on someone giving Oliver a blow job?"

"That would be correct."

"In the yoga studio?"

"In the yoga studio."

"Oh my God! That's so...so...wrong! I do *yoga* there." She started to laugh loudly. "Boy, is he ever the spiritual Don Juan."

"You're telling me. I thought he *liked* me."

"Obviously he liked you. He kissed you. It just seems he likes a lot of women."

"Should I be hurt?"

"Are you kidding? You're a married woman! You should be relieved that more didn't happen. I was going to tell you, I just never got around to it."

"What were you going to tell me?"

"That Oliver's been gaining a bit of a reputation for introducing some sexual yoga poses to his favorite students."

"He said the universe brought us together."

"Ha! His cock brought you together."

"You're so crude."

"Hey, I didn't kiss the man. Anyway, I guess he got in a lot of trouble at his last studio for having his way with one too many students. Sort of ruins the atmosphere for class."

"Where did you hear this?"

"Emma Lawson. She practices next to me. She's my yoga-mom buddy. Speaking of which, you should have stayed in the mommy-baby class. Carol definitely wouldn't have taken advantage of your vulnerable condition." She laughed again.

"You think this is really funny."

"It *is* really funny."

I thought about this for a moment. Considering the way I upset my mother and the fight I had with Drew and the relative disaster my life had become, Oliver's sexual exuberance seemed pretty damn funny. "You're right. It is really funny."

"So what was it like?"

"What?"

"His penis, of course."

"Immense."

"Just like I thought!" I could practically hear Melody slapping her thigh in the background. "Oh, man, we have to get together. I want the whole story moment by moment. But right now I have to take Sarah to my mother's."

"Something special?"

"Sunday family dinner. How about coming over Friday?"

"We'll see. Things are a bit of a mess right now."

"Oh, right. I'm sorry. I read about that missing boy in the paper this morning. How is Drew handling it?"

"I don't know. I haven't seen him. He left last night."

"Have you read the paper?"

"No, I haven't read the paper. I've been seeking out my sexual guru, as I already told you."

"You might want to take a look."

"Really?"

"I'll talk to you later. I've really got to get out of the house now before Sarah loses it. It's my window of happy baby opportunity. Call me soon."

When I got home, I said good-bye to Priscilla with a promise to see her the next day, and sat down to play with Zach. Drew still wasn't home, and I couldn't do anything, couldn't think of anything, couldn't figure anything out. I checked the messages to make sure no one had called for me. There were about ten business calls for Drew about the missing boy, but nothing from my mother. In an attempt to improve my mood, I crawled around with Zach on the floor and tickled him and sang the "Itsy Bitsy Spider" for him a hundred times.

You don't imagine, do you, when you are a small girl of say ten or eleven, that your life will be changed by a penis, a vagina and some boisterous bodily fluids? I read somewhere that statistically the first year of a child's life is the hardest for a couple's survival, which makes you wonder, doesn't it, why we ever came up with the design of the nuclear family in the first place since it evidently doesn't work very well. I think my own defense would have to be temporary post-mortem insanity, or could I just plead ignorance? I'd suffered through raising three of my four half-brothers from infancy on. I'd babysat for dozens of families. I thought I knew what I was getting in to. But no matter how hard you think it is, nor matter how hard people say it is, it's much, much harder.

They have these programs for teenagers where they have to spend a night with a doll that's programmed to cry at regular intervals. Apparently, this is an effective method of birth control. I once met a pediatric nurse who said pediatric nursing was the best method she'd ever come across. Yet all the mothers I ever spoke with, every mother who gave me unsolicited advice when I walked around with newborn Zach wailing from his six-hundred-dollar travel system stroller (for that much money, it should make them quiet), would say the same thing to me: Enjoy it. It goes so quickly.

In the early months, I longed for this advice to be true. I'd wake up each morning after patching together five hours of sleep in one-hour increments and expect to find a ten-year-old in the bassinet beside me. I couldn't understand why he hadn't already reached his first birthday. If it went so quickly, why did it feel so slow?

I know I asked a few women, including Melody Who Knows All, what they did to survive. The useless advice I got from all of them, regardless if they were strangers or friends, was "You get through it." Even those crazy people with their newborn twins seemed to think all one had to do was rise to the occasion. Personally, I wanted some real advice. Something *specific*. I wanted to close my eyes tight and find when I opened them that I knew what to do and that the baby had miraculously become a man, and a nice man, at that.

On the upside, I wouldn't trade Zach in for anything, not for a trip to Paris or a lifetime of lottery winnings or eternal life or the chance to be a saint (sounds boring anyway, and lonely), and not even to have my father back. I decided somewhere along the way that Zach was my reward for a depressing childhood. He was also his own reward for the challenges he offered me. Touching him, holding him, loving him, watching him become a person—like a real person—was a gift I'd never known to long for, as a kid, as a young adult, as an adult. I'd never known how satisfying it would be, the sight of his smile, the snuggles in the morning. If I'd known, maybe I wouldn't have felt so misplaced all my life. I would have known where to end up. Anyway, I'm here, and even though I'm crazier than before, and somehow less free and different and more tired, I'd rather have this mess and Zach than not have Zach at all.

With some heroism on my part (my scarlet letter being very heavy to tote around and my heart being somewhere in the vicinity of my knees), I managed to fix dinner for myself and Zach and spend the last hours of his day watching him walk and tumble, walk and tumble, a sight that did more for me than several weeks on a therapist's couch could ever achieve. Zach, at nine months, with a relatively small short-term memory, had no idea of the chaos that was swirling around him. He giggled and gurgled, and we read *Goodnight*

Gorilla six times before I nursed him to sleep. I took a quick trip to the mailbox once he was soundly asleep to pick up the day's paper. "Academy Boy Still Missing," read the front-page headline. I began to read.

Clarkville Academy, the once-prestigious private boy's high school that for years has struggled to survive, has confirmed that Caleb Phipher has been missing since late yesterday. His whereabouts are not known and searches through the night have not turned up any clues.

Phipher, a sophomore from Worcester, Massachusetts, did, according to the Academy's Media Relations Director, Ann Vine, leave a note. "We've given the note to the proper authorities," Vine said by phone. Sources say that the note specifically mentioned Andrew McGuire, the current headmaster, although the nature of the connection is not clear. Mr. McGuire was reached by phone late last night but was not present at the school at the time Phipher went missing.

"Phipher is an intelligent, unique individual," McGuire said. "I am certain we will be able to locate him quickly and safely." McGuire said that he knows all the students, but knows Phipher particularly well.

McGuire, who's been attributed with rescuing the academy from financial ruin and foreclosure, has been headmaster for four years. "I don't doubt that he will do everything in his power to make this situation work out positively for everyone involved," Cynthia Taylor, chair of the English Department, said. "He has an incredible way with the students."

Little is known about Phipher, 16, who entered the school this fall. Teachers report that he is quiet, hasn't participated in group sports, and lives in a dorm on campus for new freshmen and a handful of new sophomores. Most students begin the academy as freshmen.

The incident has been reported to Phipher's parents, who refused to comment when they were reached at their Worcester home—"

I put the paper down. I'd read enough, or at least enough not to embarrass myself the next time I talked to Drew. I kept wracking my memory to see if I'd logged any facts about this Caleb Phipher. Drew must have talked about him, but then there were so many Clarkville boys with so many problems, how's a wife to keep track?

Okay, so I did feel a little guilty for not remembering anything. It hardly seemed like a case of kidnapping. I mean, what were the chances this kid would show up at the bottom of a lake somewhere? It's more likely he ran away to southern California to start his movie career. Or maybe he went to New York City to a naughty girls' show and couldn't break away. I thought briefly about the possibility of Drew getting fired over the incident, and it only made me happy. But why was he mentioned in the note? I couldn't even begin to imagine. I was starting to feel like a possible guest on the *Dr. Phil* show, and that's just not the kind of television show I wanted to make my debut on.

I needed some relief.

I headed to the computer and stared blankly at the screen for about five minutes before I opened up my email account. I'd been waiting for an email from Jake. It seemed I'd been waiting for an email from him for the longest time, ever since our back-and-forth over the actual facts of our breakup a decade ago.

And there sat an unopened email from Jake Philips himself. Given my current state of affairs, I wasn't so sure opening it would be a good idea. At least I wouldn't find a picture of some gorgeous blonde giving him a blow job. I'd had enough voyeurism for one day. Possibly for a lifetime.

To: jmcguire@fanfare.com
From: jakephilips@lunerpress.com
Are you still out there? Never heard back from you. So we're still on the topic of our late, great love affair. You say I left you because there wasn't a spark? God, was I ever a teenager back then. I don't believe it. You were the first woman I dated who I actually liked. We talked to each other. I thought you broke it off with me to date Drew—isn't that what happened? And then before I knew it, you were married. Well, I do have an imperfect memory. But I was thinking the other day about your little dip in the school pond. On Halloween night. In your costume. What did you say when you plunged in? "Come on in, the water's great?" It must have been freezing. You were one wild child. I seriously doubt that I ever thought you were boring. In fact, I liked you because you weren't. And for the record, I wish I'd jumped in after you. You know what I mean? You only live once. —J

Maybe it was the sheer emotional exhaustion from the day, but I sat reading and rereading Jake's email until my eyes strained. Could he be right? Could I have remembered it wrong all this time? No, I distinctly remembered dating Drew with the hopes of making Jake jealous, of making him grow up, of making him want to marry me. And now, was he saying that he had? Was I reading too much into his words? And isn't that the trouble with email? I couldn't hear the sound of his voice, I couldn't see the expression on his face. And I wanted to. I wanted to see his face. If I saw his face, I would know, I would know something I needed to know. I loved his face, his squat nose, his curly hair. I think I always had, that teensy-weensy bit.

It's a mess here, I wrote quickly.

I told my mother the news about Donny last night. I don't think she's ever going to speak to me again. She never gets mad and she got seriously mad, for her. She threw her napkin down! You know my mother, that's practically like throwing pottery around the room just to hear it shatter. And Drew's got a bit of disaster, some kid's gone missing. I won't even go into the details about my philandering yoga teacher. At least I'm over my mastitis (that's that booby problem I told you about).

   And for the record, you really did leave me. I half-dated Drew hoping to win you back. Foolish, I know, but I thought it would change your mind.

I pressed send. I waited. I waited and waited. I went to the bathroom and checked on Zach and ate some popcorn and watched some lame TV and then I came back.

To: jmcguire@fanfare.com
From: jakephilips@lunerpress.com
You did?

Now, what was I supposed to do with that? The words hung suspended on the page. They said everything. They said nothing. The white space around them meant something, I knew it did. It was filled with longing—but was it my longing for Jake, or his longing for me?

Twenty-five

I WOKE IN THE EARLY DAWN WITH ZACH'S NOSE pressed directly into my armpit. "That must be aromatic," I said to his sleeping body. I'd had the bad taste to wake up before the sun had fully risen. "Ugh," I said, pushing off the covers. Early mornings are for virtuous people, of which I am adamantly not one. When I noticed Drew's side of the bed hadn't been used, I searched the house for him. How long could it take to find a missing person? And why hadn't he bothered to call me? I called his cell phone, which clicked me instantly to voicemail. Great. I did it again, just to make sure. He must have turned it off. I left a message, "Your wife wants to know where you are."

I grumpily made some coffee feeling neglected by everyone. Oliver had passed me over for another yoga student (paranoid thought: was my kissing *that* bad?), my mother (I checked the machine and my cell phone three times) no longer liked me and was probably snuggled up with Coach Donny even as I moped around the kitchen. Drew, what could even be said about him? He'd deserted us for the world of adolescent drama. And Jake. "God damn it, Jake," I said, to my granite countertops. He'd broken my heart and somehow *I'd* gotten it wrong? Had I been the one to break his heart? Oh, please, tell me it wasn't true.

I grabbed the phone and my coffee, went to my favorite chair and called Beth.

"There you are."

"I'm always here," she said.

"Not when I called yesterday."

"Okay. So not always. I've had a lot going on, if you know what I mean."

"No, I don't know what you mean."

"Why are you acting so short?" she asked.

"My life is over."

"A bit over the top, maybe?"

"It feels like it anyway."

"Well, I've reached nirvana," Beth said. "You're never going to believe it. I know you have all this stuff going down, but I've got to give you the good news first, then you can fill me in on the suburban wife's tales of drama."

"Beth! I need you."

"Oh, please let me go first. I'm just bursting."

I took a deep breath, just like Oliver had taught me. "Go ahead," I said. I could be gracious for a minute, couldn't I?

"You remember David Martin?"

"The nerd? From college? The one you lusted after at the reunion? The one you've been shagging? The one you've fallen in love with?"

"That would be the one."

"Of course I remember him. I *have* been paying attention to you, you know."

"We're getting married!" Her squeal practically blew off my eardrum.

"What do you mean, getting married? You can't get married. You're Beth. You're never getting married. You're constitutionally against marriage. You think of it as a sinkhole. You're the hip, wild, single gal. The next thing I know you're going to call and say you're giving birth to twins and can't stop baking cookies."

"I know. I know." Her laugh was pure joy. "I can't believe it myself. It hasn't been very long but you know when things are right—well, why would you do anything else? It seems so obvious to the both of us. I want to show you the ring. Can I send you a picture? It's breathtaking."

"God, Beth, you're wearing a diamond?"

"I am. It's love. It's totally, completely love. I've never felt this way before."

"Then I'm happy for you. Really. If a little bit stunned. You're lucky." I *was* happy for her. Still, her news made me sad, like my whole world was coming apart at the seams. Or more precisely, like everyone had fallen in love except me. And everyone was lucky in love except me. Had I made the wrong decision all those years ago?

"Oh, don't be sour. You're lucky too," she said. "You've already got a husband. And a baby. Now let's talk about the important details. Will you be my matron of honor?"

"Of course, of course," I said, although the thought of it tired me. On the other hand, maybe I could turn it into a real line of work, make some money off all my efforts. Surely there were brides somewhere who needed a rent-a-matron.

"Oh, thank you! It's going to be so wonderful! And you know the best part? I'm going to ask for a transfer to the U.S.!

We'll be in the same country again!" I could hear Beth tripping over her own happiness, and somehow, it made me feel much more alone in my rocking chair than I'd been before she called. I *had* felt that happy myself once, hadn't I, when I'd been getting married. But where did that happiness go? Is happiness like a toilet paper roll? Do you run out? Do you have to slip on a new roll? Can you even buy new rolls, or do you get a prescribed amount at birth? How could I have used all of mine up in under seven years?

"Joy?"

"Oh, sorry. I'm still here."

"What's going *on*?"

"I was just thinking about toilet paper rolls."

"In that case, you really do need some help. Tell me everything."

"There's not time."

"Start somewhere."

"No, I mean it. There's not time. I hear Zach. He just woke up. I've got to get him changed and nursed and settled and happy."

"You mean I don't even get to hear about your Adonis yoga teacher?"

"The one who kissed me and then moved on to another susceptible suburban mother? Is that the one you're talking about?"

"Get out!"

"I should have known he didn't really want me. I've got circles under my eyes the size of small swimming pools and the gut of a sixty-year-old beer-drinking bachelor."

"That's enough, Joy. You know you're beautiful. And it's not funny anymore, being so mean to yourself; you didn't used to be so self-deprecating. It's not flattering."

"Neither is motherhood."

"Actually, it seemed quite flattering on you—when *I* saw you at least. You're a natural mother."

"I am?" That was the nicest compliment I'd had all year.

"Oh, yeah. I thought you knew that. Anyway, conserve your energy. I need your help! I'm going to be a bride!"

And there she went, my last feisty, stubborn, radical friend, giving way to female hysteria and the lure of white taffeta. You might think that the last straw would have come sometime before this moment, say when I kissed Oliver, or when Caleb went missing, or during one of my countless arguments with Drew. But no. The last straw came when Beth broke her nuptial news. That was it. I couldn't take it anymore. I had to take charge of my life, and possibly everyone else's too. I didn't want to feel things spinning out of control any longer, not my mind or my heart or my vagina or my marriage or my weight or my mother or my mother-in-law or my night's sleep or my husband or my best friend or my sanity. I didn't want to be postmortem anymore. I wanted my life back. But what were the chances of that happening? It's not like I could stick the baby back up in my womb. Besides, I liked him in my life. Zach was the best thing since microwave popcorn. I couldn't go back. But how exactly could I go forward when I'd left myself behind like the old skin of a snake? How exactly could I pull it all together when it felt like someone had died the day Zach was born, and that someone was the only me I'd ever known?

Twenty-six

I SPENT THE MORNING ALONE WITH ZACH IN A CO-coon of domesticity. I seemed to be trying to show myself how normal everything was. Until I read the morning paper. "Clarkville Boy Still Missing: Headmaster Implicated."

Hmmm. Now this really was news. I hadn't seen Drew in something like thirty-six hours. And since he hadn't returned any of my calls, I was as eager to know what he was up to as the rest of Clarkville. The article, however, was less alarming than the headlines, and isn't that always the case? Apparently the note that Caleb had written mentioned Drew by name and no one else. Actually, it said, and they reprinted it in the paper, "If Mr. McGuire finds me that's the only way I'm coming back."

"This is so terrible," Priscilla said, practically busting down our door.

"Hi, Priscilla."

"I'm a wreck. I couldn't sleep. Did you see the morning's headlines? What are they trying to say? That my Andrew kid-napped the boy? It's not possible."

"Oh, Priscilla, don't worry. It's just for shock value. I know Drew. I'm sure he's out there saving the kid from some kind of hormonal tornado."

Priscilla scrunched up her face in distaste. "Oh, I wish my Walter were alive. He'd know how to help Andrew out."

"By the way, have you heard from him?"

"Oh, God!" She clutched her chest. "You haven't heard from him either?"

"No. I thought maybe he'd called you."

"This is so awful. Even if this boy manages to come back, what will it mean for the future? Surely Andrew will have to step down from his position. The bad press will ruin his reputation."

"I don't know about all that, Priscilla." She looked terrible, once I got a good look at her. Her eyes were sunken and red, like she'd been up all night crying. "Here," I said. "Say hi to Zach." I passed him into her arms. "He's almost due for his nap."

"Oh," she cooed at him. "I'll give him a bottle and rock him."

"Okay, I'll just heat up some breast milk." I'd started pumping milk expressly for the purpose of letting Priscilla give him a bottle.

While I took the bag out of the freezer, Priscilla said, "Where do you think he could be?"

"I have no idea."

"Kids now are so wicked," she said. "Shooting people in schools and causing all sorts of trouble."

"I don't think that's what this is about, Priscilla."

"But do you think he's safe?"

I stood in front of the sink running hot water over the bag of frozen milk. "He's fine. I'm sure—"

"Because I couldn't bear to lose him," she said right over my voice. "Not after my Walter."

"Oh, Priscilla," I said, turning around. "It's not that bad." She was clutching Zach to her chest with such ferocity I was afraid she might hurt him. I put the milk down and went over to take the baby from her arms, but she misunderstood my open arms and leaned into them for an embrace. I wrapped my arms around her and Zach, who was grunting a bit.

"He's all I have," she whimpered. "He's all I have."

And then some sort of angel of kindness swept over me and forced me to say these words, "No, Priscilla, that's not true. You have me too, and you have Zach."

And that's when she started to cry in the most awkward, noisy, coughing, choking, *wet* (she *was* leaning on my shoulder) kind of way. It made me feel like I had cooties, the authentic variety that you acquire in junior high school when some boy (who you actually have a wild crush on) manages to touch you during one of those enforced team games. Truly, there was visible snot on my shirt, but I kind of liked her in that moment. Or, at the very least, I knew how she felt; I'd lost someone I loved too.

Priscilla put Zach down for a nap. Then she volunteered to take a nap in the guest room. I got the distinct impression that she didn't want to go home. With the house quiet and Drew becoming somewhat of a missing person himself, a small yawn of emptiness opened up inside of me. I think this may be the very hole I'd been filling with M&M's since Zach's birth. Meanwhile, I could not find any M&M's in the house, or, for that matter, chocolate—of any kind, including baking chocolate, which I may well have eaten out of pure desperation. I didn't like the quiet. I didn't like it at all.

I called my mother.

I could practically hear my heart beating like horse's hooves barreling down the prairie.

"Hellooo," a voice said.

"Mom."

"Oh, Joy, she's gone out."

"Aunt Hilda?"

"The very one."

"I'll just try to get her on her cell phone."

"She's left it here."

"She *left* her cell phone?"

"I think she may have gone camping."

"*Camping?!* My mother? You must be mistaken."

"I generally am," she said pleasantly.

"I need to talk to her. I need to apologize for the other night."

"She said she'd only be gone a few days. She left the cell phone with me in case I needed it, when I go out for my walks. She traveled with Donny. He carries his own."

"Right," I said. I'd been pacing the family room filled with anxiety over talking to my mother. Now that I knew it wasn't possible, I sat down in my favorite chair. "Well, thanks, Aunt Hilda."

"Thank you for calling," she said in a singsong voice.

I was quiet for a moment, thinking. "I've been having a hard time," I said.

"I know hard times. They know me. We go way back."

"Oh, I'm sure. And my hard time is probably nothing in comparison. It just seems I've got myself into a little mess."

"Let me tell you something. I may not be your mother but I *am* old and old people know things, or at least that's what I thought when I was young. Now that I'm old, I'm not so sure, but that's not what I want to say to you. What did I want to say to you?" I could practically hear her wracking her brain.

"I don't know. Something about my life being a mess." Then I thought of something. "Hey, Aunt Hilda? You know how you read my fortune? Do you remember telling me about some man, some other man in my life? Do you remember what you said he looked like? Do you know anything about him?"

"I don't remember anything about anybody. But I'll tell you this. As long as you're alive, you're as free as you let yourself be."

"Right," I said absently, frustrated. "Thank you."

"You aren't trapped, you know. No one is ever trapped. The world is bigger than your brain, haven't you noticed?" She laughed, a glorious sound if I'd ever heard one. I wished it was loud enough to fill the silent house.

When I hung up with her, I dialed Diana, feeling more and more desperate to get some good advice, although I wasn't even sure of the question I wanted to ask. It was like having an itch on your back, the kind that you can almost reach but not quite, and you need someone else to find it, identify it, relieve it. You don't even have the words to say where it is—up, to the left, near the shoulder blade? You only know when it's found.

"Thank God you're there," I said at the sound of Diana's reassuring hello. "I'm in a bit of a funk. And there's no chocolate in the house. And Oliver's got a new girlfriend and Drew is off finding a missing person—"

"I know. I read about it. It's terrible news. I hope that boy is okay. You never know in situations like this. Sometimes it's suicide," she said in a whisper.

"I feel like everything's fallen apart. I told my mother about Donny and she won't talk to me. I don't even know if what I told her is true, although I thought it was at the time. In fact, I don't know anymore why I did that. Do you think that I'm jealous of her? That all along I've just been wanting what she has? Love?"

"I don't know. I can't say. I—"

"It's this email I got from Jake. It's shaken my whole foundation."

"Oh." Her voice got low, conspiratorial. "What did he say?"

"I don't know if he said anything, really. Or maybe he said everything. I can't figure it out. It's driving me crazy. He seems to remember that *I* dumped him, that I left him for Drew."

"But that's not what happened."

"I know. But what if I had it wrong? Or what if I didn't have it wrong but it's all right now? Do you know what I mean?"

"I'm not following. Maybe it's Addicus. He hasn't napped today. He's like a wild animal. It's very distracting."

"I'm sorry. Should I call later?" *Please say no.*

"Of course not."

"Thank God. I need someone to talk to!"

"Tell me what he actually wrote."

"It wasn't the words he wrote, it was the tone. It made it seem like he regretted breaking up with me, that he wished he had me now."

"Really?"

"That's how it seemed to me. How can you really tell in an email? But you know what the worst part is?"

"Too sharp," I heard her say to Addicus. "I'm sorry. I'm listening. Something about the worst part."

"The worst part is that I feel like I've been waiting a decade to have him say those things to me, to finally love me again, to want me again. Even after everything, life with Drew and marriage and Zach—I just really wanted that from him."

"And now that you have it?"

"I don't know," I started to cry, despite myself, and I could hear in my tears the same silly blubbering noises I heard from Priscilla, which just made me cry all the more.

"Oh, Joy."

"I think that I love him . . . that I always loved him. . . . When I was with him, I felt so lucky. I felt so much like myself. I look at my mother in her joy over Donny—I felt like that! It makes me feel my marriage with Drew was built on a false premise. In some ways I always intended to get Jake back. That's no foundation for love, is it?"

She was silent for a few moments. "No. I guess not. But you wouldn't really leave Drew, would you?"

Would I? The house seemed to echo the question. I might as well have been in a Hitchcock movie, it felt so much like something ominous was due to happen at any moment. I never thought of divorce before. I never wanted to be like my mother, in and out of marriages. I wanted a family that would stay together—nobody dies and nobody leaves. And that's why I married Drew, because he felt the same. "I can't give Zach a stepfather," I said. "I don't want him spending every other week with Drew; that wouldn't be fair to either of them."

"Of course you don't. Nobody wants that. But that's not how things happen, or at least that's not the *reason* things happen."

I heard a stirring in the other room, Priscilla, probably, waking from dreams of Walter. I wished, for a moment, that I loved Drew the way she loved Walter. What was it my mother had said that night I told her about Donny? Go find your love? Go live your love? Wasn't it something like that? Something like what Oliver said over and over again. "You have to dive deep," Oliver said during one particularly memorable class. "It's important that you know your heart. Dive into the stillness inside of it and hear what it has to say."

And I hadn't, had I, all this time, listened to that heart, listened to all that it knows, stopped in the stillness to hear? Well, damn if it wasn't time to start. As Jake said, you only live once. And me, I'm the girl who dived into the pond on the last day of October in New England. I could bear the cold. I could risk the plunge. I was brave, wasn't I? Or at least, once, a long time ago, I had been.

And I could be again.

I tiptoed to the office and wrote Jake an email. All of a sudden, I knew what I needed to do to correct that teensy-weensy little mistake I'd made so many years ago.

Twenty-seven

THE WOMAN IN THE STALL NEXT TO ME LET OUT A STAC-
cato fart and an unnerving moan. I don't know
about other people, but I am not a fan of public bathrooms.
There is something profoundly awkward about listening to a
stranger poop two feet away from you. Not seeing the person
doesn't solve the problem for me. I'm of the mind that all
public bathrooms should be single stall, privately enclosed. I
peed and washed my hands quickly (neither of which are easy
tasks when you have a large infant strapped to your chest) in
the hopes of dashing out of the bathroom without having to
set eyes on the pooping woman. It was just way more intimacy than I wanted to have with a stranger.

But then airport bathrooms are nothing if not strange. At
the sink, a twenty-something woman was brushing her teeth
vigorously while listening to an iPod. She was bound, no
doubt, for Nepal or some other exotic place that appeals to
wanderers. I looked at Zach in the mirror. He smiled at his
own reflection. I wore him like a badge of honor, like a mark
of identification, a measure of the love I had gained and the

freedom I had lost. I was not a wanderer anymore. Did the young woman wonder what I was doing there, at JFK Airport on a Tuesday afternoon? Probably not. I am no longer an object of curiosity.

"Cute," she said after she spit into the sink, nodding in Zach's direction.

"Thanks," I said, and then I picked up my small carry-on bag and walked out.

My flight was scheduled to leave at 7:30 p.m., which meant I would arrive in London for the morning, though it would feel like the middle of the night. I didn't mind this, but I was worried about Zach. And how would he do on the plane itself? At least I always carried the secret weapon with me—my breasts. Breastfeeding Zach is such an effective method of making him happy/getting him to sleep/quieting him down/ feeding him/consoling him/being close to him/cuddling with him/getting him to stop crying that I can honestly say, though it may put me in a camp with the zany, braless-swinging-breast-hippies, that I will breastfeed this child for as long as he will allow me to, up to and including the teenage years. From what I've heard, they're pretty terrible. Why not?

I took my place with my fellow travelers at Gate 7, sliding into one of the world's most uncomfortable seats. You have to wonder who designs these places. Are they worried someone will be tempted to linger? Like you love the airport so much you just can't leave, so they have to make the place as unappealing as possible to avoid this phenomenon?

I noticed Zach's head lolling off to the side, a sign that sleep was imminent. This was good, because at least he wasn't screaming, and not so good, because I wanted him to save his sleep for the airplane so that he wouldn't be screaming *then*. I could already see that I wasn't going to make any friends with the fellow passengers. One sight of the baby attached to my front and they practically grimaced with anticipated anger over his fussiness. Everyone has their story of flying on a plane with a raging maniac baby or a rabid toddler. I said a little prayer to the sleep gods hoping he'd conk out for most of the trip.

A man near me jostled his leg incessantly. That's at least as annoying as a crying baby, isn't it? He made me nervous. He was reading a book but he kept shifting in his seat every ten seconds. What was he so anxious about? I had a brief, horrifyingly paranoid thought that maybe he was a terrorist of some kind. At right about that moment he looked over at me and smiled.

"How old?"

"He'll be ten months in the middle of December."

"He's adorable. My son is seven months."

"Oh, that's great."

"I always miss him when I travel."

"I bet. I haven't been away from Zach for more than a few hours."

"Same with my wife. She's very devoted. You're lucky, anyway."

"Oh, I know," I said without thinking. And then I thought: Was I lucky? I certainly hadn't been feeling very lucky. Or *acting* very lucky.

I took a granola bar out of my pocket and started eating. The man went back to his book. Zach began to gently snore. About every third minute I debated getting up and running. What was I doing anyway? Who, exactly, did I think I was, some Hollywood celebrity with her own television show? What right did I have to do something so dramatic?

The dreadlocked teenager sitting across from me turned

his iPod up so loud I could hear Bob Marley crooning that I shouldn't worry about a thing. Enough ganja and I would probably feel the same way. Only I didn't. I felt like there was a very lot to worry about.

My cell phone rang. My heart leapt straight out of my body and onto the floor. I searched for it frantically, terrified of who it could be. Was it Drew, finally returning my calls? I still hadn't heard from him. I'd left another message for him while driving to the airport, something like "Call back now or forever hold your peace." But what if it was Jake, responding to my email?

"You are so *not* coming to London!" Beth's voice came screaming through the phone. "Good grief, girl, what's got into you?"

"I've got to see Jake. I've got to see him in person and work this out for myself."

"You are so not in love with him. It's been a decade!"

"Then why does my heart leap every time I get an email from him? Why do I still remember the sound of his voice and the feel of his body wrapped up in mine, sleeping?"

"I don't know. Because you're sentimental, that's why! What about Drew?"

"What about Drew? I realized I only married him to make Jake jealous, to try and win him back—"

"That's ridiculous. I was at your wedding. You were over the moon!"

"We didn't have a wedding," I wailed.

"Details. Civil ceremony, whatever. You cried. I remember that. You told me you'd finally found the Ken to your Barbie."

"He did seem good, it's true, back then. But my heart was with Jake. My heart has always been with Jake."

"Then why aren't *you* with Jake?"

"That's what I've been asking myself!" I almost jumped from my seat. She actually got it, she got what I was saying. "That's why I'm coming to London."

"Does he know this?"

"Of course. I emailed him."

"Did he email back?"

"There wasn't time. I sort of planned all this in a hurry."

"You can stay at my place obviously. I can't believe you had to ask me. And you're taking a taxi over my dead body. I don't know why you even suggested that. Hey, does your mother know about all this?"

"She's the one who encouraged me, kind of. She told me to find my love or something like that. She thinks I'm jealous of what she and Donny have."

"Maybe you are."

"That's outrageous. He's a rotund, cowboy-boot-wearing new-age, sexuality uncertain, underemployed old man!"

"Like love cares about any of that," she said. "You know the upside of this whole thing is that you'll be able to help me go dress shopping! Hehe." She sounded quite pleased.

"Perfect timing. My marriage is unraveling and yours is just set to begin. Talk about depressing."

"Hey, aren't you happy for me? I've finally found a man who's changed all my thoughts about marriage."

"No, it's great, Beth. Of course it's great. I'm just not feeling very chipper right now. In fact, I feel a little sick to my stomach. I want to get all of this solved. I feel like if I can just put my eyes on Jake again, I'll know everything I need to know."

"Then you will," she said. "You will know, Joy, you spunky thing. I'm glad to see your wild side is making a much overdue appearance. You always were a spontaneous person. Now, call me the second the plane lands, okay?"

"Okay," I said. I heard the loud smack of a kiss on the other side of the phone and we said good-bye.

I flipped the phone closed, embarrassed that maybe the man next to me had heard her. Beth has a tendency to speak loudly, like she's talking to a deaf grandmother. It's not one of her better qualities. The man smiled at me briefly. I smiled at him. Did we just share a moment? Thank goodness for the kindness of strangers. I certainly didn't feel like anyone else was in the mood to be kind to me. Of course I hadn't heard from my mother, and I desperately needed her advice. In fact, more than anything, I needed to talk to my mother.

Feeling like an orphan, I picked up a newspaper someone had left on the chair beside me and began to read in that un-reading sort of way you can do when your mind is elsewhere. In other words, I read about three different articles without absorbing a single word. I had no idea what I'd read about. The constant interruptions, the flights being called, the shuffle of people walking through the wide concourse behind me, all of this distracted me. I checked my watch. Half an hour to go before boarding time. At least the flight hadn't been delayed. I took out another granola bar and started in on it. I was about halfway through my munchathon when I noticed two men walking down the aisle purposefully, as if they were hell-bent on reaching me.

And one of them happened to be my husband.

"Joy." Drew stood in front of me. The man he'd been walking with wandered over to the enormous glass windows to look out at the flickering lights of planes coming and going in the night sky.

I looked up at my husband's face. He looked strained, exhausted, unshaven and very, very, worried.

"What are you doing here?" Drew was the very last person I'd expected to show up. I hadn't seen him in days; he hadn't even returned my phone calls. How had he found me?

He held up two tickets and flapped them in the air. "My friend and I are headed to St. Thomas. One-way. Small price to pay to see my wife."

"Are you serious?"

"They don't let you in here without a ticket. So, yes, I'm serious. But what I really want to know is if *you're* serious. What are you *doing* here?"

"I came for the comfortable chairs," I said, laughing. "Great food. To check out the recent remodel of Terminal Eight."

"It's not funny."

"It's *not* funny?"

"Joy."

"Why don't you sit down? Don't make a scene."

"That's what you care about? I just coughed up almost two thousand dollars for a trip for two to the Carribbean that I'm not actually going to take just so I could talk to you, and all you care about is my making a scene?"

"Not even close; I care about a lot of things. I care about my son, first of all, which is more than you can say. I care about myself. I care about my life. I care about having a marriage with a human being and not a ghost. I care about all my friends and my family and my future and the quality of programming on prime-time television, and I care about this child. Did I say that? That's what I care about, most of all. And second to that is me. But maybe you haven't noticed us. Maybe we have to run away, make the headlines, to get your attention." I couldn't help it. I'd begun to shout just the smallest bit. The teenager across the aisle turned his iPod off like he *wanted* to hear what I said.

"I mean, let's start at the beginning, shall we? You, my adoring spouse, my birth coach, decided to go on a trip just around the time of my due date. Good idea or bad idea? What do you think?" I held up my hand. I could see that Drew wanted to speak. "Oh, but there's more! You spend the first few months of your son's life *in absentia,* consumed with helping other boys, other children, and leaving me to essentially be a single parent. When I bring this up to you, you bristle, you defend. You act like it was *my* idea, since I was the one who wanted to stay home. Yeah, I wanted to stay home with Zach. Sure, I wanted that house in the suburbs, the same as you. I wanted a nice life, a nice home. I wanted enough money to not have to work—but at what cost?

"Don't you get it, Drew? I was alone all that time. You were gone when I needed you the most. And then in some kind of freak moment we make up about the whole birth incident, but what does that change? You start to bathe Zach. Well, gee, you deserve a prize then, don't you! What does that mean? That you've been parenting your son for ten minutes a day! Go, you! What a triumph."

"But—"

"And there's more still. A few conjugal relations here and there—for what purpose? To relieve you of a few sperm? Where's the love been, Drew, all this time? You know what I think? I think it's never been there. I think all these years have been a fraud. I think our whole marriage is built on a false premise, and it took this baby drama to reveal the truth. If our relationship can be thrown into total chaos with just one child—one!—then there can't be much to it. It's nothing. It's a flimsy bit of nothingness. A mistake. A charade. An enormous error in judgment."

I noticed that my new friend, the man with the seven-month-old son, was staring at me. In fact, I'd drawn a bit of an eavesdropping crowd. You'd think marital dramas didn't happen all the time in the American Airlines concourse. I couldn't be the only disgruntled wife who'd argued with her husband at Gate 7, could I?

Drew sat down next to me. He leaned over his thighs and put his head in his hands.

"You're right," he said into his hands.

"Excuse me?"

"I *said* you're right." Now, this was headline news. This was the biggest thing since chocolate and peanut butter had found each other. Drew took his head out of his hands and looked over at me. "I've been a jerk—but I never intended to. I know that doesn't help. I thought I was ready." I looked at him quizzically. "For a baby. I figured if I could take on running a school, I could certainly handle being a father. I guess I freaked out."

"You *guess*?"

"I did. I know I did. Look, Joy, I got really scared, even before the baby came. And then when he was born, well, we just didn't have much in common." I laughed. Despite myself, I loved Drew's uncharacteristically funny moments. "And you seemed to know what to do. You could make him stop crying when I never could."

"You didn't try."

"I did try."

"For five seconds."

"I couldn't nurse him. That's what he wanted. And of

course Clarkville really needs me. There's always more to do there than I ever have time for. You didn't seem to mind my being gone so much before the baby came. I didn't think that would change—"

"How can it not?"

"I just didn't *know* that then. I guess it's been easier for me to work. At least I know how to do that."

"But what about the summer?"

"The garden was easier too. Anything was easier. I've never been around babies."

"But he's your son!" I said.

"I know." He shook his head. "I fucked up. Everything you said about what's happened this year is right. I just couldn't deal with it. I mean, Joy, you've been . . . different. We used to talk about things and watch movies and you'd listen to me about work. You wanted to have sex and dance and play with me. None of that happens anymore. And you kind of freaked out yourself." I bristled. "Spying on Donny?"

"That was legitimate. I have to look out for my mother."

"How about leaving me to go find your college boyfriend in London?" I heard the man next to me take in a breath of surprise. I couldn't bear to look at him; we'd shared our moment; what did he think of me now? "Honey," he said, putting his hand on my arm. "You've been a little crazy since Zach was born."

"And for good reason! I've had to do everything alone. It's been about seven hundred million times harder than I expected it to be. I've been bored and isolated and lonely. When I look at myself in the mirror, it's like looking in a fun-house mirror."

"I know," he said quietly. "I wish I could have helped you. I messed up."

"Only totally."

"But you didn't make it easy. You've been hard to talk to, hard to reach. I have been trying with Zach lately."

"Too little, too late," I said. "Besides, it's not even about all of that. I just think I love Jake, and I need to find out."

Drew looked away from me, at the man standing at the windows, his back toward us. He was almost motionless. "I don't believe it."

"It's not for you to believe! We're not talking UFOs here. These are my feelings."

"Right on," the boy across from me said, and he flashed me the peace sign.

"When I first met you, Drew, I'd just broken up with Jake."

"I know that. I know all about that."

"I don't think I ever got over him . . . and I'm sorry to say that I think my feelings for him were part of why I married you."

"What are you saying?" He looked alarmed.

"I might have married you to make him jealous."

"I don't believe it." He glanced over at the boy across the aisles as if waiting for his comment. "I *mean,* I know that isn't the case."

"How can you know that? You aren't in my heart."

"But that's the thing. I *am* in your heart. I remember what it was like. We both knew almost immediately that we wanted to get married. You told me how happy you were to finally be in a relationship of equals. You and Jake hadn't had sex in a year!"

I winced, feeling the reaction of all the passengers nearby. Beautiful. Better even than daytime television. All my private affairs hung on the airport laundry line, except instead of Dr. Phil, I had Dr. Ganja. (He wasn't doing too bad a job either.)

"Look, Drew. I've got to figure this out for myself. These past nine months have taught me something about myself. I don't want to be the person I am when I'm with you. I want to be the person...the person Jake knows, the person Jake makes me feel I am. He understands me. And supports me. He helped me with the whole Donny thing when you were too busy to even care. He knows who I really am, the free me, the fun me, the alive me. With you I'm just dead."

Drew put his head back in his hands. "That's not fair," he said. "If you had a baby with Jake things would have changed too. You can't blame everything on me. Our lives have changed; we both need to grow up and accept that. We can't live the way we used to, neither of us can. I can't keep working like I did before I had a baby, and you can't keep being a fly-by-the-seat-of-your-pants person when you have a young infant. We have to carve out a new way to live. And you know what? I think it will be better. Look what we've gained." He reached over and gently stroked Zach's sleeping head.

"We will now begin boarding flight six eighty-seven to London's Heathrow Airport at Gate seven," a voice called out over the loudspeaker. "Passengers holding green boarding passes and parents with strollers boarding now, please."

I looked at Drew. He looked at me. The teenager across from us looked at both of us. Nobody moved.

"Who's that guy?" I asked Drew, pointing to the man at the window.

"That's Caleb."

"*The* Caleb? The one who's been missing?" Drew nodded his head. "What in the world is he doing here?"

"I just found him. Then when I found out about you there wasn't time to drop him off. I rushed straight here."

"How did you find out about this? I've hardly told anyone."

"You told *someone*."

"No. I didn't." I thought for a moment. A sinking sensation hit me, deep in the belly, the way you feel right before you lose your lunch. "Not Jake?"

"He called me."

"But why would he do that?"

"He thought it was only fair that I knew. You know we've been emailing back and forth a little. He's my friend too, after all."

"How did he even have your number?"

"It's on all my emails."

"Now boarding passengers in first class for flight six eighty-seven to Heathrow Airport, first-class passengers only please."

"Where did you even find him?" I pointed to Caleb.

"It's a long story. If you come home with me, I'll tell you."

I couldn't look at Drew. I started to count the crumbs on the floor below my feet.

"Go with the one love," the teenager said. He was rocking gently with his eyes closed. That may be the only moment in my life when being an adolescent seemed preferable to being an adult. Or when being a serious pot smoker seemed like a very wise decision.

"Come home," Drew said. "I'm sorry. I'm sorry. I love you. Look at me, please." I looked at him. "I don't know how it is for you. I can't revise our history. But I can tell you that when I first found you, I felt so happy, so lucky. I didn't marry you for any reason other than I loved you and wanted to be with you. That may not fix everything. I've screwed up, and I know it. It took Caleb to help me see that." I raised my eyebrows. "It's a long story. Anyway, please. We both messed up. All this time, I felt like we were in totally different places. But you know what I figured out? We're actually in the same place.

We've just been reacting to it differently. If we could share our stresses over Zach instead of running from each other . . ." He sighed. "It's only going to get better. Please, give me another chance. Come home."

"Now boarding passengers in coach, rows one to five," the voice called out. I looked over at the counter to see an attractive middle-age woman speaking into a microphone. She caught my eye and smiled sympathetically at me, as if she too had been a part of my great public discourse with Drew.

The man beside me, my stranger friend, grunted and stood up, a large black briefcase in one hand. What would he say? I wondered. I looked into his face. I noticed things I hadn't before, old acne scars, the beginning of jowls, a nick on his neck from shaving. He avoided my gaze at first and then he looked at me, and something about it, something about the kindness in his eyes opened up the dammed rivers of my heart.

"Good luck," he said, and then remarkably, he reached out and grabbed my hand, holding it for the briefest moment, as if I were someone he loved dearly, someone he loved and had to leave behind. His hand was rough, clammy. I saw a few dark, thick hairs on his thumb. It made me feel such tenderness toward him, an ocean of compassion for what we are, just merely human, imperfect, with hair in the wrong place and our histories written all over our faces. And then he let go. I watched his wrinkled backside walking away. I noticed he was overweight. He didn't look back.

"Joy," Drew said, trying to pull me back. "Come home. Please. We're a family."

"Now boarding rows one to ten for flight six eighty-seven at Gate seven, rows one to ten only please."

I stood up.

Twenty-eight

DECEMBER 22, THE DAY OF MY MOTHER'S WEDDING, dawned bright and freezing, perfect white muff weather. While the sun rose, Zach enjoyed his latest discovery as I gave him a special must-look-your-best morning bath. This discovery was none other than his penis. I think this may have been God's Christmas present to him. He'd noticed it before, of course, but recently he'd really *found* it. It became his favorite bath toy. Sometimes I could hardly get his hands off of it to put a diaper on. He would look at it quizzically then look at me. "That's your penis," I'd tell him over and over again, like a strange recording from some basic anatomy class. "That's your penis." Being the modern, open-minded person that I am, it didn't bother me that he occasionally felt more fondness for his penis than he ever felt for any of his toys (although I think I can say now, as a veteran mother, that no young baby actually needs a toy. Give him a spatula, an ear bulb, a bottle of sesame seeds, a paper towel roll and various sizes of Tupperware and life will be grand). I did have to draw the line, though, at his propensity to tug on his penis while I nursed him. It just reminded me too much of the sex I had in college.

"It only gets worse," my mother said. "Wait until he's a teenager with a penis."

"Mom," I squealed. "Gross."

"That's life, sweets," she said.

She'd started talking to me again, ever since I made a personal apology to Donny. I went to his office late on a Thursday evening. It was snowing for the first time, those flakes that fall slowly and don't amount to anything but make you feel sentimental just the same. It's weather foreplay for snow enthusiasts who are just aching to get to a ski slope and risk death for the thrill of plummeting downhill strapped into enormous elf shoes. I guess I'm just not much of a daredevil. I'm also really bad at skiing. What I do resembles tumbling and falling much more than anything else.

That night I found Donny in his office, packing.

"What happened?" I asked, looking around at the room full of boxes.

"I gave it a try. I didn't end up being very good at it." He shook his head, but he smiled. "It was fun for a change. Just one of those things I'd dreamed of doing during retirement."

"I'm sorry."

"Don't be. I'll move on to other things now. I actually have a list of about twenty things I want to do."

"No, really, I'm sorry. I sort of feel like it's my fault."

"Why would it be your fault?"

"I don't know. I guess I'm feeling generally guilty—for what I did."

"You know, Joy, it's okay. No harm done." He sat down in one of his cushy chairs.

"So you're really a professor?" I asked.

"Well, not in a while. I retired early." He laughed. "I always wanted to be a little more bohemian than a stuffy Yale professor specializing in military history."

"That was your thing?"

"I know. Dull."

"Can I ask you something?"

"You can ask me anything." Said with his southern accent, it seemed that he really did mean it.

"What's the deal with the group for gay people? And I found you online talking about gay people in the military."

"Oh, right." He laughed again. "I did start going to a group for gay people and their friends and family right after my brother came out. The news really tore me up; I didn't know how to react. He has a family, two grown children, a beautiful wife. Then I started attending the PFLAG meetings—that's for people whose children and friends are gay—and I got so involved that I began writing a bit about the issue. And because I know about the military, I was asked to write in to a magazine as an online 'expert' and occasionally contribute to chat pages. It felt like something I could do to support my brother. No doubt you uncovered that little tidbit."

"So you're not gay?"

"No, I'm not gay." He couldn't help chuckling. "Is that what you were afraid of?"

"I was afraid of a lot of things. Like losing my mother. I always have been."

"I'll tell you one thing, Joy," he said, getting up and coming over to me. He pulled me into one of his breathtaking hugs, which I endured on account of feeling so totally foolish for what I had done. But I did make a promise to myself not to just let him hug me at random. He *smelled*, like garlic and something else, something I couldn't quite put my finger on.

8

Ketchup, maybe? "As long as your mother is with me, I won't let anything happen to her." He pulled away from me. "Sound good?"

I nodded. After some more small talk about wedding plans, I made my escape.

"One more thing." I had my hand on the doorknob. "Why haven't you been married before?"

"Oh, I have. I was married when I was quite young. My wife died. We were only married a year before she found out she had stage-four breast cancer. And after that? Well, I didn't find anyone until I met your mother. But it was so worth it, the whole wait. She would be worth waiting for a hundred years."

So they had that in common, I thought, heading out. Dead spouses. Well, Drew and I had dead parents in common. That's not too bad for a bond, is it?

I bundled Zach up before I plopped him in his car seat. The gymnastics required to get him in and out of his bunting with mittens attached would lead me directly to the Olympic trials. (Have you ever put a mitten on a ten-month-old? It's like putting a shoe on a snake.)

My cell phone rang.

"I'm just running out the door."

"Oh, my goodness, I totally forgot. Today is your mother's wedding."

"The long awaited."

"I'll call you later."

"Did you need something?" Diana was always too polite to come out and ask me for anything.

"I had a little bit of a favor, actually."

"Hit me."

"Will you come for the birth?"

"Are you kidding?!"

"I'm sorry. Is that too much?"

"No, of course not. I'd love to be there. I want to see this little potato make its grand entrance. I will totally be there."

"Oh, thank you, Joy. I don't know what I'd do without you. I'm so glad you didn't make it to London."

"I wouldn't have minded a little European vacation."

"I would have missed you terribly," Diana said.

I would have missed her too, but that's not what I was thinking when I stood up and took my place in line to board the plane. Drew looked as though he could cry. I got my tickets out and, right at that moment, the elusive Caleb trotted over to Drew's side. They engaged in a conspiratorial conversation during which I wondered briefly if they were formulating a plan on how to get me out of the airport against my will. I took a step to the left, out of the line, so I could hear them better. I can't stand people whispering in public; it's so rude. It doesn't really give one any other choice *but* to eavesdrop.

I could only make out about every third word, which didn't quite help me get the whole jumping-off-the-bridge story (Caleb, of course, not Drew) that I later learned about. However, I did hear Drew's voice, quiet and reassuring, meeting every statement of Caleb's with an "I see." "I understand." "Of course." I realized quickly that despite the fact that I, Drew's wife, was boarding a plane and leaving him for another man—or at least the possibility of another man—Drew and Caleb were not talking about me. Much to the surprise of my self-consumed ears, they were talking about Caleb. I was so moved, I didn't have time to be offended. Listening to Drew's kindness, remembering that it was part of what attracted me to him, and hearing how it softened Caleb's heart, reminded me of something I *had* forgotten.

I loved this man, my husband.

Then Caleb came over to me.

"Hey," he said. "Your husband's pretty cool."

"Thanks."

"It's a bummer he quit."

"What?" I looked over at Drew. "Because of *you*," I said, looking back at Caleb. A flash of anger hit me; what right did this kid have to mess up Drew's life?

"No," Drew said, stepping over. They called my plane again. I didn't move. I wanted to know the dirt, and I didn't want to get it from across the sea. "I put in my resignation before all of this happened."

"What? Are you crazy?"

"I took a position at Harborside. Dean of Students. Never more than forty hours." Harborside is a coed day school in Branford. "It's a drive, but it will free up a lot of time." He saw the questions in my eyes. "Slightly less salary. And you know, if the commute is a problem, we can think about moving."

"I can't believe it." I couldn't have been more surprised if he'd told me he was going in for sex-reassignment surgery, although this was much better news. I really like Drew as a man.

He ran a hand through his smooth blond hair. "I've missed a lot. I want to be around more."

"Why didn't you say so? Why didn't you tell me?"

"I'd been waiting to hear from Harborside. I wanted to make sure it was a done deal. And then all of this happened." He gestured toward Caleb, who seemed to be enjoying the conversation a little more than I would have liked.

"See?" Caleb said. "He's a smart guy. Good planning, man."

He slapped Drew on the back. It seemed my escapades had gone from voyeurism to exhibitionism, and frankly I wasn't too keen on either of them anymore. All of a sudden, I wanted to be alone—like in my own bathroom, in my own living room, with my own husband, without a couple dozen strangers looking on.

So I went home.

Later, all the facts came out about Caleb's disappearance, how the search party found him on top of the tallest building in Bridgeport (sixteen stories, to be exact) threatening to jump. When Drew arrived, he talked him down. The media went wild, of course. He *had* saved someone's life. Then Clarkville offered him double his salary if he stayed. He was a hero, after all.

"Ready?" Drew said then, ambling over to the car in his finest dark wool suit, ready for the wedding.

"Hey," I said. "You're more dressed up than you were for *our* wedding."

"You like it?"

"It's okay."

"Okay? Is that all I get?"

"Pretty good, is that better?"

"It's better."

"How about handsome? You look as good as you did at twenty-five."

"Ah, that's more like it."

We got in the car for the big drive down to the Temple of Divine Light and Energy where I would meet up with my mother and her Texan-style big hair. "How will I know it's you?" I asked her on the phone the other day when she mentioned her plans for a far-out southern coiffure. "Should I look for the two-foot bangs?"

* * *

The ceremony went perfectly, but what wedding doesn't? All the pretty music and the gang of well-dressed people and promises of eternity, who wouldn't enjoy that? I stood at the front of the hall beside my mother who stood beside Donny who had indeed worn a kilt, or anyway some kind of renaissance man-skirt. But to his credit, he cried through his vows. Very sincerely too. I thought of Jake as I stood up there, who it seemed I would never marry, not the first time, not the second time. I would keep missing the chance to marry him. And for a moment, I missed him like I miss Zach when I'm away from him for a few hours. But that wasn't true. The person I missed was me—the younger, unencumbered version of myself. And who was going to give her back to me, that young, free woman? Nobody but me.

I looked out into the enormous congregation of well-wishers. There, in the front row, sat Drew, with Zach on his lap, gleefully gnawing on a cookie. (I suspected Priscilla as the source of this evil act, but it was keeping him quiet so I decided not to complain. Besides, making "no" gestures from the altar didn't seem like good form.) After our grand wedding party recession, I went back into the large white hall to join Drew and Zach so we could ride together to the reception.

"That was unique," Drew said as he drove.

"Which part? The kilt? The electric harp music, or their twenty-minute-long vows?"

"I've got to hand it to your mother. She really knows how to do things with style."

"Next to her, I feel like a toad."

"Next to you, I feel like the frog who became a prince."

"Don't sweet-talk me."

"You know, I was thinking. Maybe we should have a wedding. You never got all that stuff, the dress, the flowers, the big band. We never had all our people together. Would you want to do that?"

"We're too practical to have a wedding. What with species dying, forests being decimated, people starving everywhere. How about we just take thirty thousand dollars and give it away to hungry people?"

"Think about it, Princess Grump-a-Lot, because I'm serious. It could be really fun." And then he reached over, took my hand, and held it.

All my brothers, Marcus, Aden, Trevor and Danny, were at the reception. They spent a lot of time holding Zach, playing with him, passing him around the table, showing him spoons, throwing him in the air. Which was really nice of them, considering the fact that they're all just about at the age when you don't think about anything but your penis and generally run screaming from babies and the unfortunate connection between them and sex. I bet they all went out and bought a few boxes of condoms after the reception, just in case.

They sat at a separate table with some of my mother's friends. I sat at the head table, with my mother, Aunt Hilda, and Donny, who had, by the way, changed costumes and now wore a pair of cowboy boots and a white tuxedo. My mother put Drew at the table with the kids because he had to sit with Priscilla, and I'd expressly forbidden my mother from seating me at a table with the Torturer.

"What did you think?" she asked, sipping from a flute of champagne.

"Your best so far, Mom." And hopefully the last. If I had to go through another round of being her matron of honor, I wouldn't just *talk* about losing it—I would lose it.

"You holding up okay, sweets?"

"Me?" I scoffed. "Motherhood has virtually killed me, but other than that, I'm hunky-dory." I stopped for a moment to think about this. "Actually, it's marriage that has virtually killed me—or maybe it's the combo? Like two for the price of one? Go Crazy Quicker, get married *and* have babies."

"Some things are worth it," my mother said. "Children, for example, are definitely worth stretch marks."

"Well, that's a relief." And here all this time I'd been thinking I'd end up selling Zach so I could afford laser surgery on my stomach. One less thing to worry about.

"You aren't wishing you were in London, are you?"

"I wouldn't miss this for the world."

"That's not what I meant, honey."

"I know what you meant. And no, I don't wish I were with Jake." I looked over at Drew. He'd just gotten up and taken Zach out onto the dance floor. "Drew was right; I've been a bit crazy; I'm not sure I would have wanted to be married to me this year either. I suppose we're equal. I was just as awful as he was."

"You know," my mother said, turning in her seat to face me, "your father wasn't the best husband in the world."

"What are you saying?" I'd never heard my mother utter a single bad word against my dad.

"Just that he was human, honey. And in life you don't get to call all the shots. You don't get to turn people into what you wish they would be. For that matter, you can hardly make yourself be anything other than what you are. And you don't get to say who lives or dies, or who stays or goes, or when love

376 □ Samantha Wilde

will or won't work. You think you'll be able to, when you're young. But then you realize life is better just lived, not played like a game or planned like a meeting or fought like a war."

"I know. I know." I'd heard my mother's best wisdom many times before.

"And you love him." She said it like a statement. "Look at them." She pointed to Drew and Zach. Drew had Zach in his arms and was swinging him in circles on the dance floor. "You and Drew share something no one else can ever share."

"And that would be?"

"Zach. No one else will ever love him the way you do—except Drew. And if you want my personal opinion—"

"I do."

"No one else will ever love you the way Drew does. A man who forgives your mistakes is worth forgiving." My mistakes? I thought of Oliver's kiss. I thought of Jake's emails. And there were others, weren't there?

"You know, honey, I've never thought of this before but Drew is a little like your daddy." I turned to look at her. "Not the way he looks, of course. It's just something about the way he's holding Zach right now. It makes me think of Paul." She shook her head, smiling, remembering a time I would never know. Her face softened and for a moment she belonged to another world, the world of her youth and her innocence. "Give him time. We all need time to grow into things, even the best of us."

"Oh, Mom." I leaned into her, and she reached an arm around to hug me. "You really think so?" I looked again at Zach and Drew. "Thank you, I needed to hear that."

"Don't leave me out," came a southern-drawling, cowboy-boot-wearing historian turned life coach, as he attempted to wrap his arms around both of us. What a way to ruin the moment. He smelled like shoe polish. If it hadn't been his wedding, I would have passed on the happy family moment. As it was, what could I do? It wasn't so bad, anyhow. His faults didn't involve poverty or sexual preferences that didn't include my mother. A tendency for excessive hugging can't be the worst quality in a person, now can it?

Drew brought Zach over to me after the baby drew the attention of half the room with an ear-piercing scream that I'm certain could land him a supporting role in a horror movie. Priscilla toted along behind Drew as if she couldn't be left alone at the table to make normal wedding small talk. (And for all I know, she really *can't* make wedding small talk. For all I know she can only make Walter talk.)

Ever since the slobbering incident, I'd been hoping she'd soften to me. But then I reminded myself that my life, though it had recently taken on the dimensions of a fictional tale, existed exactly in the realm of fact. Fact Number One: Priscilla is a nasty old hag.

"I'm off to the bathroom," Drew said.

"You're still nursing him," Priscilla said, looming next to my chair.

"That's right. Same as yesterday."

"And in public."

"That's right. Because he's hungry."

"I can't say I approve. It's not healthy to go on for so long like this. It's not natural. It's not right. My Walter would never have tolerated it." She did look truly disgusted; I have to give her points for honesty. In my matron gown, I had to lift my whole breast out to get my nipple to Zach. I think the sight of my bare breast pretty much made her feel she'd turned on the porno station, not that she'd ever turned on a porn station, of course. I doubted the woman even had genitals.

"Priscilla, sit down." She did. Zach continued to nurse contentedly as I leaned forward and looked her in the eye. "I don't know if your mother-in-law spent her time telling you what to do, criticizing your mothering and making you feel unwelcome. If she did, then you have some idea how I feel. But I bet if she did, you put your foot down. I feel that a grandmother's job is to love the baby—not to undermine the mother. And honestly, I don't care what Walter would do. This is about my life with my son. *You* got to raise your son the way you wanted; can't you let me do the same?" Then I smiled because it felt so good. It felt like I'd been constipated for years and had finally taken a dump.

"Oh," she said, stunned. "I see."

"It's hard enough to be a mother," I said. "Don't you remember any of that?"

She looked down at Zach as if he'd just landed in his spacecraft in front of us. "Remember? I can hardly remember yesterday." She sat silent for a moment. "I guess it was hard." Then she said it again, more quietly. "I guess it was harder, that first year." For thirty seconds we were two mothers, two women who had something in common, not like mother and daughter-in-law—she who stole the son away.

"But I do have to say I don't think it's safe to have Zachary sleeping in the same bed with you and Andrew. I think he's a little old for that."

"Well, he's mostly in his crib now, anyway. Thank goodness. I'm getting more sleep."

"Good," she said, satisfied to have the upper hand. Still, a terrible possibility had opened itself up. Maybe we weren't so different after all. (Don't ever quote me as saying that.) As she walked away, I thought about the fact that one day I'd have a grown son. Would any woman be good enough for my Zach? I'd like to think so. But I had plenty of time to make up some wicked rules for my own reign of mother-in-law terror. I'd probably be pretty good at it too.

While my mother and Donny danced the two-step, Aunt Hilda entertained me with stories of my father. She had three champagne flutes on the table in front of her. It occurred to me that she probably shouldn't drink so much, given the fact that she took medication, but how in the world would I be able to tell when she wasn't acting normal? She'd pulled her hair back into her characteristic bun and had on a purple tunic kind of thing under which, no doubt, she had hidden her fortune cards. She had a ring on each of her fingers and smelled of incense. In five minutes, I learned that my father had been a fat baby, a late walker and a late talker. Talking with Aunt Hilda felt like opening a secret trapdoor to my life. Just hearing her speak somehow made sense out of the chaos of my life. Don't ask me how. Things don't work like that. In fact, I have no idea how things work. I leave that to other people, people with jobs and incomes and titles and letters after their names. I am a mother. I know diapers. I know crying. I know rocking. I know boredom.

"Look, honey," Drew said, interrupting my special Aunt Hilda time. He was holding onto the sleeve of a haggard-looking woman holding a baby the size of a melon—roughly.

"Hi," I said.

"Remember Alice Tate?" he asked.

"Sure," I said, although I didn't remember Alice Tate. The only Alice, as a matter of fact, I have ever known—and not too personally either—was Alice on the *The Brady Bunch*. Oh, and the one who went down the rabbit hole. However, I had to assume that the poor, tired woman in front of me had to be Alice Tate.

"From Clarkville Academy," he said. "In the English department. You met at the Christmas party last year."

"Right. Of course. How are you?"

"She's had a baby," Drew triumphantly pointed out.

"I can see that."

"Where's your little guy?" she asked. I pointed over to Priscilla, who was holding a snoozing Zach in her arms. Despite the rather catchy country tunes, Priscilla stood motionless. She would make a great pole, if she ever needed to act.

"It really does get easier," I said to her, without thinking. "Once they do more than cry and feed." I reached up and touched the baby's toes.

"Really?" Alice looked at me. The whites of her eyes were streaked with red. "I'm whipped."

"That won't change," I told her with a half laugh. "Zach can go six hours now."

"Six hours, really?" Alice almost swooned with lust. "Oh, I'm so tired."

"Is he a preemie?" I asked. "I don't think Zach was ever that small."

"He's six weeks! Eleven pounds, too." She smiled.

"Really?" I couldn't believe it. Zach could never have been that small, that fragile, that vulnerable.

"They're moving to Finney Hill," Drew said with a touch of pride, as if he himself had arranged the move.

"Wow. We'll be neighbors. I'll have to give you my number. We can have a playdate."

"I'd love that," she said. "I've decided not to go back to Clarkville. I'm going to be home full time."

"In that case, you'll definitely want to call me."

"I will," she said, as if she'd won the lottery. "I really will."

"Oh." I touched the baby's foot again. "It goes by so quickly." Drew looked at me. "Did I just say that? Please forgive me, Alice. I haven't had a drink since the baby was born. The champagne must have gone straight to my head."

Zach woke up early crying on Christmas morning. We had some high hopes that his bottom teeth were finally going to arrive after, oh, I don't know, *six months* of teething. In addition to more sleep for me, teeth would mean a great increase in Zach's food repertoire, although he'd mastered the art of gumming tofu very well. I dragged myself out of bed, checking the time. It was just before five, the worst time for Zach to wake up, being, as it was, not really night and not really morning. In other words, too late to go back to sleep and too early to get up. I pulled him out of the crib and wrapped him in his blanket. Then we rocked together in his nursery chair while I nursed him. He suckled hungrily for quite a while, which made me worry that maybe I hadn't shoveled enough oatmeal into him the night before. All the old women I knew would give the same advice when I asked: How did you get your babies to sleep through the night? "Fill up his tummy," they'd say, and I'd certainly tried. But stuffing him until he could be served as the Christmas turkey never seemed to make a difference. He just woke up when he wanted to.

That early dawn, I must have rocked him for more than an hour. I couldn't fall asleep, like I sometimes do, and for the first half hour I couldn't fight the feeling of injustice that welled up in me every time I heard Drew snore. Why wasn't I snug in bed? Why hadn't I slept an uninterrupted night in almost a year? What had I done wrong to deserve that kind of punishment? Just being born a woman—was that it? Had we never moved beyond the surface psychology of the Garden of Eden?

I had begun to acknowledge, with horror and wonder, that my initiation into the cult of mommyhood was almost complete, and as a result of my months of tandem living with Zach, we had grown into each other, the way you sometimes see trees that at first appear to be two, but on further inspection you realize are joined at the trunk (my tree-watching vacations have finally come in handy). I could sing a song and stop his hysterical tears. I knew just which book he wanted to look at on any given day. I'd developed a knack for putting my hands on just the right size spoon for him to chew on. I no longer knew what it meant to eat a meal slowly in silence. I'd thrown out every single pair of pants without a drawstring waistband. I shopped at the grocery store for mashable food. When I saw Melody or Diana we spent most of our time talking shop: naps, eating habits, nighttime sleeping, good, bad, and neutral behaviors, irrelevant plastic toys, irrelevant experiences: orgasm, moviegoing, fancy restaurants, sleeping in.

And because of all that, I had this creeping sense of accomplishment, like I'd actually done something over the course of ten months, even though day by day it appeared that I didn't do anything at all except nurse, change diapers and complain. "Look how far I've come," I said to Drew the other day. "Remember the days when figuring out how to do the laundry and take care of the baby simultaneously had seemed like astrophysics. Look at how good I am at this!" And he did. He noticed how I could swing the baby onto one hip, with four grocery bags in the other hand; how I could make dinner for all of us while entertaining Zach with just a spatula and a measuring cup. When, I wanted to know, would they start the Mama Olympics, because I wanted to enter, and, frankly, I wanted to win. It occurred to both of us that despite Drew's almost complete withdrawal from Zach's babyhood and my little ventures into crazy land (kissing my yoga teacher, eating twenty pounds of M&M's—how I wish that were an exaggeration—and Jake, oh, Jake), I'd done a really good job.

"I'm proud of you," Drew told me quite seriously. It felt so nice to hear, it was better than foreplay. "You're an amazing mother."

On that early Christmas morning, I looked down at the top of my boy's head, at his wild dark hair, which had started to curl in the center so he resembled the early eighties punk rockers with their full heads of hair half lifted into a mohawk. He was as beautiful, as perfect, to me as anything I had ever seen. He was also getting bigger. The fact that he was almost walking only confirmed my suspicions. We would never go back; we would never go back to his size 0 onesies or the days of wrapping him burrito style and setting him in the bassinet. We would never go back to the hours and hours spent on tummy time or the shocking, overwhelming, unimaginable wonder and joy and relief that I felt when I first heard his wailing cry and knew my baby was fine, was alive, had arrived breathing into our crazy world. You would have thought I'd known it already; that Zach would only grow in one direction. But I didn't know it, somehow, because of the intensity of the work of motherhood, its absolute present-mindedness, until that dawn, when I realized with sorrow and with pride that he was on his way.

It choked me up. It really did. When I put him in the crib, I had tears streaming down my face, and I stayed, for a long while after, watching him sleep, even though I was so tired, was so jealous of Drew fast asleep. I stayed and stared. I guess I'd lost a few things along the way, some of the things Drew got to keep. But hadn't I gained something too, something he didn't get? I stood another moment. I didn't want to leave. It was the closest I'd ever come to watching time, and boy, was it bittersweet. "I got lucky when you came along," I whispered down to Zach's sleeping baby self. Eventually, I tiptoed out, knowing it would take me a long while to fall back asleep, if it happened at all. I curled into bed next to Drew. I saw a smile, like a baby's fleeting sleep smile, move across his face. For a moment, he looked just like Zach.

acknowledgments

I have been waiting my entire life (well, since I was six), to write an acknowledgments page. As you can imagine, over those twenty years (or so), I've amassed an enormous number of people who need thanking. That said, I will make every effort to focus on thanking people directly involved so that I don't need to write another book just to fit everyone in.

You, for buying this book.

Christina Hogrebe, my agent, for showing me kindness, being consistently cheerful, patient, helpful, supportive, and, of course, for selling this book and keeping me in M&M's for a whole year!

Meg Ruley and all the rest of the good folks at Jane Rotrosen Agency for taking me on and making a long-held hope a reality.

Danielle Perez, my editor, whose comments made this a much, much better book, and, of course, for buying this book. I am quite lucky to work with such a gifted editor.

Bantam Dell, and all those behind the scenes whose names I don't know, who have turned this book from an electronic document into the real thing.

I seriously and sincerely hope I make all of you wonderful people lots of money. And me too. (So I can be like Angelina Jolie and adopt lots of babies.)

Jan MacBeth, who taught me writing at Walnut Hill. I have remembered you all these years for your inspiration, wisdom, encouragement.

Clare Nunes, teacher, advisor, mentor extraordinaire. Beloved to me, always honest, hilarious, compassionate, a truly gifted teacher. *My* bright star.

Bill Oram, the legend. If you are lucky enough to go to Smith College, take his classes. He changed my writing.

Luc Gilleman, lovely in all ways, great teacher, unsurpassed thesis advisor, and very funny (in his own way), but don't leave academia for the stand-up life, you have kids to feed!

Elinor Lipman, whose class I adored, whose books I adore, and for reading my manuscript, a decade later, and in a rough draft no less. I am so thankful to know you.

Jessica Brody, fellow Smithie, for wonderful emails, excellent advice, kind words, and much needed support as a writer.

All the mothers in my life, friends, role-models, saints, especially:

Jenn, Ann, and Pam, for coming to my house for toddler mornings, and unwittingly helping this book along in many ways,

Jen Skaggs, who listens, good friend, funny and kind,

Sarah Grover, for help on titles, good company, long friendship, much wisdom,

Sara Prentice Manela, for more help on titles, and on the cover, and for great mommy stories and support, for a lifetime of friendship. I wish you lived next door!

Becki Rosenfeldt, for walks and talks and for moving in at just the right moment,

Gwen Leaf, who came at the beginning with food and kindness and continues to make the trek, occasionally, to be with us,

Michelle Hammer, best mommy friend ever, queen of patience and long suffering, who went through it with me, ruthlessly honest, truly funny, deeply compassionate, who fed me so many meals (thanks to you too, Dave!), who loves me as I am, who I love and thank God for every day.

Katherine Silvan, dearest friend. I hear your voice and feel happier about everything. Confidante, spiritual teacher, wonderful mother.

The Goddesses, Supriya, Lisa, Susan and Ann, for years together, for your beauty. Each time we meet is a gift to me. I am so lucky to have you.

Elizabeth Hanly, from the Nuns (I should thank them!), mystical lady, gentle friend, a woman who *knows.*

Josh and Laura, no one like you, especially for the phrase "we didn't have much in common!"

Sheri Perelman, best yoga teacher, for countless life-sustaining classes and for the great word "wasband."

Kate Scott, best friend, home away from home. I love you.

Sarah Evans, who keeps reminding me who I am, for all our years of friendship, for being there, all hours, without judgment.

Those who took care while I worked: Jenny Webb, Kerri Craig, Melissa Huey. When you have babies, may someone equally good help you with them. And especially to Alicia Beaupre and her outstandingly wonderful family, for being the absolute most excellent neighbors ever.

Janice and St. John Forbes for helping me with the babies, loving them and supporting my work.

My yoga students, the Love Team, Agape supporters, for all your divine sparkles.

My children, Ellias and Adeline. There would be no book without you. Precious, incomparable, for showing me the deepest love, teachers of patience and kindness, you won't know until you have your own children what you have given me, but there is nothing, nothing better.

Neil, for our beautiful children, for making it possible for me to stay home with them, which has been a tremendous blessing, a dream come true, impossibly hard and infinitely more worthwhile. Incomparable father.

My brother, Josh, my stepfather, Charley, and my mother. Good family. There in hard times. Cheerleaders. For help, advice, babysitting, patience and for believing in me, despite the occasional evidence to the contrary.

My mother, who read this book, said it was "the one." What can't I thank you for? You gave birth to me! It was all worthwhile, it's official. Boarding school, college, six pairs of pink shoes. May I be lucky enough to have your career.

Agape. The One who makes all things possible. Thank you.

SAMANTHA WILDE is the mother of two children born in under two years. A graduate of Concord Academy, Smith College, Yale Divinity School and the New Seminary, she lives in western Massachusetts with her husband and children. She is the daughter of novelist Nancy Thayer. When she's not mothering her toddler and baby, she writes, teaches yoga, and moonlights as a minister. Although she hardly sleeps, she's never once been tempted to give her children away to the highest bidder (well, almost never). She's currently using nap times to write her second novel for Bantam Dell. Visit the author at wildemama .blogspot.com.